MW01133257

MAYHEM'S CHILDREN

M A Y H E M   W A V E   S E R I E S #3

FROM THE
BESTSELLING AUTHOR OF UNHAPPENINGS

For Judah!

XO

Mayhem's Children
Mayhem Wave Book 3

Copyright © 2017 by Edward Aubry

All rights reserved.

No part of this book may be reproduced in any form or by any electronic or mechanical means, including information storage and retrieval systems, without written permission from the author, except for the use of brief quotations in a book review.

CONTENTS

PART 3
PROTÉGÉE

[PART 1]
PROGENY

SABOTAGE

Wrigley Field survived. So much of the city of New Chicago had been built from scratch over its nine-year history it bore little resemblance to its namesake. The Mayhem Wave wiped most familiar buildings out of existence, leaving in its wake little more than wilderness and scraps. Yet Wrigley stood, carrying the torch for a world all but gone. Reasoning that no better symbol could be found for perseverance in the face of apparent hopelessness than the Chicago Cubs, the founders of the new city declared Wrigley's survival an omen, and a national pastime was reborn.

On opening day, nearly eight years after saving the world, Harrison Cody took his son to a ballgame. "You want a beer?"

Mitchell looked at him with a mixture of amusement and uncertainty. "I think corruption of a minor is still a real thing. Also, ick."

Harrison laughed and waved to a vendor. "Suit yourself."

Mitchell's relationship to Harrison defied traditional definition. Harrison had been his adopted father for less than a year, before Mitchell's father returned from a magically-induced oblivion. Though no longer legal family, they stayed close over the years, and with Mitchell about to turn eighteen, these outings would dwindle. He hoped the ballgame would give them an opportunity for some eleventh-hour bonding, but Mitchell spent a fair portion of his time staring off into space. Two innings in, when he managed not to notice a two-run homer, Harrison took him for a walk.

"Talk to me," he said. "What's going on?"

3

"Nothing," said Mitchell, without making eye contact.

"Nothing, nothing?" asked Harrison. "Or nothing you want to talk about."

Mitchell shrugged. "The second one."

"Hey, this is me." Harrison put his hand on Mitchell's shoulder. "Anything you tell me is privileged information. If you need to vent, I'm your guy. Remember? All the perks of having a parent, and none of the pesky judgment?" He paused there, then lowered his voice. "If you're in trouble, you know how many strings I can pull with a single phone call, right?"

"I'm not in trouble."

"Is it school stuff?"

Mitchell shook his head.

"Girl stuff?"

Mitchell laughed at that. "I wish."

"Throw me a bone, sport. You're safe here. Besides, I've got all kinds of patronizing advice to offer."

Mitchell finally looked at him. "It's dad stuff."

"Oh," said Harrison. "Shit. I'm sorry."

"No, it's okay," said Mitchell. "It's just a thing. He's... I don't know. I just feel like he doesn't get me."

A small beep came from Harrison's shirt pocket, and he sighed in irritation. "Hold that thought." He removed an object the size and shape of a pen, and spoke into it. "Cody."

It spoke back to him in a female voice that sounded full despite the tiny speaker. "We need you to come in, sir."

"Why?"

The voice paused, and Harrison frowned. As an assistant director in the New Chicago Security Agency, he understood a call back to the office would surely mean a matter of some urgency, and he would drop everything to address it. He did however consider himself entitled to demand an explanation for why he would need to leave his son alone at a Cubs game, especially in the middle of a sensitive conversation.

After a bit, she said, "It's a missing persons case."

That made things less clear. "Who? Missing persons is a police matter. Why are we getting involved in this?"

"That's all I'm authorized to say," she said.

"This is a secure line, Felicia." Harrison took a moment to look at Mitchell and put his finger to his lips. Mitchell nodded. In truth, the likelihood that Mitchell could hear enough of what came from that speaker to understand it was slim. The technology was designed for stealth, with a narrow range of audibility. "And I need to know."

Another pause. "Hold, please."

Mitchell gave Harrison a questioning look, still not speaking.

Harrison shrugged.

After a few seconds, a reply came in the crisp, British-accented voice of the NCSA director, Alec Baker. "It's Siobhan Roark."

Mitchell's eyes went one degree wider. That one he heard.

"Understood. I'm coming in right now." Harrison put the device back in his pocket.

"Go," said Mitchell.

Harrison pulled out a small PDA, and fidgeted with it. "Sorry about this. I'll call you later today. I just transferred fifty dollars to your card."

"For what?" asked Mitchell.

"In case you decide you need ten hot dogs." He put his hand on Mitchell's shoulder. "Let's finish that conversation as soon as I can get away, okay?"

Mitchell nodded. Harrison took in the hangdog look on his son's face, with a new, added level of worry. This new situation, and new uncertainty, compounded whatever personal problems Mitchell had.

One of his twenty-nine adopted sisters had gone missing.

"Talk to me."

The New Chicago Security Agency housed its headquarters in a reclaimed office building. They had imprisoned Harrison here once. Now he had an office and a staff. His assistant Felicia met him at the door and handed him a small data device as they walked to the elevator. She looked considerably younger than her thirty years, with a mop of black curls on top of a fair-skinned, slender face. Her professionalism belied any youthful first impressions she might give.

"Miss Roark failed to report to work yesterday morning," she said. "No one has reported contact with her since approximately seven a.m., when she left her home. Her boyfriend was the last person to see her, and reported her missing this morning."

"Is he a suspect?" Harrison opened a file on the small screen with his thumbprint and skimmed it as they talked.

"Not at this time. The police aren't ruling him out, but so far his story holds up."

Harrison nodded, carefully omitting his opinion. He had met Siobhan's boyfriend on at least one occasion—though he couldn't recall his name at that moment—and he seemed like a decent guy. But admitting that at this junction might come across as unprofessional, especially if he turned out to be wrong. "What's our contribution to the investigation?"

"I recalled Blevins and York right before I called you," she said. "Agent York is with the police right now, coordinating resources. Blevins is our top man for this kind of work, but he was on a deep-cover assignment, and isn't expected back until tomorrow afternoon."

They stopped at the elevator. Harrison continued to skim the file in front of him, most of it a simple acknowledgement of how little hard information anyone actually had. They stepped into the car. "York was on an important assignment as well. On whose authority did you pull them from the field?"

"Mine," she said. "This is your daughter, sir."

He raised an eyebrow at that. By taking responsibility for that call herself, especially before contacting him, she had shielded Harrison from accusations of impropriety and misuse of agency personnel. He doubted it would come to that, but the precaution reminded him how valuable she had been to him in his role as an administrator. "Thank you."

She nodded.

They reached his floor. "Have York report to me directly. I want hourly updates. I also want to know how many people we can free up for this immediately if it turns into a manhunt, and I want those people put on call."

"Understood." She left Harrison at the door to his office.

He dropped the data device on his desk, and collapsed into the black-leather chair behind it. The New Chicago Security Agency had originally recruited Harrison as the result of a unique talent he acquired entirely by chance—a highly specialized form of telekinesis. He had been content enough with that arrangement until, on his first major mission, he proved himself of worth beyond his special talent. On his return, his contributions led to him assuming a leadership role in the agency, and eventually rising to the post of assistant director.

In the face of this new crisis, he wondered, as he often did, whether he was in over his head. Certainly, with Siobhan's life potentially at risk, it felt like something out of his area of expertise. He had that very thought when he opened his desk drawer and found the bomb.

For a moment, he stared at it, struggling to believe what he saw. The thought of someone trying to assassinate him in such a dramatic manner did not surprise him, but the absurdly crude design of the device, coupled with the extraordinarily ineffective method of detonation, gave him pause. In his drawer sat nothing more than three sticks of dynamite, wired to a timer with oversized, red LED digits. According to the clearly displayed countdown, Harrison had six hours and nineteen minutes left before the bomb blew.

Even setting aside its cartoonish appearance, and the fact he had almost an entire workday to evacuate the building, this bomb could never work. Ever since the Mayhem Event, the chemical reactions that drove conventional explosives and firearms no longer generated the energy they needed to be effective weapons. Once that timer ran down to zero, the blasting cap might get hot, but it wouldn't set off a charge. Those three sticks of dynamite would smolder and turn to ash, if they ignited at all.

For all those reasons, he suspected the object ticking down in his desk drawer was a magical weapon.

He removed the communication device from his shirt pocket and spoke into it. "Felicia, I need Special Agent Logan in my office immediately. This is top priority."

"Understood," she said.

"Baker," said Harrison without pause. By voice command, the device directed his call accordingly. "This is Cody. There is a bomb in my office, on a timer, set to go off in six hours."

"Good grief," came the reply. "Call Logan."

"Already did."

"And stay put. Anyone's guess what will set that thing off."

"Great," said Harrison, now glued to his seat.

Eight minutes later, Alec Baker entered Harrison's office. The director of the New Chicago Security Agency walked with a cane, and had done so ever since suffering nerve damage from a wound in his right leg. "Let's see it."

"Bottom right drawer," said Harrison.

Alec hobbled his way around the desk, and crouched down to inspect the contents of the open drawer. He shook his head. "Only you."

"Nice," said Harrison. "Am I right to believe this bomb poses no literal threat? Dynamite doesn't explode anymore, right?"

Alec did not take his eyes off the bomb. "It probably won't explode. I'd say it's meant to do something, though. Wouldn't be much point to go to all this trouble for no effect. Magic, most likely. Anyone's guess what that timer is counting down to."

"We're not going to try to defuse it, are we?"

Alec looked up at Harrison. "I assume by 'we' you don't mean the two of us, but no, we're not. I called in a wizard to have a look at it. Probably moot anyway if Logan gets here first."

Harrison frowned. "Wizard?"

"Wizard. And do try to be cordial this time."

Harrison's experience with wizards was limited to ways in which he and they annoyed each other. A handful of them carried over from Glimmer's world (and despite the fact the pixie had been gone for years, he still thought of it in those terms), but most were ordinary humans who had a knack for wielding magic. It had taken several years to discover there existed ways for ordinary humans to use magic at all, and despite great strides in that field since then, few natives of Harrison's world could match their magical world counterparts in skill or scope.

"Which one?" asked Harrison.

"Aplomado."

Harrison groaned. "You mean Gerry?"

"I mean Aplomado. Don't call him Gerry."

"I'll try not to," Harrison lied.

Alec glowered at him. "See that you do. This is no game to him, Cody. These people have skills you and I would have to put our lives on hold for years to acquire, if we even had the aptitude, which is doubtful. If he wants to give himself a nonsense name—"

"It's a kind of falcon."

Alec raised his brows at that. "Is it?"

Harrison nodded. "I looked it up. Apryl says it's also a bastardization of the Spanish for lead-colored. I mentioned that to him a few weeks ago. You might have noticed that's around the time he stopped calling himself Aplomado the Gray. Since, you know, he was pretty much calling himself Gray the Gray."

Alec rubbed his chin in thought. "All right, that is a bit pretentious."

"I'm saying."

A knock came from Harrison's office door. In it stood a man dressed in a gray robe, holding a pointed felt hat. He had a meticulously trimmed and completely gray (though obviously dyed) goatee, and matching long, wavy hair. "Bomb?"

"Drawer," said Harrison.

Aplomado drifted to Harrison's desk and dropped his hat on it, as Alec stepped out of his way. Behind his back, Harrison mouthed, "Gerry," which earned him a rap on the knee from Alec's cane.

"This will kill everyone in the building," said Aplomado. "I assume you already know the timer is accelerating?"

"What?" said Harrison. "No, I didn't know that."

8

"Hmm," said Aplomado. "It appears to be progressing geometrically. But even if you didn't work that out—and I would never expect you to see it on your own—the clock on your wall should have been a dead giveaway. How long has it been since you discovered this device?"

Harrison looked to Alec for help, who looked at his watch. "You called it in eleven minutes ago."

"Have a look," said Aplomado.

Harrison peered into his desk drawer, where the timer rolled over from six hours to five-fifty-nine. "It's advanced twenty minutes since then."

Alec pulled a communicator from his shirt pocket. "Level one evacuation on my authorization." Seconds later a klaxon sounded, followed by activity in the hallway outside Harrison's open door, as the staff scrambled to exit the building in an orderly but swift fashion. "How long?" he said to Aplomado.

"Nine minutes of real time. Maybe. That's an estimate, assuming the countdown function remains consistent."

"Minimum safe distance?"

"Anyone not physically touching the building is safe. This is a curse, not a bomb. When it goes off, the entire structure will be turned into a deadly contact poison. If you make skin contact with so much as a doorknob, you will die. The entire building will need to be quarantined. If you try to demolish it, the dust will contaminate the entire city."

Harrison looked around himself, trying to assess anything of value he needed to grab on his way out. As he swept past his own desk, Aplomado looked him in the eyes.

"If you need to come back for something sensitive, you might be safe in an environment suit, which you would then have to incinerate, but I wouldn't risk it. Whatever you are looking for right now, you better find it and take it with you."

"You can't defuse this?" asked Alec.

Aplomado shook his head. "It would take me at least half an hour to determine the specifics of the spell to counter it. And there are safeties in place to prevent tampering or scrutiny. It is very advanced work. Mallory might be able to stop this thing, but she would never get here in time. It is beyond me. I am sorry."

"What about Sarah?" asked Harrison. "She's already on her way."

"That might work," said Aplomado, "but I really wouldn't know. Telekinesis is outside the scope of my expertise."

As the wizard stood, and retrieved his hat, Alec said into his communicator, "Magical Agent Mallory to A.D. Cody's office

9

immediately. Override evacuation protocol for that agent, and for Special Agent Logan."

"Mallory will never make it here," said Aplomado.

"Our problem," said Alec. "Dismissed, Agent."

Aplomado nodded and departed.

"How long are we going to wait for them?" asked Harrison.

"Nine minutes," said Alec. "Which I suggest you use to find us two pairs of gloves."

Eight minutes later, two men rushed into Harrison's office, escorting a frightened and overwhelmed woman in her early forties by both arms.

"Here!" said Harrison.

They took her to Harrison's desk and released her. He pointed to the bomb, and she looked directly at it.

"Oh my God!" said Sarah Logan. "Is that a bomb?"

Harrison read the timer, now frozen at thirty-five seconds. "Not anymore." He removed the wool mittens he had secured from the lost-and-found box in the break lounge. "Thank you."

Sarah rubbed her face with both hands. "May I sit down?" Harrison pulled up his leather chair, and she flopped into it. "Are you able to tell me what just happened, Director?"

"Not much to tell that isn't already obvious. Cody found that bomb in his desk about twenty minutes ago. The first thing he did was call for you, which happened to be the correct solution." Like Harrison, Sarah picked up a highly specialized telekinetic ability on the day the world as everyone knew it ended. Her talent was the ability to stop any clock with a glance, entirely involuntary, and invariably permanent. The timer on that bomb would never again read anything but thirty-five seconds.

"Right," she said. "Got it. Just give me a few minutes to burn off this adrenaline."

"Take your time," said Harrison.

"There are about twenty undergrads right now who probably think I was just arrested."

Harrison laughed. "Sorry about that. We'll give the university a statement."

She waved away the suggestion. "The school knows I'm always on call. It's my students who don't. I'll have some explaining to do tomorrow." She looked up, with a weak smile. "It's good to see you. We should probably find better ways to get together."

"Agreed. How's Saturday? Dinner at our place?"

"Ha! You're on. Should we bring Adler, or get a sitter?"

"Bring him," said Harrison. "We'll make it a family thing."

"Done and done." She looked at Alec. "Am I finished here, Director?"

"Yes," he said. "Would you like a ride back to work?"

"Nah. Thanks, but that was my last class, and I think I'd rather just walk home at this point." She stood, and gave Harrison a hug. "Saturday."

"Five-ish," he said.

"See you then." She punctuated this with a very unagent-like kiss on the cheek. "Good day, Director Baker."

Alec nodded. "Special Agent Logan."

She strolled out the door.

"Not to change the subject," said Harrison, "but are we still moving on this missing persons investigation?"

Alec crouched down to scrutinize the inert bomb, taking care not to touch it. "I'd say we have two priority investigations now."

MELODY

Dorothy O'Neill stood in the hallway outside the Codys' apartment for a full five minutes, debating whether to ring the bell. She had no fear of being unwelcome, nor anxiety about how they would receive her. Her hesitance sprang from a different difficulty, and had anyone asked her about it, she would have been sorely pressed to articulate it. It had, in fact, become an ingrained part of her routine of late. Dorothy's visits to Harrison and his family, though fairly regular, always began this way. She doubted Harrison had any notion of how much time she spent in this hallway, poised to enter his home, and not able to do so. Most days she ventured in. Some days she went home unannounced.

Though she would never be able to express it in simple terms, the problem was not complicated; Harrison was Dorothy's father. He had only ever acted as such for a span of less than half a year in her early adolescence, the only span of her life she truly felt she had one. She knew her biological father, but he stopped being a part of her life before her ninth birthday. Both of her sisters disappeared when the Mayhem Wave came through on May 30, 2004, and her mother along with them, at least at first. When Harrison traveled to the far end of the globe a year later to help prevent the world from being destroyed, he did something that caused her mother to return. Something magical. The full explanation went over her head. What mattered was she had her mother back. But that glorious restoration came at the price of leaving the only father she had ever truly known. Ever truly loved.

"Hey, Dotty."

Dorothy jumped, startled out of her ruminations. She spun to find the source of her surprise in Claudia de Queiroz, not a welcome sight in Dorothy's current frame of mind. She had known Claudia since she was fourteen, and Claudia fifteen. Claudia had been her first friend in New Chicago, providing support she sorely needed at the time. She had also been responsible for Harrison being arrested the day they arrived, which set an ambivalent tone for their relationship. They grew close within days of that meeting, but the closeness held an edge of wariness. In the years since, it had ranged from strained to confusing.

Around the time Dorothy was sixteen, Claudia began to treat her with deliberate indifference, and Dorothy came to believe that Claudia didn't see her as interesting enough, or cool enough, to be a true friend anymore. As a result, she spent most of her adolescence pining for Claudia's respect. Seeing her now reaffirmed her pining had never faded. She offered her best attempt to be blasé. "Hello, Claude."

"You heard about Siobhan?" asked Claudia.

Dorothy frowned. She had braced herself for some snarky rejoinder, Claudia's usual form of conversation. "No. What happened to Siobhan?"

Claudia gave her a quizzical look. Even in confusion, Dorothy found her striking. The skunk stripe in Claudia's hair—which Dorothy long assumed to be an affectation until discovering she had a hereditary condition called poliosis—cut a stark contrast to her dark, Brazilian complexion. Dorothy felt upstaged by Claudia's appearance, particularly compared to her own pale skin and straight, strawberry blonde hair. Trading in her thick glasses years earlier in favor of corrective eye surgery had helped boost her opinion of her own appearance, but standing beside Claudia, she felt generic.

"No one knows," said Claudia. "She's been missing for two days. I thought that's why you were here."

Dorothy resisted the impulse to tell Claudia she had no need to justify visiting her own father. Apart from not being eager to discuss her true reason for being there—for hoping to find some comfort with family in a rough patch of her life—this unexpected information pushed aside any rivalry between the two of them. "I didn't know that." Like Dorothy, Siobhan Roark was—at least nominally—one of Harrison's adopted daughters. Of the women who shared that distinction, Siobhan was one of the few Dorothy considered a close friend. That she had gone missing triggered in Dorothy not only a fear for her safety, but also guilt as she tried to recall when they last spoke.

"Well, I'm sure they'll be glad to see you," said Claudia.

13

Dorothy nodded, not sure who "they" were, and too self-conscious to ask.

After a moment's awkward silence, Claudia said, "Did you knock?"

"Oh!" said Dorothy. "Uh, no."

Claudia reached past her to rap on the door. After a few seconds, it swung inward, and the sight of Harrison's wife Apryl greeted them. She hugged each one in turn, without preamble. Dorothy wished she could find comfort in the gesture.

Apryl pointed to Claudia. "Coffee, one sugar, no cream." She turned her finger to Dorothy. "Chamomile tea with honey."

"Yes, please," said both, and Dorothy smiled, remembering why she had come here in the first place. Not even in the door yet, and already being cared for.

Apryl led them inside, where Harrison and four women sat around the dining room table. They had extended it with leaves, implying more expected guests. Of the four who had arrived ahead of her, she recognized three of Harrison's adopted daughters, and Sarah Logan, in the middle of a discussion. Harrison waved Claudia and Dorothy over to join them.

"I'm just saying we shouldn't be so quick to jump on the idea she doesn't want to be found," said one of the women at the table as Dorothy pulled up a chair. Sharp features, slender frame, straight brown hair pulled back in a ponytail, this was Melissa Lear. Like most of her sisters, Dorothy did not know her well. With her sat Rebecca Wheeler and Anna Bruce. Dorothy knew Anna better, but was surprised to see how much weight she had put on since the last time they saw each other. "Hi," Melissa said to Claudia and Dorothy with a nod.

"Hi," said Claudia.

"That's not what I'm saying at all," said Rebecca. Of the people here, Dorothy knew her the best, but mostly on reputation. Rebecca had been the oldest of the captives, and had taken on the role of den mother through their ordeal. Whether from natural inclination or necessity, she had risen to the challenge, and every one of them still treated her like a leader. After Harrison rescued them, she gladly handed those reins over to him, and then the girls' returned parents, but that respect endured. Slightly below average height, she wore her dirty blonde hair in a girlish bob. But what she might have lacked in visual command she made up for with assertiveness, intelligence, and charisma.

"I'm only asking if anyone has seriously considered the possibility she ran away on her own. I'm as happy as anyone to send the entire government of New Chicago looking for her. I just think part of that

14

effort should include looking for her in places she might have gone on her own."

"Of course we are," said Harrison. "That's standard. What little we have to go on doesn't point in that direction, though."

"Becca has a point," said Anna. "Maybe you should be weighing that possibility more heavily. Siobhan isn't… quite right in the head."

"She was a sex slave when she was fourteen years old," said Rebecca. "Are any of us seriously right in the head?"

Anna winced, and Melissa buried her face in her hands. "Christ," said Anna. "Do you have to talk about that?"

Rebecca leveled her gaze at Anna, and said with slow deliberation, "Talking about it is how I survive, Anna. And we can't pretend that's irrelevant to what happened to Siobhan just because it makes people uncomfortable."

"Excuse me." Melissa rose from the table. She bolted for the bathroom and slammed the door.

Anna gave Rebecca an unambiguous I-told-you-so look.

Rebecca sighed, and rubbed her temples. "I know, I know." Appearing to notice Dorothy and Claudia for the first time, she told them, "She'll be okay."

"I know," said Claudia, and Dorothy remembered something she rarely considered. For a few hours, Claudia had been a prisoner with those twenty-eight girls. They were all rescued before Claudia suffered any abuse, but she experienced the fear of its inevitability during those few hours, and many of the girls considered her one of their own, as did she. They all thought of Dorothy as their sister, as well, but that bond now felt like a shadow of the one they shared with Claudia.

"What do you mean not right in the head?" asked Sarah.

"It's hard to explain," said Anna. "Do you know what I mean?" she asked Rebecca.

Rebecca shrugged. "I don't know. She's always been kind of spacey. Is that what you mean?"

Anna shook her head. "It's more than that. Like she's not always there. Or she says random things that make no sense."

"Like what?" said Harrison.

"Like I don't remember," said Anna shortly. "It's just a feeling I have about her. I never said anything about it because I didn't want to be rude."

Dorothy pondered whether she had anything to contribute to this conversation. She had never seen the side of Siobhan Anna described, and she questioned how well she knew her. Apryl came in and handed Dorothy a mug, which she took gratefully. She held it in both hands, letting herself feel the warmth as she drew in the flowery scent of the tea. "Thank you."

"Thanks," said Claudia. She sipped her coffee.

"My pleasure," said Apryl. "Can I freshen anyone?"

Anna drained her own mug and passed it to her.

"How have you been, Claudia?" asked Apryl. "I haven't seen you in a while."

"Decent," she said. "Also, single. Mickey dumped me."

"I heard. I'm sorry. You all right?"

Claudia took another sip of her coffee. "Yeah. Thanks. That was kind of a train wreck waiting to happen anyway. If he hadn't called it off, I probably would have."

"Plenty of other fish in the sea," said Harrison.

"Thank you, Captain Cliché." Claudia raised her mug to him. "And, no thank you. Boys are assholes. I'm out. From here on, it's chicks, or nobody."

Rebecca laughed. "You're about due for a girlfriend anyway, aren't you?"

"Yes, ma'am. You doing anything after the meeting?"

"I had a date with my husband, but I might be able to cancel."

"Oh, let's you and me paint the town red, baby!"

Claudia and Rebecca clinked coffee mugs. A round of laughter followed. Dorothy did her best to politely join in. Claudia had never been shy about her bisexuality, and as much as Dorothy wished otherwise, it always made her uncomfortable. As New Chicago society grew from scratch, cultural norms regarding sexuality had broadened greatly, in part from the new reality that for people from different worlds—not all of them, strictly speaking, human—relationships were now possible, healthy and acceptable. Relationships between people of the same gender no longer held the distinction of being all that unusual by comparison. And yet, some tiny part of Dorothy still found that part of Claudia alienating. Perhaps it was her Catholic upbringing, or maybe simple prudishness. More likely than either of those, Claudia made her uncomfortable in general, and this aspect added another layer to that.

"Hey." Apryl nudged Dorothy. "You should pop in on Melody. I'm sure she'd love to see you."

Dorothy seized the opportunity for a break, and got up from the table. "Thanks. I'll do that." They exchanged polite smiles, and Dorothy went down the hall to Melody's room as the discussion about her missing sister continued without her. This entire event had blindsided her. What she hoped would be a visit to her father in search of support had not played out that way at all, and her own troubles seemed woefully self-centered in light of Siobhan's disappearance. So, she welcomed the chance to regroup in the company of her twenty-ninth and youngest sister.

She knocked gently at the door and eased it open. "Hey, Little."

In the small bedroom, two children, engaged in some elaborate game with dolls, looked up from their play. The older child, Sarah's seven-year-old son Adler, had clearly been roped into the activity, a task he would have grudgingly taken on in his role supervising Harrison and Apryl's five-year-old daughter Melody. She had her mother's black, wavy hair, and her father's blue eyes. Unlike Adler, she also had a feature that reminded everyone who met her how the world was now a very different place. Both of her ears rose to slight points.

"Dorrie!" The little girl leapt up as she shouted her favorite approximation of Dorothy's name, and threw her arms out.

Dorothy grabbed her mid-leap and held her in a great hug.

"Are you here for the talk?" asked Melody.

"No," said Dorothy. "I'm here to see you."

"Are they still talking?"

Dorothy set Melody down. "Yes, they are still talking. Hi, Adler."

Adler waved without speaking.

"What are they talking about?" asked Melody.

"Boring, grown-up stuff. What are you playing?"

"They're having a birthday party!" Melody pointed to an assortment of dolls in various scales, surrounded by random toys and objects most likely intended to represent decorations, or perhaps cake. "And then they're going to rob a bank!"

Dorothy laughed. "Are they, indeed? Can I assume that was your contribution?" she asked Adler.

"No," he said. "That was her."

Melody beamed.

Dorothy shook her head and smiled. What could it be like to grow up in this world, never having known the one that came before it? What would Melody's idea of a bank robbery be? And what role would imagination play in a world where imaginary things were commonplace?

"Can we come out yet?" asked Melody. "I want a glass of water."

"Probably not. I can get you a glass of water if you need one."

"Okay!" Content with Dorothy's imminent return, Melody returned her attention to the party scene laid out on her floor.

"How about you, Adler?"

"Sure," said the boy.

"Be right back." Dorothy headed back to the kitchen.

Melissa had emerged from the bathroom looking pale, her hands wrapped around a glass of ice water on the table. Dorothy walked in to take a sip of her tea before carrying out her mission for the children.

"Did Siobhan ever do or say anything you thought was a little off?" asked Rebecca.

"I don't know," said Melissa. "Maybe. I always thought she seemed very together, but sometimes I felt like she had a harder time recovering than any of us. Like she was trying too hard to do the wrong things." She held up her hand to ward off a response from Rebecca. "I know, I know, everyone is different and there's no 'right' thing for all of us, but sometimes it just felt like she was moving backward. Like she would reminisce about it, sort of. It's hard to explain. She asked me once if I ever thought about going back there, to see that hole in the wall one more time, and I wasn't sure if she was talking about reliving the escape, or reliving the other stuff. She wasn't like that all the time. I have my own ways of dealing with things that probably don't make sense to anyone else, I'm sure. I'm not judging her. You asked, and that's my answer."

After a few seconds of dumbfounded silence, Rebecca said, "You should have opened with that."

"What?" said Melissa.

"My God," said Anna. "Would she really go back there? On her own?"

Melissa waved her hands in front of her. "No. There's no way. She never said she was going to do that. She never even said she wanted to. All she did was ask me if I ever thought about it. And I don't. Not ever. It was just weird to me she did. That's all."

Harrison already had his communicator out. "Felicia, I need the most recent surveillance images of the Lone Star Kingdom. Specifically, the palace."

"On it," responded the little speaker.

"Alec," said Harrison, "I would like permission to intensify the manhunt to the southwest quadrant extending from the city, to a radius of three days' walking distance."

After a few seconds, Baker's voice came back. "You think she's heading for Texas?"

"It's a possibility. I'm following a lead."

"Understood. You have a go," said Baker.

"Thank you," said Harrison. "Felicia?"

"I heard. Already in motion."

Harrison put the device back in his shirt pocket. "Please tell us everything you remember about that conversation," he said to Melissa.

"Dad, I'm telling you, there's no way," she said. "Siobhan can't even get herself to a job interview. She would never head to Texas alone."

"Maybe not, but it's the best theory we have right now." He paused. "And I honestly hope that's exactly what this is."

No one offered a contrary opinion, for reasons Dorothy found entirely clear. As much as the prospects of Siobhan's survival alone in the wild were not hopeful, the alternative was vastly more worrisome.

[3]

MAYHESPHERES

"Thank you, Dad."

Harrison rolled those words around in his head, for perhaps the thousandth time over the past few days. He replayed the memory of a frightened young girl, in a desperate situation and a dangerous escape. Surrounded by noise, and abused children, as frightened of him as they were of their keepers, one red-headed, freckled girl worked up the courage and understanding to see him for who he was to her.

"Thank you, Dad." It was the first time anyone had called him that. Even his own adopted children who lived with him for months called him by his first name. And he certainly didn't expect the girls he rescued that day to equate his legal gambit of claiming adoption rights over them with actual parenthood. He used the tactic to save them, and it worked. And yet, this girl took his offer at its face. A few others followed her lead. Over time, they would all come to know him as Dad, much more as an honorific than a familial title. But for that moment, she needed a father, and he became that father.

The first person who ever called him Dad was Siobhan Roark.

Four days into the search for her, that memory sustained him. Clues were spare, to say the least. The theory that Siobhan set out on foot to return to the Lone Star Kingdom provided the only promising lead so far, but an ongoing and exhaustive manhunt in that direction had so far yielded no fruit. To compound his frustration, he was too close to her to be an effective leader of the investigation, so he shifted his own focus for now to another matter: his own attempted assassination.

One of the few large structures that had been built from the foundation up in the last few years housed the Center for Esoteric Research. Most buildings were still reclaimed vestiges of the world as it had been before the Mayhem Wave, and while large scale construction gradually became more feasible, it still required an impractical dedication of resources, leaving it reserved for essential projects. Magic was one such project.

Esoteric Research purported to reconcile—as much as possible—the physical properties of the scientific and magical worlds. Earth in its current state was not strictly speaking either of those things, and people and creatures from both sides of that coin were all learning to adapt. At Esoteric, ordinary humans became wizards, and the research staff progressively revised the collective body of knowledge about chemistry and physics to include all the new properties of each field, and discard the properties that no longer held.

The government of New Chicago prioritized construction of the new facility itself when it became evident that a building with an iron frame rendered Faerie magic unworkable. They built Esoteric around three stories of aluminum bronze beams and girders, and it housed dozens of specialty rooms constructed of specific materials, and quarantined from others. The design incorporated several spells on the materials to reinforce, purify, or in other ways modify them for specific purposes.

And it was an absolute glory of Faerie architecture.

A natural stream ran through the foundation and passed directly under the main entrance, itself accessible by bridge. The designers incorporated the brook specifically to provide irrigation for the flora that formed the floors of many of the individual labs, as well as the trees that provided structural support to two of the wings. Windows of standard, rectangular, flat glass looked out near others in convex, irregular shapes, stained glass, or simply open to the elements. The mixture of fantastical and earthly design elements was, for the most part, fluid and seamless. Functionally and aesthetically, the facility represented the willful fusion of resources from the two worlds that had defined New Chicago from its inception.

As he emerged from the revolving door at the main entrance, he passed through two automatic security checkpoints. After dropping his keys and communicator in a plastic tray, he passed under the metal detector, a white, rectangular arch, virtually identical to what he would have expected at an airport or government building. Beyond that he walked through the magic detector, an arch composed of two interwoven, living vines. As he passed through it, the detection field washed him with the tingle described on the prominent warning sign mounted next to it. The main foyer transitioned from mild blur to sharp detail on the other side.

"Morning, Bill," he said to the uniformed officer sitting at the security desk.

"Morning, Mr. Cody." They exchanged polite nods.

This day, he intended to visit a lab on the third floor, accessible via an ordinary elevator (though one unusually lavish in its carpeting and woodwork for a science building), or an ornate three-story spiral staircase, carved entirely from a single sequoia log, and polished nearly to the point of reflectivity. Ten minutes early for his appointment, and in need of the momentary immersion in beauty, he opted for the stairs. He took his time, admiring the plethora of tiny gargoyles carved directly into the wood, taking note of the ones he had not seen before, and the ones that had faded away since his last visit.

The third-floor corridor displayed the same variation in style as the rest of the building, with every door entirely different from every other, rendering the numbered plates near them their least identifying features. Harrison passed two wooden doors and one lab behind an open stone arch, and arrived at his destination, behind an unspectacular, institutional door. He scanned his ID. The door dissolved into droplets of vapor, whisked upward into a fan. Once he passed the threshold, the door rained back down in a mist that gradually re-solidified. He rapped on the surface of the newly hardened door. It gave a hollow, metallic report.

"That seriously never gets old," he said.

"It does, though. Trust me." Dr. Larson studied an enormous wall monitor. A magical physicist who worked for Esoteric, she handled the bulk of NCSA business with them. She wore her straight, blonde hair in a ponytail, and a white lab coat, an inadequate visual clue to the bizarre nature of her job. But she preferred simplicity, perhaps an overcompensation for the complexity her professional life threw at her every day.

She did not turn to greet him as he approached the oversized screen. It displayed a star field, with no features of interest to a lay person apart from one star off to the right that glowed many times brighter than those around it.

"What are we looking at?" he asked.

"The Solar System." She tapped a hand-held device a few times to emphasize that. In response to commands from the remote, the screen

22

helpfully added color-coded outlines of the orbits of the inner five planets, along with circles indicating the locations of each in the image. She did this for Harrison's benefit; Larson surely already saw all of that without needing the crutch of the highlights. "Specifically, the Mayhesphere." She tapped the remote again, and a large, pale-red circle appeared, covering a large portion of the screen, and centered on Earth.

Harrison tried to track the significance of this circle, and came up blank. It spanned the gaps between the orbits of Mars and Venus, crossing both. Mars itself was clear across the sky from it, on the far side of the Sun, with Venus barely inside it. "I don't know what that is."

"Yes, you do," she said. "It's what everyone calls the Mayhem Wave."

"Wow. I had no idea it extended that far." In truth, he had given that matter no thought whatsoever. The Mayhem Wave completely reorganized the surface of the Earth and its physical and chemical properties in the space of a single day. Had he bothered to consider what became of that energy after that day, he would have assumed it had dissipated. The notion it had continued beyond the Earth into space had never occurred to him. "When was this image taken?"

"About a day ago," she said. "Which is as close as we can get to real time. This image is from a probe we launched two days ago via teleportation spell. Travel time was instantaneous, but unfortunately data transmission is still limited by the speed of light, and the speed of the equipment on the probe."

"Yesterday? It's still out there? Is it still expanding? Is it still changing things? How long have you known about this?" That she would spring this on him at a time when he had much more personal matters that needed his attention agitated him. This visit to Esoteric was supposed to be about the magical bomb planted in his drawer. He wasn't ready for another round of end-of-the-world level crisis.

"Yes, yes, that's what we're trying to learn, yes, and about an hour," said Larson. "In order."

"Is it dangerous?" asked Harrison.

"Not as far as I can tell from what we know. If that changes, I will certainly apprise you." She finally turned to face him, with no terror in her eyes, behind the pair of wire-rimmed glasses she never removed. "At the moment, we are trying to track the changes to Venus and Mars, both of which have now passed through the Mayhesphere at least once. Once we compile a complete profile of either planet, we will be able to start assessing potential hazard. The general thinking at this point is it's already done whatever it's going to do the Earth, so there's no threat there. Unless it's creating hostile life on other planets, I don't see any immediate cause for concern." She put down the remote. "But that's not why you're here."

"No, it isn't," he said.

"Cody!" came a voice from the door.

The bomb from his desk flew across the room directly toward him. "Shit!" He lurched to catch it before it hit the floor. He succeeded, and stared at the three sticks of dynamite in his hands.

"Oh, don't be such a baby," said the new arrival as the door shimmered back into place behind her. Dr. Garrett, a member of Larson's staff, wore a lab coat as well but had adorned it with a stick of celery on a pin, a nod to Doctor Who and an implication she considered her job on par with that of a Time Lord. She had gelled her short, black hair up into spikes. "It's just dynamite. You could hit it with a sledge hammer and it wouldn't do anything but break."

"Yes, well, it's a little hard to shake off the silly notion that dynamite is dangerous." He gingerly set the bomb on a lab table. "It's pretty deeply ingrained. I watched a lot of Road Runner as a kid."

"You are so adorable when you're about to wet yourself," said Garrett.

"Thanks?" said Harrison. "What's the deal with the bomb?"

"It's a bomb. Three sticks of dynamite, one detonator, one timer. The timer is frozen, but you know that."

Harrison turned the bomb over in his hands, now simply three sticks of dynamite taped together. "Where's the timer?"

"Still looking that over. Your agent did a number on it, a little beyond what we expected to see. Everything else checks out as advertised though, including the detonator. Might have even gotten a good crack out of the blasting cap, since they used a tube filled with gasoline and sealed with wax. Wouldn't blow the dynamite though. Might have gotten hot enough to ignite the nitroglycerin, but it would just burn. You'd be looking at a scorched desk, but that's about it."

"And the spell?"

"No trace of it," she said. "Every scan we were able to run shows this to be a fully mundane object."

Harrison frowned. "I don't understand. Are you saying this was never cursed? Gerry seemed very sure it was. Said it was very advanced work, whatever that means."

"Aplomado," corrected Larson. Harrison waved away the interruption.

"No," said Garrett. "I'm saying it's not cursed now. Maybe your agent wiped the curse when she stopped the clock. Maybe it burned out on its own. No way to be sure. Aplomado said it was advanced work? Those were his words?"

"I'm pretty sure," said Harrison.

"Well, apart from Mallory, we don't have anyone more advanced than he is. I doubt he would toss that word out without meaning it. Maybe the curse was designed to cover its own tracks. A high-level spellcaster might have been able to rig that. Or maybe Aplomado was just lying about the bomb being cursed. Whatever the reason, it's not there."

This gave Harrison pause. "Why would he lie about it?"

Garrett shrugged. "Why do wizards do stuff? Not my department. All I can tell you is it's clean. Do you want it back?"

"Yes." He looked at it warily. "Send it to NCSA forensics, please. Curse aside, there's still the matter of where it came from."

"Good luck with that."

"Thanks. Is Sparky here?" he asked Larson.

"Should be," she said. "Do you need her for something?"

"Nah. Just wanted to say hi. Thanks."

The door dissolved for him on his way out and reformed behind him. Sparky normally worked in research, testing found magical objects or finding magical explanations for unexplained happenings. Nearly a decade into this mixed world, opportunities for discovery continued to abound. She had demonstrated an unusual level of insight into magical analysis when she first arrived in New Chicago. Originally assigned to be liaison between Esoteric Research and Faerie, she often found her talents sought for various studies, and she developed a taste for the work. Oberon sent a sprite to take her place as go-between, and she had been a regular staff member of Esoteric ever since.

Harrison took the spiral staircase down to the ground floor before getting on the elevator to descend the remaining two levels to Sparky's lab in the subbasement. Even down here, the lab entrances were of diverse appearances and materials. Harrison passed through a set of beads hanging on strings from the open doorway to her lab, tolerating the mild shock that always accompanied entrance. The shock paled in comparison to what an unauthorized intruder would feel attempting to pass the beads.

An array of skylights lit the room, magically ignoring the four floors of building directly overhead. Harrison originally assumed the sun that shone in those skylights was an illusion, until the time Sparky opened one for fresh air.

"Goggles," said Sparky as soon as he entered.

He pulled a set of safety goggles off a hook near the doorway, and strapped them on. Unlike the scratchy plastic goggles from science classes in his youth, these were made of brass and leather, with crystal clear (and magically indestructible) glass lenses.

Sparky hovered near a lab table, wearing a miniature version of those same goggles, a tiny lab coat, and nothing else. Her orange-and-yellow streaked butterfly wings flapped at alternating speeds, from blindingly fast to ponderously slow, as she examined a wooden box with a glass lid. "Be right with you." She held her hands out in front of her, palms facing each other. With a moderately loud crackle, a small arc of orange energy formed between them. Her iridescent orange hair sparkled in response. The crackle increased in volume as the arc became a sphere, which she held over the glass lid of the box and released. It dropped unimpeded into the container, which briefly glowed then faded. From there, she flitted to a wall intercom and kicked a button. "Got it. Inert, and ready to be archived. You can come pick it up any time."

"Will do," said a voice on the other end. "Thank you."

"What are you working on?" asked Harrison.

She flew to him and hovered in front of him, pulling the goggles off and perching them on her head. The lab coat hung open, exposing her otherwise nude form. He had long since stopped finding that shocking or awkward. "Magic wand. Got a request from Spellcasting to freeze it for storage. What brings you here?"

"You mean Esoteric, or your lab?"

She rolled her eyes and smirked. "I know why you're in my lab. I meant Esoteric."

"Somebody planted a cursed bomb in my desk drawer."

"Damn! Nothing irreversible, I hope?" She moved back and forth, scanning him with her eyes, no doubt looking for a donkey tail or something.

"We stopped it before it went off," he said. "But thank you for your concern. I was just here to get a report from Garrett."

"Which you totally could have done over the phone. You do know these excuses you make to see your pixie crush are transparent to everyone, right?"

"As I keep reminding you, it's not a crush. It's a friendship."

She kissed him on the nose. "Whatever. You wanna grab lunch? They're serving eel in the cafeteria today."

"That sounds awful."

"It is! It totally is." She bobbed her way over to the doorway and hung her goggles on a hook. "Come on, you can tell me about your bomb over slimy fish."

"Siobhan is missing," he said.

She frowned. "Red? Gone? What are you talking about?"

"She went missing four days ago. We kept it out of the media because of her connection to me. But that's all I've been doing all week."

"Holy crap." The pixie tapped her chin in thought. "You're not telling me this personally, are you? This is professional."

He nodded. "That's why I'm here. I want to bring you in on this."

"Now I feel really bitchy for making fun of you." She pouted.

He smiled at that. "Don't worry about it."

"Over it." She flew back to the intercom and kicked it again. "Hey, this is Sparky. Tell the boss I'm going on vacation. I'll be back in about a while." She closed the line again, and flew back to Harrison. "I'm all yours."

"Who were you talking to?"

"No idea. Whoever was listening. It'll be fine. I take it I'll be working in your building until further notice."

"Affirmative," he said.

"Then we better get that eel while we can."

He laughed. "Sure."

"I still say it's a crush."

He shook his head. "It's not."

"Whatever. Oh, crap!"

"What?"

She pouted again. "Am I going to have to wear clothes?"

[4]

DOROTHY

The University of New Chicago rose to be the most prestigious institution of higher learning in the country not merely as a function of the lack of alternatives. In fact, it competed with more than twenty colleges and universities, already well organized and endowed. Nor did it enjoy success because of the population concentration, with The City of New Chicago being the broadest and densest of the several dozen urban centers that had grown from the ruins of civilization. While those factors certainly contributed, the real source of the University's success lay in the unyielding drive for excellence of its founders and staff. The world stripped away every proper resource for higher learning, and a dedicated band of educators founded The University of New Chicago less than two years after that event, to send the world a simple message: we will not abide that.

Sarah Logan earned her PhD in mathematics at this university, and the administration heavily recruited her shortly after to come on board as a professor. They similarly recruited Dorothy after she earned her second Master's degree before her twenty-first birthday. She chose to continue pursuing her studies instead, personally vowing to remain a full-time student as long as feasible, not from some fear of finding a career, but from a genuine addiction to knowledge. At some point she would slow down enough to begin teaching, but for now, her graduate assistant stipend more than adequately supported her modest lifestyle, and the work brought her more joy than anything else in her life.

And so, two days after stumbling upon a meeting in Harrison's apartment that prevented her from coming to him with her need for personal support, she sought solace in her comfort zone, and the advice of someone there. She found Sarah in her office shortly after lunch, and rapped on the open door.

"Dr. Logan?"

Sarah looked up from a stack of papers, and offered a look of pleasant surprise. "Hi there! Come in!" She got up to pull an armful of journals off a chair, and set them on top of a similar pile on a table across from her desk.

"Thank you," said Dorothy.

"And stop calling me Dr. Logan."

Dorothy smiled. "I like calling you Dr. Logan. And I very much look forward to being called Dr. O'Neill."

"I'm sure you do," said Sarah, in a conspiratorial tone. "Between you and me, it does give me a bit of a rush some days. Other days it just makes me feel old."

Dorothy took a moment to mentally chart the progress of gray streaks in Sarah's hair. She would never mention this to Sarah directly, but she found those earned gray hairs to be strikingly beautiful and distinguished, and fantasized about her own hair transitioning from rose gold to silver.

"What brings you here?" said Sarah. "Is this about your doctorate? How is that coming along?"

"Very well, thank you," said Dorothy. "And no, I'm just here on a social call."

Sarah's eyebrows went up a notch. "Is that a first? Dorothy O'Neill paying a visit just to be social? Don't get me wrong, I am delighted, but I think I know you a little better than that."

Dorothy smiled again, and looked away. "I need advice."

"I'm listening."

She paused. "This isn't easy."

Sarah said gently, "Take your time. Everything okay?"

Dorothy shook her head.

"Personal or school?"

"Personal."

They both left that word alone for a second.

"You didn't come to Harrison's for that meeting, did you?" said Sarah.

"No."

"I thought something was up, but I wasn't sure whether to ask. Is this something you need to talk about with Harrison?"

Dorothy sighed. "No, I don't think so. I only went there because he always listens. I didn't expect him to fix anything. I just thought I could talk to him without worrying he would judge me. Then I found out about Siobhan, and now I feel guilty for wanting to bother him with my problems."

"Okay, why don't we back up a bit," said Sarah. "First of all, don't ever feel guilty for having problems, or for needing help. That said, you are right to think this is not a good time for Harrison to be there for you. So I commend you on your second choice. I am all ears, and no judgment. What has you so despondent?"

After a tense pause, Dorothy said, "Heartache."

Sarah laughed lightly at that. "Really? Oh, this truly is a first."

"Is that funny?" asked Dorothy, genuinely confused.

"It is," said Sarah. "Heartache is always funny. And it's always tragic, especially for someone your age. Is this a crush, or a breakup?"

"Breakup."

"Whose idea?"

"His."

Sarah drummed her fingers lightly on her desk. "Well, I won't lie, that does make things harder. Honestly, I had no idea you even had a boyfriend. I feel very out of touch right now."

Dorothy looked away. Blush burned her cheeks, but she refused to give in to self-consciousness. "It's okay. It was only a couple of months, and we didn't exactly advertise it." An understatement, to be sure. Dorothy did not have a particularly robust social life, and no one would have noticed a difference in her behavior if not specifically looking for it.

"It can be hard no matter how long it lasts," said Sarah. "Are you okay? Did he hurt you?"

"He's not like that," said Dorothy.

"Just trying to cover all the bases. Is it bad? If this is depression, you know you can see a counselor through the health center, right?"

Dorothy shrugged. "I tried that. It's frustrating for me to talk about my problems with people who obviously aren't as smart as I am."

"Can't fault you there. How about your mom?"

"We don't really connect as well since I moved out," said Dorothy.

"Okay, what about your peers?"

Dorothy smiled bitterly at that. "Dr. Logan, I am twenty-three years old, and a year away from my PhD. How many 'peers' do you think I have?"

Sarah frowned. "Fair enough. Listen, Dorothy, as far as I am concerned, you are family. If you need me to be your support system right now, I can do that. If you need to talk about it, I'll listen. If you need someone to take care of you, I can do that too. I know this sounds simplistic and obvious, but I promise you it gets better. That doesn't mean it won't hurt for now, unfortunately. But everyone goes through this, and everyone recovers. For real. For now, just do what you can to feel good about yourself, and give it time. Okay?"

For a moment, Dorothy did not respond. Finally, softly, she said, "He was...my first."

Sarah's eyes went wider and softer. "Oh, honey..."

A knock came from the open door. "Dr. Logan?" Two of her students stood outside her office, one male, one female, both sheepish and looking confused.

Sarah bit her lip in apprehension. "This is my office hours. I need to help these kids."

Dorothy nodded stoically. "I understand." She got up to leave.

"Hey," said Sarah, "we can talk about this some more if you need to. I'm free here in about two hours. Think you can hold out that long?"

Dorothy let out a dry and embarrassed laugh. "I guess I'll find out."

"I mean it, young lady. I want you back here at three o'clock sharp. We can go out for ice cream or something."

"I'll be back. Wouldn't want to miss ice cream." After debating trying to hug Sarah, and concluding it would appear unprofessional in front of her students, she left.

With two hours to kill, and trapped in the uncomfortable uncertainty of whether coming to Sarah was wise or simply humiliating, Dorothy turned to a staple source of distracting amusement: her little brother. She took out her phone and tapped the picture of his face that sat in a position of prominence on the screen. At this time of day, Mitchell would be in class. He would not be able to take the call, but he would see it, and find some excuse to call her back. Mitchell was a decent student, with sufficient respect from his teachers to give him leverage to manipulate them. They had done this before, multiple times, and Mitchell always managed to find the right thing to say to get himself lawfully excused from class long enough to return her calls.

Mitchell and Dorothy were nothing like each other. Where she was reserved, he was gregarious. Her insatiable thirst for learning went completely unreflected in Mitchell's plans to abandon his education after high school. They had one thing in common: the bond they shared from their brief stint as Harrison's children, a bond that had flourished over the course of their adolescences and young adulthoods. For all that Mitchell represented her opposite, she still counted him her best friend. And he made her laugh, which would come in handy at that moment. Ten minutes on the phone with Mitchell would likely be enough joy to sustain her for two hours of waiting to shed her deepest worries with Sarah. She made the call, and left a message.

Forty minutes later, still waiting for some acknowledgement from him, she abandoned the idea that anyone actually cared about her, along with her plans for ice cream with Dr. Logan, and went home.

[5]

MISSING PERSONS

W
e need to talk about getting some pixie-sized furniture in my office." Sparky hovered in Harrison's doorway, wearing a peach-colored, diaphanous gown that hung loosely on her shoulders and legs, but clung to her torso like a second skin, leaving exactly nothing to the imagination. She struck the image of a model in a Maxfield Parrish painting, but smuttier.

"I didn't assign you an office," said Harrison from his desk.

"Oh. Well, maybe we should start there."

"Or we could revisit our conversation about the dress code."

She offered a confused look. "I don't see the point in doing that. Maybe we could talk a little more about exactly what it is I'm supposed to be doing, and how much easier that will be in my own office."

Harrison stood. "Walk with me."

She followed him out the door, hovering about two feet away from him.

"For the time being, you are with me. I am juggling two unrelated investigations, and I need another pair of eyes to catch anything I miss. When I have a specific task for you, I'll let you know." He passed his assistant's office and poked his head in. "What's the status of that list I gave you?"

Felicia looked at her computer screen briefly before responding. "Contacted all but two so far. Katherine Gable is on a dig in Utah, and currently in a communication dead zone. We have an agent traveling to the site to inform her in person. And Kari Crenshaw's whereabouts are currently unknown."

Harrison frowned. "That can't be right. She should have been the easiest one to find." Katherine and Kari were two of Harrison's adopted daughters, and now the last two to be informed of Siobhan's disappearance. Nine of the twenty-eight no longer lived in New Chicago, and Felicia had been tasked with tracking them down and notifying them.

"One would think," said Felicia. "I spoke to her CO this morning. Sergeant Crenshaw is overdue to report for duty following a weekend liberty."

"AWOL?" asked Harrison, shocked.

"Evidently," said Felicia with no sign of emotion.

"That's crazy. Kari is a decorated marine. She would never desert. Did her CO offer any clarification of that situation?"

"I didn't pursue it," she said. "Would you like me to call him back?"

Harrison thought for a moment. "No, that's a military matter. They'll handle it. Damn it." He shook his head. "I can't worry about that right now. This is a crappy time for her to throw away her career, though."

"Yes, sir," said Felicia.

"Keep me posted on Katherine. I'm headed down to forensics."

"Will do."

"She has an office," said Sparky.

Felicia looked up at the pixie with her usual deadpan.

"I'm just saying, she has an office, and it seems like she gets a lot done. You get a lot done, don't you?"

"You have no idea," said Felicia.

"Leave the nice agent alone, Sparky," said Harrison.

She pouted.

"Sorry about that," he said to his assistant.

"No worries." She went back to her work.

"Come on." Harrison escorted Sparky to the elevator, where they descended to the second floor.

"What's down here?" she asked.

"Forensics lab," he said. "It's actually not that different from what you do at Esoteric. We have scientists who examine physical evidence for clues to where it came from, among other things. I had Larson send them the bomb from my office two days ago, and I haven't heard anything yet. I thought a personal visit might give them a little encouragement to step up their work a bit."

"You want me to intimidate them?" she asked, scowling.

"Probably not necessary, but we'll consider that Plan B."

"Okay." She made a practice face, growling.

In the lab, Harrison found Agent Aldridge looking at something in a microscope, and silently hoped it was related to the bomb. If he noticed the two of him entering his workspace, he gave no indication.

"You busy?" asked Harrison.

"A little bit," said Aldridge shortly. "Something you need?"

"Your attention would be nice."

Aldridge sighed, lifted his face away from the lens and rubbed his eyes. "Oh, Cody." He put his glasses back on. "You're here for your dynamite?"

"Not really interested in having it back," said Harrison. "Just want to know what you've learned about it."

"Not a thing," said Aldridge. "The dynamite itself is standard industrial grade, and looks like it was manufactured circa 1990. Anyone's guess where it came from, but it's obviously a pre-Mayhem relic, not a new product. We might have gotten some information from the gasoline in the blasting cap—whether it was siphoned from a pre-Mayhem source or obtained from the new refinery—but it completely evaporated when the girls at Esoteric broke the seal."

"What about the timer?"

"Yeah, Logan really did a number on that," said Aldridge. "I've never seen her work before this. It's pretty amazing. We couldn't get that open at all. Couldn't even scratch it with a diamond-tipped drill. There's some debate here about whether the thing might be quantum locked, but it's warm to the touch. Either way, it's a much more severe result than anything else we have on record for her. I was going to recommend she come back in for a new evaluation, in case her power has somehow evolved. That's your call, though, not mine. Anyway, it's a shame that we can't get it open, because it looks like it was hand-made. If any part of that bomb was going to tell us who made it, it would have been that clock."

"Ugh," said Harrison. "So that's it then? Complete dead end?"

"Looks that way. The parts are all tagged for the vault. Unless you have other plans for them, I'll send them down."

Before Harrison had a chance to tell Aldridge to do that, and close the book on this aspect of the investigation, Sparky zipped between them and hovered her transparently garbed body menacingly in front of Aldridge's face. "Oh, no you don't! That's quitter talk! If anyone from Esoteric gave up on an assignment that quickly they'd find their butt on the street before they could get to the end of their lame excuse!"

"What?" Aldridge sputtered.

"Hey!" Sparky pointed to her face. "My eyes are up here! Maybe if you spent less time checking out the hot pixie and more time doing your job we'd have these bad guys behind bars by now!"

Aldridge made several awkward attempts to look in directions other than Sparky's before finally looking at Harrison. "Help?"

"That's enough, Sparky."

"Harrumph!" she spat loudly at Aldridge, before flitting back to Harrison's side.

"Thank you," said Harrison to Aldridge. "Send those parts to the vault. If you think of anything you didn't already try, call me right away."

"Right," said the scientist, now perspiring.

Harrison took Sparky into the hall. "What was that?"

"Plan B?" she said innocently.

"Yeah, don't do that again. I need you not to be freaking out my agents." He flicked a loose fold of her garment. "You do realize that your nipples are actually more visible in this than they would be if you were naked, right?"

She grinned. "I know! I am rocking this thing! Right? I can make it stick to my crotch, too! Look!" She held her arms out and closed her eyes in concentration as the gown constricted itself about her abdomen.

"That looks uncomfortable," he said.

"It totally is," she said with her eyes still closed, and a slight wince. "I'm trying to decide whether it's worth it."

"Do I need to requisition a uniform for you, Agent?"

Sparky opened her eyes, and her face sank. "No." She pouted, and the bottom half of her dress released itself, draping loosely back down.

Harrison's phone chirped. He pulled the communicator out of his pocket on reflex, before remembering it didn't ring. He checked his personal phone. The screen read, "Apryl at work."

"Shouldn't you be teaching a class right now?"

"I love you too," said his wife.

"Seriously."

"It's my planning period," she said. "Did I catch you at a bad time?"

"No time is ever bad for you," he said.

"Aww!" said Sparky.

Harrison held his hand up and glared at her. She timidly withdrew. "What's up?"

"Marty Bell left a message on our home line this morning and I just saw it forwarded to my voice mail. Mitchell ran away again."

"Aw, crap." Harrison thought back to his last conversation with Mitchell, interrupted more than a week earlier, and never resumed despite his promise to the boy. One more ball for him to drop in the wake of his larger responsibilities. "Details?"

"Just that they had a fight and Mitchell stormed out. Marty wanted to know if we had him."

"We don't."

"I know that," she said. "Do you want to call him, or should I?"

"And tell him what? Mitchell has a car and an attitude. He could be anywhere. I assume this happened yesterday?"

"He didn't say. I can forward the message to you if you need to hear it, but there really isn't anything else." While Harrison formed a reply to that, she said, "Don't you dare blame yourself."

"Yes, ma'am," he said. "And yes, I'll take care of it."

"Love you!" she said.

"I love you, too." He pocketed the phone.

"Now can I say aww?" asked Sparky.

He pulled his communicator and spoke into it. "Felicia, please call Martin Bell and tell him my wife and I do not know where Mitchell went, and offer my sympathy and apologies for being too busy to call him personally."

"Got it," she said.

"Wow," said Sparky. "For a big hero like you, that was curiously cowardly."

"Yes, well," said Harrison, "if I called him myself, I'd probably be less kind than Felicia will be. Come on."

They returned to the elevator, and to Harrison's office, where he found a gray, pointed, felt hat on his desk. "Great." He looked around for the wizard who went with the hat, and wondered if Aplomado's annoying arsenal of talents included invisibility. With the sound of a tiny wooden crack, the wizard stood up from behind Harrison's desk, and sat in his leather chair. He held a dark brown splinter about eight inches long in front of his face, scrutinizing it.

Harrison's jaw dropped. "Is that a piece of my desk?"

"It is," said the wizard, his eyes still on the piece of wood.

"You jerk!" said Harrison. "What the hell are you doing?"

Aplomado showed no sign of offense. "Looking for residue of the curse on that bomb. I am told that none of your various inspections have yielded fruit." He released the splinter, and it dropped smoothly into one of the sleeves of his robe.

"Garrett says the bomb wasn't cursed at all," said Harrison. "Is it possible you were wrong?"

"Of course," he said. "It is absolutely possible that someone went to the trouble and risk to place an object in your desk that would appear extremely menacing while in fact being completely inert, and it would somehow put out false magical evidence of a non-existent curse. Possible, but idiotic to believe. I do not trifle with the possible, Mr. Cody. There are more than enough mundane agents to cover that field."

"By which, of course, you mean, 'I apologize for the unauthorized entry and property damage, Assistant Director.' Are you even assigned to this investigation?"

"Self-assigned," he said.

"Well, assign yourself the hell off it," said Harrison.

Aplomado stood and picked up his hat. "I will let you know what I find from the wood fragment. And I would appreciate you sharing any of your findings with me as well. It will save me the time of keeping track of your efforts."

"Share this finding," said Harrison under his breath. While he weighed the relative costs of allowing this arrogant prick to meddle with his investigation or going over his head to file a complaint against him with Baker, a nagging memory slipped into his consciousness. Garrett had speculated Aplomado might have lied about the curse. If so, to what end? And why would he return to this office to so brashly perpetuate his version of this story? The possibility seemed more concrete now, but also more confusing. Before he had a chance to compose a proper statement about whether the wizard would be permitted anywhere near his office or his evidence again, Sparky zipped between them.

"Just who do you think you are?" she shouted at Aplomado. "This man is your boss, you insolent freak!" The wizard received this hostility with much more poise than did Aldridge. "You'll be lucky if he doesn't have you locked up for breaking his desk! How dare you waltz in here like..." She paused, staring at him dumbfounded as he failed to react to her rant. "Are you looking at my eyes?"

"I am," he said.

"Hey Jackass!" she shouted, pointing to herself indignantly. "My tits are down here!"

[6]

BLOOD

The Pre-Mayhem Memorial took up a full city block. A three-story concrete structure encased a courtyard, the entire thing open to the sky. Paths and hallways ran through it, connected by ramps and stairways, with no underlying symmetry. Walkways followed curves and obtuse angles. And throughout, along every footpath on every floor, ran walls covered in names. They honored loved ones, or acquaintances, of the residents of New Chicago, the one common element they shared that they had not been seen since May 30, 2004. Occasional exceptions dotted the list. Persons who turned up after the building of the memorial had their names covered over with simple brass plates that read, "Found." But those represented the tiniest fraction of the names on those walls, which even numbering in the tens of millions, themselves represented the tiniest fraction of the people lost that day.

Dorothy waited patiently on a stone bench near the top of the structure. This high up, with no sheltering overpasses, the fact of the sunny day and slight breeze added a layer of comfort she sorely needed. As she sat, alternating between taking in the beauty of the weather and reading a book, several people and families strolled by, some stopping to point out a name and talk about a lost one, others on their way through the labyrinth to whatever wall held their goal, and some simply using this venue for a walk on a lovely spring day. Several fey creatures of various shapes and sizes ambled or flew by, searching for the names of their own lost kin. On a lower level, the distinct clip-clop of a centaur drew closer, ever so slightly distinguishable from the sound of a pure horse.

As the hoof beats grew louder, Dorothy looked up from her book. A bearded, male centaur approached her, a rider's arms around his chest. He stopped near the bench and knelt on all fours to let his passenger climb off. Dorothy stood and embraced the woman.

"Hello, Mother."

Theresa O'Neill kissed her daughter on the cheek, then said to her ride, "Thank you so much."

"My pleasure, I assure you." He stood and continued on his way.

"Hello, darling," she said to Dorothy, out of breath. She looked past her daughter to the departing centaur, and watched him round a corner out of sight. "What a rush."

"Been there, rode that," said Dorothy.

"Me, too. Doesn't make it any less exciting." Her eyes lingered on the spot where she last saw him. "Quite a looker, I don't mind saying. Do you think he has a girlfriend?"

"I think he has a penis the size of your forearm."

Theresa gazed away in thought. "You don't say."

"Did you bring anything?"

Theresa sat on the bench and patted it for Dorothy to sit with her. "Not this time. Did you?"

Dorothy picked up a paper box from the floor under the bench and opened it. A small chocolate cake, with the number 19 written on it in frosting, and two forks, rested inside.

Theresa smiled warmly at the gesture, then stood and went to the wall. She had come here so many times she did not need to scan it to find the names. Directly across from the left edge of the bench, at about chest height for her, she found them. Loraine O'Neill. Fiona O'Neill. She crouched down a bit, closed her eyes, and whispered a prayer. "Happy birthday, Loraine," she said at last, and kissed the stone gently.

Dorothy watched all this from her seat. She had her own conversation with her sisters before Theresa arrived. Her mother brushed the wall one more time with her fingertips, then sat, picked up a fork and took a healthy bite of cake.

"Does this get any easier?" asked Dorothy.

Her mother pondered this question while she swallowed. "I want to say no. I really do. They were my children. My blood. And I loved them more than you could possibly understand. I still love them." She poked the cake once more, and held a morsel of it in front of her. "Yes. It gets easier." She popped the cake into her mouth.

Dorothy did not respond, or ask for an explanation. She felt it too. Nine years had passed since losing her two younger sisters. Eight subjective years had passed for Theresa. Time did not erase their love for the girls, but it did dull the pain of their loss.

"This is good," said Theresa. "Where did you get it?"

"I baked it," said Dorothy.

Theresa looked at her in awe. "You bake? When did this happen?"

"I have three college degrees, Mother. I am capable of learning new skills, you know." Dorothy picked up her own fork, and sampled her work.

"Where is Brad today?" asked her mother.

"I wouldn't know," said Dorothy without making eye contact.

Her mother stopped short on her third trip into the cake. "Oh dear. I'm sorry. When did this happen?"

"About two weeks ago. It's not important."

"Two weeks. Has it really been that long since we saw each other?"

"Longer," said Dorothy, with no judgment in her tone. "I've been busy."

"Are you all right?"

"I'm fine." Dorothy filled her mouth with cake to forestall having to answer follow-up questions.

"You know I would love to see more of you," said Theresa. "I worry about you spending so much time alone, especially if Brad is out of the picture now."

Dorothy continued to chew, mentally composing a polite rebuff to this invitation. She loved her mother, but her independence mattered more to her now than it ever had. At fourteen, she had survived on her own for several months with no human contact, and she wished her mother could have seen that version of herself. For all Dorothy's intelligence and resourcefulness, Theresa still felt compelled to nurture her.

"Do you have friends you can lean on?" asked her mother.

Finally swallowing, Dorothy said, "I'm fine." It was both a dodge and a lie. She wasn't doing well, and she did not have close friends to shore her up. Her comment to Sarah about having no peers reflected a reality she had grudgingly come to accept. Even in a semi-magical world full of freaks, no one understood her. However, even as she rolled that familiar thought around her head, she remembered one person who might count as a peer. Someone who shared her age and her intellect, even if she had chosen a different path with that mind. She might even have the right kind of perspective to share, if Dorothy ever had the courage to open up to her, as she had recently gone through a breakup of her own. Unfortunately, that person was Claudia, who barely got along with her on a good day. It might be worth setting aside her pride and discomfort to reach out to her.

Her phone vibrated in her pocket. The screen showed a photo of Harrison with his family. She answered it, grateful for the diversion. "Hello?"

"Hi, Dorothy," said Apryl. "Have you been in contact with Mitchell?"

The question stung. "No. Why?"

"He ran away again. His father hoped he was with us, but he isn't."

Dorothy sighed. "He'll come back, He always does."

"I know. I just wanted to check in with you so that when Marty calls back I'll have something to say to him. If Mitchell does contact you, please direct him to his father right away."

"Which father?" asked Dorothy, half-seriously.

"Either would be fine. Harrison is a little preoccupied these days, so he's better off calling Marty, but if it's Harrison or nothing, then he should call us."

"Understood. I will pass that along."

"Thanks," said Apryl. "How are you doing?"

"I'm fine," she said. "I'm with my mother right now."

"Got it," said Apryl. "Have a good day!"

"You too."

As Dorothy pocketed the phone, her mother asked, "Who will be back?"

"Mitchell. He ran away. Again."

Her mother took this in silently, and had another bite of cake. After a pause, she said, "I'm glad you have him."

"Who, Mitchell?"

"Mitchell, Harrison, your little step-sister. All of them. I'm glad you have family, even if it's strange, pseudo-family. I'm glad you stayed close to them." She put her arm around Dorothy. "You're still my little girl, you know. Still my blood. The only blood I have left." She trailed off there, sniffing. "Oh my. I think I lied about it getting easier."

Dorothy held her mother as she cried it out.

TIME

How many of these are we going to do?"

Sarah Logan sat at a long table, with a sleep mask parked on top of her head, and an array of objects spread out before her. Most were ordinary clocks, in a variety of styles and mechanisms. Analog, digital, windup, electric (both battery powered and AC) and one very old clock run entirely on counterweights. All frozen, entirely from suffering her gaze. An egg beater, a Teddy bear, a pinwheel, an electric stapler, and several other objects and devices whose exact nature was unclear also sat before her. In every case, her ability did not affect the control objects.

"I'm not sure. Please bear with us." Dr. Garrett gathered up the clocks, tagging each one with a code, and carried them out of the room on a tray.

Sarah drummed her fingers on the table. "How long have I been here?" For Sarah, every bit of information she received about the passage of time had to be verbal.

"Less than half an hour," said Harrison.

"Seems longer," she said. "Not that I even remember what half an hour feels like anymore. Sometimes I think my students conspire to end my classes early because they know damn well I can't call them on it."

"You can trust me," he said.

She sighed. "I do. I had just forgotten how tedious and frustrating this is. Remind me why I am doing this?"

"We think the data we have on your telekinetic ability is out of date," said Dr. Larson. "It's been nearly seven years since we ran any proper tests, and your field use of the ability had some surprising results."

"Surprising how?"

Larson fidgeted with a PDA. "It's better if we tell you after the tests are finished."

"Is this something that should concern me?" she asked Harrison. "Please be straight with me."

"I don't think so. They won't tell you because it's a mental ability, and they are afraid if you know what the new thing is you'll make it happen on purpose. Is that right?" he asked Larson.

"No," she said. "But it's close enough. Ms. Logan, can you tell me everything you recall about how your ability works?"

"It's Special Agent Logan," said Harrison.

"It's Dr. Logan," said Sarah. "And I thought you had all that information from when we did this dance years ago."

"Again, because the ability is largely mental, your understanding of it may be relevant."

Sarah sighed. "If I remember this correctly—and there is a very good chance I do not—my ability is a reflex, or something like that. Whenever I see a clock, my subconscious identifies whatever parts make it go, and then I telekinetically make them stop moving. I think it's like what Harrison does with locks, only my thing works on sight instead of by touch. Did I get it right?"

Larson read off the screen of her small hand-held device. "He used more jargon, but that's a near verbatim summary of Tucker's initial report."

Tucker. Harrison could not remember the last time he heard that name. It must have been years. It took him by surprise, as did the rush of guilt that followed on its heel. Hadley Tucker trusted him, and accompanied him on his mission to rescue Glimmer. It cost him his life. Under similar circumstances today, Harrison would be able to cope with sending an agent to his or her death. He had to be able to handle it to do his job, and everyone under his command understood the risks of their profession. But this happened long before he was expected to make those life and death decisions for a living, and Hadley had never been anything but a scientist. It still stung, and it clung to him in abrasive remorse.

"Good for me," said Sarah.

Garrett returned, carrying something covered with a drape, heavy enough to need both hands. She placed it on the table with a *thud*.

"What's this?"

"Cover your eyes, please."

Sarah pulled the sleep mask over her eyes. "Covered."

"I'll need complete silence for this." Garrett pointed at Harrison. "So no smart-alecky remarks from you, punk."

Harrison held his palms up with an exaggerated look of innocence on his face.

Holding her finger over her mouth, Garrett removed the covering.

A narrow, rectangular object sat on the table, about two feet tall, and made almost entirely of glass. It comprised dozens of compartments, some of which had moving parts, and most chambers were partially filled with water. They drained into each other at various rates, and the pressure of this water drove the moving parts in their tiny, slow ballet.

"Are we recording?" asked Garrett.

"We are recording," said Larson.

"Please remove the blind."

Sarah lifted the mask off her head. She frowned at the object in front of her. "What is that?" No one spoke. She looked at Harrison. "Seriously. What is that?" He shrugged. She looked at it from different angles, then laughed. "Oh! That's cute. I've never seen one of these. It's a clock, isn't it?"

"There we go," said Garrett.

"You saw it?" asked Larson.

"You betcha."

"Mark the time she identified it. We'll go back over the recording and find the lag between when she saw it and when it stopped." Larson keyed something into her handheld computer.

"It stopped?" asked Sarah. "Was it moving before?"

"Before you took off the blindfold," said Harrison. The delicate movements had ceased. This was now and forever a frozen glass sculpture.

"Oh," said Garrett, who had moved closer to inspect the clock. "Oh! Come see this!"

Harrison and Larson moved in closer, as Garrett pointed to a drop of water suspended in mid fall. The tiny, irregular spheroid hung there with no regard for gravity or its own fluid state.

"Wow," said Sarah. "I had no idea I could do that."

"I told you," said Garrett to Larson. "Did I tell you?"

"What just happened?" asked Sarah. "Is this the new thing you were looking for?"

Garrett grinned, in a display that flaunted her lack of scientific detachment on this topic. "You, Miss Special Doctor Agent Logan, are a time freezer."

She stared at the giddy scientist. "Meaning?"

"Meaning you don't stop clocks," said Larson. "You stop time around them. More precisely, it appears that you slow time. Garrett's estimate is that you take it down to one second every twenty to fifty million years. From the data we gathered today we should be able to narrow that interval considerably."

Sarah's eyes bugged slightly as she shrunk back from the table.

Harrison looked at Larson. "This isn't anything to be alarmed about, is it?"

"Probably not. The practical effect is basically the same. This just means we understand the mechanism a little better."

"Why didn't you catch this earlier?" asked Sarah. "With all the tests I went through when I first got to Chicago, how could you miss something like this?"

"We missed it," said Larson, "because it wasn't there. The clocks we have from 2003 have all been taken apart and reassembled several times. What you did to the bomb timer was entirely new. It looks like your power has evolved. We've seen that already with Cody and de Queiroz. The reason we never saw it in your power before is the observed results of what you do have never changed, or changed in ways too subtle to draw attention."

"May I be excused?" asked Sarah. "I do believe I am about to vomit."

"Oh." Larson stepped back. "Yes. Certainly."

Sarah stood and briskly exited the lab.

"If her ability has evolved it stands to reason Rutherford's might have as well," said Larson to Harrison. "We have recent data on you and de Queiroz, but we haven't tested him in years."

"She's right," said Garrett. "We should get him in here."

"What about Apryl?" asked Harrison.

Garrett looked at her notes. "Hmm. We have much more data on her already. Is she still teleporting? That wasn't in her original bag of tricks."

"Maybe? I would have to ask her. It was actually one of the first things she was able to do, but she needed a machine for it at the time. She didn't do it on her own until a few years later."

"Well, then, we've probably already seen her upgrade," said Garrett. "We can have a look if you want, but Rutherford is the closest snake right now."

Harrison pulled his communicator out. "Felicia, please have Special Agent Rutherford report to Esoteric at his earliest convenience." Bob Rutherford—who called himself Dallas, though failed to appreciate that no one else did—was, along with Harrison, Sarah, Claudia and Apryl, the fifth telekinetic in New Chicago. His power had only ever been useful for

46

making dice roll snake eyes, or making coins land tails. If this ability had evolved since it was last tested, Harrison needed to know.

"Should I tell him why?" she asked.

"No."

"Understood. I was about to call you. We have updates on Gable and Crenshaw."

"Did you find them?"

"No," said Felicia. "And you should know their situations are worse than that. Are you able to hear this news, or should I take it to Baker first?"

"Oh, God. Tell me."

"Two agents just returned from the Utah dig site. The camp was destroyed, and they found remains of seven individuals."

"Katherine?" said Harrison with a calm that belied the fear in his heart.

"Still unaccounted for, along with one other person. We have the site quarantined. Early indications point to a demon attack, or possibly some type of non-real indigenous wild beast." Non-real indigenous was NCSA parlance for beings not originally from Harrison's world. Those people had been attacked and killed by a literal monster.

"Keep looking for her," he said. "What about Crenshaw?"

"Her command is no longer treating her as AWOL. She is now considered MIA. Her ID was recovered. It was cracked, and had traces of blood that matched her type."

Blood drained from Harrison's face, and he willed himself to stay sharp. "Are these disappearances related?"

"Given the timing, we have to assume they are, sir. All three."

"Damn it. Call Crenshaw's CO. Tell him our resources are at his disposal for whatever search they are conducting. Or start one if they haven't already done so."

"Got it. Anything else?"

He hesitated. "I don't know."

"Sir, if I may, assuming the pattern holds, there are still more than twenty women at risk," said Felicia. "It might be time to consider something more proactive."

"You mean assign a detail to each one of them? How quickly can we make that happen?"

"Actually, I was thinking more in terms of protective custody. We could house them on the seventh floor. I can have the ones who live locally brought in immediately, if that's what you want."

Harrison hesitated in the face of this suggestion. When he first met those women, they were being held against their will. His entire relationship with them was predicated on his role as the hero who freed them. Now his assistant asked if he wanted to lock them up again.

"Sir?" said Felicia. "Do I have a go?"

He gave himself a moment to be certain. "Yes. You have a go. I want every one of my adopted daughters brought to the NCSA facility in protective custody."

"Right away. Any special instructions?"

"Affirmative. There are six women on that list coded 'Hermit.' They are not to be contacted until I make arrangements to bring them in, which will be in about ten minutes. Is that all understood?"

"Yes, sir."

"And Felicia," he said, "when I say all my daughters, that includes the ones who do not live in New Chicago."

"Understood."

"Make it happen." He pocketed the communicator.

"Am I allowed to ask what just happened?" asked Garrett.

Harrison held up a warding hand, and pulled out his phone. Twenty seconds later, he got an answer.

"Harrison? Is there news?" said Rebecca Wheeler.

"Yes, and it's bad. I'm sorry to lean on you like this, but we have an emergency. I am pulling all my daughters in for protective custody."

"Oh, God," she said. "What's happening? Is Siobhan dead?"

"I don't know," he said. "And I can't think about that until the rest of you are safe. I need you to help me bring in the hermits."

"Oh," she said. "Oh, they are not going to like this."

"They are going to fucking hate it, and I am sorrier about this than they will ever believe, but that can't be my problem right now."

She paused. "We're in a lot of danger, aren't we?"

"I think so," said Harrison. "I hope I am wrong, and when you're all accounted for, I hope I can tell you how wrong I am. But yes, I think so."

Silence.

"Becca? Are you going to be able to hold it together? I need you on this one."

"Dad, I'm pregnant."

Harrison froze. "There are so many things I want to say right now."

"I know," she said.

"I need you safe."

"I know."

"Can you do this?" he asked.

"Yes. Am I going to see you when we get there?"

"I promise you will," he said. "Are you home?"

48

"Yes."

"Then stay put. I am sending you an escort."

"Okay," she said. "See you soon."

He swapped the phone for the communicator again. "Felicia, whichever agents are heading out to collect Rebecca Wheeler are to follow her directions when they get there. She is in charge of bringing in the six coded Hermit. As of now, she is the deputized ranking agent on that retrieval, on my authority. I'm coming in now. Keep me posted on this operation."

"Understood," said Felicia. "Will do."

Harrison pulled a watch out of his pocket, where he had concealed it from Sarah. Already four o'clock.

"Hey, Harrison," said Garrett. "Is everything going to be okay?"

"I hope so," he said. "This is going to be a long night."

[8]

PEERS

New Chicago had exactly one radio station, a relic of the pre-Mayhem world, dating back to 1980. The Mayhem Effect had drawn some objects and structures through time—either from the past or the future—to their final resting place in 2004. The radio station, fully equipped to 1980 standards, served the needs of New Chicago as a society newly getting its feet on the ground. Over the years, the equipment remained essentially the same. DJs played whatever vinyl records and cassettes they found in the bins. They held thousands, more than enough to maintain variety, but that stock rendered them an oldies station in perpetuity.

One of the first DJs to work there was Claudia de Queiroz. For the first few months of its operation, only her voice went over the air, for a simple reason: only her voice would reach the entire country. Claudia possessed the ability to throw sound over huge distances. Her normal speaking voice could be heard at distances up to four miles, if she chose. With a microphone in front of her and a tower to broadcast, she could be received to a radius of fifteen hundred miles, 5-by-5. Beyond that, the signal faded. Given her ability to reach the entire continent, she became the natural spokeswoman for immigration and recruitment.

This all happened when she was fifteen years old. Now almost twenty-four, Claudia remained in broadcasting as her chosen career. That, and part-time national security superhero work, as needed.

Dorothy had never been to the station before. Opening up to Claudia would be tricky enough, and she didn't want to do it over the phone. She hoped visiting Claudia at work would provide neutral ground. Or maybe it was a stupid idea, born of desperation. Either way, here she was.

Because of her close connection to a high-ranking government officer, Dorothy rarely had trouble getting in doors. A single swipe of her ID typically sufficed to persuade anyone guarding an entrance. She never abused this power. She used it this day.

Finding Claudia proved easy. Talking to her did not. Part of that came from her own reluctance, the rest that Claudia worked in a soundproof booth, currently locked, and lit with an "On Air" sign. Dorothy waited patiently in the outer room. She watched Claudia through the large window, and listened to her on the monitors. At the moment, she was enthusiastically pulling a record that had finally been scratched to an unlistenable series of skips and pops. As with so many aspects of Claudia's life, Dorothy found herself intimidated by how easy she made it look to be a celebrity.

"Aaaand, that one's a goner, folks. Rest in peace, ABBA's Greatest Hits, Volume 2. If any kind souls out there have copies they would like to donate to the cause, please, please, please let me know."

Claudia, initially facing away from the window, spun her chair around in mid-sentence, laughing at her own comment. When she caught sight of Dorothy, her eyes lit up excitedly, if briefly. She held up a single finger while she kept talking.

"Taking a break now, people. Enjoy fifteen minutes of continuous music." She pressed play on a cassette deck, and removed her headphones. The light over the door changed, and Claudia emerged from it, grinning. "Dotty! What are you doing here?"

Dorothy's heart rate accelerated. She pushed past the anxiety. "How soon is your shift over?"

"Six," said Claudia, her face poised on the edge of confusion. It was four-thirty. Ninety minutes to wait. "Why?"

"Are you doing anything after?"

"No. Are you... Do you want to do something?"

"Yes," said Dorothy. "Well, I mean, no. Not do something. I, uh... Can we just talk?"

Claudia's eyes narrowed. "About what?"

Dorothy had no prepared response to that question. The notion that Claudia would want a preview to this conversation had not occurred to her. "You're not in trouble or anything." This attempt to reassure Claudia did not have the desired effect.

Claudia frowned. "Why would I be in trouble?"

"You wouldn't," said Dorothy.

"Then why did you say that?"

"Because you're not. In trouble. You're not in trouble." Dorothy shook her head. "Forget I said that. It was stupid." Her heart pounded, from a combination of nervousness and embarrassment. She hadn't even gotten to the part where she would make herself vulnerable by asking Claudia to be her confidant. "Maybe we... never mind. Forget I said anything. I'm sorry I bothered you at work."

"Okay," said Claudia. "Either tell me what's going on, or don't. But please don't do weird, passive-aggressive shit. If you have a problem with me, be straight about it. Then I can tell you you're wrong, and go back to work."

"No!" said Dorothy. It came out with more force than she intended, and Claudia took a wide-eyed step back. "No, I don't have a problem with you. I mean, that's not why I'm here."

"So, you have a problem with me, but you're here for something else?"

"I want your help!" she snapped. "I need someone to talk to. And apparently I am extremely bad at asking for that, so never mind."

"Talk about what?" asked Claudia.

"Something personal. Can we just drop it? You can go back to work."

Claudia did not appear less confused by this explanation. "Something personal? Why bring that to me?"

"I'm beginning to wonder that myself," Dorothy growled.

"No," said Claudia. "I mean... Actually, I guess that is what I mean. I thought you didn't really like me."

"Why would you say that?" Dorothy heard the words come out of her mouth, and mentally slapped herself for playing such a manipulative card. She knew why Claudia would think she didn't like her, even though that represented an inaccurate oversimplification of her feelings on the matter. However, the question having been put out there, Dorothy did find herself interested in Claudia's answer. Given she always assumed it was Claudia who did not like her, Dorothy was curious whether Claudia's interpretation of their relationship mirrored or contradicted her own.

"I..." Before Claudia could form the rest of that idea, her phone rang. Dorothy silently raged at the timing. Claudia read the screen. "I should take this." She thumbed the screen and held the phone out in front of her. "Hello?"

"I need you to come in, Claudia," said Harrison. Claudia had put him on speaker. Dorothy found herself grudgingly impressed by Claudia's successful one-upmanship in the category of manipulative behavior. Neither of them would dare voice this conflict with Harrison listening.

"Come in? Come in where?"

"We have a situation," he said. "I am pooling as much talent as I can in case we need to use it."

The bitterness drained from Claudia's face, replaced with caution. "What kind of situation?"

"A Code Red," he said. "I believe there is a viable threat against my adopted daughters. I'll give you details when you get here."

At this piece of information, Dorothy's heart accelerated.

"Wait, what?" said Claudia. "What kind of threat? I have Dorothy with me right now. What should I do?"

"Dorothy is there?" said Harrison. "Why?"

"We're not sure." Claudia looked directly at Dorothy with steel in her eyes. "What do I need to do to protect her?"

"Dorothy is not a target," said Harrison. "Only the girls we rescued from Texas. There is a chance that may include you, which is another reason I need you to come in. We have agents out right now collecting them all to put them in protective custody. I trust you can make it here on your own?"

"What should I do?" asked Dorothy.

"Go home," said Harrison. "I will be in touch. Please be in my office by five thirty, Special Agent de Queiroz."

The dismissal stung Dorothy, and she glared jealously at Claudia for once again trumping her relationship with Harrison.

"Ooh." Claudia's face sank. "You called me 'agent.' I hate that."

"Get used to it." He hung up.

"Looks like we need to take a rain check on whatever the fuck this is that we're doing right now," said Claudia. "Better skedaddle."

"Not a chance," said Dorothy. "I'm going with you."

"You heard what Daddy said, sweet cheeks. This is big girl stuff."

"This big girl has a security clearance that gets me in the doors of that building any time I feel like dropping by. So you can either walk over there with me, or we can walk over separately at the same time. Either way, that's where I'm headed."

Claudia glared at her. "I need to talk to my station manager first. Stick with me and keep your mouth shut."

"Yes ma'am, Special Agent ma'am," said Dorothy, sharpening her bravado for the huge task ahead of it. Whatever this was about, it threatened her family, and in ways she never expected, it hit her hard with a need to protect them and a thirst for vengeance against those who would do them harm.

[9]

LOCKDOWN

Around five o'clock, they started trickling in. Harrison waited in the front entrance to greet the arrivals as they came through the metal and magic detectors. An agent entered the building, keeping close to a flustered-looking woman with a piece of carryon luggage. She saw Harrison and made straight for him. He checked the name Meghan Rosso off a list on his PDA.

"Dad? What's going on?"

"Hello, Meg," he said. "I'm sorry about all this. We have a possible situation, and I want to bring everyone here so I can be sure you're safe. Hopefully it will just be for the night."

"Does this have something to do with Siobhan?" she asked.

"I'm not able to give you details yet," he said. "Why don't you get settled in, and when the others get here we can have a talk and bring you up to speed. Okay?"

"Holding cell?" asked the agent who escorted her into the building.

"What?" she shrieked, plain terror in her eyes.

"No!" said Harrison. "Dear God, man, use your head! Seventh floor apartments. These people are to be treated as guests." He looked at Meg, now shaking. "I'm sorry. We're still getting some of this sorted out. Are you okay?"

She nodded nervously.

"We're taking you upstairs, to a nice room with a comfortable bed and a decent view. We have to double up rooms, but you can choose who you bunk with. Try to relax if you can. I'm going to be here for a while, but I will check in on you before it gets too late."

"Thank you," she said, her manner sheepish and frightened. At least she didn't blame him for this. Others would.

As her escort took her to an elevator, Harrison pulled out his communicator. "Felicia, would you please contact all the agents we have in the field right now and tell them these women are to be taken to the apartments, not the holding cells?"

"Isn't that obvious?" she replied.

"Not so much, evidently. Let's just get the word out so we don't have any more surprises."

"Will do," said Felicia.

Harrison tucked the communicator back in his pocket.

"What's this all about?"

Harrison looked over his shoulder. Sparky hovered behind him, wearing a tiny burlap sack. The words IDAHO POTATOES appeared across the front, upside-down, hand-written in felt tip marker.

"We're taking in some guests tonight," he said. "Isn't that itchy? That looks itchy."

"If I say yes, will you let me take it off?" she asked.

"No."

"Damn it!"

"Definitely getting you a uniform." As Harrison said that, two more women entered the building under escort.

"Those are your kids," said Sparky. "Aren't they?"

"Yes. We're bringing all the Texas rescues in for the night, in protective custody. I have reason to suspect they are being targeted."

"Because of Red?"

"Yes, Siobhan and now two others. Do you remember Kate Gable and Kari Crenshaw?"

"No and Yes," said Sparky. "Kari's the soldier, right?"

"Marine," said Harrison. "Master Gunnery Sergeant. Kate is a paleontology student. They are both missing now as well, which we discovered when we tried to notify them about Siobhan. Hang on a second."

The new arrivals had broken away from their escorts and made a bee line for Harrison, both towing suitcases. "Not cool," said one of them, almost as tall as Harrison, slender, with black hair to her shoulders framing a scowl on her face.

"I'm sorry, Jess. This isn't being done lightly," said Harrison. "There's a good chance you are all in serious danger. We need to be sure everyone is secure."

"I'm sure you do," she said. "While you're busy securing us, try to remember the last time we were all locked up for our own good. That's still a pretty fresh memory for some of us."

"I know."

"This is going to break people," she said. "And you know exactly who I'm talking about."

"Yes, I do," he said. "And that's why they are going to need a lot of support tonight. I have to have you on my side, Jess."

"Screw you, Dad. I'm on their side tonight."

"That's all I'm asking."

Jessica held up her index finger. "This goes on longer than one day, I'm getting a lawyer."

Harrison nodded. "Okay."

She walked past him to the elevator. The other arrival, a woman a full head shorter than Jessica and quite a bit heavier, followed behind. Wavy brown hair, swarthy complexion. Harrison checked off the name Christine Rivera.

"Christine…" said Harrison.

"Just don't." She held up a single palm, and refused to look at him as she walked past.

"They're angry," said Sparky.

"They have every right," said Harrison. "They have major problems with trust, for some very good reasons. The fact they trust me as much as they do is a huge deal, and for some of them, this is going to feel like a betrayal. Some will feel protected, some will feel imprisoned, and some of them are going to feel things I wouldn't be able to explain even if I understood them, which I probably wouldn't. And as soon as I get a head count of twenty-five, I will let them all yell at me, or thank me, or throw tomatoes, or whatever. I would rather make them all angry with a mistake than lose one of them forever because I was afraid of hurting their feelings. They will see that, eventually." He sighed. "But not tonight."

A lone woman came through the door. Slight build, youthful face, topped off with a mass of blonde ringlets. "Dad?" she asked as she made it through the detectors. She set her bag down long enough to give him a hug.

"Hey, Britney," he said. "You okay?"

"I think so. At least I am now. Are we in trouble? All I heard was I had to come in right away."

"Not trouble," said Harrison. "We're just taking some precautions. It will probably turn out to be nothing."

Britney smiled. "You are so cute when you're lying. Where do I go?"

He pointed to the elevator. "Seventh floor. Find an empty room or someone you want to bunk with."

"Are you staying here, too?"

"I sure am," he said. "Along with a couple dozen agents."

"Good." She stood on tiptoe and kissed him on the cheek before making for the elevator.

Two more came through the door. Harrison ticked them off his list. Erin Wells. Virginia Carter. Harrison greeted them both, to various degrees of frustration and worry, and sent them upstairs. In the midst of this activity, Dorothy and Claudia came through the front door.

"Reporting for duty, Assistant Director," said Claudia in the snarky tone he had come to know so well, but with a bitter edge to it he couldn't place.

"I thought you were going home," he said to Dorothy.

Before she could respond, Claudia said, "Sorry, boss. Tagalong here insisted on crashing the party."

"Actually, I'm glad," he said. "We're doing intake here on a lot of frightened and angry young women. A familiar face or two might help ease the tension. Would you two mind going up to the seventh floor and making some rounds? Check in on them? Offer to get them something to eat, or drink, or read, or whatever?"

"We would be delighted," said Dorothy, with an expression he also recognized well: smug. Something was happening between these two, but he didn't have an ounce of energy to devote to caring about it.

"Thank you so much," he said. "You should probably know that a huge part of your job is going to be listening to Jessica Williams tell you what a piece of shit I am."

"I'm okay with that," said Claudia.

"As I thought you would be," he said. "Just let them vent. Whatever it takes to make them feel like they have some control here. Frankly, I'd like to feel that myself."

"Got it," said Dorothy, giving Claudia a little smile. "Shall we?" She sauntered off to the elevator, a clearly disgruntled Claudia following in her wake.

"What's their thing?" asked Sparky.

"Don't know. Don't care. Bigger fish to fry at the moment." His phone chirped. Becca's face greeted him on it. "Hey. How are you doing?"

"Four so far," she said.

"How are they?"

"No one flat out refused," she said. "That's better than I expected."

"That's good, I guess. Are they with you?"

"No. I had your people lend me six female agents, and I've been dropping them off one at a time as I go. They should start getting there soon. Just stay out of their way and you should be okay."

"Nice work. Thank you," said Harrison.

"Thank you for putting me in charge," she said. "I think that has helped. It's a little weird to be giving orders to your people, though."

"It's not weird to them," he said, with no idea if that was true. "How soon will I see you?" He glanced to his right as he spoke, more from nervous fidgeting than anything else. Activity in the building was somewhat heightened this evening, with additional agents stationed on the main floor. A man in a familiar Hawaiian shirt moved past two of them and around a corner out of Harrison's sight.

"Two more stops. Half an hour, maybe?" said Rebecca.

Harrison's eyes traced the spot where the garishly dressed man had last been, weighing the advantages of dropping everything to pursue him and find out who he was against his need to stay on top of the intake of two dozen frightened women. "Shit," he whispered.

"What?" said Rebecca.

Harrison shook his head vigorously and returned his attention to where it needed to be. "Nothing. Sorry. Godspeed. See you soon."

"Thanks." She hung up.

"Who's this?" Sparky pointed to the metal detector. A woman walked through it, no taller than five feet, with a tiny frame. She had a knapsack on her back, and looked at the floor as she moved.

"Shandra Walker." He turned to face away from the new arrival, holding his hand loosely by his side. "Don't look at her, please."

Sparky covered her eyes with her hands. Not subtle, but Harrison ruled it adequate.

After about half a minute, a piece of paper brushed his hand, and he closed his fingertips on it. Shandra kept walking past him, still looking at the floor. "You can open your eyes now."

Sparky spun around to watch Shandra walk head down into an elevator. "What just happened?"

"We don't make eye contact, and we only communicate through writing," he said. "Her rules. They keep her going. I don't question them. At least she communicates with me at all."

He held the sealed envelope up to read the word "dad" handwritten on it, and nothing else. The note inside similarly said only, "I'm scared." He tucked it back in the envelope, folded it and stuck it in his back pocket.

"Can you go get me a piece of paper, a pen and an envelope, please?"

"Back in a jiff!" She zipped away.

He checked Shandra off his list. Anna Bruce came in shortly after. Check. That made eight. Nineteen of his rescued daughters lived in new Chicago. The other nine (including two missing) lived out of town, some very far. None of those would be coming tonight, nor would Siobhan. Eight down, ten to go before he could rest easy. The next morning he would begin the process of fretting about the seven stragglers.

As Anna entered the elevator, Alec walked out of it. He made his way across the room, leaning on his cane the whole way. "Bit of a circus tonight?"

"We have it under control," said Harrison.

"Could have given me a warning," said Alec. "Not that it matters."

"Did I overstep my authority?"

"Not at all. Enjoy your slumber party, Cody."

He looked back at the door as another woman entered. She had a significantly larger suitcase than those he had seen thus far that day, her escort was a five-year-old girl, and he was very much in love with her.

"Daddy!" Melody raced through both detectors without pause and threw her arms around him. He picked her up and held her tight, with her chin resting on his shoulder.

"Hey, beautiful!" he said to Melody, his one and only daughter by blood.

"We're sleeping over!" said Melody into his shoulder.

"I see that," said Harrison. Apryl had finally made her way through the detectors with her oversized rollaway. "What a lovely surprise," he said pointedly to his wife.

"Oh, quiet, you. You need all the help you can get and you know it." She looked around her. "Nice place you have here, but the lobby is a little cold. You need some more comfy chairs. Maybe a fountain."

"Mind yourself, Mrs. Cody," said Alec. "I've counted the towels in your room. See they are all still there when you leave."

"And your bellhop could be a little less surly," she said.

"Yes, well," said Alec, "enjoy your stay. If you need me, I will be back tomorrow morning at the usual time. Until then, you have this, as you say, under control." He departed.

"You do know we don't have a room for you, right?" said Harrison. "We will barely be able to sleep eighteen in the seventh-floor rooms as it is. When the others come into town, I don't know where we're going to put them."

"You have a pullout couch in your office, don't you?" she asked.

"I do," he said. "And a lovely leather chair from which to watch the two of you get a good night's sleep."

"This is why I love you," she said.

He gently returned Melody to the floor, and gave her a kiss. "Don't forget to brush your teeth," he said to his daughter.

"I already did," she said. After a moment's glare from her father, she amended, "I mean, I was just about to."

"Good night, sweetie. I'll be up in a bit." He gave a Apryl a kiss as well, of a different nature. "Wait up for me?"

"I'll give you until twelve," she said. "After that, no promises."

"That will have to do. You know the way?"

"I sure do. Tallyho." She dragged her luggage away as Melody made a dash for the elevator.

Shortly after that, two more women entered the building. Jennifer Howell and Maria Perales, two of the six women he had sent Becca to retrieve. Two female agents escorted them, one of whom was under five feet tall, with pale-blue skin and high, pointed ears poking through a mane of thick black hair, and dressed in the standard issue black suit. Harrison turned away from the new arrivals.

Jennifer and Maria were two of six residents of New Chicago who had made it clear that under no circumstances did they ever want to see Harrison again. There was no hatred there, but he knew things about them they couldn't bear anyone knowing, so individually, over the years, they had cut him—and everyone else from the group of twenty-eight rescues—out of their lives. He honored that need with no hard feelings, and it did not put a dent in his feelings of fatherly protectiveness over them. The fact two of them arrived at the same time was probably hard enough on them. Compelling them to come to his place of work without warning crossed a line that might do them serious emotional harm. But, weighing that against the alternative, he had no choice.

Harrison walked over to the security desk, with his back to Maria and Jennifer, and they slipped past him. Ten down, eight to go.

Over the next hour, he ticked six more names off his list. Kristina Morris, Teresa Washington, and Emily Lewis all came in avoiding direct contact with him. Melissa Lear, clearly flustered, sought support from Harrison and accepted it. Mary Kelley was friendly and understanding, and Danielle Brown was downright chatty.

During that hour, Sparky returned with Harrison's paper, envelope, and pen. He asked her to wait long enough for him to write, "I know. Hang in there. We love you." He sealed the note and gave her instructions to deliver it to Shandra. She left him to continue his vigil.

Two to go. Brooke Witherspoon, and the woman sent to find her, Rebecca Wheeler. Another half hour passed with no sign of either. Right as Harrison was about to check in with Rebecca, Jessica decided to return to the front entrance for another round of protests.

"Am I a prisoner?" she asked.

"Can we not do this right now?" said Harrison. "Please believe that I understand—"

"You understand nothing," she said.

"Maybe I don't, but you're not going to fix that tonight."

"I'm asking. I want to go out for a cup of coffee. Can I do that?"

"Ask Dorothy for a cup of coffee," said Harrison. "She'll take care of you."

"I don't know," she said. "I really like this little coffee shop near my house. I'll just pop out and get us both lattes, okay?"

"Jessica, I love you dearly, but we cannot have this conversation tonight."

"So, I am a prisoner. I want to hear you say it."

"Oh, for God's sake!" he barked.

Before he had a chance to finish that thought, Rebecca came in the front door with two agents and her husband. She marched through the detectors to get to Harrison. The two agents, still ostensibly under her command, hung back. "Brooke is gone."

"Oh, no," said Harrison.

"What does that mean?" asked Jessica.

"She's not home. We checked her mother's house, and the hospital. Her phone is going directly to voice mail."

"Oh, shit," said Harrison. "Why didn't you check in?"

"I don't know," she said. "Maybe because this is my first manhunt-slash-lockdown? This was a long, difficult day for me, Dad."

"I'm sorry. You're right. Come here."

He held his arms out, and she embraced him. She went limp in his arms, physically dumping the tension that had sustained her throughout her several-hour mission.

"Oh, God," she said. "She's gone. What do we do?"

"I'll take it from here. Get some rest." He kissed her forehead. "And I know this timing is not ideal, but congratulations. I am very, very happy for you."

"We're not telling anyone yet."

"Mum's the word," he said. "Get some sleep."

The two agents they came in with took Rebecca to the elevator. Her husband lingered.

"You and I need to have a conversation about whether my wife works for you," he said. "Because I think she doesn't. We should get on the same page there."

"Blake, seriously, that's just one more conversation I am not having today. You would have to get in line behind Jess anyway." He put his hand on Blake's shoulder. "The only thing that matters to me right now is Rebecca's safety, and the safety of twenty-seven other women. Take care of her now, please. Yell at me later."

"I will," he said, and followed Rebecca to the elevator.

Harrison looked at Jessica. Her eyes had gone wide, and she avoided his gaze. He took out his communicator. "Top priority manhunt. I need Brooke Witherspoon located and brought here immediately."

"I'm on it," said Felicia. It surprised Harrison to hear her voice, as she would normally have left the building by now. Her dedication to duty in this crisis added one more notch to his gratitude for having her on his staff.

"Now," said Harrison to Jessica. "We were talking about coffee?"

Jessica had closed her eyes. She made two fists, curled her arms to her chest, scrunched her shoulders, and generally attempted to curl into a ball while still standing. Tears flowed freely from her closed lids.

He put his arms around her and held her. "Let's get you back upstairs."

She nodded, and they walked.

10

ROOM SERVICE

Dorothy and Claudia stood together in silence, waiting for the elevator. The walk to NCSA headquarters had been chilly. The beautiful sky from early afternoon gave way to accumulating clouds, and a cold front began to make its presence known. Dorothy was glad she brought a jacket. Unfortunately, no jacket could insulate her from the chill coming off Claudia. Her cry for help at the station had gone horribly wrong, escalating to a pointless conflict. Perhaps working together would give them a chance to start over. "What's on the seventh floor?"

"Apartments," said Claudia. "Efficiencies. More like hotel rooms with kitchenettes, really."

"Why do you have hotel rooms in a government building?"

Claudia shrugged. "They were here when we found the building. Most of HQ is reclaimed office space, but that floor is totally different. It's a pre-Mayhem building, so it could be a floor from a hotel that got transplanted here."

"That's weird," said Dorothy.

"I've seen weirder. They're pretty nice. I stayed in one for a few weeks when I was fifteen. That was before New Chicago was a country. We were still sorting everything out. When the NCSA claimed this building, they kept that floor the way they found it. Sometimes it's useful to have some beds ready."

"Like now?"

"Yup," said Claudia. The elevator arrived, and they boarded.

They rode the seven floors in silence, and Claudia stepped out as soon as the doors opened. Unlike the dull, industrial gray everywhere else in the building, the carpet in this hall displayed a blue and silver pattern, vaguely floral, but abstract enough to be anything.

"I'll take the left." Claudia walked off and knocked on a door. A few seconds later someone let her in.

A moment's solitude allowed Dorothy to question the past hour of her life, and the bizarre rivalry between them. Her momentary joy at Harrison validating her—taking her side in a conflict he could not even see—confused her now. She wished she could trade it in for a reset button and a second chance at that visit to the station.

Dorothy knocked on the first door to the right.

"Come in," came a voice from within.

Unlike a typical hotel room door, this one opened freely from the outside. Within she found a spacious living area with a table and desk, two twin beds, a small kitchenette, and a door leading to a bathroom. That these rooms had been transplanted into an office building was a distinct possibility, but surely even in that theory, an oversimplified explanation. The Mayhem Wave had randomized the world so comprehensively that juxtapositions like this had become a norm.

The room's single occupant sat on a bed, holding a book. "Dorothy? Are you my roommate?"

Despite the unhappy facets of the current situation, Dorothy smiled at Meg Rosso. She knew all of Harrison's Texas rescues, but some she considered friends more than others. When she first met them all, she naturally gravitated toward the ones closest to her age, and those bonds held over time. She had also stayed close to Christine Rivera, Britney Hinson, and Jess Williams for that reason. The youngest of the group, and another close friend, Siobhan, would not be here tonight. That momentary realization gave her sad pause.

"No," she said. "I'm actually here working tonight. Is there anything I can get for you to make your stay more comfortable?"

"You're not on the list?" asked Meg.

"Apparently not. Harrison says I'm 'not a target,' whatever that means." Meg's eyes bugged slightly, and Dorothy mentally kicked herself for the choice of words. She plowed ahead. "Are you hungry? Can I get you something to eat?"

"I did skip dinner," said Meg.

"What can I get for you? A sandwich? A salad? A cookie?"

Meg smiled at that. "Sandwich. Turkey, if you're taking orders. Or are they already made up?"

"Nothing is made up," said Dorothy. "But there's a kitchen downstairs, and a deli half a block from here. Give me an hour and I'll find you turkey. Cheese? Mayo? Lettuce/tomato?"

"Swiss if you can find it. Nothing else." Meg put the book down and got up. To Dorothy's surprise, she gave her a hug, atypical warmth for Meghan, whom Dorothy considered a bit of a dark soul. "Thank you for coming. This is weird, and not fun."

"I know," said Dorothy. "That's why I'm here."

"Are you staying?"

"I don't know. I guess if they need me to, I will."

"If I don't get a roommate, can you stay here?" asked Meg.

"I'd like that. Let me see what the situation is. You're my first stop. I have sandwich orders to take. But yes, I would like that."

Meg offered a weak smile, and the tiny victory pleased Dorothy. "Then I won't keep you. See you soon?"

"With turkey. I promise."

"Good." For an instant, the darkness returned to Meghan's eyes, and she fell back into her book.

Two rooms later, Dorothy headed to the kitchen with orders for hot chocolate, chili and oatmeal cookies. In the pantry, she found a can of chili, a loaf of wheat bread, hot chocolate mix, and a box of oatmeal cookies. In the refrigerator, she found cold cuts and cheese. It took her about fifteen minutes to heat the chili, make the sandwich, mix the hot chocolate and put three cookies on a plate. As she arranged these items on a tray, Claudia came in.

"Chicken soup, tea, and pineapple," she said.

"Pantry," said Dorothy, pointing.

She returned to the seventh floor for her deliveries, and to take new orders. In the time she had spent downstairs, four more women had arrived, including Shandra Walker, who took the other bed in Meg's room. Dorothy had no space in her head for disappointment over having her spot taken.

On her third round of orders, Dorothy found a single room still unoccupied, and took a moment for a bathroom break. Her core temperature slightly elevated from the constant activity, it finally occurred to her to take her jacket off. She hung it on a hook in the bathroom, staking her claim to the room and its single bed.

This went on for another three hours. Much of that time she spent making small talk, catching up with old friends and getting to know acquaintances better. Some of the guests wanted to be left in peace, and she provided that service as well by fashioning "Do Not Disturb" signs for them.

At ten o'clock, content that everyone's immediate needs had been met, she took a break. Harrison had left his post by the main entrance, which told her that intake had finally ended for the night. She approached the security officer at the front desk, a satyr she had seen in the building before, though she did not know his name. He looked about her age, but she suspected he had decades on her, based on the length of his horns.

"Is my father still here?" she asked.

"In his office, I believe."

"Do you need to see my clearance for me to go up there?"

"No, you're good, Miss O'Neill." He punctuated this with a smile that bordered on flirtatious, and gave his goatee one subtle stroke.

"Thank you." On her way up, she reflected on how satisfying it felt to contribute. The women staying here did appreciate her care, and the presence of a familiar, friendly face. Charged with this curious sort of optimism, she might, perhaps, find a way tomorrow to earn Claudia's appreciation while she was at it.

11

HEREDITY

With seventeen women accounted for, and a search underway for one more, Harrison retired to his office. His workspace was significant, designed for meetings, and a comfort that went with the prestige of his position. It also served as a bedroom in the event he ever needed to sequester himself at work.

Ordinarily, he would sleep on the couch. It had a pullout mattress, but if he had a pillow and a blanket, he typically didn't bother with it. Tonight it was open, made, and occupied by one child. He gently kissed her forehead, and she stirred enough to make a single, cute *smack* with her lips, then went right back to sleep.

"Are they all here?" asked Apryl from an armchair across from the bed, wearing a t-shirt, sweatpants, and slippers.

Harrison went to his closet and put his jacket and tie on a hanger. "All but one. Still looking for Brooke."

"Oh," said Apryl. "Do you think she's trying to avoid you?"

He shrugged. "I hope that's it. Doubt it, though. I sent Becca to persuade her to come in. Unless one of the other girls tipped her off, I don't see how she would even know we were coming for her."

"Do you think she'll turn up?"

"I'd rather not say," he grumbled. "But I'm not going to be able to sleep until I know one way or the other. What are your plans for tomorrow?"

"Emotional support. Once they're settled in, they're going to need an advocate outside the agency."

"Being my wife won't earn you any points right now, I'm sorry to say."

"No," she said. "But being their stepmother might. Those girls all know me, and most of them like me. I think they'll appreciate having a woman who will stand up for their needs. If I'm wrong about that, I'll back off."

"What about Melody?" he asked. "I'm not going to be able to watch her, and with you being den mother, you won't either."

"You don't have a day care? I assumed you had a day care."

"Not so much."

"Rats," she said. "I guess I'll have to juggle her. Maybe your guests can take turns sitting."

"I'm not so sure they're going to be up for that. We'll figure something out."

"What are their living conditions?" she asked. "If I'm going to take this on, I should probably have a sense of what to expect. Are those rooms comfortable? Are their basic needs going to be met? Privacy is the big one. What about food?"

"The rooms are nice. They are going to be crowded though, especially when the out-of-towners start showing up. We are probably going to need cots. I'm hoping to feed them whatever they want. We have a decent cafeteria, and we can afford whatever takeout or catering they need on top of that for as long as they are here. I put Claudia and Dorothy on room service detail tonight, so hopefully that will help them all feel a little more at ease."

Apryl sat up. "Dorothy's here?"

He nodded. "She came here with Claudia. I put them both to work right away. She seemed happy to do it."

"Well, there's our sitter."

"Oh," said Harrison. "Good point. I'll try to catch her before she leaves."

Apryl got up from her chair and sat on the bed. Watching her daughter sleep, she said, "We are safe here, right?"

"Very much so. I would never bring all those women here if it weren't." Harrison plopped down in the chair Apryl had vacated.

They sat in silence for a while, absorbing the events of the day. "I worry about her," said Apryl finally. "She's getting old enough to figure out her parents aren't normal, you know."

"We're normal."

"We have superpowers."

"Yeah," he said. "But other than that. Besides, I'm not sure 'super' applies to mine."

"You know what I mean. What is that going to feel like, when she figures out we can do things no one else can? Things she can't?"

"Would you rather she could?" he asked. "I don't think that would make her any happier."

"Are we sure she won't?" asked Apryl. "I mean completely, absolutely sure?"

"As sure as we can be," he said. "But if you want to go down that road again, I can talk to Larson about setting up some more tests. I'm sure she'd love to get Melody back into her lab."

"Is Larson the one with the crush on you?"

"No," he said. "That's Garrett. And she doesn't have a crush on me."

"She just flirts with you every time she sees you."

"She's outgoing."

Apryl gave him her best deadpan.

"It's not every time," he tried.

More staring.

"Anyway, she's not my type. I'm much more into outrageously beautiful Latinas."

"A weak save," she said, "but I'll allow it."

"Seriously, do you want me to call her? Melody and Adler have both been through so many tests, I can't imagine they missed anything. What we have isn't genetic. They are normal kids. But if you want to keep looking for something, we can do that."

She brushed Melody's cheek. "I just don't want her to feel like she's not special."

As Harrison pondered the best way to respond to that, a voice came over his communicator. "Assistant Director? This is Grant."

Harrison took out the device and stepped away from his sleeping child. "What do you have for me?"

"Not much," said the voice. "We're at Witherspoon's residence right now."

Behind Harrison came a knock at the door, and Apryl said, "Yes?"

"Apryl? I didn't realize you were here." Dorothy's voice. He let Apryl field this visitor.

"There are signs of forced entry," continued Grant. "The front door lock has been picked. There was also a dish of food upside down on the kitchen floor. That's not much to go on, but it might be evidence of a struggle. We've searched the apartment for Witherspoon, and she is not here."

Forced entry. A struggle. This had moved well past the realm of coincidence. The women he rescued from childhood slavery were being systematically taken. "Understood. Keep a detail posted there until further notice. If you find anything else, let me know right away." He pocketed the communicator. For a moment, he allowed himself to grieve for his own stupidity in waiting too long to round up his daughters to protect them, then dismissed that feeling as irrelevant. They were under his protection now, as would be their remaining seven sisters once his people brought them to the city. His thoughts turned to his youngest daughter, his true child, and he came back to sit with her. He brushed her head, thinking about the world she was growing up in, and the dangers it presented, and silently thanked the universe she would be spared this particular peril.

"Talk to me," said Apryl.

"There are signs of a break-in at Brooke's apartment," he said. "It's real."

"Oh, no," said Dorothy. "She's not here? I thought they were all here."

"We're down one," said Harrison. "And now it looks like she's not coming. Grant says her front door was picked, and there may have been a struggle."

"How did the agents with Becca miss that?" asked Apryl.

"I don't know," said Harrison. "Maybe because I put her in charge and she didn't know what to look for? They should still have been more thorough, with or without orders."

"What does that mean?" asked Dorothy.

"It means we have a serious problem, and that I was right to bring everyone here. I only wish I had done this yesterday."

"Do not blame yourself for this," said Apryl.

"Oh, I don't," he said. "I know exactly who to blame. There is only one group that would take an interest in these women, because there is only one thing they all have in common."

"Lone Star," said Apryl.

"Lone Star," said Harrison.

"But why now?" she asked. "It's been eight years. What possible reason could they have for rounding up the girls at this point?"

"I didn't say I knew why," said Harrison. "Just who. And where. We have a trip to plan. As soon as we have the last seven secured here, I am taking a team to Texas. We are going to bring my daughters home and end this."

12

HOW TO GET OVER IT

At almost midnight, Dorothy finally made her way back to her room, exhausted. The news of Brooke's disappearance on top of everything else had sucked the life out of her, and now Harrison spoke like they were about to go to war. Dorothy had no frame of reference to cope with this level of crisis. She needed to get some sleep. Maybe tomorrow she would be equipped to continue caring for her charges in the face of what would certainly be new fears.

She poured herself a glass of water, and sat down at the table in the kitchenette. Looking at the bed, she remembered she brought nothing here. No pajamas, no toothbrush. One night of icky mouth would be a small price to pay for the work she and Claudia had done, as would be one night of sleeping in her underwear. She finished her water, got up and unbuttoned her shirt. At that moment, from behind the bathroom door came the sound of a toilet flushing, followed by the sound of running water. Half a minute later, Claudia came out of the bathroom.

They both froze.

"Well," said Claudia. "This is awkward."

"I thought you went home," said Dorothy.

"I thought *you* went home," said Claudia.

"This is the only room that isn't taken."

"I call dibs?" Claudia grinned imploringly.

"I was here first."

Claudia frowned. "Nuh uh."

Dorothy pointed to the bathroom. "Happen to notice a jacket hung on that door?"

Claudia looked behind her. "Oh. Um, then I guess we can share?"

They both looked over at the single twin bed. Then they looked at each other. Dorothy fished a quarter out of her pocket. She held it up with the head side facing Claudia. "You get the bed." She turned it around to show her the tail. "You get the floor."

"Fine," said Claudia.

Dorothy flipped the coin into the air and stood back to watch it land.

Claudia lurched forward and snatched it out of the air with surprising speed. She held it in front of Dorothy, showing her the head side, then placed in on the table with a loud *whap*. Dorothy looked down. The tail looked back at her. When she looked up, Claudia already taken the comforter from the bed to fashion into a sleeping bag. Claudia baffled her completely. Strangely, this renewal of their inexplicable conflict diverted her from the larger situation happening around her, and she welcomed that.

"Why do you think I don't like you?" asked Dorothy.

Claudia dropped one of the bed pillows on the floor near the head of her makeshift bedroll. "What was the personal thing you wanted to tell me?"

"I asked first."

"I don't recognize your authority to ask first, and I took the floor. What was the thing?"

Dorothy sat down at the table. After a beat, she asked, "How do you get over a breakup?"

"Oh." Claudia pulled up a chair across from Dorothy. For a moment, all she did was stare, with a glazed look to her eyes. She snapped her fingers, gazing off into space.

"Brad," said Dorothy.

"Brad!" Claudia thumped the table. "I swear that was on the tip of my tongue. What happened?"

"He broke up with me."

"Got that part. Why?"

Dorothy fidgeted. "Why did Mickey break up with you?"

"He got bored and found a girl he liked better," said Claudia.

"Oh." Dorothy looked at the table.

"What happened with Brad?"

Quietly, she said, "He got bored and found a girl he liked better."

"Oh, shit!" said Claudia, laughing.

Dorothy looked up. "What?"

"I was just kidding about Mickey. He called it off because we weren't clicking."

Dorothy looked down again. "Great."

"How many times have you called him asking for one more chance?"

Dorothy thought before answering. "Twice."

"Okay," said Claudia. "You're done now. You only get two tries, and you used those up. Next: this is only a question, not a suggestion. Have you had any thoughts about suicide?"

She thought about that one too. "Not that I would act on."

"Right. Close your eyes. I want you to picture something."

Dorothy closed her eyes.

"Ready?"

She nodded.

"Melody at your funeral."

Dorothy's eyes snapped open in shock.

"You're done with that now, too," said Claudia "See? We're working down a checklist."

"Is that how this works?"

"More or less."

Dorothy nodded, feeling a mild sort of enthusiasm. "What's the next one?"

"Did you cry yet?" That one made her less enthusiastic. She took too long to find a way to answer, and Claudia said, "You didn't. I bet I even know why."

"Why?" said Dorothy as evenly as she could.

"Because smart girls don't cry. You're a brain. You've always been a brain. Me? I'm a heart. I cried over Mickey, and I didn't even like him that much. But not you, right? Smart girls don't cry."

Dorothy hesitated, then shook her head. "No. I didn't cry. And I'm not going to. What's the next one?"

Casually, Claudia asked, "Did he fuck you?"

Dorothy's heart tried to punch its way out of her chest. "I beg your pardon?"

Smirking, Claudia leaned back in her chair. "I bet he did. And if I know you—which I feel pretty sure I do—you lost your virginity to him, too. Am I right?"

Dorothy trembled and blushed. She wanted to leave, but experienced the beginnings of a head rush, and feared if she stood she might pass out. "You don't get to ask that."

Claudia leaned in closer, and all the joviality drained out of her face. "Did. He. Fuck. You."

"We…" Dorothy had no idea how to say it. Had sex? Too common. Did it? Too juvenile. Boffed? Schtupped? Boinked? These terms raced unbidden through her head. Finally, she heard one that helped her find her dignity, and she sat up straight. "We made love."

"No, you didn't."

"What?" she said, mildly shocked. For a moment, she imagined she even managed to get sex wrong, and what they did somehow didn't count. "What do you mean?"

"The ones who make love?" said Claudia. "They stick around. The fuckers walk away."

Dorothy's head-spin righted itself. The fuckers walk away. He walked away. "Fucker," she whispered.

"What's that?" said Claudia.

"That…" Dorothy worked up the nerve to repeat it. "Fucker."

"Sing it, sister."

"That fucker!" she shouted.

Claudia laughed. "Now we're cooking!"

"Oh, God!" Dorothy's throat constricted. She succeeded in fighting the tears off for a solid two seconds. Then they came, followed by the barking sobs. She buried her face in her arms on the table and let loose. She barely heard the scrape of Claudia getting up from her chair through her own weeping. After what felt like a minute, Claudia pulled up next to her, and put her arm across Dorothy's shoulders. She reached up and held Claudia's wrist while the sobs flowed out and finally settled down.

When she finally regained the strength to look up, Claudia sat close, with a warm smile that triggered her self-consciousness about the red mess she surely presented by now. Her face was covered in moisture, and her eyes burned. Claudia handed her a roll of toilet paper. She tore off a length, carefully folded it, and blew. When she pulled the soaking tissue away from her nose, Claudia courteously held up a small wastebasket for her convenience. She disposed of the wad, tore off another, and dabbed her eyes.

"And that," said Claudia, "is how we do that."

[13]

HISTORY

Harrison woke shortly before sunrise, having spent the night in his leather desk chair and the previous day's clothes. He took a moment to grab a fresh shirt, underwear, and socks from the suitcase Apryl packed for his entire family, before waking her.

"Hey," he whispered.

"Mm," she said.

"I'm going to the gym to take a shower. Then I'm headed to Esoteric. Lots to do today. Dorothy is somewhere on floor seven. I might be back by lunch." He waited for a response. Mesmerized by the beautiful sight of his wife and little girl curled up in so blissful a slumber, he almost put off starting his day. Almost. "Did you get all that?"

"Mm hm," she said, eyes still closed. "Esoteric. Dorothy seven. Back by lunch. Call me with news."

"I didn't say anything about calling."

"That's me, dope," she said. "Call me if there's any news."

"You're okay with the girls?"

"I've got this," she said. "Go."

He kissed her once on the forehead, and got a smile for the gesture. Another kiss on Melody's head, and he was off.

One shower and change later, he left the building, headed for the Esoteric

Research facility. En route, he checked in with Felicia. "Any word on the out-of-towners yet?"

"Two secured so far," came her voice over the tiny speaker. "Ashley Adams, and Elizabeth Cahill. They should be here by noon. Still waiting to hear on the rest."

"Thank you," he said. "Please check in on all five of the others right now and give me a status report. We lost one last night. I do not want a repeat of that."

"Understood."

He pocketed the communicator, in a continued state of appreciation for his assistant. Felicia Kestrel came on board the NCSA three years earlier as a field agent, and discovered herself not physically suited for the work. Though able to handle the stress and the emotional demands of the job, her reaction time was too slow in virtually every exercise, and despite having the build of a ballet dancer, she had some agility issues that made her a liability in rigorous assignments. In short, she washed out.

Fortunately for Harrison, her intellectual gifts did not go unnoticed. Alec assigned her to his staff, where she had played the part of his right hand for the past year. What she lacked in physical grace she more than made up in mental stamina and swiftness. Harrison had complete faith that she would handle any task he set her on with competence, thoroughness, and speed. More than once in the past year he caught himself realizing her excellence gave him opportunities to get soft, so he made it part of her job to keep him on his toes.

On his arrival at Esoteric, he went straight to Larson's lab, taking the staircase two steps at a time. He did not pause to notice the turnover of tiny gargoyles, and knew from experience they would find that disappointing. Some other time.

"Taylor Richardson secured," said Felicia. "No contact on the others yet. Ashley Adams is in the building."

"How are they holding up?"

"I wouldn't know, sir," she said. "Would you like me to interview them?"

Harrison made a mental note that Felicia was not in fact perfect. "No, give them space. Dorothy and Apryl are going to handle advocating for them. If they bring you any concerns, please address them immediately. Our guests are to be given anything they want, short of release."

"Understood."

He swiped his card at Larson's door, once again enjoying the show as it dissolved into mist before his eyes and resolidified behind him. He found her staring at the wall monitor again, this time with two other people, both wearing lab coats. One was a man Harrison guessed to be in his mid-thirties, the other a slender woman with close-cropped hair and the darkest skin he had ever seen. It took a moment to recognize her as an elf. She looked about twenty years old, which probably put her at least two hundred. Both scientists split their attention between the wall screen and whatever work they were doing on hand-held computers. All three of them managed to completely ignore his entrance.

"Hey there," he said. "Has Rutherford checked in yet?"

"No," said Larson, without turning to greet him. The man did look up at this point, and gave Harrison a courtesy nod. The elf did not acknowledge him.

"Felicia, I need an immediate recall on Special Agent Rutherford," said Harrison into his communicator. "Have him brought directly to Esoteric."

"On it," she said.

"I need that reevaluation of Rutherford's ability," said Harrison to Larson. "Can we fast track it? If he's advanced anything like Sarah has, I need to know exactly how much."

After several seconds of no response at all, Larson said, "Are you talking to me?" Her eyes stayed on the screen.

"Yes," said Harrison.

"Oh," she said. "No, we can't fast track that. I need you to see this."

Harrison had anticipated obstacles to the plethora of things he needed to accomplish this day, but not lack of cooperation from Larson among them. "Doctor, I have a very full schedule today, and Rutherford's eval is high priority. Can this wait?"

"You're going to want to make time for this," she said.

"Not to put too fine a point on it, but there are four women who are one distraction closer to dying for every side project I make time for today. This really has to wait."

"They will all be dead in less than a year, along with everyone else on the planet."

It would be a long day indeed. "You have my attention."

"Come here."

Harrison moved toward the large screen. It showed the same image as the last time he saw it, including the highlighted orbits and the circular overlay of the Mayhesphere. "Did it move?"

"It's been moving this whole time," she said. "I told you we were trying to figure out if it was still expanding. Well, it is. Not at a constant rate, but definitely expanding. Pulsing, in fact, like a huge, expanding heart."

Harrison gulped. "That's awful."

"Yes, it is. If our computations are correct, it should intersect with the sun in three hundred one days, plus or minus twelve."

"I assume that's bad," said Harrison. "Will it change the sun?"

"You better believe it," she said. "Do you remember what the original purpose of the Mayhem Wave was?"

"To free Rhu'opihm," said Harrison. He hadn't used that name in years, and he experienced a moment of queasiness speaking it.

"Well, yes, that," she said. "But I mean the ostensible reason."

"To wipe out the guns."

"Correct. In the wake of that wave, some fundamental properties were altered. Gun powder no longer explodes. Neither does nitroglycerin, C4, and a host of other former explosives. A few common substances like gasoline still pack a punch, but for the most part, bombs are a thing of the past."

"The sun isn't a chemical bomb," said Harrison. "It's a nuclear furnace."

"Correct," she said, "and it will continue to burn. As far as the rest of the universe is concerned, our star will continue to be a star. Unfortunately for us, it turns out the Mayhem Wave also affected some properties of fusion and fission reactions, presumably as a neutralizer for nuclear weapons. Those processes still work the way they always have, with one modification. Fission reactions release eight percent less energy than they used to, and fusion reactions release twenty-four percent less. Those are averages, but they will suffice to lay out the problem."

"Oh, shit," said Harrison. "Would that translate into a twenty-four percent drop in surface temperature?"

"No, but close enough. Our preliminary estimates show an average surface temp drop of sixty-five degrees Kelvin."

"Which will be cold enough to kill everything," said Harrison.

"No, it won't," said the dark elf who had ignored Harrison earlier. "Helioseimology projections put the temperature decrease as negligible for at least a thousand years."

"Yes," said Larson. "Thank you, Aulthresh, we have been over this. That assumes solar activity consistent with pre-Mayhem patterns, which will no longer apply when the wave hits."

"Wait," said Harrison to Aulthresh. "Go back a step. Thousand years?"

The elf turned her attention to Harrison for the first time. As with most elves of his acquaintance, first eye contact came with a rush, a natural human response to her beauty. Elves generally represented an ideal of humanoid perfection, and Aulthresh was no different in this respect, though the nearly-shaved head did manage to offset the effect enough to keep it from shutting down the conversation.

"Photons in the Sun's core are densely packed, and in a constant state of violent collision with each other. It is virtually impossible for a single photon—and the heat it carries—to escape that chaos. Therefore, it can take tens of thousands of years for it to finally reach the surface." Aulthresh explained this in a wispy soprano, ornamented with a slight accent at once both alien and familiar. "Even if all the reactions across the entire star drop their energy output by twenty-four percent, the heat you feel today is already thousands of years old, as will be the heat you feel tomorrow, and tomorrow after that."

"So," said Harrison, "by the time we start to see a measurable drop in Earth's surface temperature, we will all be long dead."

"Speak for yourself," said Aulthresh. "This will certainly be a problem. It just won't be yours."

"Or it will," said the other scientist, extending his hand. "Rick Gorecki. You're Harrison Cody, aren't you?"

Harrison took his hand. "Yes. Hi. Not to skip the niceties, but what do you mean it will?"

"Gorecki thinks the Sun will collapse," said Larson.

Gorecki held his hands out in front of him, holding an imaginary sphere about the size of a basketball. "The sun has two forces acting on it at all times. It's massive, so there's a lot of gravity trying to push it into a smaller ball. But it's also hot, which creates outward pressure as the material expands. A sudden drop in thermal output..." He glanced at Aulthresh. "...even taking into account existing solar dynamics, could give gravity just the edge it needs to drop the corona right down to the ground." He punctuated this by slamming his hands together.

"The Sun does not have a ground," said Aulthresh.

"You know what I mean."

"The Sun collapses to a dwarf star?" said Harrison. "Does it stay hot?"

"Well, sort of," said Gorecki. "But that turns out not to matter anyway, because if the collapse is hard enough..." He illustrated his next point by bringing his hands together again, then clapping loudly and throwing his arms wide. "Boom."

"Bounce back," said Harrison. "Explosion."

"Something like that."

"I gather that won't take thousands of years?"

"Weeks," said Gorecki. "Possibly days."

"Except none of that is going to happen," said Larson. "It is well established the Mayhem Wave is capable of exerting its influence retroactively. The drop in temperature won't be gradual, or even sudden. It will always have been that cold. Which puts us back at the first scenario. The oceans will freeze over, among other things. Some deep-sea life might survive."

"Or something completely different and unexpected could happen," said Gorecki. "Because magic."

Aulthresh rolled her gorgeous, black eyes.

"For now," said Larson, "we are assuming the cold scenario is the most likely. It might be possible to sustain a small human colony for some time, but that doesn't look promising enough to be a solution."

"May I assume you have a better plan?" said Harrison.

"Plan might be an optimistic word. We do have a possibility, but at the moment, we're not sure if we can control it." She touched a control under the screen, and another circular overlay appeared inside the Mayhesphere on the screen, nearly the same size, and concentric with it.

"What's that?" asked Harrison.

"You made that," said Larson. "That's the counter-bomb wave. We discovered it last night. It's expanding in almost the same pattern as the Mayhesphere, but slightly faster, and at a different pulse rate. The good news is that when it catches up, they will both be completely neutralized."

"The bad news is that you think that's not going to happen this year."

"You got it. Current projections put the collision at three hundred eighty-two days, plus or minus fifteen."

Harrison rubbed his face. The energy he had spent the past two weeks devoting to the cause of protecting his daughters now felt like a complete waste. Even if he succeeded in keeping them safe, and even if he managed to find the missing four and bring them home, they all had ten months to live. "Tell me you can fix this."

"We can fix this," said Larson. "We just don't know how yet. The counter-bomb was a spell, and it's going to take another spell to enhance it. We have had less than twenty-four hours to study this, but I feel confident we can find a way to correct this problem in time. We're going to need resources, though. And wizards."

For a fleeting moment, Harrison considered assigning Aplomado to this project, to get him away from the NCSA, but the thought of trusting the fate of the world to that man was more than he could stomach. "I can give you Mallory. Maybe one or two more."

Larson's eyebrows went up a notch. "She's good."

"Very good," he said. "No point in sparing the talent on this one."

"That's very generous."

"Mm hmm," said Harrison.

"You're negotiating to have that eval done today," said Larson.

"One day of Garrett for ten months of Mallory? That's a steal."

She thought for a moment. "You can have her for two hours."

"Starting as soon as Rutherford gets here," said Harrison.

"Done."

"It's a pleasure doing business with you, Doctor."

"And you, Assistant Director," said Larson. "Now, unless you have any further requests, we have a world to save."

He smiled. "I'll be on my way. Please have Garrett forward any findings to me directly and immediately." He gave Aulthresh a smile she ignored, and Gorecki a small wave he returned.

Felicia spoke again. "Margaret Collins is refusing to cooperate with agents."

"Damn it," he said. "Let me talk to her."

As he passed down the corridor, waiting for the call, he glanced into whatever rooms happened to be open. In the second open door he caught sight of a technician wearing a Hawaiian shirt, which amused him. Sparky was indeed used to a different standard of professionalism here. He made it nearly to the stairs before he recognized the shirt. Hadley Tucker wore it the first day of their expedition to find the source of the Mayhem Wave, an expedition from which he did not return. He had also seen the same shirt fleetingly in NCSA headquarters the night before.

Harrison swept back to that open door to look inside, only to be greeted by a technician wearing an ordinary lab coat, and a dryad who wore nothing. "Can I help you?" asked the wood sprite.

Before he could respond to her, the speaker on his communicator cut in. "We had a deal!"

"Hello, Peg."

"Don't give me that!" she said. "We had a deal! You can't do this!"

"Ordinarily I would agree—"

"You can't come take me from my home just because one of them went missing. I trusted you! You said I would never see you again! Any of you!"

"It's four," said Harrison.

"Four what?"

"Four people missing. Siobhan, Kate, Kari, and as of last night Brooke."

"Oh." This slowed her down, barely. "Can't you just leave me with a bodyguard or something?"

"Whatever took Kate killed at least seven people to get to her," he said.

A pause on the line followed this information. "I don't..." She left the idea unfinished.

"I won't sugar coat this, Peggy. Your life is in serious danger, and I need you secure."

"What about what I need, Dad?" Even in her rage, and her conviction to have him out of her life, she used the title.

"You need you secure, too," he countered.

Another pause. "Can I have some time to think about it?"

"I wish we had that luxury, but no. You need to come right now." He left unspoken the threat that his next step would be to have her arrested. It would break his heart, but he would not hesitate.

"All right," she said. "But I don't want to see them when I get there, and I don't want to see you."

"We will arrange that."

"Goodbye." The quiet background hiss on the line ended. One more accounted for. Three to go.

[14]

FAMILY

Dorothy woke at six o'clock. Her body, being a creature of habit, resisted attempts at rest after that moment, every morning. She rolled over. Claudia lay curled up in the comforter on the floor, face down in a pillow, dead to the world.

She picked up her clothes from yesterday and tiptoed to the bathroom. After stripping off her underwear and taking a brief but wonderful shower, she redressed in all the same garments. First order of business today as soon as she could break away would be to get herself some clean clothing. She gargled with tap water, a poor substitute for a morning brush. Hair still wet, she went out to greet her day.

First stop was Harrison's office, though he had already left. Apryl sat up in bed, looking over a handwritten to-do list. Melody slept on.

"Isn't that what you had on yesterday?" asked Apryl.

"I didn't realize I would be staying the night when I got here," said Dorothy.

"You'll probably have time to go home and pack today. Are you planning to ride this out?"

"I guess so," said Dorothy. "I didn't exactly have a plan yesterday. I just thought I would try to help."

"Well, I'm definitely going to need you today," said Apryl. "I'll start circulating around ten o'clock. How long can you watch Melody?"

"As long as you need me to."

"Why don't you take her home with you once she's up and dressed. She can help you pack. Besides…" Apryl leaned over to give her daughter a kiss. "I don't want her to spend all day in this facility. It's not exactly kid friendly."

"I'd like that," said Dorothy. "How many days should I pack for?"

"I have no idea. We packed for four. It will probably be longer than that. Is staying here going to interfere with your school work?"

"No, it's all independent right now anyway."

Melody shuffled and rolled over. "Hey, Melody, Dorothy's here."

The little girl looked up with bleary eyes and said, "Dorrie," with a broad smile before falling back asleep, placing a warm tickle in Dorothy's heart.

"Did you eat anything yet?" asked Apryl.

"No. I was going to grab breakfast in the cafeteria. Should I wait for you?"

"Probably not," she said. "I won't be ready for a while and you have a long day ahead of you. You should eat while you can. Can you suffer in yesterday's grubbies until nine thirty?"

Dorothy laughed. "Sure."

"Meet me back here then. Melody will be dressed, fed, and ready for your packing adventure."

"Sounds good."

As Dorothy headed out, Claudia appeared in the door. Dorothy attempted to greet her with a smile, but Claudia, unusually focused, missed it. "Hey," she said to Apryl. "Is Harrison in the building?"

"I don't think so," said Apryl. "He left for Esoteric before I got up. You could check with the front desk to see if he ever came back."

"I'll try that, thanks," said Claudia.

"Would you like to join me for breakfast?" asked Dorothy. "I'm heading down to the cafeteria." For a moment, Dorothy relished the idea of a fresh start with Claudia. After their heart-to-heart the previous night, she felt they were finally connecting as true friends.

"Can't, sorry," said Claudia. "I'm supposed to be doing superhero stuff today. I need to find the boss."

It wasn't until Claudia spoke to her directly that Dorothy realized Claudia had not yet acknowledged her at all. Even responding to her, Claudia had trouble maintaining eye contact. Somehow, they had gone back to awkwardness, for no reason Dorothy could discern. Maybe Claudia felt she opened up too much, and now she felt embarrassed, except Dorothy had been the vulnerable one in that situation.

"All right then," Dorothy said in a clipped tone. "See you at nine thirty," she said to Apryl. "Excuse me." She slipped past Claudia without looking at her.

Insufferably frustrating woman.

Shortly before nine-thirty, Dorothy returned to collect her little sister. They strolled the half-mile to her apartment from the NCSA building through the beautiful spring day.

"Are we sleeping over again tonight?" asked Melody.

"I think so, Little," said Dorothy. "We might be there for a few days."

"Why are we staying at Daddy's work?"

Why indeed? In what possible context could Dorothy spin this story that would make sense to a five-year-old? The truth was they were staying there because their extended artificial family was in danger. Artificial or not, family was family. That much she would understand. But the nature of that trouble? Dorothy herself did not fully grasp it. Even having spent her formative years in a world and a culture where the impossible was commonplace, she had a hard time truly comprehending the threats that surrounded them every day of their lives.

"Do you know Becca?" she asked Melody.

"Uh huh," she said.

"You know she thinks of your daddy as her daddy too, right?"

"Lots of people do," said Melody. "Like you!"

"That's right," said Dorothy. "We're sisters, right?"

"Yeah!"

"Well, there are a lot of girls who are our sisters, too, even if we hardly ever see them. And Daddy is worried about them right now, so he wants to keep them all together."

"Why is he worried?" asked Melody. "Are they in trouble?"

Yes. They were in terrible trouble, and Dorothy tried to imagine what it would feel like to be, as Harrison put it to her, a target. For a moment, she allowed a wisp of selfish relief to flow over her she would never voice to anyone. Dorothy held deep concerns that terrible things might happen to her sisters, might already be happening, and might already have happened. But if she had to pick one sister to protect, it would be Melody.

"They didn't do anything wrong, if that's what you're asking. Daddy just wants to take care of them. That's all. Like he wants me to take care of you when he can't, and when mommy can't. Only right now, there are too many people he wants to take care of, and he can't do it by himself. So we're there to help."

"Are we their babysitters?"

Dorothy thought on that. "Yes, that's pretty close."

"I want to help!"

Dorothy smiled at Melody's joy in the face of a peril she could never fully appreciate, refreshing and infectious. With all the crises in her life, both personal and on a larger field, she could think of no better tonic than a walk on a beautiful day with her little sister.

"You are helping, sweetheart."

15

PLANS

Halfway back from Esoteric, Harrison got another notification. "Alicia Sullivan is secure," said Felicia. "Still no contact on the last two."

"Good. Keep that news coming." As he spoke into the communicator, Claudia approached him from the NCSA building. If she had business at Esoteric, she hadn't said anything about it, and he needed her back at base. Her part-time agent status made accountability for comings and goings vague sometimes. He made a mental note to address that after this crisis.

"We have updated surveillance of the Lone Star Palace, as well," said Felicia. "You're going to want to see this."

"Newer than the photos I saw three days ago?" he asked.

"Yes, and there are signs of activity."

Harrison upgraded his hunch to suspicion, the only likely suspects in the abductions of those four women being the bastards who held them captive in that building. That someone had now returned to that place threw up a red flag. "What kind of activity?"

"It's better to show you," she said. "How soon will you be back here?"

"I'm on my way right now. Maybe ten minutes."

Claudia caught up with him.

"Where are you headed?" he asked her.

"Looking for you." She spun on her heel as she met him to walk with him. "I need something to do."

"You have something to do," he said. "I want you with Apryl and

Dorothy. The three of you have twenty-plus women to keep happy and one little girl to entertain. That should be plenty to keep you occupied all day."

"I need something *else* to do," she said, without making eye contact.

"Can we not be brat girl for one day, please? I have a lot on my plate today, and I need you where I need you." After a few seconds of no reaction to that, he said, "If you and Dorothy have some personal squabble right now, put it on hold. Is that understood, Special Agent?" Irritation crept into his voice, and he rode it for effect.

"It's not a squabble."

"Well, what the hell is it?" he asked, a fraction of a second before remembering he didn't care.

"The more I'm around her, the more I feel like I can't live without her."

With no time to deal with drama, and no desire to coddle the people working for him, he nearly got off a rehearsed response before Claudia's words registered. When they did, he stopped walking. "Wait, what?"

"What?" cried Claudia, shock in her eyes.

"What did you just say?"

"Nothing! What?"

He took a deep breath. "Claudia, I have exactly..." He looked at his watch. "No time at all to deal with this, so here's how this is going to work: You're going to be straight with me about any personal issues that might jeopardize our handing of the current situation. Then I'm going to give you orders, and you will follow them. Got that?"

She nodded.

"Good. Now. What is going on between the two of you?"

Claudia's face fell into an expression of defeat. "It's just a crush. If you need me to handle it, I'll handle it."

"I need you to handle it. Does she know?"

"I sure as hell hope not," said Claudia. "Have you met Dorothy?"

"How long has this been a problem?"

"I don't know. What time is it now?" she asked.

"One thirty-five."

She made a thoughtful face, and began calculations on her fingers. "Then... about... eight years."

"In other words, always," said Harrison.

Claudia shrugged. "Pretty much."

"You do understand you have literally picked the absolute worst day to bring this to me, right?"

She nodded.

"Then we're together on that, at least. Okay, here's what happens next.

For now, you hold it together, because you're a big girl. There will be plenty—and I mean *plenty*—of work today for all of you, so you probably won't be around her much as it is. When you see her, you will regard her as a colleague, and treat her accordingly. At the end of the day, we will come up with a long-range plan. Got all that?"

"Yes," she said.

"Good. Now, it will take us a few more minutes to cross the distance to the NCSA building, so that's how much time you have for us to take off the badges and talk like people, if you want to. Do you?"

"Sure," she said.

"All right then. Let's start with: What exactly are your intentions with my daughter?"

Claudia laughed at that. "Entirely honorable, I assure you, sir."

"So..." he said. "Love at first sight? Dorothy was fourteen."

"A smoking hot fourteen, with the mind of thirty-year-old," said Claudia.

"Hmm. I guess that's a fair point." He feigned shock. "Hang on! Is that why you had me arrested? You were trying to get her alone?"

"Shit!" said Claudia. "I wish I'd thought of that. No, I had you arrested because you were a dick."

"Fair enough. So why is it suddenly a problem? Or has it always been?"

Claudia shrugged. "Meh. It comes and goes. It's always worse right after a breakup. Stupid Mickey."

"Asshole."

"Right?" she said with enthusiasm.

"Is this helping?" he asked.

"A little. It's stupid, and it'll pass. The timing sucks."

"Yeah," he said. "Amen to that."

───────────────

Harrison stopped next at Felicia's office. "Let's see them."

Felicia turned a monitor to face him. With the specific technology available to them, flyover surveillance was an inexact science. The monitor showed a grainy image of the castle where he spent a few hours, during which he rescued twenty-eight girls from slavery, and started a fight that ended with several people dead. Not a happy memory.

He could not pick out much detail, but some things were clear. The Windex blue moat had grown over with brush and pond scum. From this angle, he could make out the edge of the gaping hole in the second-floor wall where they had torn an escape route by ripping out a barred window. "This looks exactly like the one you already showed me."

"It is the one I already showed you. I wanted to give you a baseline. Take a look at this one." The image scrolled off screen, replaced by one from a different angle, taken under different lighting conditions, and slightly fuzzier. "Do you see it?"

"What am I supposed to be seeing?" She switched the picture back to the original, left it there for a few seconds, then showed him the new one again. Given they were not from the same point of reference, it was difficult to make out what would have changed.

"See it yet?" she asked.

"No." Harrison did not enjoy this game, but it was necessary. If she told him what to look for, he might see it by power of suggestion. He had to be able to replicate her observation to confirm it. "Go back again." He looked at the first shot, studying every detail he could find that seemed relevant. On this third pass he took note of things other than the building itself. The moat. One edge of a pen used to house horrible monsters (thankfully not visible). The surrounding overgrowth. "Okay. Give me the new one." She switched images again. He took in the environs once more, from the different angle. "Wait. Go back." She switched it back. "Forward." The image shifted again. "Drawbridge."

"That's what I saw, too," she said. Tricky to spot at first glance, ivy and moss covered the drawbridge, signs of disuse. The fact Texas had gone from desert to jungle after the Mayhem Wave made this sort of precision work difficult even without the technological limitations. But there was a difference. In the second photo, a clear seam of light cut across the middle, and the bridge perched at a different angle, even taking into account the altered perspective of the camera. In the first photo, it was down. In the second, raised.

"That's a good catch, Agent Kestrel."

"Thank you, sir," she said. "Does this mean we will be focusing on the castle in our investigation?"

"Yes, it does," he said. "That's where I was headed anyway, but this clinches it. How soon can we have a flier ready?"

Felicia opened a schedule to check. "Maybe as early as tomorrow morning. Probably not until Monday."

"Please put together an assault team," said Harrison. "And I want additional surveillance of that structure. As much as possible for every moment between now and mission time."

"Understood. Will you be leading the team yourself?"

Harrison hadn't given that as much thought as he should have. "Probably."

"Special agents? Wizards?" she asked. "How much power do you want to bring into this?"

"I'll have a list for you in an hour." He didn't have an answer to that question yet. However, Felicia's use of the word "power" did give him an idea of who he wanted to bring on this.

They were going to need a babysitter.

16

THIS THING

Dorothy and Melody returned to the NCSA mid-afternoon, bearing a suitcase. By this time, Apryl had successfully lobbied to have two offices converted into lounges, one of which would be completely off limits to anyone but the women in protective custody, and the other intended for them, but open to visitors. She also arranged catered dinners for the next four evenings, and cafeteria vouchers for breakfasts and lunches. Those women choosing to remain isolated in their rooms or the lounges were to have their meals delivered. They were otherwise permitted to visit the cafeteria, and other non-classified areas of the building, with minimal escort. Some of these concessions came easily, others required more work on her part, but she got them all.

Dorothy heard some of this from the guard at the front desk, and the rest from some of the more gregarious women who chose to take advantage of their wandering privileges. She finally managed to catch up to Apryl in the open lounge, where four of her charges were watching a movie.

"Mommy!" said a delighted Melody, who ran to Apryl's arms.

She scooped up her child in a smooth motion and planted her on a hip. "You are getting very big!" Melody responded by hugging her more tightly. "What did you do today?"

"We went to the park," said Melody. "And we rode in a taxi, and we had big pretzels."

"Not in that order," said Dorothy.

"I'm sure it was fine," said Apryl. "You ready to swap?"

"You mean you get one Melody and I get twenty special guests?"

"Tag," said Apryl. "You're it. They're pretty well taken care of at this point. If you and Claudia just try to pop in on the lounges and the hall maybe once every hour or two, you should be fine."

"I can do that," said Dorothy. "Melody was good today. We never had a proper lunch though, just the pretzels we got from a street vendor. You might want to feed her."

"Are you hungry, Sweetie?" asked Apryl.

"Sure," said Melody.

Apryl laughed. "That doesn't sound very urgent. I think we'll hold out for dinner. It's Mexican tonight."

"Mmm," said Melody. "Taco."

"Close enough."

"I think I'll get a sandwich before I head upstairs," said Dorothy. "They're okay, right?"

"They're fine. Go eat."

Dorothy went from there to the cafeteria. She ordered a grilled cheese sandwich and a tea. The same ID that got her into this facility also got her a lunch pass, which she discovered when she tried to pay. When she emerged from the order line into the dining room, she spotted Claudia, sitting by herself at a small table near the window. For a moment, Dorothy considered pretending she didn't see her, but she caught herself, disgusted she would fall into that behavior so easily. This stupid game had to end. She walked directly to Claudia.

"Hi," she said, still standing.

Claudia looked up, and casually said, "Hey," before going right back to her food.

"Mind if I join you?"

Claudia did not look back up, and for a moment, Dorothy thought she might be deliberately ignoring her. Finally, she said, "I'm actually headed back upstairs. My break is over." With that, she stood and picked up her tray, half a sandwich still visible on it. "See ya."

"Hey," said Dorothy, hoping to catch her for even a few seconds, but Claudia kept her back to her, and continued walking. "Hey!"

Claudia stopped, without turning around.

"Come here, please," said Dorothy.

Claudia's shoulders slumped. She turned around and came back to the table like a scolded puppy. "What do you need?"

Dorothy put her tray on the table. "Sit down, please."

"I really have to—"

"No, you don't. Apryl already told me you and I are fine for at least an hour, which also means, by the way, that you apparently aren't doing any 'superhero stuff' today at all. So." Dorothy pulled out a chair and planted herself in it. "Sit, please."

Claudia hesitated. "Dotty, seriously, what do you need? This isn't a great time."

"I need you," she said, "to sit down."

Claudia resigned, put her tray back down, and sat. She picked up the half sandwich on her plate, and took a bite.

"This thing has to stop," said Dorothy.

Claudia perked up at that, looking curiously nervous. "What thing?"

"This thing." Dorothy pointed to herself, then Claudia, then herself again. "This thing between us. This thing we do. This undercurrent of hostility. I like you, Claudia. I look up to you. And I'm tired of this pointless rivalry, when we should be friends."

"Maybe we just don't get along," said Claudia around a mouthful of sandwich.

"Then that's the thing that has to stop," said Dorothy. "Listen, those things you said to me last night… That's why I came to you. I trusted you because I thought you were the only one I know who is smart enough to understand me."

Claudia looked up at that, an odd sort of surprise in her eyes. It faded to something starker. "I was just trying to push your buttons."

"I *needed* someone to push my buttons," countered Dorothy. "What you said was exactly what I needed to hear. I knew you of all people would know how to talk to me about this, and I was one hundred percent correct about that. So don't you dare belittle what you did for me."

"I didn't cure you," she said. "You're still going to hurt over Brad."

"I'm not stupid. I know that. But I also know I can defend against that hurt by remembering what a fucker he is." Saying the word gave Dorothy a tiny, giddy thrill.

Claudia smiled. "He really is."

"I know. And no one else in my life had the courage—or I guess the vocabulary—to make me see that." Dorothy put her elbows on the table and rested her chin in her hands. "I think you might be my best friend, Claudia."

Claudia's eyes went wide on that. "I… don't know what to say."

Dorothy laughed softly. "Well, that's a first. Try this: just say you agree we should stop sniping at each other. This friendship matters to me, and I don't think I ever saw that more clearly than I did last night. But the little jabs are poisonous, Claudia. We treat each other like we don't get along,

but we do." Dorothy looked down, considering her next words. "I know…
I'm not very much like you."

"That's for sure."

Dorothy looked up and pointed at her. "Don't interrupt, please. I'm
not much like you, but that should have stopped mattering as soon as we
grew up. I want to be able to talk to you without worrying what stupid
thing you're going to mock next. And I want you to trust that I'm not
going to try to one-up you, which I only do because you intimidate me."

"I intimidate you?"

"Yes, and there I said it. Which means it doesn't have to matter
anymore." Dorothy stopped there, well aware she had by now overloaded
Claudia with an emotional neediness she herself barely understood.
"Claudia, you and I are two of the smartest people either of us know. We
can figure this out. And don't tell me you don't care. I saw your face when
I fell apart last night. You do care, and you are kind, and you cover it up
with this tough girl façade so no one can get close enough to see who you
really are. But that ship has sailed. I saw you, I know you, and I like you.
And I want to be friends. Real friends. Not weird, snippy, almost friends."

With that, both women sat in silence for a few seconds. Finally,
Dorothy said, "I feel as though I've probably said enough at this point."

Claudia nodded.

"Can we do this? Can this be real, please?" Dorothy held her hand out
to Claudia. "Can we start over, right now?"

Claudia hesitated. She reached up and took Dorothy's hand. Dorothy
smiled at her success. The handshake lasted a bit beyond the purpose it
was meant to serve, and she gave a little squeeze. Claudia squeezed back,
and let go.

"Thank you." She winced. "Was that too much?"

Claudia stared at her with peaceful eyes. "Oh, I think that was just
about right."

17

TEAM

A bout twenty minutes after viewing the aerial photos of the palace, and while still in Felicia's office compiling his list of operatives to make up the team sent to retrieve the kidnapped women (and he forced himself to assume they were all still alive), Harrison got a call from Esoteric.

"Cody? Are you busy?"

"I feel like we talked about this already," he said to Larson.

"Yes, yes," she said. "I was just being polite. It's not really in my skill set. I need you back here as soon as you're able."

He frowned. A return trip to Larson's lab was not on his very-full-and-already-behind-schedule agenda. "Why?"

"Because Rutherford is here for that fast-tracked evaluation, and we have had some major surprises. I assumed if this was urgent enough to put my day on hold, you would want to see the results."

Harrison made a mental note to bring in experts to train his people on how to communicate their findings over the phone. "I appreciate that, but I really have quite a lot to do. At the moment, I am trying to determine who my most valuable field agents are for a rescue mission."

"Rutherford may very well make that cut, if you see what we just saw," she said.

Harrison growled. "How long can you keep him there?"

"He's your man. He will stay here as long as you tell him to."

"Give him a magazine. It's going to be at least an hour."

"All right. See you then," she said.

He pocketed the communicator, and spent another two minutes fretting over his list before putting it aside.

"I'm heading back to my office," he said to Felicia. "Do me a favor and jot down any recommendations you have for the extraction team. You know these people's strengths at least as well as I do."

"I'm sure we're thinking of the same people already," she said.

"Even so. Please keep me updated on our last two stragglers."

"I will."

Harrison covered the short distance down the hallway back to his office in less than a minute, but in more than enough time for another interruption.

"Hey!" came a shout from behind him. In the time it took for him to turn around, Sparky had already circled him twice, a small black and orange blur.

"Is there a problem?" he asked.

She stopped, and hovered in front of his face. In place of the burlap sack, she now wore a black jacket and tie, and black slacks. She held her arms out wide to display the objectionable attire. "Are you for real with this?"

"Until you can figure out how to dress appropriately, yes," he said.

"Why do I have to dress at all?" she asked. "You people are such prudes! I never had this kind of trouble at Esoteric."

"Different environment," he said. "Different standards."

"Do you have any idea how restrictive this is?" She grabbed her throat. "I... I can't breathe!" She issued some entirely unconvincing choking sounds, and her face took on a bluish hue.

"Yes, I know how restrictive the suit is," he said. "It's the same thing I'm wearing."

She stopped. "Oh. So it is. Well, poo. I'm out of ideas. Can't we just agree that I've learned my lesson, and let me go back to not wearing anything?"

"As amusing as I find this, it may surprise you to learn that your dress code issues are low on my list of priorities today." He scrutinized her for a moment, with an idea. "How fast can you fly?"

"Pretty fast," she said.

"Glimmer fast?"

She laughed at that. "Oh, pumpkin, you have a greatly inflated notion of what pixies can do if you think we're anything like her. She was all of us. The fastest, the brightest, the strongest, all added together and multiplied up. Your standard issue pixie is a lot humbler than that."

"I'm not sure you're using the word 'humble' correctly."

"You know what I mean. I'm not her."

"Yes, you are," he insisted, gently pointing to her right hand.

She looked at the missing finger there, and backtracked. "Okay, well, yes, I am. But I'm not all of her. I'm the tiniest fraction of the speck of dust under her fingernail." She put her hands on her hips and gave him her best pissy stare. "If you brought me here as a stand-in because you miss your cutie, I should go back to my lab where I can be naked in peace."

"Sparky," he said, "I know exactly how much you are and aren't her. You're not a stand-in. You happen to have talents that I find useful, apart from anything Glimmer might have been able to do. And I like you personally, which you already know."

"Oh," she said. "Yeah, I did know that."

"Right. So seriously, cut the crap. How fast can you fly?"

"Mach two."

"See?" he said. "You could have just said that. Thank you. I'm putting together a rescue team, and you're on it. I just needed a clear idea of my resources."

"We're going on a mission?" she asked with excessive enthusiasm.

"Possibly as early as tomorrow."

"Which means we're leaving the building?" She waggled her eyebrows mischievously.

"Yes, Sparky," he said. "And the dress code will hold for the duration of the mission."

"Damn it!" She zipped away.

Without further distraction, he made it the rest of the way to his office. Melody sat on the bed, still unfolded, playing with two dolls and a stuffed turtle. "Where's your mom?" he asked her.

"Potty," she said without looking up. She spoke in hushed tones and different pitches, returning to whatever imaginary conversation her toys were having.

Apryl emerged from Harrison's private lavatory. "Hey, you," she said, and crossed the room to plant a kiss on him. "Any news?"

"About?"

She shrugged. "Anything. I have some updates about our guests if you want to hear them. Did Felicia tell you any of what we did today?"

"No," he said. "We've been talking about other stuff."

"Okay," she said. "Just thought you'd want to know they have all settled in. I managed to claim two offices as lounges for them, and connected with four local restaurants to provide catered meals until at least Tuesday. Tonight is Bueno Cantina."

"Mmm," said Harrison. "Tacos."

"What about you?" asked Apryl.

"Two more stragglers still unaccounted for, but I'm hoping we will have them by the end of the day. Dallas apparently has some awesome new power that Larson is willing to tell me exists, but won't give me specifics. The Lone Star Palace is occupied again as of this week, which can't be a coincidence." He paused there, thinking back on the day. "Oh, and we all have ten months to live before the Sun goes cold."

"Is that all?" asked Apryl.

"Oh," said Harrison. "No, sorry. Claudia is in love with Dorothy."

"Called that," said Apryl.

Harrison, expecting a bit more surprise from her on any number of those topics, said, "Called that? When?"

"A year ago, at least. Don't you remember me saying Claudia had her eye on Dorothy?"

He thought back a year, as best as he could. "No."

"Well, I did," she said. "Should have put money on it. Tell me about the Texas thing."

"You don't want to hear about the Sun going cold?"

"Do you have people working on that?"

"Yes," he said.

"Then leave it alone. Texas?"

Harrison sat down in his comfortable leather desk chair. "The drawbridge on the moat was raised as recently as three days ago. Someone is there, right now, and the girls I rescued from that hellhole are starting to vanish. I think that's where they are. I could be wrong, but that's what I think. I am putting together an extraction team, and we are leaving to get them soon, possibly tomorrow."

"You're leading this mission yourself?"

"Yes, I am," he said. "If you're going to tell me this is a conflict of interest, I won't argue with that, but I'm still going. And this brings me to my next topic of discussion. I have partial list of operatives, but I also intend to take special agents and wizards. If we find them there, this will end, and it will end in shock and awe, followed by their safe return. So... I need muscle on this one." Harrison let that statement sit there, for Apryl's appraisal.

She drifted around the room pensively, then faced away from Harrison and stretched her arms out. "You just called me muscle."

"That I did," he said, wishing he could see her face.

Still facing away from him, she flexed her arms. "I am pretty badass."

She spun around, excitement in her eyes. "Does there exist a butt I can't kick?"

"I don't think so," he said.

"Then I'm in."

"Wow," he said. "I really thought this was going to be a discussion. Are you actually eager for this?"

"I'm a high school teacher," she said. "How often do you think I get to cut loose with my superpowers?"

"Steady, girl. If this goes to plan, you won't be powering anything. I want to bring you as insurance, not firepower."

"Unless you need it."

"Unless I need it."

"How long are we going to be gone?" she asked.

"Hard to say. Depends what we find when we get there. We should budget a few days, but we could end up back here in a matter of hours."

Apryl sat down on the bed with Melody, still engrossed in whatever story her dolls were playing out. "How much of this did you hear, honey?"

"You're pretty badass," she said.

Harrison failed to suppress his laughter.

———

Roughly an hour and a half after he told Larson he would be back in an hour, Harrison returned to Esoteric. He found Bob Rutherford reading a magazine at the same table where Sarah had successfully frozen time inside a water clock. Rutherford was almost fifty years old, overweight, and generally unkempt. What hair he still had was overdue to be cut, and apparently unaccustomed to the company of a brush. He wore a button-down shirt half tucked into a pair of stained jeans.

"Hello, Dallas," said Harrison.

Rutherford looked up. "Howdy, Independence." Rutherford was the third resident of New Chicago to be discovered to have superhuman telekinetic abilities. At the time, he imagined himself part of a team of superheroes, and they all needed codes names, or secret identities. As each telekinetic shared the trait of being born on days of great historical significance, he assigned the code names accordingly. Harrison became Independence for his having been born on the American Bicentennial. Sarah Logan became Eagle, named for the Apollo 11 landing module, which touched down on the surface of the moon a mere four hours after she was delivered by Cesarean section. Claudia he called Tiananmen, after the massacre in China that occurred the day of her birth. For himself, Rutherford chose the name Dallas, to commemorate the death of President John F. Kennedy, assassinated only ten minutes before Rutherford came into the world.

"Sorry to keep you waiting so long," said Harrison.

"S'all right," said Dallas. "It wasn't that long."

Harrison tried to imagine how gracious he would be about being made to sit in a laboratory for ninety minutes on the whim of a superior, and conceded he would handle it with far less courtesy. "What is it you want to show me, Doctor?" he said to Larson, who stood patiently with her colleague Garrett at the other end of the table.

"I'd like to do the cards again," Larson said to Garrett and Dallas. "You're going to want to watch this closely," she said to Harrison.

Garrett took what appeared to be an ordinary deck of cards, shuffled it seven times against the surface of the table, then fanned them out face up so Harrison could see they had been properly randomized. She tidied them back into a solid rectangle. "Are you ready?" she asked Dallas.

He grinned. "Go for it."

Garrett held the deck in one hand, palm facing Dallas. She closed her hand around the deck until it started to bend, then gave one more push. The entire deck sprayed forward out of her hand in a shower of cards. Several hit Dallas in the face. He did not flinch.

Once the last card left her hand, he went straight to work scooping the cards off the table and floor. In a matter of seconds, he reassembled them into a deck.

"Spread them out, please," said Garrett.

Dallas turned the deck face up and fanned them out across the table. All fifty-two cards were grouped by suit, and within each suit neatly sorted in order from ace to king.

"Okay," said Harrison. "That is impressive. What's the probability of that happening by chance?"

"A number so small there is no reasonable analogy to make it resonate for you," said Larson. "But just for a quick comparison, if he started doing that at the birth of the universe and did it once every second without a break until this moment, he still wouldn't have done it enough times to reasonably expect this result to happen even once. Meanwhile, this is the fifth time he has done it in this very room on this very day."

"His power affects probabilities, right?"

"That's what we thought at first," said Garrett. "It turns out his power is to cheat. Watch this." She picked up the deck, removed the ace of spades right off the top, and tore it up. She opened a second pack of cards, pulled out the 2 of clubs, and inserted it to the first deck. When they ran the experiment one more time, not only were the cards completely sorted, the missing ace of spades showed clearly on top, with the extra 2 of clubs nowhere to be found.

"That's a pretty good trick," said Harrison.

"It's not a trick," said Larson. "He is using his telekinesis to rearrange the ink on the surface of the cards. He isn't sorting the deck when he picks it up, he is changing it into a sorted deck by reprinting any card that isn't in the correct position. He is forcing order out of chaos, and he is doing it at the molecular level. We think the essence of his ability is to reverse entropy."

"Pretty sweet, huh?" said Dallas.

Harrison gawked at this disheveled sample of humanity who considered his ability to fundamentally alter the fabric of the universe "pretty sweet." Somehow this person possessed the power to force order from chaos, but couldn't be bothered to tuck his shirt in the whole way. "Is that what he does to dice?" In the first demonstration Harrison had seen Dallas perform nearly nine years earlier, he rolled double ones with a pair of fair dice every time he threw them.

"No," she said. "Initially, he was just tumbling the dice telekinetically, as you would expect, and that's still what he does for that particular manifestation. But what he just did is completely new. Tucker ran similar tests with cards in 2004, and at that time, he was unable to sort them. We should start running tests to measure what happens when he tries to do something like that deliberately. I'd like to bring Logan back in as well. The fact he has moved on from the original trigger objects might mean you are all able to do that. I am very interested in whether she can manifest the time distortion with something other than a clock."

Harrison had no idea how to process the information. He found the notion of a Dallas this powerful inconceivable and frightening. As he pondered whether bringing him on this mission would be prudent or reckless, Felicia contacted him.

"Kara Patrick and Lauren Chapman are still unaccounted for," she said. "There are indications they may have been taken. Agents on both sites have now called them in as missing."

Harrison tried to form a response to that, but only managed to whisper, "Damn it."

18

DISTRACTIONS

Dorothy and Claudia spent the rest of the day checking on the detainees, securing cots for the new arrivals, and generally making themselves available for requests or concerns. The general attitude of the NCSA guests had settled into complacent resolves to make the best of the situation, which ran the gamut from enthusiastically attempting to treat this as a gathering of friends to a grudging acknowledgment of the need for protection.

At six o'clock, the caterer arrived with fixings for burritos, tacos, quesadillas, and an assortment of other Mexican dishes. Most of the women gathered in the two lounges to eat. Dorothy and Claudia took orders from the few who chose to stay in their rooms, and delivered their meals to them. With that done, they each loaded up a plate and sat together at one of the tables in the open lounge. The Codys arrived shortly after and joined them. Harrison gave Claudia a wide-eyed look of bafflement. She smiled and shrugged.

"I have a new assignment for you," said Harrison to Dorothy.

She raised an eyebrow. "Do tell." She and Claudia made a fine team now that they had sorted out their weird, pointless conflict. While the idea she had impressed Harrison enough he wanted to promote her to some other job held some appeal, she hoped it wouldn't keep her away from Claudia. She didn't want to lose momentum there.

"We're going on a little vacation," said Apryl with a wry smile. "Melody needs a nanny for a few days."

Dorothy sat up. "Vacation? Now?"

"Relax," said Harrison. "She means 'rescue mission.' It just has her pumped up a bit. I think she's looking to bust some heads."

"I am indeed," said Apryl.

"You can stay here and keep doing what you're doing, if you don't mind a sidekick," said Harrison.

"Yes, that sounds great." Dorothy would get to keep working with Claudia after all, with the bonus company of her baby sister. Win-win.

"You can stay in my office if it goes that long," said Harrison. "Private bath, spacious quarters. Bound to be a step up."

"Where did you stay last night?" asked Apryl.

"Claudia and I shared a room on the seventh floor." Dorothy looked across the table at her roommate, with a smile. Claudia shifted uncomfortably in her seat. "Only one bed, though." She pouted.

"I took the floor!" said Claudia with wide eyes.

"Yes, she was quite chivalrous about it, too," said Dorothy.

"I'll bet," said Harrison.

"What day are you leaving?" asked Dorothy. "And how long will you be gone?"

"If I can get clearance, we're heading out at dawn tomorrow," said Harrison. "Plan for three days, but expect us back in one."

"If they are gone for more than one day, you should stay with us in Harrison's office," said Dorothy to Claudia. "There are more people here now than yesterday, and we should free up the bed."

Claudia opened her mouth, then looked at Harrison with an awkward grin.

"Which brings me to my next item," he said. "Special Agent de Queiroz will be joining the extraction team. I am trying to load up on heavy hitters."

"Sounds good," said Claudia.

"Oh." Dorothy hoped her disappointment did not show. Maybe they would at least have a chance to talk again tonight before she left.

Harrison's phone chirped at him. He pulled it out of his pocket. "Ugh. It's Marty."

"What's going on with that?" asked Apryl.

He put up a finger to ask for quiet. "Hi Marty." A brief pause followed. "No, he hasn't. I promise I will let you know as soon as I hear from him. How long has he been gone now?" Pause. "That's not even close to his record, is it?" Pause. "I know." Pause. "I know. Listen, I hate to be abrupt, but I'm in the middle of an investigation, and I can't stay on the line." Pause. "Yes, I promise. Yes. Sit tight, Marty. He'll cool off. He always does." Pause. "All right. Take care." He pocketed the phone.

"What was that about?" asked Claudia.

"Mitchell ran away again. Marty was just checking in to see if I've heard from him."

Claudia frowned. "How long has he been gone?"

"Three days," said Harrison. "This is typical for him. He gets into a huge fight with Marty, storms out, hides out with a friend for a week, then comes back and they both have a good cry about it. This is at least the third time in the last year."

"Shit," said Claudia.

"Yeah. Honestly, I think Marty makes much too big a deal out of stuff Mitchell does. He wants to control his son. That wasn't possible when he was ten, let alone eighteen. I want to be supportive, and not interfere, but most of the time I just want to grab him and shake him and tell him to leave his kid alone for once." Harrison sighed. "They'll be fine. I'll have a long talk with the boy when he gets back and try to help him sort out his baggage. Meanwhile, we have other priorities. Marty's on his own."

"On that topic, who else is coming?" asked Claudia.

"The three of us, Sparky, whatever wizards Esoteric can spare for three days, and a dozen agents," said Harrison.

"Oh, shit," said Claudia. "I just realized I have no clothes here. I probably stink already. If I go for three more days, you'll all be sorry."

"I have enough outfits for four days," said Dorothy. "You can borrow two. We're about the same size, right?"

"Um…" said Claudia.

"I'm going to issue you some combat gear," said Harrison. "That's standard for something like this."

"*Thank* you," said Claudia with strange emphasis.

"I've got your back." Harrison winked at her.

"We need to talk," said Aplomado.

Everyone jumped, and Claudia shouted, "Fuck!"

"Can you not do that, please?" said Harrison.

Dorothy tried to figure out what to do with her excess adrenaline. Wizards confused her, to say the least. That this one could stroll up in the middle of a conversation without being seen she found creepy enough. That fact he would *choose* to do that greatly disturbed her.

The wizard held up a splinter of wood longer than his hand. "There were two curses on that bomb."

"Does it matter?" asked Harrison. "We stopped it."

"Perhaps," said Aplomado. "However, the contact poison curse was never the intended main effect. Whoever cast it used it as an encapsulation for the real one."

"What does that mean?" asked Harrison.

"Think of it as the piece of bacon you wrap around a pill to get it down a dog's throat," said the wizard.

"What was the other curse?" asked Harrison.

"I don't know yet."

Harrison laid his hands flat on the table. "Listen, Gray the Gray, three things: One, I'm trying to eat with my family, and you're not exactly enhancing that experience. Two, that bomb is kaput, disassembled, and in storage, and never, ever went off. And three, unless you have something to actually tell me instead of just something to use as an excuse to ruin my dinner, can you please write it up in triplicate, give one copy to Felicia, keep one for your files and shove the third one up your ass?"

No one spoke.

Finally, the wizard said, "It was my understanding that you had two investigations running. One on the disappearance of your female friends, and one on the security breach in your own headquarters. Is that wrong?"

"Yes, it's wrong," said Harrison. "The second one of those is now closed. If you want to keep picking at that scab to entertain yourself, be my guest. But please leave me out of it. Are we clear?"

"We are quite clear," said Aplomado. "Thank you for this new information. It may very well prove most useful."

"Whatever that means. Shove off, please."

The wizard bowed, and departed. Harrison shook off his annoyance, and Apryl gave him a backrub to cool him off. Dorothy did her best to roll with this extremely awkward incident, bothered in a way she would not have been able to articulate. But when she looked at Claudia, seeking some comfort in her friend, she saw an apprehension in her eyes that mirrored her own.

19

LONE STAR REVISITED

At six-fifteen in the morning, with the team assembled and clearance granted, Harrison's extraction mission was nearly underway. They took a modified version of the same fliers they had seen (and stolen) during their time as prisoners of the Lone Star Kingdom in 2005. Over the course of several years, explorers had discovered multiple examples of that technology. By 2009, reverse engineering—as well as other advances and discoveries—facilitated constructing these craft from scratch, with some alterations to the manta ray-shaped design.

Several operatives occupied the landing pad, securing equipment or otherwise prepping. Apart from two wizards, they wore body armor and blades. Invisibly, Bess, the enchanted and sentient short sword that had once been Alec's weapon, hung strapped to Harrison's belt. He and Apryl stood at a short distance from the others, keeping out of their way as they did their jobs. The final passenger arrived.

"Who got the bed last night?" asked Apryl, smiling, as Claudia approached.

"I did," said Claudia. "It was my turn."

Apryl continued to smile at her.

Claudia glared at Harrison. "You told her?"

"Spouse rule," said Harrison.

"Fabulous," said Claudia, the word punctuated by the sudden sound of the opening lick from "Layla" by Derek and the Dominoes. Claudia fumbled to get at her phone.

"Tell me that's not her ringtone," said Harrison.

"Shut up." She managed to get it out and open the call, holding the phone in front of her. "Hello?"

"Claudia?" said Dorothy. "Am I on a speaker?"

"Yeah," said Claudia. "Regulations. No closed communications before an operation."

"Really?" said Harrison.

Claudia scowled at him and waved for silence.

"Oh," said Dorothy. "That's weird."

"I know."

"You left without saying goodbye. I thought we were going to do breakfast."

"Sorry," said Claudia. "I didn't want to wake you."

"Oh. Well, I wanted to wish you luck, and a safe return."

"Thanks! Good luck with your babysitting gig."

"Ha! I don't expect Melody to be much of a challenge by comparison, but thank you," said Dorothy. "I should probably let you go."

"Yeah, the boss is giving me the hairy eye."

"I don't doubt it. Good luck!"

"Thanks," said Claudia. "Love you. Bye."

The pause on the other end of the conversation offered more than enough opportunity for Claudia to slap her hand over her mouth and bug her eyes half out of her head. Finally, Dorothy said, "I love you, too. Take care." She hung up.

"Ohmygod ohmygod ohmygod," squeaked Claudia.

Apryl's jaw dropped. "What just happened?"

"I think we just said two completely different things that sounded exactly the same," said Claudia. "Oh, fuck! I can't believe I just did that."

"Right," said Harrison. "Because this is the kind of drama I need to be dealing with right now."

"Why didn't you say something?" said Claudia. "That's why I put her on the speaker! I thought if we were all talking it wouldn't get weird!"

"You hushed me!" said Harrison.

"Because you said something stupid! I didn't mean don't talk at all!"

"It will be fine," said Apryl. "She'll assume you meant it innocently. Besides, she won't even remember it by the time you get back."

"Oh, God, I hope not."

Sparky chose that moment to flit over to the group. Like most of the party, she wore body armor. "Are we rolling soon?"

"We are rolling now," said Harrison. "Do you want to ride with us, or would you rather fly there yourself?"

"I can fly there solo?" she asked.

"Sure," said Harrison. "If that's what you want."

Sparky stripped off her body armor and dumped it on the landing pad. "Bring that along for me, will you?" She flew off nakedly.

It took an hour and forty minutes to get to the Lone Star Palace from New Chicago. Along the way, the team prepared for the possibility they would be dropping directly into combat. The two wizards spun spells about the flier to make it less likely to be detected, but not invisible. A true invisibility spell would render everyone inside blind, including the pilots.

Harrison, Apryl and Claudia were to remain in the flier until the scouting party secured the landing area, a plan that did not fit well with Apryl's desire to deal severe damage upon those who had taken her husband's daughters. Her abilities ranged from providing spontaneous power sources for devices both technological and magical, to teleportation, to other capabilities she hadn't fully explored yet. Unfortunately, for all her power, she had virtually no experience wielding it in a fight. She accepted the ruling it would be better for her to wait than rush in, but she didn't care for it.

They set down about half a mile from the palace. Far enough to retain some element of surprise, close enough to travel on foot. Three operatives set out to scout the structure. If it took them more than an hour, a dozen more would storm the castle, with the wizards laying down protection in front of them. It turned out not to be necessary. The scouting party returned less than forty minutes later.

"The area is secure," said Agent Milton to Harrison. "The building itself appears abandoned. There is no evidence of any vehicle traffic to or from the structure. The entrance is completely overgrown with vegetation. If I had to guess, I would say no one has been there in at least two years. Probably quite a bit longer."

"That's impossible," said Harrison.

"You can inspect the area yourself, sir. It's completely safe."

"Thank you," he said. "I will do that." He patted the invisible scabbard at his side for reassurance.

Harrison, Apryl and Claudia emerged from the flier under escort. The area was pure brush. Easy enough to navigate, but more savage than he expected. "Claudia, I need Sparky."

"Check in, Sparky," she said in a normal tone of voice. Anyone within a quarter mile of where she stood would hear that sentence loud and clear. At the edge of that radius, the sound waves from her voice would decay. Years of training had honed her ability to control the range of the effect with precision.

Less than a minute later, the pixie appeared, completely nude, her orange butterfly wings fluttering gracefully. "I've been around the castle three times now. I don't think there's anyone here."

"I'm going to need you to do some recon," said Harrison. "Are you okay entering the building?"

"Yepper."

"Good. I'll get your body armor."

"What for?" she asked. "I just said there's no one there. Do you really think I need protection, or is this a ploy to cover up my lady parts?"

"The second one, mostly," he admitted.

"Oh, you." She flew away.

"I want to see the bridge," said Harrison.

The party moved through the overgrowth at a reasonable pace. About ten minutes later they came to the edge of the palace grounds. Only one road led in, also covered in weeds, confirming Milton's report of no signs of vehicle traffic. They took what remained of this road to the bridge, itself covered in plant growth. Ivy wrapped around it like a botanical python, stretching the entire length.

Harrison led his people over the bridge. It proved a difficult walk. More than once Harrison imagined himself losing his balance and tumbling into the swampy remains of the castle's moat. Halfway across, he looked for the seam, but could not find it under all the plant life. Worse, he had expected to see at least some sign the ivy had been cut to allow the bridge to open, but he found it entirely unbroken, no matter how far he followed it.

"This doesn't make any sense. I saw an aerial photo of this drawbridge taken three days ago, and it was clearly raised. There's no way these plants could have completely grown over it again in that amount of time. Unless..." Harrison looked back over his shoulder, then forward again, trying to get a feel for the length of the ivy. "Unless it was a spell of some kind. I want the wizards up here ASAP. This drawbridge was open, and I want to know how they covered their tracks so completely."

Milton frowned. "Sir?"

"Yes?" said Harrison.

"This isn't a drawbridge."

Harrison stared at him, unsure what the agent meant. He looked down at the bridge again, still confused. "Explain."

"Look at it, sir. There are no hinges, or chains, or any mechanism to move this bridge. The ends are flush with the road. There are no seams. It's not a drawbridge, sir. It's just a bridge."

Harrison looked in both directions again, then walked to the end of the bridge closest to the castle. He pulled away as much of the vines as he could by hand, and looked for some indication of a break between the bridge and the connecting road, but found only smooth, unbroken pavement. Standing, he said to Milton, "Please bring me the wizards. There has to be some kind of magic at work here."

"Yes, sir," said Milton.

"Cody, I need your attention," said Aplomado. He stood before Harrison on the road to the castle, shimmering.

"Shit!" Harrison toppled over, barely able to keep himself from falling into the moat. "How did you get here?"

"I am not 'here,' and I cannot maintain this projection very long," he said, "so please listen. The encapsulated curse went active the moment you opened the drawer. It did not require the bomb to activate it. You and anyone who came into contact with that bomb or spent any significant amount of time in your office since that day have been under its influence."

"I closed that investigation." Even as Harrison spoke the words, they now sounded horribly wrong to him. "Did I really do that?"

"You did," said Aplomado, "which only reinforces my point about the curse."

Harrison felt a fuzziness to his thinking, but recognized this was not a new feeling, simply an ongoing one he hadn't identified until now. And as he allowed himself to explore that, a memory surfaced from his first trip to this castle eight years earlier. As they flew over this bridge, he had noticed from the air it was a fixed bridge, not a movable one. At the time, he thought the moat had been dug for show, not actual defense. He even put that in writing when he returned to New Chicago, in his mission report. He had come here on a completely bogus piece of evidence he should have spotted on first glance. "What was the curse?"

"Bad judgment." Aplomado's projection rippled and disintegrated.

[20]

OUT

Dorothy sat on the single bed in her shared room, staring at her phone. Love you? She hadn't seen that one coming, and it gave her an odd rush. A friendship this close would take some getting used to.

"Claudia loves you," said Melody, half-awake in her makeshift cushion bed on the floor.

"Hey, Little," said Dorothy. "I didn't know you were awake."

"Mmm," said Melody with a sleepy smile.

"How did you know I was talking to Claudia?" asked Dorothy.

Melody rubbed her eyes and looked at Dorothy curiously. "That was Claudie? On the phone?"

"Yes." Dorothy frowned. "Why did you say that?"

"Claudie loves you? Daddy said so." Perhaps to fill the silence that followed that statement, she added, "I love you, too."

"And I love you, little sister," said Dorothy, but her head had gone to a completely different place. She recalled years of awkward encounters, ridiculous conflicts, strained avoidances, and example after example after example of a fact so obvious in its new exposure she had no business denying it as long as she had.

Claudia loves you. Daddy said so. Because Claudia would tell Harrison, but never, ever tell you. Except, perhaps, by accident.

Too many emotions collided at once for Dorothy to make sense of them. Part of her, the rational part, expected this to feel like a betrayal. She experimented with feeling lied to, and manipulated, and used. But that didn't track. Claudia hadn't maneuvered Dorothy into this friendship. If anything, she actively pushed her away. This was no betrayal. But it would certainly be a challenge. In the wake of all the radical changes to the world, same-sex relationships held a place in the norm now, and a relatively tame one at that. But that didn't mean Dorothy would be able to return Claudia's feelings. That reality would hurt them both. In plainest fact, Dorothy considered Claudia her best friend now, and had on some level for a long time. She would not let this discovery from the past two days be undermined by the secret facet of that friendship now exposed.

Should she pretend not to know? Would that make it easier, or would it compound one lie of omission by doubling it? Should she try to talk it out? What if that frightened Claudia away, this time permanently? As she considered that possibility, she found she could not bear it. No, they would have to find a way to make this okay. In a day, or two days, or three days, whenever Claudia got back, they would have to deal with this.

It would be a very long three days.

[21]

BAD JUDGMENT

Harrison pondered Aplomado's parting words with utter confusion. If things were as serious as the wizard appeared to believe, why could he find no evidence of a problem? He said the supposed curse would affect anyone who spent enough time in Harrison's office, but he and Apryl had already slept two nights there with no ill effects.

He chose to abandon his inspection of the drawbridge, now somehow converted to a fixed bridge, and went to the front doors of the castle. "No, wait." He paused in his tracks. "That's not right." He looked back at the bridge. Not drawbridge. It had never been a drawbridge. "Watch yourself," he said to Agent Milton, closely following him. "Things here are not as they appear."

"Meaning what?" asked Milton.

Harrison placed his hand flat against the door. A scraping creak built up behind it, followed by a groan as the door shuddered. Two or three more wooden collisions sounded, followed by one large *bang*, and a quiet rumble that faded to nothing. He poked the door with his finger, and it swung inward. A few paces in front of him lay a broken wooden beam under a settling cloud of dust. This beam would have withstood a moderate assault by battering ram. Against his naked palm, it had no hope.

Sunlight streaming in the open doors revealed details within. The interior of the castle, every bit as aesthetically unremarkable as he remembered, now held thick layers of dust on every surface, and cobwebs along the walls and ceilings. From down the hallway came a tiny orange glow that grew in magnitude as Sparky drew nearer.

"Hey," she said. "I've been to every nook and cranny of this place, and it's totally deserted. Found three corpses in the throne room, but that's it."

"This is nuts." He turned to Milton behind him. "Bring the flier to the hangar here and set up a perimeter. We're going to figure this out."

Milton stood a hair straighter. "Respectfully, sir, why are we still here? This is clearly a dead lead."

"We're looking for…" Having no idea how to finish that sentence, Harrison left it dangling. When his phone rang, he welcomed the reprieve, until he saw who it was. He opened the call. "Marty, I don't mean to sound insensitive, but I am extremely busy right now. If you are this concerned about Mitchell, maybe you should just call the police. It might even teach him a lesson."

After a dead pause on the other end, Marty said, "The police didn't reach you?"

"No. Wait, are you saying you already called them?"

"No," said Marty. "I didn't… They found his car, Harrison. It was wrecked. There was no sign of him. I thought you might be able to help."

A red flag flashed in Harrison's mind for an instant, but it furled itself and vanished. "Let me get back to you." As Harrison killed the call, Marty returned a fraction of a syllable. Gratitude? Protest? Impossible to know. "Milton," he said uncertainly, "can you bring me a wizard?"

"Already on the way," he said. "You called for them when we were on the bridge."

"Did I?" A brief but intense spike of pain stabbed Harrison in the head. It amplified his confusion. "Never mind. I don't… No, wait, do… Ow!" Another stab. He collapsed to his knees.

"Boss?" said Sparky. "What gives?"

"Glimmer?" he said.

"Oh, damn. We have a problem, Mister Secret Agent Guy," she said to Milton.

"I see that." He pulled out his communicator. "We need those wizards now!"

For nearly half a minute, Harrison stayed on his knees, with no idea how he got there, or why he hadn't stood up again. A pair of warm hands took the back of his head, and a male voice said, "I feel it. It may take me a moment to draw it out." The hands got warmer, and the voice continued to speak, but in gibberish. Finally, the voice said, "Got it!" A loud *crack* sounded in Harrison's head, and a flash of multicolored light appeared behind his closed eyelids.

The events of the past few weeks corrected themselves in his mind from something that made perfect sense to a series of inexcusable blunders. "Oh, shit!" He stood straight up with no effort and remarkable energy. "We put them all in one building and then flew a thousand miles away from them!" He turned to the hooded face of a wizard whose name he did not know. "Find my wife. She has this same bad judgment curse. Check de Queiroz as well. Milton, you're with me." He walked briskly out of the castle to the bridge. Milton and Sparky stayed with him. The wizard leapt straight over all of them and landed dozens of yards ahead of them, in seconds. "I want us in the air in ten minutes. Can you make that happen?"

"Yes, sir," said Milton.

"Good. Sparky, fly directly to the NCSA building. Find Dorothy and tell her I was wrong. She is a target after all. Report to me as soon as you get there."

"Okey doke," said the pixie. "Do I get to ask why?"

"Because I fucked up, that's why," he said. "I thought the only thing those women had in common was Texas, but I forgot the other thing they had in common. Me. And now my adopted son is missing, which means whoever took them is coming for Dorothy too."

"Oh, crap!" she said.

"Go!"

She went.

As he got across the bridge, he got another call. He pulled out his phone expecting Marty's face. The screen read Chicago Memorial Hospital. "This is Harrison Cody."

"Mr. Cody, this is Dr. Ackerson at CMH. I am afraid I have some bad news. Your friends Sarah Logan and Warren Bennett are here, with serious injuries." The doctor paused.

"Keep talking." Harrison made it across the bridge. Several agents had gathered around the collapsed form of his wife. The other wizard pressed his hands to her forehead. Claudia stood nearby.

"You were listed as an emergency contact. You may want to come here as soon as you can. You should know that Mr. Bennett is in critical condition."

To get to Sarah, someone had critically injured her husband, probably another thing he could have foreseen if his head had been on straight. "Do you have their son?"

A pause. "No, I'm afraid only the two of them were found. Do you want to know the specifics of the incident?"

Harrison stopped. Only two found. Adler was missing. "Melody!" he shouted, and bolted. By the time he got to Apryl, she was coherent, and alarmed.

"We have to go back!" she said.

"Adler's missing."

It took a moment for that to register. "Melody!"

"I know." Harrison looked around him and did a quick head count. He pulled out his communicator. "Felicia, I need a full—"

No one there found out what full thing Harrison needed, because halfway through that sentence, Bess drew his hand to her hilt, and gave his body instructions it obeyed without question. He cart-wheeled to his left, kicking one of his own agents in the throat in the process. The breezy *whoosh* of a sword went past his head as he dodged it and came under his assailant with a stab to the abdomen. He pulled Bess upward sharply. She cut through body armor as easily as the soft tissue beneath. Harrison rolled out of the way as innards spilled out behind him. Shifting to the right, he grabbed the sword hand of the man who now attempted to impale him, then whipped around, smoothly decapitating him.

For a few seconds, no one moved. Several other agents had drawn swords, but they lowered them as Harrison turned in a cautious circle.

Traitors, said Bess in his head.

"I got that," he said. "Any more?"

I do not believe so.

"Good. And thank you, by the way."

It pleases me to protect you.

He wiped the blood off her blade using the pant leg of one of his slain opponents, then reached down and picked up the communicator he dropped.

"Cody?" Not Felicia's voice. "Come in!"

As he attempted to respond, the sound of explosions came through the tiny speaker with a clarity and volume that left no doubt as to their nature. He looked at Apryl. She had one arm around Claudia. He walked to her and took her hand.

"We can be there in under two hours," he said.

"Screw that." She threw her free arm around his waist. The bright day went black.

[22]

STORM

When the blasts came, and the city erupted into chaos, Dorothy and Melody were two blocks away, eating ice cream. The explosions were more than loud enough to be heard from inside the restaurant, but not powerful enough for their effects to reach that far.

"Was that thunder?" asked Melody. She seemed more curious than frightened.

"I don't know." Dorothy looked to the window. The walk here had been sunny and delightful, and a welcome distraction from the stresses of the past few days. As bright and cheery as the weather had been only twenty minutes earlier, thunderheads now overcast the sky, blacker than she could recall ever seeing them.

"Stay here." Dorothy got up to join several other patrons who had moved to the windows for a better view of the storm.

"I want to stay with you," said Melody.

Dorothy held her hand as they moved to the door.

One customer pointed to the sky. "What is that?" Tendrils of red smoke curled around some of the clouds, and sparks passed between them.

"We need to get back to the building," she said to Melody. "Right now."

"Is it storming?" asked Melody.

"Sort of." Dorothy left a twenty-dollar bill on the table and took Melody outside.

The NCSA building blazed on at least two floors, including the

118

entrance. In the ever-darkening sky, those flames glowed more brightly than anything else in the city. For a moment, fright and indecision gripped Dorothy to paralysis. No natural weather produced these clouds. Normally she would return to base, where she would be able to keep Melody safe. But base was ground zero right now, and she didn't have a plan B. They were half a mile from her apartment, but she had no reason to believe that would be a haven without understanding the situation better.

She needed advice, and assurances, and right before she pulled Melody back inside the ice cream parlor and hit Claudia's number on her phone, she caught her first glimpse of the giant bats.

BATS

As the three of them materialized on the street outside the NCSA building, the blackout from teleporting lingered. The burning building in front of Harrison clarified his eyes had not gone dark; the city had. Cloud cover extended far enough to blot out the sun. The clouds themselves, black with red streaks, drove home a point already obvious: they were part of an attack.

Flames engulfed the entrance to the building, as well as the third floor. Four floors above those fires twenty-two young women waited for the dooms he had inadvertently lured them to. And somewhere else in there was his five-year-old daughter, along with a woman he very much considered his daughter as well. With luck, countless NCSA agents already considered it their top priority to get them all to safety. Given three of his own assault team tried to kill him not five minutes earlier, he held little faith in that hope.

"Melody!" shouted Apryl.

Harrison blocked her from running into the burning building.

"I got her!" Claudia waved her phone over her head.

Apryl grabbed it. "Dorothy? Do you have Melody? Are you inside?" A pause. "Oh, thank God!"

Hearing these words, a small fraction of Harrison's tension bled off.

"Where are you? Wait! No! Don't say anything!" Apryl looked to Harrison with pleading eyes. "Can she tell me?"

He hesitated, as he considered the risks to his children. "We have moles," he said as evenly as he could. "Her phone is not secure."

"I can get them. Teleport them somewhere safe."

"If she gives away their position you may not have the chance."

Apryl's chest heaved. She closed her eyes and took a deep breath. "Listen to me," she said into the phone. "You are both targets. Don't come back here, and don't go anywhere anyone might think to look for you! You take my baby, and you run! You run, and you don't look back! Don't trust anyone, even if you know them! Don't tell anyone where you're going. Not even me. When we get these bastards, I will call you." She listened for a few more seconds. "Dorothy, listen to me. I love you, I trust you, and you will do this. Keep her safe." After listening to whatever final words Dorothy had, Apryl hung up.

"Where are they?" asked Claudia.

"Somewhere not in there." Harrison pointed to the building. "Which is all that matters right now." He put his hand on Apryl's shoulder. "That girl kept herself alive for half a year when she was fourteen years old."

"I know," said Apryl, steel in her eyes. "But that's not why I trust her. I trust her because she's Melody's big sister, and because our baby means more to her than anyone else in the world. Let's get this done so we can call her back." She pointed to the building again. "I need to get you and Bess in there, don't I?"

Before he could answer, Claudia shouted, "Shit! What the fuck is that?" She pointed overhead.

Harrison looked up at a cloud of bats with bodies roughly the size of minivans, and inestimable wingspans. At least a dozen circled the top of the building. In their midst hovered a man in a long, dark red robe. A broad hood enshrouded the figure's face, but in the half-light of the blotted sky, two red pinpoints of light marked eyes.

The floating man made large, animated gestures with his arms as he spun and tilted, directing traffic. Bats dove in and departed at his visual commands. As Harrison watched this ballet in horror, one bat flew close to a gaping hole in the wall, and came away from it with a sack dangling from a chain around its neck. That bat flew upward and away into the black clouds until it became invisible against the sky.

"Oh, my God." Apryl bit her knuckle. "There were people in that."

A familiar gray cloak rocketed up to the hovering figure and collided with it. Aplomado grabbed the dark wizard's wrists, and a brief struggle ensued, comprising equal parts physical grappling and flashes of light and sound. After a few seconds of this, both wizards plummeted, at a speed far greater than caused by gravity. They hit the ground at least two hundred feet from where Harrison stood, with a loud *boom* and a shockwave that nearly knocked him off his feet.

"I hope that buys us time," said Harrison. "Get me up there. Seventh floor. I have to stop this!"

"Are you coming?" she asked Claudia.

Seeing the fear in her eyes, Harrison said, "No, and neither are you. You get me in, then you come right back out again. I have Bess."

"And I have magic," said Apryl.

With no time to argue, he said, "Let's go."

Everything went dark again. When his eyes adjusted, he found himself in the seventh-floor hallway. The lights were out, making for a dim environment, but bright enough to render the quantity of bodies littering the floor visible. At least a dozen agents paid for their work with their lives. At the far end of the hall, her back to him, stood a single assassin, holding two swords at her sides. Harrison drew Bess.

We are in trouble, she said.

The woman with the swords turned and charged him. He came at her with the short sword, and rolled under her as she leapt to strike at him. With the clang and jolt of metal on metal, Bess deflected one of the swords. The other found him and bit. A glancing blow, not enough to do critical damage, but enough to sting, and to make him acutely aware of his situation. No one had ever cut him with Bess in his hand.

We should flee.

The assassin came back for another pass. This time Harrison spun around her, dodged two strokes, and knocked one of the swords from her hand. She cried out, and he froze at the sound of her voice.

Felicia.

Tucking her injured hand under her arm, she dashed into one of the bedrooms. Harrison chased after her, but as he entered, she leapt through the hole in the wall, and grabbed a chain hanging from a giant bat. She climbed the chain with her knees and one good hand, and pulled herself up by the hair on the bat's neck to a sitting position astride it. It carried her away.

Harrison braced himself for possible bat attack, thought every such creature still visible to him now flapped away in full retreat. As he stood there catching his breath, the red-robed wizard rose before him, arms outstretched. Fully visible through the gaping hole, no more than a few feet from the building, he paused as he reached Harrison's eye level.

Harrison clutched Bess, preparing to defend himself in whatever way she decreed. For a moment, he felt the familiar wash of Bess assuming motor control, and in that moment, the dark wizard locked eyes with him. They glowed red, barely bright enough to illuminate his face under the shadow of his hood. That dim red light revealed the hint of a smile, before the wizard shot upward and out of sight.

Harrison walked back to the hall, finding no sign of Apryl. Her teleportation power sometimes protected her from harm against her own will.

He checked every bedroom. Each one contained one or two dead agents, and no one else. All his daughters were gone.

[24]

WORM

Dorothy turned off her phone and pocketed it. Instructions not to trust anyone would include the possibility that phone communications were being monitored. Apryl said she would call, and Dorothy would wait for that call. Until then she had a single job: Take care of the most important person in her world. Keep her safe, keep her hidden, at all costs.

"Was that Mommy?" asked Melody.

"Yes," said Dorothy.

"What did she say?" asked Melody in a strangely calm tone.

"She said it's not safe for us to go back to the building."

"Because of the fire?"

"Yes," said Dorothy, "because of the fire. She also said we should go on a little trip, just you and me."

"Where are we going?" she asked.

An excellent question. Under instructions not to go anywhere anyone would look for her, Dorothy ruled out every hiding place she could think of. She had to get herself to someplace she had never been. New territory.

She had to leave town.

"We're going to ride on a train," said Dorothy. "Does that sound fun?"

Melody pondered this. "I never went on a train. Is it nice?"

"Very nice," said Dorothy. "It's big, and comfortable, and pretty, and fast. And sometimes they have great food."

"Yeah! Let's go on a train!" said Melody.

Relieved by the easy sell, Dorothy took Melody's hand. The Worm

124

station was only six blocks away. She had never been on the Transit Worm before, which meant in part that everything she had told Melody was a guess. It also meant that anyone looking for her in predictable places wouldn't start there. She would have to rely on the hope they didn't expect her to flee the city with Harrison's child.

Dorothy had about sixty dollars in cash on her, enough to buy two passes, and almost nothing else. She would have access to a great deal more than that if she used her card, but didn't dare risk it being tracked. Their ice cream meal would have to be enough to sustain them for now.

Given virtually everyone in the city had their attention fixed on the bizarre happenings in the sky, the two of them made it to the Worm station without incident. Waiting passengers watched news coverage of the NCSA fire on wall monitors. The crisis had not elevated to a station shut-down, but that could change in minutes.

Dorothy scanned the board. The New Chicago Worm station was a hub, with six platforms. Two of those had docked trains at that moment, one of which would board for departure in six minutes. With luck, that would be enough lead time before the government declared an emergency and trapped her here. As she paid for their passes on the eastbound train, her stomach growled, reminding her that pistachio ice cream did not constitute a balanced meal. She hoped Melody's tummy would be more easily fooled.

Once on the train they settled into what were indeed extremely comfortable seats. Dorothy waited until it pulled out of the station and into the tube before finally conceding the two of them might be, at least for now, safe.

"Are we running away?" asked Melody, the question so matter-of-fact Dorothy almost didn't hear it for what it was.

"I think we might be," she answered honestly. "You know I will take care of you, right?"

"I know," she said. "I hope we can go home soon."

Struck by how easily the child appeared to be taking the shakeup of her entire world, Dorothy said, "I hope so too, Little."

On that note, she pulled out her phone to check for missed calls, on the chance the situation was resolved and they could come back. But when she attempted to turn it on, she discovered the battery had gone dead.

[PART 2]
PRODIGY

AFTERMATH

From the seventh floor of a building whose first and third floors were on fire, Harrison surveyed the scene of carnage Felicia had left before riding away on a monstrous bat. Apryl appeared behind him, grabbed him around the waist, and teleported him back to the street. They didn't stay there long.

"*¡Ay Dios mio!* You're bleeding!" cried Apryl before jumping them to the emergency room. It startled a few people, but most barely noticed. Teleportation ranked nowhere near the top of the list of the impossible phenomena New Chicagoans had come to accept as commonplace.

Harrison touched his left flank. It stung. His hand came away much bloodier than he expected. Apryl doffed her body armor and threw it to the floor. She pulled off her shirt, stuffed it under Harrison's armor at the injury and pressed down with her full weight. "I need some help here!"

"I'm fine," said Harrison, but his own words sounded distant to him. He looked at his hand again, trying to calculate how much blood he was losing based on that sample, but managed to remember he had no idea how to do that math. A cold wave came over him, and right before he blacked out, a woman shouted.

"Coming through! That's my brother!"

Harrison never lost consciousness, though he did lose his sight. In the darkness, he was aware of people talking near him, and about him. Apryl was there. And Lisa. Except Lisa was dead. Except, wait, no, Lisa came back. One of them said something about getting his armor off. Someone else, a male voice, said something about a gurney.

Eventually, he found himself sitting in a bed, with an IV in one arm, and his sister suturing up a long but shallow gash in his side. Apryl sat in a chair near the bed, looking exhausted. "How long was I out?"

"About five minutes, you big baby," said Dr. Lisa Cody, drawing another stitch through his wound. "What did I tell you about getting hurt?"

"You said don't. Five minutes?"

"Yes. Is this a sword wound?"

Harrison took a moment to collect his thoughts. "I think so. I'm coming down from a curse I've been under for days, so I'm not one hundred percent sure of anything, but yes, I'm pretty sure that is a sword wound. And no, I can't tell you any of the details."

"Doctor patient privilege?" she asked.

"Nope."

"Big sister baby brother privilege?"

"Stop," he said. "I have major problems to deal with, most of which I caused. I will tell you anything that ends up declassified. For now, the only thing that matters to me is getting back on my feet and making everything right again. Am I going to be out of here any time soon?"

"I'd like to keep you long enough to get you hydrated and fed." Lisa clipped the last stitch. "After that, you're on your own. I wouldn't get into any more sword fights, though. You'll tear that open again if you're not careful."

"Yes, well, I'm going to get a healer on this today, so that won't be a problem."

Lisa glared at him. "You know, there is something to be said for letting your body repair itself on its own. Magic is a wonderful healing tool for emergencies, but you pay a price for that kind of treatment."

"I know," he said. "I've seen the studies."

"I wrote some of those papers," she said. "No joke, Harrison. Stay off that. Let your body do what it's designed to do."

"Not to change the subject, but I need to see Sarah Logan and Warren Bennett. They were brought in to this hospital yesterday or today, and I'm their in-case-of-emergency person."

"I saw they were here, but I haven't seen them personally. Warren is in bad shape. Is this another thing you can't tell me?"

"Sorry," he said. "I need to find Sarah and talk to her right away. I have a lot of work ahead of me today, and for the foreseeable future. And, I have to get back HQ, assuming we still have one of those. Any word on the fire?"

Apryl and Lisa looked at each other. "Which one of us are you asking?" asked Lisa.

He waved away his own stupid question. "Sorry. Still getting my head together. Do I still have my communicator?" Apryl pulled the device out of her pocket and gave it to him. "Baker," he said into it. "Where are you and how much do you know?"

"I'm standing outside our building," came the reply. "And I know it's on fire. What's the situation?"

"Oh good," said Harrison. "You're alive. The situation is that we've been infiltrated. No idea how badly. Felicia was a double agent. Not sure if she turned or if she was always a plant, but given what I saw just now she has training we don't know about. She's working with a wizard I've never seen before today, and if he created that curse bomb, he may have done even more damage we don't know about yet. All the women we were housing have been abducted, we have casualties, and you need to get yourself to a wizard right away to be checked for a bad judgment curse."

"Don't be absurd," said Alec. "I don't need to do that."

Harrison considered explaining, then abandoned reasoning with Alec in favor of an alternative. "Aplomado, are you all right?" The last Harrison had seen of Aplomado, the wizard had crashed down hundreds of feet into pavement.

"I am," came the reply.

"Director Baker is outside the NCSA building. Please find him immediately and offer assistance. Do you take my meaning?"

"Of course."

"Alec, Gerry will be there in a few minutes. He will bring you up to speed."

"Very well," said Alec. "Where are you?"

"CMH," said Harrison. "I need to check in on Special Agent Logan, and then I am coming back in. Is the fire department there yet?"

"Affirmative. Most of the flames are out now. There is still a lot of smoke."

"I should be there within two hours," said Harrison.

"Aplomado's here," said Baker. A pause on his end lasted for the better part of a minute. "Bloody hell! How did this get as far as it did? Was everyone in the building under that curse?"

"I don't think so," said Harrison. "Aplomado would know better than I would. He said it was concentrated in my office, because of that bomb. You were one of the first people to be in proximity to it, and Apryl and I stayed there for two nights, so we took the brunt of it. At least I hope so. The bigger issue is the agents who saw it happening and didn't say anything. We need to get into that building as soon as possible and find out who is missing and who is dead."

"We're going to have to answer for this," said Alec. "You do know that, right?"

"Yeah," said Harrison. "I do know that, and I can't worry about it. My only priority is finding those girls. Once they're back home and safe, anyone who wants to discuss my resignation with me is welcome to do so."

"Agreed. I'm going to find out how soon we can get into the building."

"Good. I'll see you soon."

<hr>

Sarah sat by Warren's bedside, her arm in a cast, and several bruises and bandages on her face. When Harrison came into the room, she did not get up.

"I would offer to hug you," she said, "but I am short one arm."

"How is he?" asked Harrison.

"Unconscious. Beyond that? They got the bleeding to stop. Now we are supposed to wait. Is Adler dead?"

Struck by the bluntness and calmness of the question, he honored her directness with a direct answer. "We don't know."

"This was never about Texas, was it?"

Harrison sighed. "Doesn't look like it. We don't know much at this point, but the fact they took Adler and Mitchell tells me they are after all our children."

She sat up at this. "They took Mitchell?"

"It looks that way. Marty and I thought he had run away, but the police found his car wrecked and no sign of him."

"I'm sorry."

"Sarah, this is not over. I swear to you I will personally deliver Adler back to you."

"That's not your place," she said. "It's mine. You are welcome to come along for the ride, but I'm getting my son back myself."

He nodded. "I'm heading over to Esoteric to find a healer. You're going to need that, too."

"I'm in." She stood, and carefully leaned over the comatose form of her husband, planting a soft kiss on his lips. "I will be back."

Baker's voice came over the communicator. "Cody?"

"Here," he said.

"They won't let us in the building, but they are pulling out bodies and survivors. Twelve dead so far, thirty-one injured. We are bringing in a healer from Esoteric to make sure the survivors are all stable, before we take them all to the prison. Sorting this out is going to take a day or two, at least."

"I will be there soon," said Harrison. "Special Agent Logan and I both need that healer, so keep him there, please. Do you need me overseeing interrogations today?"

"No, Cody," said Alec. "You have a rescue to coordinate. Best get started on that right away."

"Thank you," he said. "We'll be there in a few minutes. One more thing."

"Yes?" asked Alec.

Harrison thought for a moment, trying to filter out reasonable thoughts from the lingering tendrils of confusion from the curse. After finally ruling the question legitimate, he asked, "Has anyone seen Sparky?"

[26]

ERIE

Dorothy sat and stared at the whiskey sour sitting on the tray table in front of her seat. For most of the past hour, she kept picking it up, putting it down, and generally not drinking it. It was unusual enough for her to order a drink at all, let alone anything harder than a glass of wine. She couldn't recall if she had ever had a whiskey sour before, and certainly had no memory of what they tasted like. And yet, when offered her one complimentary beverage, she ordered this drink. Apart from her profound reluctance to try something she might not like, a very, very small part of her also felt that under her circumstances, she might do well not to impair her faculties.

She and Melody boarded the eastbound Transit Worm in New Chicago with no set destination. You take my baby, and you run. Those were the instructions she had to follow, and run they did. At some point, they would get off the worm, and she would figure out how to keep going on what little cash they had left. Or she would use her bank card to get whatever they needed, with the potential outcome of being traced, and abducted.

"You don't want that," said Melody.

The little girl's comment snapped Dorothy out of her ruminations. "What do you mean?"

"The drink. You don't want it."

Dorothy looked at the untouched glass, and then at Melody. Her own complimentary beverage was a grape juice, long since drunk. "No, I guess I don't."

"Good." Melody went back to looking at the pictures in a magazine.

Not entirely sure what to make of that exchange, and strangely unconcerned by it, Dorothy went back to staring at her drink, trying to remember why she ordered it. A voice came over the PA announcing the Erie station.

The Transit Worm lines represented the largest salvage and restoration project in the short history of the Republic of New Chicago. The trains arrived in the world as a product of the Mayhem Wave, and based around a futuristic technology that allowed them to run at extraordinary speeds. The underground tubes were for the most part intact. Lacking the resources to build entirely new stations, the project leaders elected to preserve the existing stations they could restore, and scrap the stations too far gone, for spare parts. As a result, fully operational stations existed in locations otherwise defined by utter wilderness. Small cities had begun to grow around these stations, much the way ancient cities grew around convenient ports. Erie Colony, gradually replacing its long-gone, namesake Pennsylvania city, held one such station.

"We get off here," said Melody.

"No, Little," said Dorothy. "We are going to ride this worm to the end of the line."

Melody shook her head. "Dorrie, we get off here."

Dorothy frowned at Melody's unsmiling face. "Why?"

"Your head is fuzzy," said Melody. "Not fuzzy like Mommy and Daddy, but fuzzy."

Dorothy shook her head. "What are you talking about?"

Melody shrugged and looked away. "You're fuzzy. We get off here." She looked back at Dorothy with wide, little-girl eyes. "Please?"

Dorothy had another look at her drink. She hadn't touched it. Why would her head be fuzzy? For a fraction of a second she caught herself thinking how irresponsible it was for her even to consider drinking. "My head is fuzzy. How did you know that?"

Melody shrugged again.

The little girl's conviction in favor of Erie as their destination persuaded her to abandon her plan. Again, for a moment, she caught herself thinking that was a terrible way to make a decision, and again the moment passed. But by now she could feel those moments coming and going. There had been a lot of them over the past few days. On her own, she would not have noticed it.

"Something is wrong," she said to Melody. "Isn't it? Something is wrong with me."

"I think so," said Melody.

Great. On the run with a five-year-old, trying to stay alive and stay hidden, and the child had a better grasp of the situation than the adult did. The worm's deceleration, initially gradual and smooth, pulled Dorothy forward as they approached the station. "Let's get off here."

"Okay," said Melody.

As the train slid to a soft halt, Dorothy and Melody got up. Their motion ended, and the doors gracefully and silently slid apart. Another announcement for Erie station came over the PA, but by then they had left the train, trying to get their bearings on the station floor.

Erie station looked much like New Chicago station, minus the level of activity. Nearly identical architecture, more than half of the storefronts were vacant, the open ones sparsely patronized. Dorothy avoided all the shops in her quest for an escalator. In the process, more than once she caught herself thinking they could afford to spend a few minutes in one shop and afford to spend their last few dollars on something nice. She shrugged these thoughts off.

A passage to the surface led them to a frontier town. One street, some businesses, some homes, and a modest population to occupy both. The afternoon sun hung low in the sky. They would need a place to stay. She could use her card to pay for lodging, but traceable activity could end with her and Melody as someone's prisoners, or worse. As she thought herself into that corner, a familiar voice came from above.

"There you are!" Sparky descended in front of her, and hovered at eye level.

"Sparky?" said Dorothy. "What are you doing here?"

"Boss's orders," she said. "I was supposed to find you and then report back. I don't think he had any idea how hard it was going to be to keep up with you. That train thingy is fast! Plus, I had to keep track of where it was. Did you know you can't see it from the air? I sure didn't! That thing is nuts! Anyway, I'm glad I found you. Everything okay?"

"You're pretty!" said Melody.

"Good eye, kid," said Sparky.

"And naked!"

"I know!" Sparky grinned. "Finally!"

"My head is fuzzy," said Dorothy.

At these words, Sparky moved in closer to look at her eyes. "Meaning what, exactly?"

"I don't know," said Dorothy. "That's part of the fuzziness."

"Huh," said Sparky. "So what do we do now?"

Dorothy took in her companions. One was only five years old, but still managed to identify a problem Dorothy had not detected, the other at least centuries older than that, but clearly a loose cannon. These were her charges now, as well as her resources.

"That," she said, "is an excellent question."

NON-REAL INDIGENOUS

"Hold still."

Crow the Healer laid his hands on Sarah's broken arm. It emitted a surprisingly loud cracking sound, and Sarah cried out.

"Ow! Oh, God damn it! Ow!" She clutched her arm, still in a cast, and clenched her teeth in pain.

Next to her stood a man at least half a foot shorter, and at least forty years older, in a robe adorned with large and diverse feathers. "You should get that cast off," he said in a quiet, gravelly voice. "You'll wanna move that arm around, okay? Let it limber up?" He demonstrated by flailing his own arm around gracelessly for a few seconds. "You want me to do your face, too?"

"Sweet Jesus, no!" she said. "Oh, my God, that hurts!"

"Lemme see your cut," said Crow to Harrison.

Reluctantly, Harrison raised his shirt to expose the sutured gash on his side.

"Hmm," said Crow, poking the stitches.

Harrison winced, but bravely endured the prodding, until the burn kicked in. "Oh, shit!" He closed his eyes and tried to find his happy place as Crow magically cauterized the wound from the inside out. The sweet aroma of burnt meat drifted into his nostrils, and he did what he could to shut it out, or deny its significance. After what felt like a very long time, Crow stood back to inspect his work.

"All done," he said.

Harrison looked down, tugging on his skin. Lisa's stitches would have left a scar, but surely nothing like the huge pink stripe staring back at him right now. The sutures remained in place, though some had partially melted.

"What do I do about the stitches?" he asked.

Crow shrugged. "Go see a doctor? Not sure what to tell you. Don't do stitches. You should have come to me first."

"Great. Thanks." He would have to return to the hospital and ask Lisa to remove them, which she would no doubt do with maximum criticism. But that could wait. "How soon before we can get into the building?" he asked Alec.

"Not today," he said. "They are still inspecting it for structural damage. The good news is it might be mostly superficial. The bad news is your office is a complete loss."

"Of course it is."

"We're relocating HQ to the lakeside facility," said Alec. "It's going to be a tight fit, but it should only be for a few days."

"Then I'm going to get started with the rescue operation," said Harrison. "Your assignment to this investigation is now official," he said to Aplomado. "I trust that's agreeable?"

"Of course," said Aplomado.

"Fantastic. First up, is there any way to find those girls using magic?"

"Not as such," said the wizard. "However, there are things I can know about them without pinning them to a location."

"Such as?" asked Apryl.

"Whether they live," said Aplomado with his customary disregard for tact.

"Get on that," said Harrison. "Meanwhile, I need someone to find out who the hell Felicia Kestrel really is. Even with Bess, I was barely able to hold my own against her, and I think she may have killed at least a dozen agents singlehandedly."

"On that note, are you ready for some numbers?" said Alec.

Harrison would never be ready for these numbers. "Yes."

"Nineteen dead, including Blake Wheeler." Alec paused there.

"Oh, God, no." When Harrison took Rebecca Wheeler into protective custody, her husband came with her, the only spouse to do so. And now he was dead, and Rebecca's baby would be born without a father. Assuming he found Rebecca in time.

"I'm sorry," said Alec crisply. "We also have seven agents missing, presumed defected."

Harrison took all of this in, pushing aside thoughts of how he would

139

tell Rebecca her husband was dead, and it was his fault. "Three of my assault team tried to kill me."

"What about the rest of them?"

"Bess says they're clean."

"Then they are clean," said Alec. "Talking of which, I will need Bess for the interrogations. When your team gets back, have them all report directly to me. I will need a nucleus of agents I can trust."

Harrison unstrapped Bess's scabbard from his belt. He surrendered her to Alec with reluctance, but a grudging acknowledgement that Alec's relationship with her outranked his. He pulled out his communicator. "Milton, are you still at the palace?"

"Negative, sir," came the quick reply. "We are in the air. Should be touching down in Chicago in about fifteen minutes."

"You left on your own initiative?" asked Harrison.

"No, sir. You told me to be in the air in ten minutes. I assumed that order still stood with you gone. Dealing with body bags took some extra time, but we left about forty minutes after you did."

"Agent Milton, my chief of staff just resigned," said Harrison. "Would you like that job?"

"Respectfully sir, I think I am more valuable in the field."

"I can work with that," said Harrison. "You impressed me today by being the only person to call bullshit on my erratic behavior. I need someone solid right now, and you're up. If you want it to be a temporary assignment, it will be. But today, you're my right hand. As soon as you touch down, send the rest of the team to the lakeside facility to wait for Director Baker, and then report to me. I will be at Esoteric."

"Understood," said Milton.

"Hey, spy guys," said Crow. "I'm done here, right?"

"Quite so," said Alec. "Thank you."

"Wait!" said Sarah. "My husband… He's in a coma. Can you…?"

Crow shook his head. "Don't do comas. You're looking for brain damage there. He'll have to work that out on his own."

"Oh," said Sarah, downcast.

Crow shuffled off. Once he was out of easy earshot, Sarah said, "I didn't realize Esoteric trained people that old."

"We do not," said Aplomado. "Crow is eighty-seven years old. The upper age bound for entry into any school of magic is forty-nine."

Sarah frowned. "I don't understand. Wasn't that magic?"

"Crow is a non-real indigenous," said Aplomado. "He's been doing that since long before Esoteric ever existed."

"Oh," said Sarah. Non-real indigenous meant from Glimmer's world.

Esoteric Affairs applied this term to magical creatures to distinguish them from common real-world animals. But ordinary humans also populated that world, as would be expected from any fairy tale, and the term applied to them as well. After the Mayhem Wave blending of both worlds, none of those ordinary humans crossed from their world to the mixed one. However, when Harrison's counter-bomb restored a substantial fraction of the missing population, it restored them from both worlds.

At first, the convention was to refer to the world of pixies and dragons as "imaginary," and Harrison's native world as "real," but those terms fell out of favor as the public consciousness moved toward an assumption of the word "imaginary" as a slight. The culture of New Chicago eventually and officially resolved to use the words "magical" and "mundane" to distinguish the worlds. In most corners, however, the old terms persisted, usually in the somewhat neutralized form of "real" versus "non-real."

Non-reals still represented less than one in twenty of the overall human numbers, but that still meant several million arrivals to a world of technology beyond their ken, and cultural differences abounded. Over the years, most had adapted, much the same as their real-world counterparts adapted to a world with magic and no guns. Unlike Crow, who stood out as a magic user, the majority of non-real indigenous humans had integrated themselves so thoroughly as to be indistinguishable from reals.

"How soon can I call Dorothy?" asked Apryl.

"I don't know," said Harrison. He looked overhead at the smoky, red-streaked clouds, still crackling, but starting to break up. As responsible as he felt for the fates of the twenty-eight daughters he had vowed to protect and failed, Apryl's question mattered most to him. Somewhere on the other side of that storm hid his only child by blood, and another daughter, the young woman entrusted with her safety. The prospect of prolonged separation from them haunted him, and he rejected that fear with all his will to do his job. He looked to Alec.

"Anyone's guess," said Alec. "You were right to be concerned about communications. It's impossible to know if the attack is over. If it's not, and if your phones are being monitored—which I feel compelled to add is entirely likely given the level of infiltration we discovered today—then you will be taking a terrible risk."

Apryl put her arm around Harrison's waist, and said nothing. Her touch on his newly cauterized wound peppered it with stabbing sensations, which he gave no outward indication of feeling. He reached out and took Sarah's hand. "We need to get to Esoteric," he told them both. To Aplomado, he said, "The only thing on your agenda right now is telling me how many of my children are still alive. How quickly can you do that?"

"Give me an hour."

"That's going to be the shittiest hour of my entire life," said Harrison, "so any minutes you can shave off it will earn you a lot of points."

"Challenge accepted," said the wizard.

Harrison nodded.

Apryl teleported them.

[28]

INTO THE WOODS

The pleasant late May afternoon gave way to evening as Dorothy wrestled with what to do next. She and Melody sat on a park bench in the middle of a sparsely populated town, with nowhere to stay, no food, and six dollars in cash. Unless she came up with a better plan, this bench would be Melody's bed tonight. For a fraction of a second, letting her sleep on this bench seemed entirely reasonable, and then she caught it again. Since Melody's comment on the worm about her head being fuzzy, she had noticed several cases of herself approving of patently stupid ideas. Either her exhaustion caused these slip-ups, or something else was going on, and the fact Melody spoke of her parents having fuzzy heads as well implied to her the latter. Unfortunately, she wasn't sure what to do about it other than to stay on high alert.

Happily, her other traveling companion could fend for herself. Sparky had stayed with them since they arrived at Erie Colony. As she tried to imagine what Sparky could do for them to keep them from going hungry, it hit her like a slap in the face, and almost slipped out of her consciousness. But she held onto the idea long enough to voice it.

"Sparky, take my card." She reached into her pocket and pulled out her bank card.

The pixie dipped down and took it in both hands.

"What am I supposed to do with this?" she asked.

"How quickly can you fly to Chicago and back?" asked Dorothy.

"Oh, golly," said Sparky. "I really wouldn't know. That's math, right?"

"How long did it take you to fly here when you were tracking us?" asked Dorothy.

"Not wearing a watch."

This was going nowhere, as was Sparky. "Listen, it couldn't have been more than a couple of hours, which means if you left now you could probably be back before it gets too late. I need you to get us cash."

"Right!" said Sparky. "How do I do that?"

"Come on," Dorothy said, getting up. "I'll show you."

The three of them walked into town, looking for a bank, and eventually found one. The technology for allowing money to trade hands was developed from scratch soon after the government of New Chicago reestablished the dollar as their unit of currency. Getting the economy up and running was a top priority, with banking one of the first types of business to get a toe-hold in the new world. Some factions wanted to abandon money altogether and get a fresh start with some other type of economy, but ultimately the simplicity, familiarity, and avaricious appeal of cash won out.

"The card goes in here." Dorothy pointed to the slot. "It will ask you to enter a PIN, which is a four-digit code. The code is 7-7-4-8. If you look at the letters, it also spells 'spit.' That might be easier for you to remember. Once you type in the code, it will ask you how much you want to withdraw. Please get five hundred dollars."

"Got it," said Sparky. "And I have to go to Chicago because that's where your money is?"

For a moment, Dorothy considered the true explanation, that if she could be tracked by her bank card, a withdrawal in Chicago would make it appear she never left the city, but decided to go with, "Yes. That's right."

"All righty then. Back in a bit." Still clutching the card in both hands, Sparky ascended and zipped away, leaving a faint orange trail. Moments too late, Dorothy remembered she had no phone now, and had missed an opportunity to get a message to Apryl or Claudia, to let them know she and Melody were okay.

"All right, Little," she said. "We now have a few hours to find out if this town has a hotel."

Melody looked at her with a strange sort of wonder in her eyes. She turned around and bolted.

It took Dorothy a second to comprehend the little girl she had left everything behind to protect had fled from her. It took another second to consider the possibility whatever fuzzy head issue she experienced had dulled her reaction time, and yet another to shake herself out of analyzing her inaction. With a three second head start, and a shockingly swift stride, Melody now had a lead Dorothy could not afford to give her.

"Hey!" shouted Dorothy, to no effect. "Melody!" She launched herself into pursuit. Given Erie was still no further developed than a random scattering of unevenly distributed buildings, Dorothy tracked her visually with relative ease as she chased her. The lack of significant ground traffic also meant no immediate danger of being hit by a car tearing across the street, although that could change without warning. As Melody reached the mouth of an alley between two small buildings, she stopped.

It took Dorothy a couple seconds to catch up to her, at which point Melody shouted, "Come on!" and took off again. Dorothy found that phrase at least partially reassuring in the sense it was now clear Melody wasn't fleeing, she was leading. Unfortunately, it looked like she was leading Dorothy away from what little civilization existed here. Once they left the main street, the colony mostly comprised dirt roads leading to parts unknown, separated by fields and forests. Melody tore straight for one that led into the woods. Dorothy finally caught up to her, and she grabbed her and scooped her up. Melody offered no resistance.

"Sweetheart," said Dorothy, "slow down. What are you doing?"

"We have to go this way." Melody pointed into the woods.

"If I put you down, are you going to run again?"

"If you can keep up I will," she said, clearly missing the point.

"Melody," said Dorothy, "we need to talk before we run. Can we do that?"

"We have to go this way."

"I know. I know we do." Dorothy could not trust herself to make rational decisions, and following Melody's lead to stop in Erie seemed to have played out in their favor so far. Until she could get a bead on the trouble with her brain, letting her little sister take the lead might be their best bet. In her head, that plan sounded both perfectly logical and completely insane. For the time being, unfortunately, it was all she had. "Listen, we can go this way if that's what you want—"

"We have to," she said.

"Then we can. But I can't run the whole way. I don't have that kind of energy. Can we walk instead?"

"It's a long walk," said Melody.

"How far?"

"I don't know."

Great. "I'll tell you what. Let's walk for now. If it gets to be too far, we can turn around and find a nice bed in town for the night, and try again tomorrow. Is that okay?"

Melody rolled her eyes at this. "It's not *that* far."

"Little, you have to work with me. Where are we going?"

Melody pointed.

"That way," they said simultaneously.

Dorothy sighed, and looked at her watch. Five o'clock. Mid May. They had maybe three hours of walking time before sundown. That was also about how much time they had before Sparky returned, if everything went to plan. Walking with a five-year-old, Dorothy estimated they would cover two miles an hour. More if they kept their energy up. Worst case scenario would put them at least six miles away from food and lodging when night fell. In the forest. With no means of protection. This was insane.

"I need you to promise me something," said Dorothy. "Can you make me a promise?"

Melody nodded, and stuck out her pinky. Dorothy curled her own little finger around it. "We will go this way for now. But promise me that if I say we have to go back, you won't run away. If I say we have to go back, we will turn around and go right back to town. If you promise me that, I promise I will take you down this road for as far as I think it is safe. Do we have a deal?"

Melody bit her lip, clearly struggling, but she didn't let go of Dorothy's finger. What conflict raged in her little sister's head? Weighing her trust in Dorothy against whatever compelled her down this road? Comparing Dorothy's words to the voices in her head? As Dorothy was about to declare her faculties impaired, and herself unfit for the task of caring for this girl, Melody said, "I promise." She gave Dorothy's finger a squeeze, which Dorothy returned with a hug.

Dorothy decided to set two hours as the maximum safe walking time away from town. If they turned around after two hours and walked back the way they came at the same speed, they would make it back with only an hour or so of darkness in front of them. That already seemed like a foolhardy risk, but compared to the plan of walking until it got dark, it felt like utter brilliance.

The road wound on. For a while, every ten minutes or so they passed a free-standing structure, some weathered, others of new construction. They passed three log cabins that reminded her of the earliest attempts to develop Chicago back into a city. She and her mother lived in such a cabin for three years, until larger-scale housing became feasible and the cabins were wiped away to make room for buildings. They also passed a gas station, long since abandoned from its true purpose, and modified into a dwelling. That would be a pre-Mayhem relic. The fact they encountered residences did make her feel less fearful of the prospect of becoming lost in the woods. In a worst case scenario, they would stray too far, and have to rely on the kindness of strangers to get them through the night. A weak plan, to be sure, but better by far than some of the alternatives.

About an hour into their journey, they came into a clearing. Several acres of land had been deforested and cultivated into a farm, growing something that pushed tiny, pale green shoots up from the soil. A dense wall of trees surrounded the field on all sides. Unbidden images flooded Dorothy's head of Melody suddenly deciding they needed to leave the path and run through the woods. She shivered.

They saw no farmhouse, or other type of construction near the crop field, which meant the farmer lived in one of the cabins or the gas station. After they reentered the forest, it gave no further signs of human habitation. Dorothy kept careful watch on the time. By six-thirty, their path had already become dim enough to make it difficult to see a significant distance ahead. Too early for sunset, but Dorothy had foolishly failed to take into account the sun would pass below the tree canopy long before it dipped under the horizon. As she was about to call off the search for whatever they were searching for, her worst nightmare came to pass. Melody broke to her right and dashed into the trees.

Ready this time, Dorothy charged into the woods behind the little girl, catching her in seconds. Unlike before, when she scooped Melody into her arms, she struggled.

"Put me down!" she cried.

"You promised!" said Dorothy. "We're going back right now!"

"We're here!" said Melody. "It's right down this path!"

Dorothy looked at her feet. In the early evening forest half-light, she could make out a trail, obviously worn by foot traffic. She looked ahead, unable to discern how far it went, or where. "You promised we would go back if I said so."

"But we're *here!*" cried Melody. "Let me show you!"

Again torn between trusting the child or trusting her own compromised wisdom, she opted for faith in her sister. "Do not run," she said firmly. "We will walk down this trail until I feel uncomfortable, and then we will turn around. You promised. Do you understand me, Melody Glimmer Cody?"

The use of her full name had the desired effect. Melody went slack in her arms. Dorothy took her hand, and set her down. With a firm grip on her, Dorothy allowed Melody to lead them down the path at a cautious pace.

A few minutes later, the trail ended, and several feet to the left of its terminus began a foot path inlaid with flat stones. The mismatched paths had a look of shoddy tailoring to them. At this stone path, the woods gave way to a clearing with a well-tended lawn, where they found another cabin. This one had a more polished look to it than the roughly cobbled together homes they had already passed. Dorothy did make a mental note of approval it was built from wood, not gingerbread. Smoke issued from a narrow brick chimney, and light spilled from a glass-paned window.

"Is this it?" Dorothy whispered.

The little girl nodded with wide eyes.

CURSE

Apryl, Sarah, and Harrison reappeared outside the front door to Esoteric. Teleporting inside the building would be impossible, given the number of magical defenses surrounding it as, unlike Harrison's or Sarah's talents, Apryl's were magical in nature.

Once inside, Harrison led them to Larson's lab. "I need a curse expert. And I need one now."

"Back the way you came, second door on the right," said Larson, only looking at them for the amount of time it took her to say that.

They found the room as instructed, where they met two humans in lab coats and an elf in an elaborate and ornate silver robe studying a miniature dragon in a cage.

"Which one of you is the curse expert?" asked Harrison bluntly.

The elf stepped forward.

"My wife and I are recovering from a curse of bad judgment, and I need to know everything there is to know about it, starting with a confirmation it's completely gone. This is NCSA top priority. Do you need to see my credentials?"

"I will need saliva samples," said the elf, gracefully extending his hand out behind him. One of the human techs handed him two microscope slides. He passed them to Harrison, and he and Apryl each spat on one. He took the slides back and squinted at them. "A complete analysis will take thirty minutes, but by this I can see that you are both clear of the dark magic. You may experience after-effects, but they will pass. What can you tell me about the curse?"

"It was encapsulated in a curse of contact poison, and implanted in a physical object, specifically a bundle of dynamite."

"Was the caster present?" asked the elf.

Harrison thought back to that day. He now knew the most likely suspect was the dark wizard he had seen during the attack. Or it might have been Felicia, given he now knew her to have abilities beyond her NCSA resume. She was not in the room when the bomb was defused, but he had no idea when the bad judgment curse became active, and she would have had plenty of opportunities to be there when it did. "I'm not sure."

"How long ago did this happen, and where?"

"About two weeks ago. I found the bomb in a desk drawer in my office."

The elf nodded. "Leave me. I will have your results shortly."

"Thank you," said Harrison. To Apryl, he said, "Hospital, please." They went outside, held hands, and teleported back to Chicago Memorial. At the emergency room front desk, Harrison asked for Dr. Cody to be paged. Five minutes later, she appeared, wearing the expected frown.

"I assume you need some charred sutures removed?"

"If it wouldn't be too much trouble," said Harrison. "Also, a cast."

"Come on," she grumbled.

Sarah stayed at the hospital with her comatose husband. Apryl and Harrison made it back to Esoteric a few minutes after the thirty they had been asked to wait. As they got to the front door, Harrison got his call from Aplomado, sixteen minutes shy of his hour.

"All thirty-two of your lost lambs are alive," he said.

"They're alive," Harrison said to Apryl, knowing she would not be able to hear Aplomado's voice over the communicator.

"Melody?" she asked.

"Yes. All of them."

Apryl gasped, and put her hand over her mouth. Tears flowed from clenched eyelids. That answered the question of how long she would able to hold it together. The tightness in his throat and the moisture in his own eyes answered a similar question for Harrison. "Anything else you can tell me?" he asked the wizard.

"Yes. The twenty-eight Texas women, the little boy and the young man are all in excellent health. Near perfect, in fact, which is in itself notable. Whoever has them is taking extremely good care of them."

"What about Melody and Dorothy?" asked Harrison, hoping the nervousness in his voice didn't project.

"Signs of exhaustion and early dehydration," said Aplomado. "No true health risks, but they will want to get some water and sleep soon."

"Is it reasonable to believe that means they haven't been taken yet?" asked Harrison.

"Yes, it is reasonable to believe that," said Aplomado. "It may be completely false, but it is reasonable to believe."

"Then I choose to believe it. Thank you."

"Are they still free?" asked Apryl.

"I think so," said Harrison. "Aplomado says their health signs are showing as different from the others." He held up a hand to preempt the obvious next question. "They're fine. Tired, but fine."

Apryl nodded. "Okay."

They entered the magic lab. The elf sat at a desk. The techs were gone, as was the dragon. "Do you know anything yet?" asked Harrison.

"No," said the elf. He did not look up.

"How soon do you think?" asked Harrison, gradually becoming aware of the event horizon to his own patience.

"Shortly."

"Listen," said Harrison to Apryl, "I need to have a conversation with Larson. Do you want to stay with me?"

"Am I going to understand or like anything the two of you talk about?" she asked.

"Unlikely."

"Then there's your answer. Come find me in the break lounge when you're done." She kissed him. "And be done soon."

He made his way back to Larson's lab. On passing through her dissolving/solidifying door, he asked her bluntly, "Could this Mayhesphere problem have anything to do with what's happening to my daughters?"

"That's really outside the scope of what I do."

He waved away the response. "I know that. What I'm trying to ask is if there is any reason to think someone might be able to influence those spheres, and what they might hope to gain by it."

She frowned at him. "Whether the spheres can be influenced and what could be gained from it are precisely the questions we are focused on answering right now," she said with an edge of impatience. "Why are you asking?"

"Because I just came down off a bad judgment curse, and the last time we spoke, when I was still cursed, I blew this off as nothing when it really means the end of the world. I'm trying to go back over my tracks and catch anything I might have missed. Someone wanted me making very bad choices these last few days, and I need to know why. If there's any chance this was one of them, I need to catch it now."

"Ah" said Larson, her demeanor more relaxed. "That does make sense. All right, here's my best summary. Intuitively, it does not seem likely to me that all those abductions are related to what we are observing with the Mayhespheres. As far as someone else trying to manipulate them, so far the only end results we can foresee are the total destruction of all life on Earth or the prevention of that, and a status quo. Neither of those outcomes would make sense to me as a goal for some adversary to have, though I concede that's more your department than mine. Is that helpful?"

"Maybe," he said. "If it's possible, I'd like you to keep those questions open. If anything in your research strikes you as suspicious, please contact me immediately."

"Honestly, Harrison, I think you may be reading things into this that are not there. If it's the timing that has you concerned, you should know this has been going on for years without anyone knowing it, and if we hadn't sent the probe, we still wouldn't know it. It's a simple coincidence that we launched it on the same week as these attacks."

Harrison winced. Coincidence was rarely his ally.

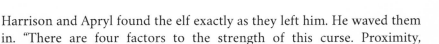

Harrison and Apryl found the elf exactly as they left him. He waved them in. "There are four factors to the strength of this curse. Proximity, duration of exposure, intelligence and age." He paused there.

"I'm listening," said Harrison.

"The curse would most likely have been tied to that room. Anyone who set foot there will have been affected. Some more than others. As a general precaution, you should have everyone who could possibly have passed that threshold in the last two weeks examined. You will also need to sterilize the room itself, which would be best accomplished with fire, if possible."

"Already taken care of," said Harrison with an edge of grief. "Duration?"

"The more time spent in that room, the worse the effect," said the elf.

"My wife and I slept there for two days," said Harrison.

"As was obvious from your saliva. You two would most certainly have been affected worse than anyone else."

"Well," said Harrison, "that's good news at least."

"What about Dorothy?" asked Apryl. "She was in and out of that room those two days."

"Is she intelligent?" asked the elf.

"Super-genius," said Harrison.

"Then given her sporadic exposure, she will probably be able to shake off the effects on her own in a matter of hours. I would still recommend she be examined and purged."

"Not possible," said Harrison. "But you say she will be all right?"

"She should, yes."

"What about age?" asked Apryl.

"The younger the victim, the stronger the curse," said the elf.

Harrison and Apryl looked at each other. Her eyes reflected his own fear. Harrison said, "Our daughter slept there two days as well."

"Is she clever?"

"Extremely," said Harrison, with hope.

"Age?"

"Five," said Apryl.

The elf raised his brows in an expression that did not inspire a sense of well-being. "She should be examined and purged without delay."

"Also not possible," said Harrison, as calmly as his racing heart would allow. "She is under the care of my adopted daughter Dorothy, but we do not know where they are."

"The accursed Dorothy?"

"Yes," said Harrison. "But you said she will be all right in a few hours, right?"

"Yes, she should. If she is protecting your child, she will need her wits about her. At five years..." He frowned and shook his head. "I am truly sorry. The curse will have affected her in ways too extreme to reasonably predict. She will be in a state of constant self-risk until the curse wears off, which could take days. If you are able to find her, you must do so right away."

Apryl put her arm around his waist and pulled him close, trembling. "Tell me Dorothy is up to this."

He held her close, and kissed her forehead. "It's a bad judgment curse, Apryl. Melody will be a handful, but she won't be in any true danger as long as Dorothy is with her." He willed himself to believe this.

"You're sure?"

"Absolutely," he said. "It's not like Dorothy is going to let Melody call all the shots."

[30]

STRONTIUM AND IAN

A pewter gargoyle knocker adorned the door to the log cabin, an incongruously ostentatious ornament in the context of this frontier town. Dorothy gently lifted it, and tapped it against the pewter plate underneath, expecting a moderate rapping noise. The hollow *boom* it produced instead startled her. For several tense seconds, she waited for a reaction from inside. The muted sounds of voices and footsteps came from within. Finally, following the sound of a latch being undone, the door swung smoothly inward.

A young boy, perhaps twelve years old, stood before her. He wore a blue oxford shirt and tan slacks, and had neatly cut and meticulously combed straight blond hair. Smiling warmly at Dorothy and Melody, he said simply, "Yes?"

"Hello," said Dorothy. "My sister and I were out walking, and we seem to have gotten turned around. Can you tell us how far we are from the city?" As the most plausible lie Dorothy could concoct under pressure, it felt like the right place to start. Unfortunately, the boy offered nothing in response but a frown of confusion. "Do you... have a parent?"

He smirked at the question. "Sort of."

"Oh, just let them in, Ian," came a woman's voice from behind him. "Let's get it over with."

Getting it over with did not hold much appeal for Dorothy, regardless of whatever it ended up meaning, but when the boy, Ian, opened the door further, Melody dashed inside. The interior of the cabin was furnished and decorated in a motley style. Persian rug on the floor, cast iron wood

154

stove, a padded folding chair and a rolling desk chair enclosing a mahogany dining room table, Formica surfaced bar with three built-in metal stools running alongside an open kitchen area, and at least two doors leading to rooms that couldn't be large considering the outer dimensions of the house. On the wood stove sat a large black pot, with something simmering inside.

A woman in a tasseled purple jacket and skirt, with white hair in an elaborate braid running down her back to her knees, stirred the pot. She was easily ninety years old, and astonishingly beautiful. The age lines running rampant through her skin did nothing to diminish her Greek goddess cheekbones, dimpled chin, or delicate nose.

"Hello," said Dorothy. "Thank you for inviting us in. My sister and I—"

"Hang it up, child." The old woman continued to stir the pot without looking up. "No one finds this place without looking for it. Whatever story you rehearsed is already nonsense. Why don't we start over?" She pulled a wooden spoon out of the pot, put it to her lips, and slurped.

Dorothy's courtesy smile faded. "All right. My sister led me here. We came into Erie Colony this afternoon, and she felt drawn to this cabin. May I assume you know why?"

"You may assume as you like," said the old woman, finally looking at Dorothy with eyes of steel gray, "but I haven't a clue." She looked at Melody, who had curled up in an armchair by the window. "That's not your sister."

"Yes, she is." Dorothy stood straighter.

The old woman put the spoon down and walked toward Melody. Dorothy prepared to spring between them, but the woman stopped. "Huh. So she is. After a fashion."

The detailed perceptiveness put Dorothy even further on guard. She attempted retreat. "I am sorry to have bothered you. I think it would be best if we went our way."

"You're cursed, you know," said the old woman.

Dorothy blinked at that. "I beg your pardon?"

"Both of you. Bad judgment by the smell of it. You want me to take that off you?"

Dorothy rolled that offer around in her head before speaking. Her feelings of uncertainty over the past day now made perfect sense, although the question of how they had come to be cursed in the first place lingered. Given the elaborate conflict they had been drawn into, and her limited knowledge of how magic should work, there must have been multiple opportunities to do that to her. With the new revelation of her predicament, coupled with an immediate chance to have it

155

resolved, Dorothy's host took on a new and obvious light. "You're a witch."

"Duh," said the witch. "You want cured or not?"

The boy watched this exchange with a smirk, and when Dorothy spared a glance in his direction, he said, "It's okay. She's just like that."

"So I hear," said the witch, scowling playfully at him.

In Dorothy's best assessment of the situation, she and Melody were not in danger. The fuzziness in her head felt lessened from earlier. "My name is Dorothy. This is Melody." She gestured to the little girl.

Melody yawned.

"We came to Erie fleeing danger, and ended up here. If you mean us harm, we are quite likely doomed, although you should know I will do everything in my power to kill you if you threaten my little girl. If you mean us no harm, then yes, we would be very grateful for your help with the curse."

The old woman looked back and forth between the two of them. "I'm Strontium. This is my boy, Ian. You're welcome to stay a bit, and I'll cure you on the house. Probably won't eat either of you. Does that suit?"

Despite herself, and surely at least partly from exhaustion, Dorothy could not help but laugh. "Yes, that suits us very well."

Strontium rolled her hand. "C'mere."

Dorothy approached her, trusting, but cautious.

The witch put her hand on Dorothy's forehead, and hummed. After a few seconds, Dorothy experienced a slight pop inside her skull, and a sudden and reassuring sense of clarity slammed her. "Thank you."

"That wasn't so bad," said the witch. "Probably would have cleared up on its own soon. Lemme see the kid." She knelt at the foot of the armchair where sat a comfortable and now drowsy Melody.

"Did you say your name was Strontium?" asked Dorothy.

The old woman sighed. "Please don't start. I took that name when I was initiated. At the time, we knew it as a legendary substance with mystical powers. The stuff of science tales, don't you know? Then the mix-up happened and I found out it's a metal that corrodes in the air and explodes when you put it in water. Not exactly awe-inspiring. If I weren't bound to the name, I'd trade it in now. Could be worse, I guess. Had a sister named Phlogiston. Can't imagine how stupid she would feel right now if she was still alive."

With the mention of science tales, and the mix-up, Dorothy made a connection. "You're a non-real."

"Again with the duh." Strontium brushed her fingers over Melody's arm, and frowned. "The curse did something weird to your kid. Never seen this before."

A small surge of adrenaline hit Dorothy. "Something bad?"

"Mm," said Strontium. "Don't think so, but definitely weird. She's not showing signs of bad judgment, even though it's for sure the same curse."

"Can you cure it?"

Strontium shrugged. "Not sure what there would be to cure. I can draw off the intended effects, but she doesn't have any. Whatever she's got, it's something else. You two staying for supper?"

Dorothy did not welcome the change of subject. And yet, the mention of food reminded her how long they had both gone without it. Her top priority was Melody's well-being, and in the absence of a clear answer to how the curse affected her, feeding her would help meet that mandate. She looked back at the stove where Ian now stood over the pot. "What is it?"

"Eye of newt soup," said Ian.

This perked Melody up for the first time since she had flopped into the armchair. She sat up excitedly. "Really?"

Ian laughed. "No. It's rabbit stew."

"Oh," she said with unmasked disappointment, and flopped back down.

"Then yes," said Dorothy. "We would love to stay for dinner. Thank you for your hospitality."

"Just to skip to the end of this little dance," said Strontium, "we don't have spare beds, but you two are welcome to the couch and the recliner."

"I don't want you to trouble yourself," said Dorothy.

"Don't kid a kidder, kid. You're two hours walk from town through a dark forest, and I already said I won't eat you. You'd have to be an idiot to turn down a place to stay."

Dorothy laughed again. She liked this witch, and her head felt clear enough now to trust her instincts. Though possible that Strontium was manipulating her, given her choices, and the surety they would be as vulnerable on the road, she chose trust. "Very well. Thank you. We will stay the night. But only the night."

"You're welcome." Strontium pointed to the window behind Melody's chair. "Is that with you?"

A person-shaped orange glow hovered in the window, accompanied by the sound of tapping on glass.

Dorothy smiled. "That's my pixie."

"You have a pixie?" said Strontium.

Ian grinned. "Nice!" He ran to the door and let her in.

Sparky flitted across the room and dropped the bank card and a wad of crumpled bills on the table. "Hey. You might want to count that. I'm pretty sure I dropped some of it. I mean, I definitely dropped all of it, multiple times, and I'm pretty sure I didn't find it all."

"This is plenty." Dorothy picked up the bills and smoothed them out. Things were certainly beginning to look up. Tomorrow she would send Sparky back to Chicago with messages, and hope they could now safely return. But for now, food, rest, and time to regroup. "Thank you, Sparky. This is Strontium and Ian. They have invited us to dinner and to stay the night. Strontium, Ian, this is Sparky."

The pixie flew a few slow circles around both the cabin's occupants. "Hi," she said to Ian, who grinned, enraptured. When she flew to Strontium, she got a knowing look instead of a grin. "Oh!" said Sparky to Dorothy. "You have a witch?"

[31]

RESPONSE

Harrison looked out the window of his temporary office. The black and red cloud cover of the previous day completely gone now, May sunshine beat down on the surface of Lake Michigan, making it sparkle.

A light rap sounded at his open door, and he looked over his shoulder. Milton stood there, short crewcut and thin lips. Out of the body armor and dressed in the standard suit and tie, he hardly looked like the same man.

"Come in," said Harrison.

Milton entered, holding a data device. "I have the final analysis of the Lone Star site, sir. And an update on Miss O'Neill. I assume you want to hear that first?"

"Yes! Please," said Harrison, attempting to quell a minor surge of adrenaline at hearing the name.

"Someone withdrew five hundred dollars from her bank account yesterday," said Milton.

"Someone? Where?"

"Here in the city. We're trying to get a copy of the security camera feed, which is proving to involve a surprising number of obstacles. Should have that by tomorrow morning."

Harrison frowned. "I don't understand. Dorothy would never use that card if she wanted to stay hidden. That's a rookie mistake. There has to be something else going on here."

"Could she have hacked into the bank?" asked Milton. "If she created a record of herself being here when she's actually somewhere else, that would be a good smoke screen."

"I don't know. She's bright, but I don't know what kind of computer skills she has. Damn it, I need to see that security feed." He shook his head in frustration. "All right, tell me about Texas."

"The State Department informs me there are at present two separate city-states independently claiming to be the true Lone Star Kingdom. Neither of them lay claim to the area around that castle, which is a lucky break, since what we did there could have been seen as an invasion. Both governments have denied any involvement with the kidnappings."

"What about the site itself?"

Milton looked at his PDA. "The throne room corpses were apparently suicides. They may have been left behind to bar the door, although given the hole you put in the second floor, I'm not sure what the point of that would have been."

"That room's exit to the hall is permanently fused," said Harrison. "Did that myself. They probably recognized it as secure. Any indication why they would want the place sealed up?"

"Negative, sir. Also, those bodies are at least five years dead. Partially decayed, partially mummified. Given that and the dust coat on every surface, it seems unlikely anyone has been in or out of that building since 2008 or earlier."

"In other words, it's a dead end," said Harrison. "Which we knew it would be. What's next?"

Milton keyed the screen of his PDA. "Agent Kestrel's weapon was recovered from the seventh floor of NCSA HQ. It's an enchanted wakizashi. A Japanese short sword. Fortunately, Eleanora was on site, and identified it as magical before anyone had a chance to touch it. It has been transferred to the containment vault at Esoteric."

"Have we learned anything from it?"

"Not so far. It's being treated as a level one magic hazard. It might be days or weeks before anyone is cleared to study it."

"Wonderful," said Harrison. "She had another sword. Is it reasonable to assume that one is magic as well?"

Milton scrolled down the screen of his PDA. "Eleanora says yes, probably an enchanted katana. She also said you were lucky to survive that fight."

"I'm aware. We can thank Bess for that. Anything else?"

Milton tapped his screen. "Interrogations of NCSA personnel have yielded eight loyal agents and one mole so far."

"Who's the mole?"

"Hunter, sir," said Milton. "Been with the agency seven months. The Director is currently interviewing the people who did his background check."

"What do we know about the attack on HQ? I thought bombs were impossible now."

"They weren't bombs, per se," said Milton. "The fire department is telling us they may have been ordinary cans of gasoline, wired to ignite simultaneously." One of the few substances on Earth that still retained its explosive properties was the family of petroleum-based fuels. Thankfully so, as internal combustion still served as the engine of choice for most ground travel, though recent advances would eventually make that obsolete. While not a convenient explosive for most military purposes, gasoline still did a bang-up job of setting a building on fire.

"Great," said Harrison. "I'll add that to the list of obvious things I should have caught. Should I even ask where we are with tracking the girls?"

"No developments since the last time you asked, sir."

"Which was?"

Milton looked at his watch. "Forty-eight minutes ago. The second anyone knows anything, sir, they will tell you. I doubt you will have to hear it from me."

"I suppose not. What about the dark wizard?"

"Nothing so far. The description you gave doesn't match any mage in the agency, or any identified magic user. That's not unusual, though. A lot of them act in secret, even the good ones."

"All right." Harrison gestured to a seat near his desk. "Sit, please." Milton pocketed his PDA, and sat, as did Harrison behind his desk. "I've done some checking up on you since rashly offering you this job yesterday."

"I assumed you would," said Milton. "Are you about to tell me I'm not the right man for the job? Because you'll get no argument from me."

"No," said Harrison. "Although I do appreciate your directness, which is the quality that brought you to my attention in the first place. Do you prefer to be called Milton, or would you like me to call you David?"

"Your prerogative, sir. Most people call me Milton."

"Milton it is. You were army before the Mayhem Wave."

"Yes, sir," said Milton. "Warrant Officer."

"I know," said Harrison. "Combat leader. I see you were also one of the first fifty agents recruited into the NCSA. We had a standing army before this agency was formed, but you didn't enlist. And yet, when this agency began recruiting you were first in line."

The decision to create a civilian agency of national security had been a controversial one, designed in part as a check against the powers of the newly forming armed services. New Chicago was a nation formed from scratch in a heartbeat, and such structures had been put in place specifically to limit opportunities for dictatorship.

The fact the NCSA fell entirely outside the purview of military chain of command provided an attractive opportunity for survivors who came from law enforcement backgrounds, or had similar skills. People with experience in the intelligence community—such as Director Alec Baker —were natural recruits. The agency also brought certain types of career criminal into the fold, such as burglars and hackers. But one occupation type was noticeably scarce in the ranks of the NCSA: soldiers. Surviving military personnel, with few exceptions, returned to their old careers, granted their previous ranks upon credible proof of credentials. Since most military survivors still had their uniforms and dog tags, that proved simpler for the most part than most other attempts at reorganization. But few of them opted out of service (as was their right under New Chicago law), and only one chose the path of civilian national security.

"Is that a problem?" asked Milton.

"Not at all," said Harrison. "I'm just wondering why you traded in your camo for that suit and tie. I could understand if you wanted to give it all up and become a farmer or something, but you still have a sword at your hip."

"I liked the structure," he said. "And I liked the work. But the army operates under a set of rules that never felt right to me. The Agency is different."

"We have rules here, too."

"The right rules," said Milton.

"I don't suppose you would care to be more specific," said Harrison.

"No, sir," said Milton.

"That's fine. You think you're the wrong man for this job?"

"Respectfully, sir," he said, "I do."

"Well then," said Harrison, "you will be happy to hear I've decided the post is temporary, and that I have another assignment right up your alley."

"Sir?"

"My top priority is to find the people who were abducted, which I choose to believe will happen soon. Once this turns from an investigation to a rescue operation, we'll need a strike team."

"You want me on that team, sir?" asked Milton with obvious enthusiasm.

"It's your team," said Harrison. "I want you to pick it, and I want you to lead it."

Milton's restrained smile transformed to a frown. "I thought you would be leading the team yourself."

"Tried that. Didn't work out so well, as you probably saw." He held up his hand. "And yes, I know I was under a curse, and yes, I know we had moles on the strike team, and moles here pointing me in all the wrong directions. But even with all of that not being true anymore, there are other side issues. I spent most of this morning on the phone, first with the President and then with the Chairman of the Joint Chiefs of Staff. As much as I would like to say how important that makes me feel, the first conversation was entirely about whether I should keep my job, which wasn't fun."

"I'm sure," said Milton.

"Yeah. The second was about why this is still a national security matter, and not yet an act of war, which was an even harder sell. The good news is that Alec and I are both getting a pass on this debacle. The bad news is the military still wants in, which I think has the potential to make this a lot worse. They are on a leash for now, but if anything else goes wrong, I won't count on that lasting. The upshot is even if I wanted to lead this mission, there are plenty of people with clout who would object." Harrison shook his head. "And I can't say I would argue with them. Getting that damned curse out of my head has made me realize this is a conflict of interest no matter how many things go right. These are my children, Milton. I can't be the one going off to rescue them, because I won't have a clear head, curse or no curse. But you can. You are the right man for this job."

Milton nodded. "Understood, sir."

"Good," said Harrison. "I need you to start putting your team together today. I want you to be able to move on this the second we know where to send you. Meanwhile, you will continue in the capacity of my assistant until you get the go order."

"Got it." Milton stood. "Will there be anything else right now? It does sound like I have some work to do."

Harrison smiled at the initiative. "No, go ahead. I expect regular reports today. Any ideas on who you want to bring?"

"Yes, sir," he said. "I will want all the telekinetic agents, for a start."

Harrison sat back in his chair. "I think that's doable. Logan wants in anyway, and I was already expecting to assign de Queiroz to the team. You may want to reconsider Rutherford, but I will leave that up to you once you have a chance to talk to him."

"That's three, sir," said Milton. "I will want all five, including Mrs. Mendoza-Cody. I recognize she is not NCSA, but she does have clearance."

Harrison stared for a moment. "Milton, I just told you I can't go."

"Negative, sir," said Milton. "You told me you can't *lead*. I won't be asking you to do that."

"Wow," said Harrison. "You want me on this team, under your command? And you want me to bring my wife, also to follow your orders? You really have a pair, don't you?"

"Yes, sir."

"That's what I want to hear." He sat back in his chair, steepling his fingers in front of him. "I must say I had not considered this possibility, but the answer is no. We can't run an op this sensitive with an ambiguous chain of command. However…"

"Yes?"

Harrison sat up. "I might consider coming along anyway. I still want you as point man. You call the shots. I carry the accountability. Something like that. I might be able to sell that to Alec. The NCSA isn't like any pre-Mayhem agency. We're still making up rules as we go. God knows we've improvised worse than this in the last nine years. I'll talk to Alec tonight and give you an answer tomorrow."

"Will you be speaking for Mrs. Mendoza-Cody, or just yourself?"

"I would not presume to speak for Mrs. Mendoza-Cody," said Harrison. "If you can recruit her on your own, you can have her. I admit to no small degree of curiosity as to the outcome of that conversation. Seeing as you have a lot more work ahead of you than you realize, you'd better be off."

"Yes, sir!" said Milton with a confident smile.

Claudia poked her head in the door. "Hey, am I interrupting?"

"Would it matter?" asked Harrison.

"Probably not."

"What do you need, Claudia?" He nodded at Milton, who turned to go.

"The guys in surveillance finished checking our phones for bugs this morning, and they're all clean. They said they don't think Dorothy's phone would be tapped if ours weren't. So, how soon before I can call her?"

Harrison frowned. "Come in. And shut the door."

Milton and Claudia walked sideways past each other as they both crossed the doorway. She pulled the door shut behind her, and stood there, looking at the floor.

"What happened when you tried?" he asked.

She looked up. "It went straight to voice mail."

"How many times, and when?" he asked, grateful for the lack of pretense.

"Only once," said Claudia. "About fifteen minutes ago. I'm sorry. I held out as long as I could."

With that easy admission and apology, Harrison understood Claudia's apparent nerves were not about getting in trouble for breach of protocol, but fear for Dorothy. And he had a remedy for that he hadn't shared with her yet. He pulled out his communicator.

"Aplomado," he said into it.

"Yes?"

"I need an update on Melody and Dorothy. Do you have—"

"They have slept, and eaten," said the wizard. "Health signs still imperfect and fluctuating, unlike the other thirty. Dorothy shows signs of an enchantment, which could mean several things, none of which would be bad news."

"So they are okay?" asked Harrison, looking directly at Claudia.

"Quite so."

"And probably not captured?"

"Again," said the wizard, "a reasonable but completely unverifiable interpretation."

"Thank you. Keep monitoring, please." He pocketed the communicator. "She probably turned the phone off for safety. Or the battery died and she didn't bring a charger."

Claudia nodded with large eyes.

"Aplomado has orders to alert me the second he sees any signs he thinks are worth concern. They're my kids, Claudia. I have my eye on them."

Claudia nodded again. She bit her lip.

He stood and walked around his desk. "Come here," he said with his arms open.

She crossed the room in silence, then curled up in his arms and wept into his shoulder.

[32]

RANDOM

Dorothy recounted her money. Three hundred eighty-six dollars. Between Chicago and Erie, Sparky had managed to lose one hundred twenty dollars in cash, which Dorothy wrote off as the cost of measuring the Pixie's reliability, convincing herself it was money well spent. It would cost fifty-four dollars for two worm passes back to Chicago, leaving three thirty-two. That should be more than enough for a hotel room for one night, a phone charger, and three meals. If their exile lasted longer than one more night, she would need more cash.

She took a sip of her tea, something herbal and exotic, a flavor she did not recognize. Poison? Unlikely. Passing up an entire night's opportunity to kill Dorothy in her sleep only to poison her over breakfast made no reasonable sense. She had slept in until nearly noon, a reminder of the stress of the previous day. When she woke, she found her hostess had prepared tea and scrambled eggs. Melody had already been up for some time.

Strontium emerged from one of the side doors, still wearing the purple fringed outfit from the day before. Dorothy stuffed the wad of cash back into her jeans pocket, silently adding a change of clothes to the list of things she hoped it would buy. As much as the witch still looked radiant wearing the same thing at least two days in a row, Dorothy had an aversion to feeling dirty, and sleeping in her clothes definitely counted. "Thank you again."

"No bother at all," said the witch. "You moving on soon?"

"I think we should," said Dorothy. "We have about two hours walk ahead of us to get back to Erie Colony, and things to do when we get there."

"Erie Colony?" said Strontium. "That was yesterday. Never make it there in two hours now."

Dorothy frowned. "It took us two hours to get here from town. We're rested now. We should be able to make it back in the same amount of time, if not better."

"Child," said Strontium, "we're not there anymore. That was yesterday."

Dorothy leapt up from the table and bolted for the door. "Stupid!" she shouted at herself. She threw the door open, hoping to see the Erie forest. The sight of Strontium's well-tended lawn greeted her, surrounded by a grassy plain to the right, and a beach to the left. "Aaugh! Stupid! Damn it!" She whirled on Strontium. "You knew this would happen!"

"Sure I did. What does it matter? I told you no one finds this place without looking for it, and you said you were running from danger. You're safe here. What do you care where we are?"

Dorothy struggled to contain her rage, which would serve no purpose against someone more powerful than she. "We're stuck here now! Right?"

"You can leave whenever you want!" said Strontium. "I don't care!"

"But I don't know where to go!" shouted Dorothy. "I don't know where we are! We could be a hundred miles from the nearest fresh water! Do you even know where this is?"

"Of course not," said the witch. "That's the whole point of a Random Cabin. If I don't know where I am, nobody does. Really, child. You would think I had done you wrong. Aren't you trying to hide?"

"Yes, but—"

"Well you don't get more hid than this!" said Strontium. "And you're welcome, by the way!"

Dorothy stepped outside to cool off. As furious as she felt, the witch made a salient point she couldn't counter. Was this any different from Apryl telling her not to use the phone? Or her choosing not to use the bank card? Not knowing her location added one more layer of concealed information, in this case a layer hundreds of miles thick. The midday sun beat down on her, and perspiration beaded on her forehead. Wherever they had gone, it had a warmer climate than Erie. As much as that made her feel better about her situation, it also reminded her how grubby she felt in yesterday's clothes, which she now further soiled with sweat.

Strontium followed her outside.

"Where's Sparky?" asked Dorothy.

"Swimming," said Strontium. "This is a beach after all. *She's* not mad at me. That one knows how to make the best of things. And you know, a swim sounds like a grand idea. We only have a day here. May as well take advantage of it." She poked her head back in the door. "Who wants to go in the water?" she asked the children.

"Me!" they both shouted.

"Well, come on then." The two children jumped up and ran to the door with Strontium.

"Melody didn't bring a bathing suit," said Dorothy, with attempted bitterness.

"Well then, she'll fit in just fine." With one child on each hand, Strontium walked down to the shore.

Dorothy stood in the doorway with her arms crossed, trying to think of the right scathing thing to say. "Stupid," she whispered to herself.

Down on the beach, all three of them stripped off their clothes and splashed around in the waves.

"Damn it," she said finally, and stormed after them. Halfway over the dune, Sparky caught up with her.

"Hey," said the pixie, her orange hair slicked over with seawater. "You coming in?"

"No," she said. "I am coming down to the beach to scold three irresponsible swimmers for going in the water without a lifeguard."

"Somebody is grumpy today."

Dorothy stopped. "Do you even understand our situation? Are you even capable of comprehending where we stand right now?"

"You and the kid are on the run from whoever kidnapped those twenty-eight girls, and Mitchell, and Adler," said Sparky. "You were both under a curse of bad judgment, but she wasn't affected for some reason, so that's worth keeping an eye on. You left town in a hurry, and no one back there knows where you are, which is now irrelevant anyway because neither do you. Melody led you to this witch somehow, which is also pretty interesting, and she put you up for the night and fed you rabbit, which was pretty darn nice of her, considering how snarky you were just now. Oh, and you lied to me about why I had to go to Chicago for the money, but that's okay, we're still friends. Does that about cover it?"

Dorothy started walking again, at a more casual pace. "How did you know I was lying?"

"I didn't, but I figured it out," said Sparky. "I'm guessing you wanted me to go back there to make it seem like you never left town, right?"

"Yes," said Dorothy.

"See? Not as dumb as I look. You could have just told me, but you didn't. Meanwhile, old lady here didn't tell you she lives in a cabin that picks itself a new backyard every night. Maybe that was the wrong thing to do, or maybe she didn't think it was important for you to know. But as far as I can tell, she did you both a huge favor, and now you're being pissy about it. Not really my place to butt in, I know. Just tossing out some observations."

"What if we never get home?" asked Dorothy.

"Like that would ever happen," said the pixie. "Pumpkin, you give the word and I'll drop everything to find Chicago and come back in a flier. I have until midnight. And if I don't find it in time today, I've got all day tomorrow to try from wherever we are then. Okay, so she surprised us. I still say this is a good gig for you. Ride it out. Have some fun. The water's great, by the way. A little cold, but I took care of that."

"Fine," said Dorothy. "For now. But I'm taking you up on that offer to find Chicago, and it will probably be tomorrow."

Sparky giggled. "Done." She shook her head vigorously, spraying Dorothy in the face with tiny droplets of salt water, and zipped back down to the beach.

Dorothy walked the rest of the way. Strontium and Ian had dug a pool in the sand for Melody to splash around in, rendering her lifeguard concerns moot. All three of them were buck naked.

"You're all going to get sunburned," she said to Strontium.

"Nah," she said, smiling. "I've got stuff for that."

"I'm sure," said Dorothy.

"You going in? The water's warm."

"So I hear. Not much of a skinny dipper."

Strontium shrugged. "Suit yourself." Leaving Melody to play in her pool, and Ian to work on a sand castle he constructed around it by hand, she went back into the ocean and crouched down in the water, bobbing up as waves came in.

A drop of sweat broke free from Dorothy's temple, and found its way down to her right eyebrow. She wiped it away. Now keenly aware of the temperature, she felt the lure of the water. She kicked off her shoes and socks, and began rolling her pants up before realizing how little that would accomplish. She took off her jeans and left them on the sand.

As she walked down to the water's edge, the sand transitioned from loose and hot to dense and cool, and finally wet. She scrunched her toes in relief, letting the beach mud ooze between them, and it soothed her more than she expected. A wave broke in front of her, and raced up the beach to cover her ankles in deliciously cool foam.

The briny smell of the spray brought her back to childhood memories, pre-Mayhem. Trips to New Jersey to visit family punctuated by days at the beach, swimming, building sand castles, strolls on the boardwalk with French fries and pizza. She closed her eyes and let herself go there. The distant roar of the ocean provided hypnotic white noise. The cry of a gull pierced the air, possibly her imagination auto-correcting her environment to the Jersey Shore. She took a few steps forward. Water brushed past her calves. A wave surged over her knees.

She opened her eyes and looked straight ahead, at nothing but water stretched out to the clear horizon. Another wave covered her legs, and she took a step backward to keep her balance. Finally, a wave broke over her that soaked her shirttails and underwear, and she gave in, dropping down to her knees to let the water roll over her clothed torso. She dunked her head down and up, spitting out water and pushing her hair back over her face.

"Not so bad, is it?" said Strontium from behind her.

Dorothy turned around to look at her. Only her head was visible, bobbing up and down with the waves above her crouched form.

"No. Not bad at all." Dorothy looked back up at the beach. Melody and Ian both sat in the pool now, pushing wet sand from within to fortify walls that kept crashing down onto them. Sparky weaved back and forth above them. "What are you running from?"

"I'm not running," said Strontium.

Dorothy faced her again. "No. The house does all the running for you. So, what are you hiding from?"

The witch looked at her with serious eyes, for the first time since meeting her the day before. Then she looked away. "It's not me I'm trying to hide."

As Dorothy tracked Strontium's gaze, it fell on the pool of splashing children.

33

HADLEY

"That's her."

Harrison replayed the ninety seconds of footage from the ATM security camera once more. In it, the pixie fumbled with the card, dropped it, picked it up again and successfully inserted it. Her entire body heaved with relief at achieving that much. She went through the elaborate and awkward process of asking for and scooping up a stack of bills, which she clutched along with the returned card, and flew off in a flash of orange light.

"Definitely her. This is good work, Milton. You said this was two days ago?"

"Correct. I have someone cross-checking for other sightings of the pixie. No word so far."

"Does this give us any reason to believe they are still in the city?"

"Not necessarily," said Milton. "All it really tells us is that Sparky has access to Miss O'Neill's bank account, or did two days ago."

"Well, that's big all by itself," said Harrison. "I think it's safe to assume Sparky is with them, which means they are a hell of a lot safer, no matter where they are."

"It is my duty to point out there are other possible explanations," said Milton. "Not the least of which is the pixie is working for the enemy."

"Noted," said Harrison. "And thank you. Don't ever stop keeping me on my toes. I choose to take this one on faith though. I know Sparky too well to believe she would turn against us. This is good news. How are we coming on finding the others?"

"We have a weak lead as of this morning, but nothing concrete yet. I'd rather not get your hopes up with a guess as to how that will play out."

"I appreciate that. And your strike team?"

"Assembled, less yourself," said Milton. "Do you have an answer for me yet?"

"What did Apryl say?" asked Harrison.

"She said no." Milton presented this information with utter detachment, surely masking disappointment at his own failure to achieve the impossible.

"That was to be expected," said Harrison. "What about Rutherford? You still want him?"

"He's a bit rough around the edges, but he has a power that might be useful. I plan to keep him in reserve, but yes, he's coming."

"All right, then," said Harrison. "I'm in. Here's the deal: on paper, this is my op. Officially, you are subordinate to me, and your assignment is advisory. Our unofficial understanding is that I will take one hundred percent of your tactical advice. Alec agrees that this mission is a conflict of interest for me, and he agrees that you should be making the big decisions. But he also agrees that I can't answer to you in the field. Too much potential for confusion and hazard. As long as it's completely clear to you that I am in charge, I will stay the hell out of your way. Do we have an understanding?"

"That's not optimal," said Milton.

Harrison shrugged. "Then I have to stay home. How badly do you want me on this run?"

"Badly enough to compromise. But to be frank, my biggest concern is that you will step in and pull rank at exactly the wrong time. You'll be under stresses no one else will. I need to know you won't kill a good plan with a knee-jerk reaction."

Harrison smiled at that. "You don't know me very well, Milton. It's much more likely that I'll charge out on my own and leave you all behind."

"That would be your prerogative. Is there anything else?"

"No, just keep me updated on that lead."

"Will do."

Milton left Harrison alone with his ruminations. In two days, they had only identified one mole, who had yet to provide them with useful information about their adversary. His children, even the captured ones, appeared to be safe and healthy, but that could change at any moment. He took what strength he could from the heartening news of Sparky as Dorothy's guardian pixie.

Harrison stood and walked to his window. Looking out over the lake, he took out his phone and called home. Apryl picked up on the first ring.

"Is there news?" she asked.

"Sparky is with Dorothy and Melody," he said.

"Oh, thank God!" said Apryl. "Are you sure? Did you hear from them?"

"We have security camera footage of Sparky using Dorothy's bank card to get cash two days ago," said Harrison. "That tells me she doesn't want to pay for anything with the card directly, to avoid detection. The fact Sparky got the cash right here in Chicago might mean they left town and sent her back here as a decoy. Dorothy is smart; that's the kind of move she would make."

"Two days ago? How can you be sure she's still with them?"

"Because if they got separated Sparky would have come back here, and pixies are notoriously difficult to kill. The most likely scenario is she is still taking orders from Dorothy."

"You think they're safe with her?"

"For now," said Harrison. "I don't want to jump to any unwarranted conclusions, but this does make me feel a lot more secure. Sparky is an excellent lookout, and she packs a punch in a fight."

"Good." Apryl paused. "Your boy Milton came here this morning to recruit me. Was that your doing?"

"Absolutely not. I put him in charge of assembling and leading the strike team for when we go to rescue the girls. I also told him if he wanted you he would have to ask you himself."

"Well, tell him I'm in."

"Wait, what?" said Harrison. "He told me not five minutes ago you said no. I assumed you would say no."

"I did say no," she said. "And now I'm saying yes. You tell me our baby is safe for now, and I believe you. But she's never going to be safe for real until whoever is after her is found and stopped. I've been thinking about this all morning. If she's safe with Dorothy and Sparky, then I can't just sit here waiting for the rest of the world to protect her. That's my place."

"Apryl," he said gently. "I'm on the strike team. And I can't promise it will be a safe or easy assignment. I'm catastrophizing here, but worst-case scenario, we fail, and our daughter becomes an orphan."

"Fine," said Apryl. "You can stay home."

"Apryl…"

"No, listen," she said. "I have to do this. If I don't, and something goes wrong, I will never forgive myself for sitting here on my hands. Besides which, you know full well I am one of the most powerful assets you have for something like this. I don't like playing this card, but if one of us has to stay home. It should be the lock-pick, not the powerhouse."

"Let me think about it," he said.

"Think all you want, but it's not your decision."

He sighed. "All right, then I'll think about staying home."

"We can talk tonight," she said. "I love you."

"I love you too." As the words left his mouth, he caught sight of a man standing on the lakeshore. From this distance, he appeared a speck like all the other specks down there, but in a strikingly loud and familiar color. It wore Hadley's Hawaiian shirt, the same one he caught sight of in Esoteric a few days earlier, and in NCSA Headquarters a few days after that. "Hey," he said, keeping his eyes on that figure. "I have to go. See you tonight."

"Okay," she said. "Bye."

He put his phone in his pocket without taking his eyes off the shirt, and pulled out his communicator. "Milton, I need you to take a man in for questioning. He is standing on the lake front north of my window, and he is wearing a green Hawaiian shirt."

After a brief pause, Milton responded, "All right. Sending two men out right now."

Harrison watched as the man on the shore did nothing but stand there. After about two minutes of this, two agents walked up to him, and straight past him. "You have to be freaking kidding me," Harrison whispered. Into his communicator, he said, "Milton, I need you in my office right now."

Milton entered less than a minute later. "Sir?"

"Come to the window, please."

Milton complied.

Harrison, whose eyes had not strayed from their target, pointed and said, "Do you see that?"

"The lake, sir?"

"Standing in front of the lake," said Harrison. "A man. About your build. Green Hawaiian shirt."

Milton stared in that direction. "Is he fairly obvious?"

"You'd have to be blind to miss him," said Harrison.

"Then it's someone only you can see, sir." In the post-Mayhem world, observations of impossible things rarely prompted confusion or the need to lie about them.

"Possibilities?" asked Harrison, eyes still on the man.

"Illusion," said Milton. "That could be a curse, but we'd probably have caught it in light of this week's events. A wizard might be able to cloak himself from some people but not others. You'd have to ask one of them about that; it's not my specialty. Um… It could be a mundane hallucination, brought on by stress or drug use."

"We'll rule that one out," said Harrison.

"Yes sir," said Milton. "Ghost, perhaps?"

"Oh, shit. Why didn't I think of that? I'm going outside. I think he wants to talk to me."

"Would you like an escort?"

"Bodyguard?" He looked down at the ghost of his friend. "No, I'm good."

When Harrison got to the lakefront five minutes later, Hadley's ghost stood there patiently. He walked up beside his dead friend. Both men looked out on the lake.

"How long have you been haunting me?" asked Harrison.

"Not long," said Hadley. "A few days, I think. Time doesn't work exactly the same for you and me, I'm afraid."

"I'm sorry about what happened to you," said Harrison. Countless times he wished he had the opportunity to say those words over the last eight years. Finally hearing them, they sounded exactly as inadequate as he knew they would. Hadley had been killed by a single shot to the neck, as Harrison watched in horror, on a mission Harrison had asked him to come on against his wishes. Murdered by their enemy for the sole purpose of upsetting Harrison. It worked spectacularly.

"Bygones," said Hadley. "That's not why I'm here."

"Why are you here?" asked Harrison, doing his best to shake away the memory, and the guilt.

Hadley's ghost shrugged. The gesture had a slightly blurry quality to it. "Even if I knew, I probably couldn't tell you. But I don't know."

"Listen" said Harrison, "I can't believe I'm actually saying this, but we're kind of in the middle of a thing right now, and I can't afford to be distracted. Why don't you come with me over to Esoteric? I'm sure they would love to see you."

"I've been there," said Hadley. "They can't. See me, that is. You're the only one, and believe me that's not by my choice. You should also know the thing you're in the middle of is connected to my being here. I don't know how yet."

"Oh," said Harrison. They stood in silence for a bit. "I am glad to see you, you know."

"I think that's good," said Hadley. "There's a lot I'm still sorting out."

"I'm not going to keep you a secret," said Harrison. "No one else can see you, but they'll believe me that I can. My assistant already believes me. And like I said, I can't afford to be off my game right now. Is that going to be all right?"

"Truly, I have no idea. Haunting is a very new experience for me. I don't know the skills that go along with it, if that's even an appropriate way of putting it."

Harrison couldn't help but smile at that. "Still the scientist." Hadley's words more fully processed. "If this is your first haunting, what have you been doing for the past eight years?" Harrison's concept of ghosts centered on them trapped between earthly existence and a proper afterlife. He dreaded the thought of a Heaven from which Hadley had been ejected. Or a Hell.

"Nothing," said Hadley's ghost. "Not a thing. I didn't exist."

"I don't understand."

Hadley turned to look at Harrison for the first time, with eyes that were not eyes, and said, "The last eight years have been oblivion for me. That made sense. This new state is confusing." He paused there. "Whatever brought me back here brought me back from absolute nothingness. I imagine it's something quite significant."

Harrison had no words for this idea, and so he was grateful on more than one level when Milton's voice came over his communicator. "Sir? Are you all right down there?"

"I'm fine. Coming back up in a minute, with a guest." He looked at Hadley. "You ready to come inside?"

"I really have no way of knowing," said the ghost, before following Harrison back to the building.

34

FAMILY

Day three of Dorothy's stay in the Random Cabin took place somewhere cold and snowy. The cabin itself stayed comfortably warm, between the wood stove and whatever magic kept it going. Shortly before noon, Strontium put on a heavy coat of multicolored fur, and left Dorothy with the children for almost an hour. She came back with a salmon. Ian went out back and pulled vegetables from a garden that somehow managed to weather the extreme cold, and they had two meals of fish.

Day four they lived in a swamp. The lawn formed an island, surrounded by impassable muck and copious insects. They had gator that day. Day five they found themselves on bare rock, breathing cold, thin air. That day Dorothy had her first taste of mountain goat. Day six passed by on a grassy plain that stretched to the horizon in all directions. Dorothy learned how many mice it takes to feed a family of four for an entire day. Each day Strontium took these hunting trips alone, and with apparent joy.

And for Dorothy and Melody, each day meant one more day out of contact with their loved ones. Starting on day three, Sparky honored her promise to find Chicago, at least in the attempt. Each day she found they were too far away for her to make it there and back in the hours remaining before midnight. And each day, Dorothy became more apprehensive about their prospects.

For the first few days, Dorothy remained cordial with her host, but guarded. The witch seemed harmless enough, but trust did not come easily for Dorothy, and her wariness guided most of their interactions. Strontium's friendliness remained consistent, and while Dorothy found it difficult to trust her, she found liking her easy enough.

Melody's demeanor was another matter. It took her no time at all to bond with Ian, and the two children spent all their waking time together. Ian slipped into the role previously occupied by Adler Logan, as Melody's surrogate older brother and willing foil. Melody took on small chores, which Dorothy at first assumed gave her a sense of importance. However, after a few days had gone by and Melody's enthusiasm for housework grew instead of fading, it grew clear she genuinely considered herself a member of the household, and took that responsibility seriously. This factor more than anything ultimately drew Dorothy out of her self-imposed shell.

On the evening of the eighth day, Strontium spontaneously animated two cloth dolls to entertain the children. She had them dance a waltz on the dining room table, and when Melody applauded and begged for more, the two dolls hopped down to the floor, where they set up a checkerboard and played out a game. They took their moves with great deliberation, often walking around the board to survey their positions, and tap their little felt heads as if in deep thought.

Strontium observed all this from a chair across the room with a smile, and with no indication of how much effort she exerted to perpetuate the show, or whether the toys had simply asserted their independence.

As the children gawked and laughed, Dorothy pulled up a small stool next to Strontium. "Is magic something you learn? Or is it something you're born with?"

"A little of both, I suppose." Strontium turned to face Dorothy with amused eyes. "Hang on, are you actually talking to me?"

Dorothy bit her lip. "I'm not very good at being a guest."

Strontium laughed. "You don't say."

Dorothy frowned. "I'm not upset with you anymore."

"Didn't think you were. You just haven't decided how you feel about staying here. Can't say I blame you. Not entirely, anyway. You and the girl are free to go any time you want, you know."

"You know we can't do that."

"Fiddlesticks!" said Strontium sharply. "We've been walking distance from three different settlements since you got on this ride. You send that pixie out every morning to find your city, but there's other ways home. I'm betting that little girl's mother has a phone, right?"

Dorothy looked at Melody, still absorbed in the dolls and their game. Her mother did indeed have a phone, but the last instructions Dorothy had gotten from Apryl by phone were to trust no one and stay out of sight. Strolling into an unknown town to ask for help from strangers did not qualify as following those instructions. Neither did taking up residence with a witch and her boy, she supposed, but it seemed safer somehow by comparison. She looked back at Strontium. Spontaneously, she asked, "Are you a good witch or a bad witch?"

"Asked Dorothy," said Strontium with a straight face.

"Don't tease. I'm asking you for real. We've been here a week, and I don't know how much longer it's going to be. Melody and I aren't your guests anymore. We're your boarders. And I want to know what that means for my little sister and me."

"You're not boarders," said Strontium.

Dorothy's heart sank, visions of being tossed out at the next town now overtaking her other concerns. "You won't let us stay?"

"Hell, yes, I'm letting you stay. You aren't boarders." She pointed to the children. Ian had engaged in a silent argument with one of the dolls, involving a lot of stern looks and head-shaking. Melody looked on in dreamy admiration. "You see that? You're family. World of difference."

"Oh." Dorothy had not foreseen this development, and she thought back on how more evident it would have been if she had been paying attention instead of brooding. "You didn't answer my question," she pointed out nervously.

"Are you a good person, or a bad person?" asked the witch.

"Good," said Dorothy without hesitation. After a beat, she added, "I think."

"You want to know if I'm a good witch or a bad witch?"

Dorothy nodded.

"Well, that's not for me to say, is it? I am who I am. Haven't eaten you yet, so that's worth considering."

Dorothy laughed. "Indeed."

"We can scare up two more beds," said Strontium. "Give me time and I'll even be able to give you rooms."

In the face of Strontium's warmth, sincere and infectious, Dorothy felt the first tentative stirrings of that elusive trust. "Thank you."

"You're welcome. Who are you running from?" asked the witch.

Dorothy sat up at this. "What makes you think we're running?"

"You said you came here to hide."

"Maybe we only needed to hide for the night," said Dorothy.

"Three chances to get off and you're still here. You want to go home, but you don't want to be found. That's a runner. So, who are you running from?"

Dorothy hesitated. "I don't think I should say."

"Child," said Strontium, "you are my sister now. That's not going to be optional, so you may as well admit to it. This is *our* home now. Your dangers are my dangers. And fair is fair, I'd like to know what those dangers are."

Dorothy took a deep breath, and a leap of faith. "I have twenty-eight adopted sisters, and something or someone has taken some of them. Maybe all of them by now. I really don't know. And I don't know who, and I don't know why, but if they came for my sisters, they are coming for me, too. And they are coming for Melody."

"That sounds like the middle of a very long story," said Strontium.

"It probably is. I wish I knew the beginning. Or how it ends." Dorothy thought for a moment about how to word her next question. "Are your dangers my dangers?"

Strontium shrugged. "I guess. Don't have too many dangers, though."

"Who are you hiding Ian from?" asked Dorothy. The notion of them all on the run from two different enemies daunted her, and she needed whatever power she could glean from knowing details.

Strontium met that question with a silence that stretched long enough to trigger the beginnings of fear in Dorothy. Finally, she stood, and walked to the kitchen, out of earshot of the children, beckoning Dorothy to follow. "I'm not hiding Ian from anyone. I'm hiding everyone from Ian."

Dorothy looked at the sweet, gentle boy she had come to know over the course of a week. Kind, smart, helpful, polite, an ideal child in every respect. But in the world after Mayhem, nothing was ever what it seemed anymore. "Why?"

Strontium sighed. "He breaks things."

Dorothy contemplated the wide variety of possible meanings to that phrase, and found them too diverse for proper understanding. "He breaks things?"

"I don't want to say more than that. He's a good boy. We have a good life. He's happy, and everyone else is safe. That's all that matters."

Everyone *else* is safe. Not what Dorothy wanted to hear. "Are we safe?"

"From Ian?" asked Strontium, shocked. "Of course we are! You know my boy. He'd sooner give his life than hurt you or your sweet one."

"But he breaks things."

Strontium looked away. "He hasn't broken anything in a very long time. I don't think he even remembers it anymore."

"But you won't tell me what it means."

"No," she said. "And if we keep him here, I won't ever have to."

Ten days into their trip in the random cabin, Dorothy and Melody woke to find a new wing had grown onto the building overnight, consisting of two small, furnished bedrooms. Melody spent much of that morning jumping on her new bed.

Sparky continued her daily searches for New Chicago, showing no sign of growing weary with the task, nor frustration at her lack of success.

Dorothy assumed some of Ian's kitchen duties, in part to pass the time, in part to free him up to spend more time keeping Melody happy, and in part because she genuinely wanted to contribute. Over two weeks, she discovered more about cooking game than she thought possible. She learned which meats had to be aged to be palatable, which ones had to be boiled to render them tender enough, and which ones could be grilled right away. She left butchering duties to Ian, initially because she felt too squeamish. Once she overcame that discomfort, Ian still insisted, for fear she would not have the dexterity or eye to properly remove the foul glands of some of their catches. The day he successfully skinned and dressed three skunks, she conceded the point.

On day fourteen, Dorothy woke early and ventured outside. A wall of dry heat greeted her when she opened the door. The cabin was nestled in a stretch of low brush. In front of her, at a distance her mind struggled to calculate, lay a sprawling river, enclosed by sheer cliffs and populated with majestic buttes. She emerged from the house, gradually accepting the scale of her surroundings. Her eyes fixed on the far cliff wall, she paced the length of the front lawn. In parallax, the distance became intuitively farther and farther, until she estimated it must have been many miles. Dorothy had never seen the Grand Canyon in person. Every description she had ever read, and every photo she had ever seen of it, now proved woefully inadequate to convey its simple magnitude, or its colossal beauty.

"I love this place," said Ian from behind her.

The voice startled her, and she turned to find him sitting in a lawn chair. "I didn't see you there."

"That's okay," he said. "You had better things to see."

Dorothy looked back over the vista, still trying to wrap her head around something that big. She felt a sudden pang of regret the cabin had materialized in the bottom of the canyon, depriving her of the view from the top. There would never be enough time in one day to climb up to see it. "Have you been here before?"

"I'm pretty sure we've been everywhere before," he said.

It only occurred to Dorothy that moment how many times this boy must have seen the world change around him. Thousands of days, with every morning a new locale. It stood to reason he would have revisited some sites multiple times. She attempted to compute the number of times he would have been likely to see this canyon, via probability and the law of large numbers, before conceding there were too many variables in play for her to truly understand what his life must be like. "Do you like jumping around like this?"

His brow furrowed, and he hesitated. "I think so."

These jumps were all he knew. He had no frame of reference to know whether he liked them or not. She lacked a similar frame of reference. She had spent the past eight years of her life in New Chicago. Getting her own apartment when she turned twenty represented the most adventurous move she had made in that time. These past two weeks excited her more than she would readily admit. Though she held firm to the goal of finding home, she began to understand how much she would miss the adventure, and it surprised her to learn this about herself.

As Dorothy looked out over the Colorado River, she adjusted her sense of their altitude to higher than her earlier estimate. Ahead of the house lay a few dozen yards of low brush, but beyond that a rocky outcropping dropped off out of sight. Perhaps from the edge of that cliff she could get a better view. It might turn out to be ten feet to the bottom, or half a mile. No way to know without looking. She glanced down at her jeans, and ruled them adequate armor against the scratchy undergrowth. With a new-found sense of adventure, she sallied forth.

Ten steps in, Ian called her name. She turned to ask what he wanted. In that moment, the pain hit her.

She grabbed her ankle in surprise. Looking for thorns, she found two red spots on her white sock. The reality of their source hit her at the same time as a new surge of pain, like burning oil injected directly into her blood.

She shrieked. In response came a rattle, like a maraca from Hell.

Desperately trying to remember anything she had ever learned about rattlesnake bites, she came up blank. All the old movie remedies—tourniquet, knife cut, suck out the venom—were bunk. Beyond that, she had no idea. The entire bottom half of her leg burned with a fire beyond her imagining. She tried to limp back to the house, and fell.

As the cold overtook her, she recognized it as shock. Her last coherent thoughts related to Sparky protecting Melody, wishing she could resolve things with Claudia, and a detached, intellectual understanding of the vast distance to the nearest hospital.

She never truly lost consciousness, but her awareness of her situation became dreamlike and scattered, marked by her certainty of only pain and fear.

At some point, she became aware of movement. Words of concern drifted past her, then words of reassurance. Flashing back to the last time she felt cared for in a moment of vulnerability, she managed to ask, "Claudia?" Someone responded, but not in a way she found discernible, apart from the recognition of a voice not Claudia's, and the remembrance Claudia was thousands of miles away

Gradually, and dimly, she came to understand she rested in a bed, her entire leg now numb. She lifted the blanket, expecting to find the limb black and horrific. Her jeans gone, the leg looked swollen, but not as ugly as she feared. Slightly pinker than its mate, otherwise intact, and moist with a balm. An herbal scent hit her nostrils.

"How do you feel?" asked Strontium.

Dorothy turned her head to the witch by her bedside in a rocking chair. "Like a stupid city mouse. I had no idea anything could hurt that much. How long was I out?"

"Couple hours. You're lucky the boy was out there."

"Even luckier you knew how to take care of me. Thank you."

"Pish, posh," said Strontium. "I'm sure at some point you'll save my life, too."

"Did you do magic on my leg?"

Strontium made a vague gesture with her hand. "Herbs, mostly. I did top it off with a little spell. You should be up stepping on snakes again in few hours."

Dorothy laughed. "Indeed." With her leg under control, the rest of her body now asked for attention. Specifically, her stomach growled. "I skipped breakfast."

"Well, if you feel up to eating, I should introduce you to the last phase of your treatment." The witch stood and left the room. A minute or so later, she reappeared carrying a bowl containing a few chunks of white meat with steam rising off them, and a fork. It smelled like chicken.

"Is that what I think it is?" asked Dorothy, a bit reluctant to hear the answer.

"Yepper. You'll need this to anchor the spell. Little revenge goes a long way, too."

Dorothy sat up and took the bowl. She speared a piece of meat, and cautiously put it in her mouth. The chewy rattlesnake flesh tasted bland, but oddly satisfying, both physically and emotionally.

"Who's Claudia?"

Strontium asked this as Dorothy took her second bite. Chewing, she gave herself a moment to decide how to answer that question. "A friend back home."

"You asked for her while you were delirious with the pain. Pretty sure you thought I was her."

"I remember," said Dorothy. "You were rescuing me. Claudia rescued me recently. It was easy enough to conflate the two of you while my head was spinning. You should take it as a compliment. She's my best friend."

"Is she, now?" Strontium asked with a curious smile and bit of a twinkle in her eye.

"Yes, she is." As Dorothy said this, she felt the beginnings of a blush, but chalked it up to the snake venom.

<hr>

Early in the morning on day twenty-six—fried partridge day—Sparky set out on another attempt to locate New Chicago.

"I feel good about this one." She rubbed her palms together in anticipation of the day's work ahead of her. "I think we're at least on the right continent this time."

"You said that on wombat soup day," said Dorothy. "Which was pretty obviously incorrect."

"Yeah, but I've got my bearings now," said the pixie.

"Well, good. Shall we run down the mission checklist?"

"I think I've got it by now."

"Humor me," said Dorothy, smirking.

"Yes, ma'am."

"Item one?" said Dorothy.

"Locate Apryl, and tell her Melody is happy as a clam and getting fat on wild animals."

"You can skip the fat part."

"Righto," said Sparky.

"Item two?"

"Find a map and tell the good guys where we are."

"Good," said Dorothy. "Item three?"

"Phone charger." The pixie held up three fingers on her right hand, emphasizing, perhaps unconsciously, the missing index finger on that hand. "Glimmer's Wound" was the popular term for this affliction of every surviving pixie.

"What kind?" asked Dorothy.

"The battery kind, not the plug-in kind," said Sparky. "Right?"

"Right." If Sparky's mission succeeded, she wouldn't need the phone. But if it failed, and she still managed to bring back the charger, they would be able to communicate with the NCSA, at least for a while.

"Then I high-tail it back here. I've got this, boss. Any last instructions?"

Dorothy hesitated. "Before you leave, if you have time, find Claudia, and tell her..."

After a beat, Sparky said, "That's not a very clear message."

"Just tell her I'm all right," said Dorothy. The real message, still taking form in her head since the rattlesnake incident, would be more complicated. It could wait.

"Got it. Locate Claudia and tell her to stop worrying about you."

"Say it more kindly than that, please. Tell her I am doing well, and that I hope to see her soon."

"You guys are buds, huh?"

Dorothy thought about that question, in its simplicity. "She's my best friend. And I only just figured that out before this all fell apart. I might be dead, for all she knows, and I don't like the thought of what that must feel like for her." Dorothy left unspoken that she had no way of knowing whether Claudia herself was alive. They last spoke briefly and in panic, with the city in chaos, and the organization Claudia worked for under attack by forces unknown. The unbidden image of Claudia's grave rushed into Dorothy's consciousness. In her desperate attempt to push it away, she said, "Please tell her I miss her."

"Miss her," said Sparky. "Got it."

"No!" Dorothy caught herself up short. "Just... say the thing about hoping to see her soon." Things between Dorothy and Claudia, assuming they both survived to see each other again, were far from resolved. Dorothy saw Claudia as her best friend, itself a new and important discovery for her. However, she also discovered that Claudia had feelings she could not admit, feelings she would assume Dorothy knew nothing about. That would be a tricky conversation. She blushed again at the thought of it.

"Maybe you should write it down," said Sparky.

Dorothy took a deep breath to find her center, frustrated that of all the myriad challenges thrown at her over the last week, not knowing where she and Claudia would stand with each other flustered her the most. "Just tell her I am all right, and that I hope to see her soon, please."

"Okey dokey. I think I got it all, chief," said the pixie. "I'll see you before midnight, hopefully with the cavalry."

"Godspeed."

Sparky flew up a few hundred feet in a graceful spiral, then zipped away, leaving a faint orange trail and tiny sonic boom.

Dorothy watched the pixie trail dissipate. Her eyes lingered there well after the last few sparks faded from view. "Please let today be the day."

At the stroke of midnight that evening, the children asleep with bellies full of partridge, and Strontium inside reading a book, as Dorothy sat on the front lawn waiting for Sparky's return, her environment shimmered and faded from a brush-covered field to a grove of orange trees in full blossom, clearly visible by moonlight.

"Oh, damn," she whispered.

35

TROUBLE

Nearly four weeks after his daughters were taken from him, the hunt for them finally turned up a solid lead. Harrison sat in a conference room plotting a rescue and desperate to launch it. On a wall monitor, he scrolled through image after image from a surveillance drone of a compound deep in the forests of what was once southern Maine. The area itself, a camp of sorts, consisted of a dozen or so small boxy buildings surrounded by an elaborate stone wall with turrets on the corners. Like so many things in the post-Mayhem world, it had a blended aesthetic of the commonplace and the exotic. The buildings, arranged in approximately staggered circles, enclosed a central courtyard comprising paths through a flower garden.

Nothing about this specific setup appeared unusual or suspicious; in the wake of the population surge following the counter-bomb, hundreds of small communities had sprung up in a variety of configurations. Some merged and became small nations unto themselves, others maintained neutrality, and were left in peace. New Chicago was by far the largest sovereign nation to establish a presence in the Western Hemisphere, and while they held an official policy of non-interference, they frowned on smaller nations with more intrusive goals.

Standard procedure on each discovery of a new settlement began with a survey, first by aerial reconnaissance, later by diplomacy. New Chicago recognized the independence of over seventy such microstates, and enjoyed trade relations with many of them. Flyover images of this new community, however, did show cause for concern.

One image showed a woman in three-quarter profile, laughing. In Harrison's opinion, and that of several experts in the agency, this woman was Jessica Williams, one of Harrison's twenty-eight Texas rescues. The other image showed a woman dressed in a black hood and armbands, wearing a samurai sword on her back. Harrison recognized both the sword and the woman wearing it. He had a smaller version of the same blade locked in a case in the basement of this building, and she used to work for him.

None of the other women had yet been identified by face and name, but enough people populated this community that they could all be there. From the available information, no more than a dozen or so people ever left or entered the village through the massive gate on the stone wall. Because the only picture of Jessica showed her laughing, and because she appeared to have the run of the compound, Harrison found it difficult to discern the level of threat to her.

"What are we still doing here?" asked Dallas Rutherford. Overweight, unskilled in meaningful physical activities, and pushing fifty, he left no doubt to everyone else in the room why he was still there, as opposed to out on a rescue mission. That didn't mean they couldn't sympathize with his frustration. Milton brought him into this meeting, along with the other four telekinetics and Aplomado, because his power made him a valuable resource. That no one had requested his opinion was not apparent to him.

"Because we can't rush into a situation we know nearly nothing about," said Harrison. "Without a clear idea of their defenses, or a decent extraction plan, we would be rushing into a fight. Our goal is to get them all out alive. Dealing damage to their captors is a secondary concern."

"You have no idea what you're talking about," said Dallas. "Do you?"

"Actually, the reason I put Agent Milton on this operation is precisely because he does know what he's talking about, and those are his recommendations, and his reasons," said Harrison. "But yes, screw you, Dallas, I do know what I'm talking about, and I'd like to remind you that you work for me. If you could see about shutting the hell up, I'd be delighted not to bring you up on disciplinary charges."

Apryl came up behind him and put her hands on his shoulders. "Don't let him rattle you. We all want to get out there. He's just the only one with no internal editor."

"You should get your ghost pal to go check that place out," said Dallas.

"I can't do that," said Hadley. The ghost stood near the door to the conference room. Several people had already walked past him without seeing him, though every one of them managed to avoid colliding with or passing through him.

"He can't do that," said Harrison, "as I have already pointed out multiple times."

"I'd like to hear that from him," said Dallas.

The beginnings of an ache stirred in Harrison's temples. "Dallas, please stop talking."

"Someone is coming," said Hadley.

"What do you mean?" said Harrison.

"What does who mean?" said Sarah Logan. "Are you talking to the ghost again?"

Harrison put his hand up to shush her, but before he could ask Hadley to elaborate, Sparky came shooting through the door in a shower of orange lights. She stopped short in front of Harrison's face. Scratches dotted her arms and legs, and a smear of something tarry tracked across the left side of her face. "We have a problem."

"Sparky!" shouted Apryl. "Where's Melody? Is she all right?"

"I don't know and I don't know." Sparky looked back at the doorway. "Do you all know there's a ghost in here?"

"Focus!" shouted Harrison. "What's that on your cheek?"

She frowned, then drew her finger across the smear, pulled it away and looked at it. Her eyes flew open in horrified shock. "Ew! Ew! Ew! Napkin! Napkin!" Milton managed to get a tissue into her hand before she completely fell apart, and she scrubbed furiously at her cheek and finger. She threw the soiled tissue to the floor, and flew around Harrison to hide from it behind him.

"What is that?" he asked again.

She gulped. "Goblin blood."

36

GOBLINS

Dorothy sat alone in a wooden lawn chair as the sun crept over the edge of the orange trees. Thousands of blossoms splayed out like tiny white starfish. Some trees had the beginnings of fruit, small, hard, and dark green. They looked for all the world like limes, and Dorothy might have mistaken them for such, or unripe lemons, but for the smell. She knew the sweet, citrusy aroma of orange blossom well, and she had spent the night outside under its blanket for comfort.

She stretched her arms out, watching the wide blue shawl draped over them slide gracefully toward her shoulders. She had not worn her own white shirt and blue jeans since the day she went swimming, although they waited for her in a dresser, laundered and neatly folded. She and Strontium were close enough in size to make borrowing outfits from her ideal, particularly with a magical cinch or tuck here and there. Dorothy's need for fresh clothes every day satisfied, she felt no compulsion to wear her own. Now, dressed in a flowing blue fringed skirt, black sheer top, the shawl, and knee-high leather boots, she felt entirely out of her aesthetic, but cherished the change from simplicity to a touch of wildness. If Claudia could see her in this getup, she would laugh, and tell her she looked like she had fallen off a Stevie Nicks album cover. Imagining her making that joke, Dorothy felt momentarily warm, and smiled. The tiny joy did not last long.

Strontium emerged from the front door of the Random Cabin, up with the dawn as was her habit. She drew in a deep breath through her nostrils, and loudly sighed out her pleasure at the fragrance. This first moment of the day, so pure and beautiful, beckoned Dorothy. Strontium looked so radiant, as if she hadn't just rolled out of bed, surrounded by lush trees and lovely scents. Dorothy desperately wanted to drink it in and have it be all that mattered. But she could not.

"You're up early," said Strontium.

"Or late," said Dorothy.

Strontium crossed her arms and scowled like a concerned parent. "Tell me you didn't sit up all night."

"Sparky's gone."

"Already?" said Strontium.

"Still," said Dorothy.

"Oh." Strontium's face fell in realization. "Well, that's a tough break." She sat down on the grass beside Dorothy's lawn chair, expressing no concern about planting herself on the dew-covered ground, and sure to be magically dry by the time she stood again.

"I think this arrangement just turned permanent," said Dorothy to her host.

"Their loss, our gain," said Strontium. "You know you still have choices, though. Don't ever think you're trapped here."

"It's not that simple," said Dorothy. "This is a big setback. I don't know what to do next."

"You'll figure it out."

"I wish I could believe that." As much as she accepted Strontium's words intellectually, deep down, she thought only of her failure to return Melody to her parents, and that she would never see Claudia again.

═══

Dorothy kept her news from Melody. For the day, at least, she should be allowed to think she would go home soon. Melody had been as accommodating as one could reasonably expect from a five-year-old ripped away from her parents for four weeks, and Dorothy knew that with anyone but her big sister she would have fallen apart by now. But politely, patiently, and with a strangely mature understanding that this was not really a vacation, the questions about going home had begun. And soon those questions would be answered permanently, and negatively, and Melody and Dorothy would cry together, their hearts both broken. But not today.

Dorothy sat outside on the lawn, while Ian taught Melody how to play chess, on a board carved into a tree stump. They sat opposite each other on stone stools, and stared at the board. Melody already knew checkers, as Ian discovered earlier in the week when she beat him handily in what he thought was her first lesson. Strontium had gone off to hunt whatever game would be this day's food, but judging from their surroundings, Dorothy suspected it might be something along the lines of raccoon. For her part, Dorothy used the day to read, a favorite leisure activity she had neglected of late. As it happened, Strontium's library, well-stocked with spell books, also included a smattering of literature from the real world, perhaps to better understand it. On chapter two of *Anna Karenina*, the goblin arrived.

Dorothy saw him when she looked up to give her eyes a break, and gasped. There had been no warning, no sounds of him approaching, no brush moving in the distance. The yard went from no goblins to one goblin in the blink of an eye.

He stood there, scratching his back and the side of his head with a knobby wooden club. He wore armor, fashioned from dull metal, held together with leather straps and no small amount of twine. That he had managed to come through the orange grove in that ensemble without making appreciable noise unnerved her. He stood about five feet. That gave Dorothy a seven-inch advantage she had no idea how to use, particularly as this fat creature surely weighed three times what she did. His skin was a greenish-gray, or perhaps a grayish-green, depending on the angle of the sunlight, bumpy, and covered in patches of thin hair.

He looked at Dorothy, and as she locked eyes with him, her attempts to find intelligence there met with failure. As calmly as she could, she ran through every scenario she could imagine of what would happen next. Her prospects of disarming him were not great, but if he made any move she considered a threat, she would buy the children the seconds they needed to get into the house and lock the door with her life. As she thought this, his gaze shifted to the children, and she prepared to spring.

"What ya playin'?" he said, his voice unexpectedly squeaky for so brutish a creature. The children met his question with a silence Dorothy found terrifying, but the goblin seemed to think simply awkward. He waved his hand. "Sorry. Don't mean ta interrupt. Go on."

"It's chess," said Melody.

For the first time since this new arrival, Dorothy looked at her sister. Her expression indicated curiosity, by contrast to Ian's unconcealed panic.

"He's teaching me. Do you know how to play?"

"Melody, sweetheart," said Dorothy, "don't bother the nice man."

The goblin started at this, and turned to look behind himself, which he did in both directions. "Is there a nice man?" he asked, a hint of confusion or perhaps fear in his voice. Dorothy ruled that moment of uncertainty to be her window of opportunity, but it passed. "Oh!" He guffawed. "You mean me! No, I ain't no nice man. I'm a goblin, see?" He held up his club as evidence.

"I never saw a goblin before," said Melody.

"And I never seen chess before! So, how about that?" He laughed again.

For a moment, Dorothy considered the possibility that this creature was harmful only to the eyes, and that perhaps he posed no threat.

He made a horrible hawking sound, spat a gob of green goo onto the ground (most of which ended up on his foot), and smacked the club loudly in his open palm, repeatedly. "You can bring the chess with you. I like it."

"Oh damnation," came Strontium's voice from the side of the house. She stood there holding two dead raccoons, and an expression of severe irritation. "A goblin? A goblin! I can't leave the house for an hour without a piece of dung goblin dropping in?"

"Now look here—" said the goblin.

"No, you look here!" She dropped the animals with as much indignation as she could muster. "This is my house! Don't you dare drag your smelly carcass around my pretty lawn!"

Dorothy stood. The goblin focused his attention on Strontium, revealing he could only direct it to one thing at a time. She carefully sidled over to the children. Ian sat frozen in fear. Melody looked somewhere between confused and bored. "We should go in the house," she whispered. Her plan, as best as she could form one, involved racing inside and locking the door, then hoping Strontium feared this goblin as little as she appeared.

"Oh, no you don't!" The goblin clumsily trotted to the door of the house, clattering as he went. Apparently, his hearing made up for his less impressive qualities. That put Dorothy and the children between the goblin and the witch, the worst tactical position on the field. As she tried to regroup in her head, things got worse.

"What's this?" came the voice of another goblin, newly appeared behind Strontium. Before she could scold him as well, he had an arm around her, and a sword at her throat. "Is this them?"

"I think so," said the first goblin.

"We was supposed to find two," said the second. "These is more than two."

"That's better than less than two. Let's take 'em all and throw out the ones we don't need."

"Sister," said Strontium.

Dorothy locked eyes with the witch.

"Stay inside. Lock the door."

"Shut up!" said the first goblin. "You ain't goin' in there!"

"And sister," said Strontium. Her face had gone extremely pale, and her eyelids fluttered. "You're reading the wrong book."

A lot of things happened very quickly after that.

The goblin holding Strontium began to smoke. Before he had a chance to scream properly, flames completely engulfed him, as well as the witch. Though bright, they did not radiate enough heat for Dorothy to feel them, even at less than five feet away. They did however provide more than sufficient heat to do their job. The blaze consumed both bodies within seconds, leaving a pile of fine, smoldering, gray ash, into which the sword dropped without making a sound.

At the sight of his partner being immolated, the other goblin charged, holding the club over his head. Dorothy attempted to pull Melody out of harm's way, but in the fraction of a second it took to get her hands on the little girl's shoulders, Ian shouted, "No!" and threw his hands out in front of him, palms facing their attacker.

The goblin's armor exploded off him. The blast faced away from the children, and several pieces of armor shrapnel struck the wood on the sides of the cabin with loud *bangs*. Every scrap of metal, leather and twine sheared away, leaving him completely denuded. Uninjured, but suitably surprised, he stopped his charge and dropped his club.

"I can see your willy," said Melody.

The goblin, still in a state of shock, looked down to confirm this observation, and in that moment, Dorothy finally saw her chance and took it. She scooped the sword out of the ashes and ran straight at him, screaming, whether from rage or terror unclear even to her. The goblin looked up at the noise at the exact moment she impaled him. Even with the sharp blade, it still took a great deal of effort to push the weapon through his fat torso. As she did this to him, he tried to punch her, but only succeeded in pulling her in closer.

They both toppled over, the goblin on his back with Dorothy still holding the sword, and still trying to push it in further. She yanked it to the side. Black and foul tissue herniated out of the open wound. The goblin shrieked, and eventually gurgled, as stygian ooze streamed from his mouth. Dorothy held onto the sword, cutting and digging with it as much as possible, until his wail became a death rattle. It took a very long time for that to happen.

Finally, panting, she felt Melody's hand on her shoulder.

"He's dead," she said.

Dorothy rolled off the corpse, and kept rolling across the lawn, letting the slight downward incline carry her away from it. The immediate threat vanquished, she sobbed uncontrollably.

After a minute or so of this, Melody said, "Dorrie?"

She willed herself to stop crying, and sat up. Both children sat on the grass next to her.

"What do we do now?" said Ian.

Dorothy looked from the sloppy, black mess of death she had caused to the ashy remains of the person who likely had saved them all with her sacrifice. "We stay in the house. And we lock the door."

37

INTERFERENCE

"Goblin blood?"

This outburst belonged to several people in the room, including Harrison. "What happened to Melody?" he asked sharply.

"She got away," said Sparky. "The goblins didn't even see her. But it took me too long to kill them all, and I didn't make it back in time."

"Sparky, I need you to slow down," said Harrison. "Where are Melody and Dorothy, and what happened with the goblins? In that order, please."

"Melody and Dorothy are in a Random Cabin. I was with them for about four weeks, but I didn't make it back in time yesterday and it left without me. They could be anywhere now."

"I don't know what a Random Cabin is."

"Oh," said the pixie. "A Random Cabin is a house that moves itself every day at midnight to somewhere else. There's no way to know where it will go next."

"Hence random," he said.

"Right! I kept leaving in the morning to find this place, and going back before midnight so I could stay with them. Yesterday I was on my way back after dark, and I found six goblins creeping up on the cabin. I killed them, but it took too long. By the time I got back to the right spot, the house was gone."

"You killed six goblins?" said Milton. "How?"

She shrugged. "A little magic, a little violence. You know. Anyway, when I missed the house I went back to looking for Chicago. This place is way farther north than I thought it was! Oh, hey." She hovered over to where Claudia stood, visibly anxious. "Dorothy says she misses you."

Claudia's eyes went a few degrees wider, but she said nothing in response.

"No, wait." The pixie scratched her head. "That's not right. She said she hoped to see you soon. Yeah, that was it. First she said she hoped to see you, then she said she missed you, then she said just tell you the hope to see you thing. Got kinda turned around there. Sorry."

"That's okay," said Claudia quietly. "Random Cabin? Are we ever going to find them?"

"You can track that," said Hadley's ghost.

"What?" said Harrison.

"How?" said Sparky.

"Can you see Hadley, too?" asked Claudia.

"There are magic detectors in all the GPS satellites," said Hadley. "I saw that when I toured Esoteric a few days ago. I guess the mental block on using magic with technology is gone now?"

"That lifted when Rho'pihm vanished," said Harrison. "We've made a lot of progress since then."

"Progress on what?" asked Aplomado.

"Hadley says we can track the cabin using the GPS satellites," said Harrison.

Aplomado thought for a moment. "Tell him he is correct."

"Tell him I can hear him," said Hadley.

"How does that work?" asked Harrison.

"A Random Cabin is imaginary world magic," said Aplomado. "Very useful for hiding against adversaries who can't travel a thousand miles in a single day, but quite useless against the tools we have in the blended world. We can ask the satellites to identify the pattern of its movements over the last few days or weeks, and use that to find its signature."

Harrison held up his hand as he took out his communicator. "The only detail I need is how long that will take."

"Minutes," said the wizard.

"Larson," said Harrison into the communicator, "we need to borrow the GPS satellites for a few minutes. Highest priority."

"For what?" she asked.

He handed the communicator to Aplomado.

"We need to find an object of magical teleportation," he said. "Random relocation once a day at precisely local midnight. Run a magical sweep through the data from the last two weeks looking for an object with that behavior, and track its present location."

"Give me five minutes," she said.

"Is this good news?" asked Claudia. "Can we find them?"

Harrison looked to Aplomado and Hadley, both of whom nodded.

"It's mixed news," said the wizard. "If we can track them, so can the enemy. Those goblins were sent there, meaning there are probably more of them today."

"We launch this mission right now," said Harrison to Milton. "Starting with a trip to that cabin."

"Hold up," said Dallas. "What happened to waiting until we had enough info? I don't want to charge into a death trap."

"What?" said Harrison. "Five minutes ago you couldn't wait to get in the air! Those two are the only ones left who haven't been taken, and we have a chance to save them!"

"This is reckless!" shouted Dallas. "And don't even try to claim it isn't personal."

"Special Agent Rutherford!" barked Milton.

Dallas jumped at the sound of his name.

"Stand down," said Milton through gritted teeth. "The assistant director is absolutely right. You will get in line, or you will sit this mission out in a cell. Are we clear?"

"Yeah." Dallas slouched. "Yeah, sure. Sorry." He turned a chair to face away from the group and sat in it.

An early report from Larson broke the tense silence. "I can tell you Florida for certain. Give me ten more minutes and I can narrow it down to a square mile."

"Florida," said Harrison to Sparky. "Is that enough to get you there?"

"Show me," she said.

He keyed a screen on the conference table, and a map of North America appeared on it. He highlighted New Chicago, and marked a circle around the center of the Florida peninsula.

"See you when you get there," she said, and zipped out the door.

Harrison looked at Milton, who nodded, and said, "Let's do this. Communicator, please." He took the device from Harrison, and said into it, "We are heading to the landing pad right now. Once you have the coordinates, please upload them to the flier."

With that, Harrison followed Milton out the door, to rescue his daughters while they still had time.

38

GIBBERISH

The door to the Random Cabin locked with a simple Dutch bolt, in polished brass. Dorothy had a hard time believing it provided substantively more security against goblins than if the door had been fastened shut with a Velcro strip. Surely Strontium had magical protections in place, or she wouldn't have advised her and the children to stay in the house behind this lock. Dorothy trusted this idea, and chose to believe this advice had not been the final, deranged words of a lunatic.

The two dead raccoons lay on the floor in the kitchen area. Dorothy scrutinized them from her seat at the table. She had no idea how to cook raccoon, but would likely need to figure it out. They could go a day without food if they had too, but as a long-range plan, she would have to take Strontium's place as both hunter and cook if they were to survive.

As soon as they came inside, Melody took a set of tiny wooden figures out of a chest on the floor, and set them up for her usual imaginative play. The figures were old toys of Ian's he claimed to have outgrown. Dorothy suspected on seeing them over the last few days that they might well have some further significance to the witch of the house, but she had now missed her opportunity to ask.

"Is she coming back?"

Dorothy broke her gaze away from her little sister. Ian stood at the window. From that angle, he would barely have the vantage to see the pile of ash, all that remained of the woman who had cared for him.

"I don't know," said Dorothy honestly. She had seen too many impossible things in her life to accept without question the reality or permanence of Strontium's apparent death, so easily offered for their safety. In the absence of evidence otherwise, however, she would need to proceed as if the witch would never return. Watching Ian gaze out the window in his sadness and worry, she thought back to the moment outside that had truly turned the situation in their favor. "Ian? Can I ask you about what you did earlier?"

"Sure," he said, still looking out the window.

Dorothy got up and walked over to him. Tentatively, she rested a hand on his shoulder. He neither flinched nor moved closer to her. "How did you…" She considered how to word the question. Attack the goblin? Strip his armor off? She didn't grasp exactly what she had seen, let alone how to describe it. Finally, she simply said, "…do that?"

"It was an accident," he said. "I break things."

Melancholy colored his voice, and a note of guilt. Dorothy may not have fully understood what she saw, but one thing she found entirely obvious: that was no accident. "I know," she said softly.

"Did Strontium tell you?"

"Yes," said Dorothy. "But she didn't tell me anything other than that. I don't really know what it means."

He shrugged. "It doesn't mean anything. I break things sometimes. It's not on purpose."

She crouched down to meet him eye to eye, and he broke his gaze away from the window to look at her. "You saved us, Ian. I don't think you did anything wrong. You saved Melody, and me, and you saved yourself. And that means a lot. Please don't feel bad about doing that."

"You killed the goblin."

"But I couldn't have with that armor on him." Dorothy fought back a mild nausea at the memory of her long, upsetting attack and butchery of the monster. When Ian did not respond to this logic, she tried a probing question. "Is that magic? Is that something you learned, that you don't like doing?"

"No," he said. "It's something in me. Strontium tried to fix it, but she said she didn't know how."

Something in him. Not magic. Dorothy made a connection, and looked hard into his eyes. "Ian, how old are you?"

"Eleven," he said.

This number provided the piece of the puzzle Dorothy noticed but couldn't identify when she first met him. Eleven was the least common age of all humans in the post-Mayhem world, for a simple and unfortunate reason. The Mayhem Wave came on May 30, 2004, nine years earlier. Most babies and toddlers who survived that event did not survive it for long. The few immediately found by responsible adults had a chance, but the ones left on their own faced starvation and monsters, with no defense. Even the counter-bomb returnees a year later had a sadly high mortality rate for very small children. Strontium must have found him right away, and cared for him, to his excellent fortune. "Do you know your birthday?"

He shook his head. "We mark it on the Winter Solstice."

Naturally, he wouldn't know the date. Strontium would have found him as a toddler with little coherent knowledge of his previous life. Dorothy, however, did have an idea of his probable birthday given his age, and the fact he had a super-human power that magic could not cure. By her best guess, Ian came into the world on September 11, 2001, the day Americans lost their sense of safety in the global theater, the day a cruel act of monumental violence took thousands of lives. If they ever got back to New Chicago, she would take him to Esoteric Studies, where he would learn the extent of his power, and how to control it. And he would meet Claudia, and Harrison, and the other people like him, who shared historically significant birth dates, and telekinetic powers.

But if so, they had a new challenge. Each power, in some way, linked to the event that occurred on the day the person who wielded it was born. Claudia had the power to be heard at great distances, a reaction against the day that so many voices were silenced in Tiananmen Square. Harrison had the power of freedom, to bypass any lock, real or imaginary, as a metaphor for the day marking and celebrating two centuries of American liberty. Ian's power would reflect the terrible day in history that coincided with his birth, an unfair burden for such a gentle child.

He had the power to destroy.

As Dorothy wrestled with how to communicate this to him, and how to answer questions he would surely have had for his entire life, he broke the moment by saying, "I guess I should go ahead and stew the raccoons."

This startled her out of her ruminations. "Are you up for that?"

"It's my job." With that, he walked to the kitchen and pulled a sharp knife out of a drawer to skin the animals.

Dorothy had no desire to watch that process. She looked out the window to keep her mind off it, but faced carnage out there by far outstripping two butchered raccoons. Right before pulling her eyes away from the mangled, bloody goblin corpse, she caught a glimpse of the copy of *Anna Karenina* she had been reading, now splayed on the ground. She didn't think she would be able to resume reading it even if she had it in her hands, but the notion of escaping into a novel did hold some appeal.

Eyes away from the kitchen, she strolled to the far side of the cabin, where a section of wall consisted only of bookshelves.

At first, she perused the real-world literature shelf where she originally found Tolstoy, but nothing struck her fancy. Then she remembered Strontium's other parting words. Moments before burning herself to ashes, she told Dorothy she was reading the wrong book.

In the desperate hope that Strontium had left her a clue, Dorothy scanned the shelves. If a book existed here with her name on it, or some other sign, it might include a message from the witch, perhaps telling Dorothy what to do next, or perhaps even telling her that Strontium still lived. She would never share that hope aloud with the children, but at that moment, she wanted nothing more than for Strontium to come back, and keep them all safe.

As she ran her finger along the spine of each dusty tome, she hunted for anything that looked like a message. Every few books, she would pull one out that looked unusual, and open it. Each time, she found within page after page of nonsense writing. Strings of letters that made no sense, and suggested no reasonable pronunciation, accompanied by illustrations of creatures or devices she had never seen. Occasionally, she would recognize something. One book held a drawing of a dissected arthropod that strongly resembled something that tried to eat her and Mitchell when they first met Harrison. Another showed a pixie (though thankfully not dissected).

Two dozen or so books into the process, she noticed several lying open at her feet. Such disrespect for books not in her nature, she felt a twinge of guilt for dropping them there, but not strong enough to slow her down. The writing took on aspects she found progressively more interesting as she went. Many of them appeared to be written in different languages, or different alphabets. Fragments of meaning filtered through, possibly from the illuminations, possibly from root words she recognized. Once she caught herself laughing hysterically at something, but when she tried to find it, or recall what she read, she drew a blank.

"Dorrie?" said Melody.

"Not now!" barked Dorothy, instantly disliking her own tone, yet not deviating from her quest. Further and further she dug through the collection, stopping often to study the writing, which by all reasonable analysis, even what she found in languages she could read, consisted of gibberish.

At last, two thirds of the way down the wall, tucked between two much larger books, she found a volume the size of her hand, bound in fine red leather, with no title or writing on the cover or spine. She removed it gently, noticing that unlike the rest of the library, it had no coating of dust. She lifted the front cover, heart racing in anticipation. Inscribed there, she found the hand-written words, "For my Sister Dorothy."

The words looked back at her in curly and ornate penmanship, the last word quintuplely underlined in a wave that folded over itself and ended in a spiral. The ink appeared faded, as if ancient. She closed the book and clutched it to her chest, eyes clenched in victory. Drawing a deep breath through her nose, she found it gave off the scent of roses and cayenne, and she salivated.

"Dorrie?" said Melody again.

"What?" said Dorothy, irritated at the shattered moment.

"The stew is ready."

She took a few moments to process those words. "That can't be right," she said softly. She opened her eyes to the half-light of sunset pouring into the window. It had been right before noon when Ian began to skin the raccoons. Before her stood a wall of shelves, two thirds empty. Scattered about the floor, covering her feet and spread out to as far as halfway across the room, lay many, many books.

The hunger pangs hit her like a chop to the gut. Ian and Melody sat at the table, bowls of raccoon stew steaming in front of them, blowing on spoonfuls before cautiously putting them in their mouths. It smelled glorious, as much from hunger as from the rich, spicy aroma. Her own bowl, already served, waited for her at the table with a spoon and napkin.

She crossed the room, pushing scattered books aside with her feet as she shuffled. She pulled up a seat at the table, and took up her spoon. "Thank you," she said to Ian, who nodded with trepidation in his eyes. She found the stew delicious, ingredients notwithstanding.

"Are you okay?" asked Melody sweetly.

Dorothy had no idea. "Yes, Little. A bit distracted."

They ate in silence for ten or fifteen minutes. Dorothy had no words of explanation or comfort for her young charges. Something had consumed her for an entire afternoon, and she hadn't even been aware of the passage of time. The prospect of continuing as the head of this witch's household now filled her with an apprehension she could not describe, and as she mentally promised to stay more attuned to her surroundings, she noticed her left hand resting on the book, where she now understood it had been the entire time she sat at the table.

She stood with her empty bowl, and took it to the kitchen. A hand pump at the sink drew clean water from somewhere Strontium never disclosed. She rinsed her bowl, and put it in a drying rack. Holding the kitchen counter with both hands, she took a deep breath to center herself, and undo the stress of this day. Voices from outside interrupted that attempt.

"Aw!" someone shouted. "What's this! That's disgusting!"

"Oof!" said another. "What happened to him, eh?"

"I dunno," said the first, "but that makes me wanna puke! Don't that make you wanna puke?"

"Nah," said the second. "That ain't nothin'. I seen bigger messes than that poor bastard."

They spoke of the goblin corpse in screechy voices, likely goblins themselves. Dorothy looked to the table, where both children sat frozen and wide-eyed. She put her finger to her lips, and pointed down. Both children climbed off their seats and scooted under the table. Dorothy crept to the bar, where she crouched low enough to almost conceal herself, while still being able to peek over the edge.

"What do you think happened to him?" said the second voice. "Looks like he lost a fight, but bad!" He followed this up with sickening laughter.

"You suppose whoever done this to him is still around?" asked the first, notes of fear in his voice.

Dorothy looked across the room to the sword, leaning against the wall by the door, and tried to calculate how quickly and quietly she could get herself to it.

"Don't see how," said the second. "There's no cover here."

Dorothy tried to understand that remark, so foolish on its face. Setting aside the fact of the dense orange grove with plenty of hiding places, there was also the matter of the house they occupied.

"What about this here house?" said the first, echoing her thoughts, followed by the sound of wood on metal. "Ow!"

"Idiot! No one's in there! Just look at it, will you?"

"Ya didn't have ta hit me!" cried the first voice.

Whatever protection surrounded the house, its effects became clearer to Dorothy. They would never look inside, because it somehow appeared from the outside to be vacant. At least it appeared that way to one of them. Evidently it was an imperfect shield, which worried Dorothy.

While she pondered the possible reasons why one goblin might see through it while the other did not, a face appeared in the window, and looked straight at her. For a moment, the goblin looked confused, although she had difficulty reading his repulsive face. Then he said, "Hey..."

Whether he saw her, or had some other observation to share, she never learned, because his head exploded against the glass. Covered in black, tarry blood, the window now blotted out what light still shone through it from outside, and Dorothy could not see what happened without moving to another vantage point. Crashes, screams, and more crashes came from outside. After half a minute of this, all fell to silence. Finally, a soft tapping came from the other window. Motioning the children to stay put, Dorothy crossed the room, taking a moment to pick up the sword. At the other window she found Sparky knocking on the glass.

"Don't open the door!" shouted the pixie. "Let me in the window!"

Dorothy complied, carefully opening the pane and slamming it shut with the pixie inside. Sparky was covered in tiny scratches, and spattered with two different colors of blood. She flew straight to the sink, where she kicked the pump repeatedly and dunked herself under the flow.

"I am so glad to see you!" said Dorothy. "Strontium is..." She nearly said, "dead," then remembered for Ian's sake to soften it to, "gone."

"Gone where?"

"Not sure," said Dorothy. "What just happened?"

"Goblins," said Sparky. "One of them almost saw through the glamour on this house. Must be a pretty bright boy, for a goblin. You all right in here?"

"I think so." The children emerged from their hiding place, nervous, but stable. "The goblins?"

"Dead," said Sparky. "And rescue is coming. Harrison found the house using techno jiggery pokery. He should be here in a couple of hours."

A wave of relief washed over Dorothy. "That's very good news."

"Yeah. Just sit tight here. We'll have you all back home in no time. Claudia's coming, too. That should cheer you up!" Sparky grinned as she delivered this bonus news. Dorothy's heart skipped a beat on hearing it. She honestly couldn't think of anyone else in the world she would be happier to see, but also felt nervous about the conversation they would eventually need to have. One thing at a time.

"What if more goblins come before that?" asked Ian.

"Then I'll take them out!" Sparky rolled her fists in front of her face. "We've got this. I promise."

"I'm holding you to that," said Dorothy. "Kids, you heard the pixie. We're getting rescued soon. Let's clean up."

The children took their bowls to the sink. A meaningless task, but it gave them focus and purpose, which they would need to get through the next few hours. For their next job, she would ask them to help clean up the mess she made of the bookshelves. On that thought, she looked down at the little red book in her hand, and could not recall exactly when she had picked it up.

======

About ninety minutes later, more voices arrived outside. The children had curled up on the couch, and fallen asleep, most likely from stress. Cautiously, Dorothy moved closer to the door.

"This will be the pixie's work," said a male voice she did not recognize. It sounded strangely arrogant, impressive given how few words the man spoke. More importantly, it sounded human.

"Clearly," said a female voice. This one she did recognize, and it filled her with relief. "The children should be nearby."

"Perhaps the house?" said the male voice.

"Perhaps," said the woman. Like the clever goblin, they half-saw through the glamour on the house. Dorothy looked at Sparky, who had a hand up to her ear, and a finger to her lips.

"Is that them?" whispered Dorothy.

"I think so," whispered Sparky. "The woman sounds like an agent I know."

"Me, too," said Dorothy, the last of her hesitance draining away. She went to the door and pulled the bolt. Light spilled out of the cabin into the evening darkness, illuminating two people. One was a man, dressed in a gray robe and hood that made it difficult to identify him. But the other wore a familiar face, a pleasure to see.

"Agent Kestrel?" said Dorothy, finally allowing herself to relax.

The woman, Felicia, smiled. She wore different garb than her usual NCSA attire, and her dark curls peered out from under a black hood. "Hello, Miss O'Neill," she said, as she let herself in.

39

EN ROUTE

It took less than an hour to get the flier loaded and cleared for takeoff. Now into mid-afternoon, even at their top speed it would be after sundown before they reached the target site in Florida, but well before the critical time of midnight.

"Sparky is there by now," said Harrison to Apryl. She had not spoken since boarding the flier. He shared her stress at their daughter's vulnerability, but willed himself to believe this would all end well. "She will protect them."

Apryl didn't look at him. "I know."

"She took out six goblins by herself."

"I know."

Her blank expression, while understandable, concerned him. "This will be over in a couple of hours, Apryl."

"No, it won't," she said, finally looking at him. "It will be over when whoever is gunning for our child is dead."

"That's next on the agenda. Once you teleport Melody and Dorothy back to New Chicago, Milton will take the rest of us to Maine, and we will end this."

Part of Apryl's frustration stemmed from her inability to teleport directly to Melody's side right away. That power required either a working knowledge of her destination, or an intuitive sense of the right place to go, and she had neither. She nodded in response to Harrison's reassurance, but his words would mean nothing until she held Melody in her arms.

Milton got up from his seat and said something to Sarah, who nodded. He made his way back to Harrison and Apryl, stopping along the way to check in with Aplomado and a few specific members of the strike team. Harrison noted he walked right past Hadley, who sat invisibly in one of the few empty seats. When Milton got to their seats, he crouched down to make eye contact. "Mrs. Mendoza-Cody, are you clear what happens when we hit the ground?"

She nodded. "You want me on point? Is that the right word?"

"Correct. You and Logan are our heaviest hitters. If we encounter the enemy, you are to take out any weapon they have that has a power source. If you are directly engaged in hand-to-hand, you are to teleport out of harm's way without hesitation."

"That will happen whether you order it or not," she said. "It's a reflex."

"That's good. Remember, our one objective is to secure your daughter and Miss O'Neill and get them back to the city, and you are their fastest ticket home. You are not to put yourself at risk for any reason."

"If Melody is in danger, all bets are off," she said.

"Understood. Here's hoping that won't be an issue." He looked at Harrison. "Sir? You know your part?"

"I stay in the flier with de Queiroz and Rutherford," he said.

Dallas sat behind them and had thankfully managed to stay quiet for the flight so far. Overhearing this part of the plan, he chimed in. "That's ignorant. You've seen what I can do, Independence. Maybe you and the kid can stay behind, but I should be out there with the commandos."

Harrison turned around to face him. "That's not your call, Dallas."

"Well, maybe it ought to be," he said. "It's not like you're doing such a great job making decisions."

"It's an order, Special Agent," said Milton, "and you will follow it. When we get to Maine, we are going to need you, and you are not going to risk your life before that on pointless heroics. Is that understood?"

"Yes, sir," said Dallas, with no mockery or bitterness in his tone. Whatever skill Harrison lacked to keep Dallas in line, Milton had it in abundance. Harrison had not worked closely with Dallas in the eight years they had known each other, primarily because until these last two weeks, Alec generally viewed his power as a joke. His usefulness finally becoming apparent, he now revealed himself as a petulant jerk.

Apryl put her hand on Harrison's knee. "Do not let him get to you. You need to be at a hundred percent right now."

He took a deep breath and blew it out. "I know, I know. I'll be okay. In three hours you will have Melody safe back home. My eye is on the ball, I promise." He leaned in close and whispered in her ear, "I will save kicking his ass for when the mission is over. It will be my reward."

That got a weak smile from her, the first he had seen in days. Soon, this tension would be resolved. Melody would be with her mother, Harrison would be in Maine rescuing the others, and everything would be fine.

All they had to do was get to the cabin in Florida before the enemy did.

40

FELICIA

Agent Kestrel walked into the cabin wearing many knives. In addition to the sword on her back, she had at least two blades strapped to each limb of various sizes and shapes. In a world with no guns, the NCSA armed their field agents with such weapons, but Dorothy had never seen them so emphasized. Perhaps this represented a uniform she had never had occasion to see before. She briefly toyed with picturing Claudia in it. Felicia took a few slow steps around the main room, glancing into corners.

"That's a new look for you," said Sparky.

Felicia did not look at her. "Tim. Pixie."

The man in the gray robe had entered the house at this point, holding a gnarly wooden staff. At Felicia's spoken command, he thrust it upward, and a ball of white lightning shot from the tip, directly at Sparky.

She had no time to react. Her wings vanished, and she dropped to the floor. The impact made a sound like an iron bar falling onto concrete, and resonated for a full two seconds.

"Sparky!" Melody ran to her and scooped her up, then looked back at Dorothy, worry in her eyes. "She's stiff."

It took Dorothy a second to overcome her own surprise at this attack. "What have you done?" She gently took Sparky's immobile form from Melody's hands. The pixie felt cool to the touch, and stone hard, like a glass figurine. Her arms and legs all held poses partially extended and bent, matching the look of shock frozen on her face. Dorothy carefully laid her on the surface of the table, mostly on her back, her rigid limbs rendering graceful placement impossible.

As calmly as she could, she took Melody's hand, and held out her other for Ian. The boy looked at her with wide, frightened eyes, and took her offered hand. She drew both of them to her. In her quick assessment of their situation, she considered the possibility of some terrible misunderstanding, or of Felicia protecting them all from a rogue pixie (or believing so). The appearance of three armored goblins in the doorway negated both those feeble hopes.

She glanced at the sword she had stolen, propped against a chair about five paces from her current position, and futilely estimated the time it would take her to get to it and dispatch all five opponents. Her skills with a blade limited to skewering a naked, defenseless goblin, and clumsily at that, Felicia's training would surely outmatch her own.

"Is there anyone else here?" asked Felicia, still sweeping the room with her eyes.

"No," said Dorothy. The children trembled against her, Ian considerably more frightened than Melody to judge from the intensity of his vibrations. With Sparky out of commission, Ian represented their only hope of victory or escape. "Ian," she whispered. "Can you…?"

He shook his head, lip trembling.

"Are these the girls?" asked the cloaked man Felicia had called Tim. As he spoke, he lifted his hood, exposing a sickly white head, completely hairless and covered in abstract tattoos.

"They are indeed," said Felicia, finally looking at Dorothy with a sinister smile.

Dorothy locked eyes with her, and in that moment, she knew the enemy had completed their collection. And Dorothy had let them right in the door, on the trust of a familiar voice. She would have died to protect Melody against any threat, but she could not protect anyone from her own naiveté.

"And the boy?" asked Tim coldly.

Dorothy pulled Ian closer.

"Disposable, I would say." Felicia browsed the arsenal she wore, doubtless looking for the ideal tool to cut a little boy to death with finesse. With what seconds she had before that happened, and in a desperate hope she read this situation correctly, Dorothy threw out a wild gamble.

"You stay away from my son," she said, with narrowed eyes.

Felicia laughed. "Your what now?"

"My son! Under New Chicago law, I am this boy's mother."

Felicia's brows rose at this, and Dorothy's heart pounded at the hope she had pushed the right button. The assassin shook her head. "I don't think so. But high marks for effort. There is no way you were his first adult contact since Mayhem."

"No, but I was his first adult contact after your monster orphaned him. The law still applies." She stared Felicia down. "This boy is every bit as much my son as I am Harrison Cody's daughter."

Those, it turned out, were the right words. Felicia froze. "Tim?"

He hesitated. "If the child is the grandson of a Power, we dare not kill him."

Dorothy's heart, already working on overdrive, pressed hard against her chest at that statement.

Felicia pursed her lips. "Well played, Miss O'Neill."

"Thank you," said Dorothy, attempting to feel in control. It came out a bit choked, but she stood by it.

"You should know this is only a reprieve," said Felicia.

"Silence!" said Tim, glaring at her.

Dorothy took in everything she could glean from that exchange. Ian's life would be spared now, but taken later. That fate awaited all three of them. But his instant adoption had bought them some time. Time for a plan. Time for her father to swoop in and rescue them all, like the hero he was. With Felicia obviously disgruntled by this development, opportunities might arise to throw her off her game. When the moment came, Dorothy would play her secret weapon, the little boy trembling in her arms right now, who could probably kill them all with a touch. Or a thought. She held a very big gun. Now she needed time to figure out how to pull the trigger.

"Outside," said Felicia. The joy of this successful hunt, so evident earlier, drained from her demeanor.

"Dorrie?" said Melody.

"It's all right," she lied. "We're going to be all right. I promise."

The little girl hugged her as hard as she could.

Felicia drew her sword. "Outside! I'm sworn to bring you in alive. Undamaged was not part of the agreement."

"Come on." Dorothy ushered both children to the door with her arms around them. They stepped out into the cool spring night. Outside, at least a dozen goblins roamed the grounds, some with torches. Two of them spread a broad, circular blanket on Strontium's lawn.

"In the bag," said Felicia.

Dorothy walked to the cloth and sat down in its center. She put Melody on her lap, and curled her arm around Ian, sitting by her side.

"We're okay," she whispered again. "I've got you both, and I won't ever let go."

The two goblins pulled the sides of the sack up over their heads. They cinched the top shut with a loudly rattling chain, cutting off the torch light, and leaving Dorothy and her children in darkness. She pulled them tighter to her. "Hold on," she said, hoping her fear did not come through in the words.

Melody gasped, Ian cried, and Dorothy's stomach felt as though it had dropped out of her body, as the bag swiftly ascended with them inside. The sounds of their own fear disappeared under the heavy beat of giant bat wings.

41

TOO LATE

The flier reached the cabin well after dark, but still hours before midnight. Harrison was relieved to find the house still there, illuminated by floodlights from the flier, less so by the carnage surrounding it as they got closer. "What is that?"

"Goblins," said Aplomado. "Dead. One stabbed, two death by pixie, by the look of it."

"That's good, right?" said Apryl. "Sparky protected them, right?"

Harrison walked to the front of the flier, where Milton double-checked body armor and weapons. "I'm coming with you."

"Negative, sir," said Milton. "I've got this."

"Those are my daughters."

"And this is a tactical decision. Respectfully, sir, I strongly recommend you stay in the bird."

As the flier made its slow, vertical descent, more details became apparent, most troubling that the cabin put out almost no light. "Sparky should have made contact by now," said Harrison under his breath. "What is she waiting for?"

"I will let you know in less than a minute, sir," said Milton.

"David, I'm not going to wait here for news."

"Is he going?" shouted Dallas from the rear. "Cos if he's going, I'm going!"

"No, you're not," said Harrison firmly.

"Try and stop me!" Dallas unbuckled his belt.

"Rutherford, stay in your seat!" ordered Milton.

"Yes, sir," said Dallas.

Under other circumstances, Harrison would ask Milton how he did that. It would be a worthwhile topic of conversation for the ride home. For now, all he wanted to talk about was the fact Milton's authority on this mission did not extend to keeping him waiting here while they went into that house and found his little girl, or her remains.

"Agent Milton," he said, as the flier touched down.

Milton held up his hand. "Not now, sir, please. Logan, Mrs. Mendoza-Cody, I need you at the hatch."

Both women stood and moved to the side door, where they waited with obvious apprehension. Four more agents stood and prepared to follow them. Apryl's objectives were clear enough. Take out weapons, flee if attacked. Sarah's job was less obvious. Outfitted with night vision goggles, she would scan the enemy's equipment for anything that looked enough like a clock to freeze. Up against nothing but goblins with medieval weapons, this would not end up being useful, but if their opponents carried technology, locking it down might put them at a disadvantage. Though Milton reassured her the other agents would treat her protection as the highest priority, Sarah did not keep her misgivings about this task a secret.

The hatch hissed and slid aside, and in the second it took Sarah and Apryl to work up the proper courage to step down the ramp, Claudia launched herself from her seat and dove between them.

"Damn it!" said Milton. "Go!"

Sarah and Apryl jumped out the door, lighting the scene ahead of them with powerful headlamps. Claudia had not taken the time to don one of those, and raced through the dark to get to the house. The four agents followed, as did Milton. Harrison charged after them.

Agents combed the grounds with their lights, swords drawn. Sarah stayed close to one of them, looking around her with wide eyes. Apryl and Claudia nowhere in sight, Harrison had no doubt they had both run straight into the cabin. Claudia's distant cry of "Dotty! Dotty!" confirmed that conjecture as well as the conclusion his daughters were no longer here. At least one agent had entered the house with them, as evidenced by the two dancing beams of light in the windows. Mentally declaring it secure, he went after them.

Up close, the dead goblins looked predictably grizzlier than they had from the air. One of them lay naked and gutted like a fish, though with less precision than Harrison had seen from fishermen of his acquaintance. One lacked a head, its remnants spattered across a large section of outside wall. A third had been thoroughly pulverized and sprayed over the lawn. Harrison's stomach turned slightly, less from the sight of gore than from the realization that his pixie had done this.

He entered the house. Apryl and Claudia were sitting at a table, the former with her head buried in her arms, crying, the latter curiously staring at some object there. "Get the wizard!" said Claudia. She looked up at the people not running out the door to obey her command, and shouted, "Now!"

"Do it," said Harrison to the agent, who ran for the flier. Harrison shined his headlamp on the table, illuminating a human-shaped statue, in an uncomfortable-looking pose, the size of a pixie. "Oh, God." He sat next to Claudia. "Don't touch her."

"I didn't."

"Is there any sign of them?" he asked as cautiously as he could.

Claudia shook her head.

Profoundly grateful to learn that his wife wept over their abduction rather than the discovery of their bodies, he got up and crouched by her side, gently rubbing her back.

She whirled on him. "We have to get her back." She held a strikingly controlled tone for the amount of moisture covering her face.

"I know," said Harrison.

"I mean right now," she said. "We need to go to Maine, right now. That's where they have her, right?"

"We think so," said Harrison.

"Then we have to go there!"

Milton entered. "That's exactly what we are going to do, ma'am. I'd like to be in the air in five minutes, so whatever you need here, you better grab it."

Apryl took that cue to grab Harrison, and hold him tightly.

"Where is she?" asked Aplomado, entering the room.

"Here." Claudia scooted away from the table and held her arms toward it.

Aplomado moved to Sparky's immobile form, and held his hands about a foot over her body He muttered some incantations, then dipped his hand into his robe. He brought it out in a fist. Leaning over the pixie, he blew gently into his hand, spraying her with fine, white powder. It settled on her like dust. After a few seconds, she glowed orange beneath it, and issued a tiny cough, followed by a loud sneeze.

"Crap!" She sneezed four more times, each more powerful than the last. "Crap!" she shouted between sneezes, when possible. Finally, she shook herself, sending the dust everywhere, and her wings sprouted gracefully from her shoulder blades. "What did I miss?"

"We don't know," said Harrison, still holding Apryl, her head buried in his shoulder. "What's the last thing you remember?"

"Your cute-as-a-button assistant girl, covered in knives," she said. "Then somebody zapped me. Ow. Is she an assassin? She looked like an assassin."

Felicia. "Yes. And not one of ours."

"Oh," said Sparky. "Damn. We shouldn't have let her in, should we?"

"No."

"Oh, boss, that's my fault. I'm so sorry."

"Don't do that," he said. "We'll sort out blame when everyone is safe. Most of it is going to be mine, so don't do that again. I need you at your best. Got it?"

"Got it!"

"Heading out," said Milton. "Phase two starts right now."

"Hey," said Harrison to Apryl, gently. "Let's go rescue our little girl, okay?"

She looked up again, face soaking wet. "Do you think she's still alive?"

"Honestly? That's the only thing I feel completely sure of right now. Someone went to a lot of trouble to round up our children. Jessica is alive, so I think they all are."

"Then what are we waiting for?" Apryl picked herself up, took a moment to plant a kiss on Harrison, and marched boldly back to the flier.

42

GLOW

The sensation of flying provided less discomfort and terror than Dorothy expected. Though concerned the bag would suffocate them, they had plenty of room. Tiny air holes peppered the fabric, each reinforced with a grommet. Dozens of points of cool breeze brushed her skin through them. Unfortunately, they did a poor job of letting in moonlight.

Both children clung to her, in obvious fear for their lives. She had expected some crying, but they reacted to their situation with silence.

"Melody?" whispered Dorothy.

"Yeah?" said the little girl.

"How are you doing?"

"Okay." A rote answer, but she had enough of her wits about her to engage on a basic, social level, which Dorothy chose to find encouraging.

"Ian?" whispered Dorothy, looking for some confirmation there as well.

"What?" he whispered back.

"Are you okay?"

"I don't think so," he said. "Why are we whispering?"

A fair point. "I don't know," said Dorothy in a normal tone of voice. "I guess I didn't want to frighten you."

"It's not you I'm frightened of," he said.

Dorothy had no adequate response to that. They went back to riding out their journey in silence. Without a watch, Dorothy had lost her sense of the passage of time. She assumed it had been at least an hour, but it might have been two. Or ten minutes. With no idea where they were going, nor a way of measuring the speed of the giant bat carrying them, she had no way of knowing how long she should expect to stay in this bag. She hoped it would be some amount of time less than it took for the children to discover they had full bladders.

At some point, she noticed she held her book.

She caressed the leather, cool and pebbly against her hand, and tried to remember how she had kept it hidden from Felicia long enough to take it with her. Then she tried to remember why she would bother hiding it at all, or taking it with her for that matter. The important thing was she had it. That was all that mattered. And as she thought that, she noticed something for the first time, something she should have noticed before. She could see the book.

Breaking the total darkness, the red cover stood out faintly but noticeably. She tried to focus on it, with limited success, and mentally wished it were easier to see. The brightness of the red glow increased, and she could not only make out details on the cover now, but it threw off a strong enough glow she could see her fellow passengers.

Neither child wore the terror-stricken look she had prepared for. They did however look at the book with a curiosity that might be enough to distract them from thinking about how they would be treated once they reached their destination. Dorothy made it glow brighter, simultaneously realizing she had control of it.

"What is that?" asked Melody.

"It's a night light," said Dorothy. "I can make it bright enough to see by, or I can turn it off if you decide you like the dark, I think."

"Leave it on!" said both children.

The soft, red glow added a layer of desperately needed comfort to their captivity, and after a while, the bag filled with the sound of two children softly snoring.

With Melody fast asleep on her, Dorothy shifted her arms to open the book and read it. It acted as its own book light. At first, as with other books she had carefully examined in Strontium's library, unintelligible writing filled every page. In some cases, she questioned whether the symbols in front of her represented writing at all. So, when she finally tuned in to her own voice and realized she had been reading it aloud, she gasped, and slammed it shut.

The light went out, leaving her in total darkness again. She took several deep breaths, then calmly willed the book to resume glowing. It did. She cautiously opened it to a random page and found gibberish. Attempting to read it aloud, she stumbled over every potential pronunciation, and after a few minutes of this, she gave up. Something had happened earlier she did not know how to reproduce.

With a sigh, she set the book down on the cloth, resting her hand on it. The glow faded, but long before her environment went dark again, she fell asleep.

They all woke with a *thud*. The top of the bag dropped down on their heads, and in her half-awake state, Dorothy nearly screamed. She stopped herself only because Melody screamed first, and her duty as the little girl's nanny kicked in. She held Melody closer, and rocked her, making soft hushing sounds. Melody's cries became whimpers.

"We stopped," said Ian.

"I know," said Dorothy, pulling him in closer.

Chains rattled. The top of the bag opened in a circle that threw pale, white light onto them, and Dorothy shielded Melody's eyes, shutting her own. With a rustle of cloth, the bag fell away from them, exposing them to cool, fresh air. She dreaded what she would see when she finally found the courage to open her eyes. Tentatively lifting her lids ever so slightly, she winced at the light streaming in, but held her ground against it, determined to face whomever or whatever awaited her. A human figure resolved itself from blur to familiar face.

"Hello, Dorothy," said Siobhan Roark, offering the warmest of smiles, and extending her hand to help them up. "Welcome."

As Dorothy struggled to find a safe or meaningful response to this greeting from her friend, she felt around her for the book, and came up empty.

[43]

COLD TRAIL

The flier reached what had once been the Maine/New Hampshire border as the sun pushed its edge over the horizon. Another ten minutes to the compound, they made one high altitude flyover to assess the immediate level of resistance it would offer to an incursion. The images from that surveillance proved not at all what Harrison expected.

"What am I looking at?" he asked Milton. They inspected several photographs, one at a time, on a monitor in the cockpit. "What happened here?"

"Unclear," said Milton.

On the screen, a shot of the compound looked much as it had when Harrison last saw images of it two days earlier, though with no activity, and several dead goblins strewn randomly around the area.

"You're one hundred percent certain they are still alive and healthy?" Harrison asked Aplomado, for the third time in as many minutes.

"Absolutely," he said.

Harrison took valuable consolation from this information, especially now that it seemed likely his daughters' rescue would not happen as soon as he hoped. And even more so given the evidence of violence below. "Is it possible they escaped?"

"I'd rather not speculate before we're on the ground," said Milton.

"I understand," said Harrison, who very much wanted to speculate before then, but chose to keep that to himself. "I need to update Apryl."

"All right."

Harrison excused himself from the cockpit, and found Apryl and Claudia sitting in the back of the flier. Both had eager looks to them, but waited for him to speak.

"Aplomado says they are still alive and doing well," he said.

"But they're not here," said Apryl.

He hesitated. "The compound looks abandoned. We're going to check that out." He took Apryl's hand. "They are going to be all right."

She squeezed his hand. "I know. I'm... I don't know exactly how to say this. I can sense Melody."

His brows rose at this. "What do you mean?"

"I don't know what I mean," she said. "I just can. I know she's not hurt."

"Have you always been able to do that?"

"No," she said. "It started today. I can't explain it. I just know it's true. It feels like another power, but I don't understand it well enough to describe it better than that. I'm sorry."

"Don't be," he said. Apryl's abilities represented one of the more prominent unsolved mysteries at Esoteric for the past eight years. Unlike the other telekinetics, Apryl possessed powers based in magic, and she manifested new ones at random, about twice a year. Most were unspectacular, and not all of them lasted. "I'm glad you sense her. We both need that right now."

"What about Dotty?" asked Claudia, hungry hope in her eyes.

Apryl shook her head. "I don't know. If Aplomado says she is all right, I think you can trust in that. But I can only sense Melody."

Harrison's stomach experienced a brief stint in zero gravity as the flier began its vertical descent. "We're heading in to check out the grounds. Milton will probably want you with him again."

"Tell him I'll pass this time," she said. "I need to focus right now. Make sense of this feeling."

"Is he going to want me?" asked Claudia.

"I wouldn't count on it, after what you pulled last night, but I'll ask." On his way back to the front of the flier, Harrison passed Dallas, who snored at him. He considered letting him sleep, but with Apryl sitting this one out, Milton might want Dallas on the ground. He gave him a gentle shake. "Hey, Dallas."

Dallas snorted, and his eyes popped open. "What? Was I asleep?"

"Yeah," said Harrison. "Time to wake up now. We're landing at the Maine compound. It looks like there's no one there, but we're going in to see if we can find some sign of what happened to the girls. Milton might need you."

"Tell him to forget it," said Dallas gruffly. "I'm staying right here."

Harrison silently counted to five. "That's fine. You're probably safer here anyway." He tried to walk away from further discussion, but Dallas unbuckled and stood up.

"No, wait," he said. "I'm coming. What are we looking for?"

Frustrated by Dallas's whimsical approach to obeying orders, Harrison nearly didn't answer the question. But Dallas would keep asking it, and he preferred talking to him over hearing his voice. "Any kind of clue as to where we should look next."

"I thought you said there's no one there," said Dallas.

"Right," said Harrison. "So, if they've moved to somewhere else, we need to figure out where that is."

"No, that's stupid. We need to go home," said Dallas.

Harrison narrowed his eyes. "Just so I know what kind of insubordination to charge you with, am I hearing correctly you are saying we should abort this mission? Because I'm pretty sure you weren't brought along to offer advice."

"If there's no one there, we shouldn't be here," said Dallas. "This is a stupid waste of time."

"Fine. If it's a stupid waste of time, then you can sit here while we waste it without you."

"No way," said Dallas. "If you're going out there, I'm going out there."

Milton emerged from the cockpit at that moment.

"Well, that's really not up to you," said Harrison. "Agent Milton, will we be needing Special Agent Rutherford for this sweep of the compound?"

"Negative," said Milton. "You should stay in the flier, Rutherford."

"Okey doke!" said Dallas amiably, and returned to his seat.

Stuck somewhere between frazzled and impressed, Harrison asked Milton, "How do you do that?"

"Sir?" asked Milton.

Harrison could not articulate the question without it coming across as asking a subordinate to tell him how to do his own job. "Never mind. Apryl wants to sit this one out. Is that okay?"

"That's her prerogative, as we agreed when she volunteered," said Milton. "We should be okay without her. De Queiroz is to stay in the flier as well. As soon as we secure the area, she and I need to have a conversation."

"She knows," said Harrison.

"Good. Let's do this." Harrison joined him and a handful of agents out the hatch.

STADIUM

Dorothy's eyes adjusted to the light. They had touched down in the middle of a wide open field, surrounded by seats that stretched up for dozens of feet. Overgrown grass covered the field itself, although a section of it had been roughly cut down in the center, where they sat. People (or perhaps goblins) hacked away at the grass with scythes and grass whips, expanding the cleared area foot by foot. Overhead, huge arrays of lights beamed down upon them in the pre-dawn twilight.

They had landed in a sports arena. Dorothy could not tell the exact shape or purpose of the field through the overgrowth, nor identify it as a pre-Mayhem structure or something new. The seats appeared to be twentieth century design, at least from a distance, but giant, ornate columns surrounded them and stood interspersed among them, in alternating stone and wood. It felt like a space for watching some unearthly sport, and her own placement in the center of the playing field gave her an uncomfortable sense of being a gladiator.

Siobhan continued to hold out her hand, a delighted smile on her face. She wore a white and pink sun dress, and its simple beauty emphasized her brilliant red hair and freckled complexion. She radiated a sense of well-being, cleanliness and peace, like a child on Easter morning.

For weeks, Dorothy had pictured this person languishing in some squalid prison, at best. At worst, tortured and dead. "Siobhan?" she said, trying to attach some sense to her situation.

Siobhan laughed. "Hello, sister." She put her hand out farther. Dorothy took it and stood. Siobhan held her hand for a moment, looking her over, then took her in her arms and gave her a warm hug. "I'm so glad you're here," she said into Dorothy's ear. From Dorothy's perspective, there seemed to be even odds on whether that constituted a cry for help or a statement that everything proceeded according to her sinister plan. Neither of those possibilities struck her as promising.

Stepping away from Dorothy, Siobhan held her hand out for Melody. "Hello, Melody. Do you remember me?"

"No," Melody admitted without hesitation or shyness, her demeanor reserved, and almost prickly.

Siobhan giggled softly. "Well, we'll have plenty of chances to get acquainted, I'm sure. Would you like to meet the other children?"

Red flag. "What other children?" asked Dorothy before Melody could respond.

"You'll see. You'll all see. And who do we have here?" Siobhan crouched down in front of Ian. Despite the fear in his eyes, he appeared to take comfort in the appearance of Siobhan as their greeter, and Dorothy couldn't decide whether that was safe or dangerous.

"This is Ian. My *son*." Dorothy stressed that last word as a precaution against anyone else ruling Ian disposable, as Felicia had.

Siobhan's eyes lit up. "Your son! Oh my, you have been busy. How about you, Ian? Would you like to meet the other children?"

By Dorothy's count, at least four things could go terribly wrong in the next few minutes, not the least of which was Ian remembering his gift for breaking things in a way that would not help them. So, it both troubled and relieved her when he simply said, "Sure. How old are they?"

"Mostly Melody's age," said Siobhan. "A few older, a few younger. None as old as you, though. At least I don't think so. It's best if we all just go to meet them. They will all be getting up for breakfast in an hour or so. That should give us enough time to get you all healed."

Another red flag. "We don't need to be healed." Dorothy picked up Melody and held her on her hip. "We're all fine."

"Oh, I'm sure you are," said Siobhan. "But there's always room for improvement, don't you think? I'll bet you have little health issues you don't even know about. I sure didn't know about mine until they were gone. Apparently, I had a reflux problem. I can sing higher notes now. Isn't that funny?"

Dorothy considered it curious that Siobhan had cause to sing at all. "Siobhan, Harrison is very worried about you. We all are. Are you sure you're okay?"

She smiled again. "I'm fine, Dorothy. You'll understand soon. We'll get you all healed up and then I'll introduce you to the Professor. He will explain everything."

Red flag number three. "Tell me about the Professor," said Dorothy.

"Oh, he's amazing," said Siobhan. "You'll love him. You really will. He has been so good to us. Taught us things about ourselves none of us knew. He calls us Mayhem's Children. Isn't that dear?"

"Very dear," said Dorothy. By all outward appearances, Siobhan had joined a cult with very specific membership requirements. But whatever brainwashing she had endured was subtler than it might appear at first glance. Apart from the context, her behavior didn't stray far from the Siobhan she had known for years. "How many Mayhem's Children are there, Siobhan?"

"Ooh." She put her finger to her chin in thought. "Let's see. There's you, your little brother, the twenty-eight of us, and fourteen little ones." She smiled again at Melody and Ian. "Sixteen now that your little ones are here. They're going to have so much fun."

"Mitchell is here?" asked Dorothy, startled by mention of her brother.

"Yes!" said Siobhan. "And he's so excited to see you!"

Dorothy shared that excitement, but perhaps not the same way. She looked around her, assessing her options. At least a dozen people and goblins whacked away at the grass, and one giant bat sat calmly behind her. There could be hundreds of people and creatures anywhere under the seats, including her brother, her twenty-eight sisters, and at least one professor. Also at least one each of assassin and wizard, their abductors who had not deigned to greet them on arrival. Her resources consisted of one remarkably brave little girl, one boy with untested destructive potential, and her wits. Escape was not on the table, nor combat. She would have to ride this out as far as she could, and hope she could resist whatever had been done to Siobhan.

She took Ian's hand. Still holding Melody, she said, "All right, Siobhan, what happens next?"

———

Siobhan took them to a healer. Dorothy had never employed the services of one, though she had heard both Harrison's descriptions of what it felt like, and Lisa's admonishments against them. For her part, she always found the prospect of magical tinkering with her own health to be outside the boundaries of acceptable risks. In this case, she wasn't given the choice. With Siobhan's welcome wagon duties properly discharged, two goblins joined her for the job of escorting Dorothy around the complex.

They were both exactly as threatening and repulsive as the one Dorothy killed. Siobhan had no apparent problem with them.

The healer, an old woman, reminded Dorothy of Strontium, whom she missed dearly, far more than she would have thought for someone she only knew for a few weeks. Apart from her age, however, nothing else about this woman resembled the witch. Her manner was cold, her appearance decrepit, and her touch gave Dorothy the willies. She endured it long enough to feel her body realign itself ever so slightly, and other than a brief flash of pain in her chest, she came away feeling invigorated. Her energy had increased, and inspection revealed some flaws now straightened out. Her cuticles, rough from weeks of living in relative wilderness, were healthy and smooth. A pimple under the skin on her chin which had made itself known two days earlier had disappeared.

These improvements in no way abated her sense of danger. Whatever happened to Siobhan's mind came from something other than this healing process. The children went through the same procedure, with Dorothy helpless to stop it even if she wanted to, unless she could think of a way to overpower two armed goblins. And then, surely, dozens more.

From there Siobhan took them to a makeshift classroom. As promised, the children were up, and ate breakfast with their teachers. Dorothy looked toward a man she did not know. "Is that the professor?"

"Oh, my, no," said Siobhan. "You'll know him when you see him. I promise you that."

Dorothy did not recognize the other teacher, a tall woman with dark hair, until she looked up. "Dorothy?" said Jessica Williams, a bright smile on her face. She got up from her seat and ran to hug her. "They didn't tell me you were here! When did you get in?"

"About an hour ago," said Dorothy. "Are you all right?"

"I'm great!" said Jessica. "Did you meet Professor Heatherington yet?"

"Not yet," said Dorothy.

"We're doing orientation right now," said Siobhan.

Dorothy looked around this room full of children. Some of them looked back in mild curiosity, but not for long. They went about their breakfast and play without particular regard to their surroundings. They all appeared as happy as their teachers. By Dorothy's quick estimate none of them was older than eight. A single baby sat in a high chair, as a teacher fed her from a jar. One boy she knew. "Adler?"

Adler Logan-Bennett looked up from his scrambled eggs. "Dorothy?" He scooted his chair out and walked to her. "I didn't know you were here."

"We just got here," she said.

"Hi, Adler," said Melody.

"Are you okay, honey?" asked Dorothy.

Adler shrugged. "They take care of us. It was scary at first, but it's sort of like school. Are my parents here?"

"No, honey," said Dorothy. "Just me."

"Oh," he said, his disappointment fully evident, and his composure entirely different from what she had seen so far in Siobhan and Jessica. Clearly, he did not share their delight to be here nor did he imagine he would stay forever. That he lacked the obvious brainwashing of the adults gave Dorothy hope that Melody and Ian would be spared whatever she herself would soon be struggling to resist.

"We're going to drop the little ones here," said Siobhan. "They can have breakfast with the others. Are you hungry, kids?"

Melody held Dorothy a bit more tightly.

"Do you remember Jessica?" asked Dorothy.

Jess smiled again at Melody. Leaving them here was not ideal, but nothing would be, and she needed to be able to focus without distraction. And Jessica was a dear friend, no matter what had been done to her. Dorothy had no choice but to trust her children would be safe here, at least for now.

"No," said Melody again, coldly.

"Well, she is a very good friend of mine." Dorothy gently lowered Melody to the floor. "And she is going to watch over you while I go take care of some things with Siobhan. Are you hungry? It looks like they have some good food here."

Melody surveyed her surroundings, and for a moment, it seemed like she might go either way with this idea. "When will you come back?"

"Soon." Dorothy leaned over and kissed Melody on the forehead. A slight, unexpected tingling feeling grazed her lips when she did so. It startled her, but she chalked it up to a side effect of the healing process.

"Come on," said Melody, taking Adler's hand, and holding the other one out for Ian. He looked to Dorothy for guidance. She rubbed his shoulder.

"It's okay," she said. "Eat. Have fun if you can. I will be back soon."

Ian took Melody's hand, and the three of them went to a table.

As Siobhan took Dorothy to the next stop on her orientation, Dorothy asked her, "Who are those children?"

"They're like Melody," said Siobhan. "Sons and daughters of people with powers."

This brought Dorothy up short. "All of them? How is that possible? I thought Adler and Melody were the only ones. Everyone thinks that. Where did the others come from?"

"All over the world," said Siobhan.

"Wait," said Dorothy, "Harrison said there were only twelve people with powers in the world, and five of them are dead. Most of the others live in New Chicago. How can there be this many children of the ones still out there?" Dorothy omitted her belief that Ian was one of the missing two. That would only leave one person to parent all those children.

Siobhan laughed. "Do you really think there were only twelve? And that almost half of them happened to be your friends? No, there are hundreds."

"Do you have all of their children? Are they all here?"

"All but three," said Siobhan. "Soon all of Mayhem's Children will be together. Rounding up Harrison's children was the trickiest part. If we hadn't figured out how to get them all in one place we'd probably still be looking for them. But that's done now, and none of the other Powers adopted anyone, so all we have to do now is find the last three babies. The Professor is so happy he'll have us all together."

So many things about this exchange set off alarms in Dorothy's head, but Siobhan's use of Harrison's name topped them all. In the eight years Dorothy had known her, she had never called him anything but Dad. That confirmed Dorothy's brainwashing suspicions, and although the problem had no immediate fix, identifying it gave her a tiny feeling of power over it. But that was only one alarm. The others troubled her more.

"What will he do when he has us all together?" asked Dorothy calmly.

Siobhan giggled. "Silly. Sacrifice us, of course."

[45]

DUCK SEASON

The houses in the Maine compound resembled other homes Harrison had seen rise from the ruins of earlier civilization. They all showed evidence of construction with advanced technology, from whatever building materials nature provided. It made for an odd mixture of the crude and the sophisticated. Wooden framed houses with slick polymer siding sat alongside huts made entirely from fused gravel. Several houses stood out by their ordinariness, clearly remnants of the pre-Mayhem world. At least one hybrid of twentieth century American architecture and otherworldly magnificence stood among them. Brick walls merged seamlessly with marble pillars, covered in meticulously carved relief.

Harrison had visited several such communities, typically built up around a nucleus of pre-existing structures. Like New Chicago, they grew from there, although at a microcosmic scale to what had bloomed around him in his home city. The only thing this hamlet lacked was activity. It took the better part of an hour before Milton declared the entire compound secure, but it had been obvious to everyone in their first five minutes there these buildings were all abandoned.

The team found a total of eleven dead goblins scattered throughout the complex, some discovered inside buildings, but most lay on the open ground, cut to ribbons, with the shattered remnants of their armor strewn about them. Weapons still protruded from several, including one specimen who had been pinned to a wooden wall with an ornate

230

longsword, and another split nearly in half, with an axe buried in the notch.

"We're supposed to think this was a fight," said Harrison to Milton. He stood near the stripped and skewered goblin pinned to the wall, and touched the pommel of the sword that held him there. It felt cool and tingly.

"You really shouldn't do that," said Hadley. The ghost had followed Harrison on this excursion through the barren homes, occasionally interjecting an opinion, but mostly staying out of the way. "You should know that any randomly found sword in the world now runs about a five percent chance of being cursed, and a slightly higher probability of being enchanted."

Harrison drew Bess from her sheath, and held her at an angle to the longsword, viewing its reflection in the surface of her blade. That image of the sword glowed pale green, infused with magic, but anyone's guess what type. He weighed the risks of pulling this sword out to keep, and opted against. Pretty, but not worth the potential danger. He could ask Aplomado to inspect it first, but wizards typically kept weapons they found without ever revealing what they knew about them.

"Yes, sir," said Milton, oblivious to the exchange with Hadley. "We are. But this was no fight."

"No." Harrison looked around him. "These weren't soldiers. They were sacrificial goats. They were killed and left here to make it look like these people fled an enemy."

"It's not very convincing." Milton pointed to two different slain goblins. "Neither of those show any sign of struggle. One of them has a dagger in his throat the same size as a sheath on his own belt. They were executed with their own weapons, and they let it happen."

"That's crazy. They must have known we would see through this."

Milton shrugged. "Maybe they thought we wouldn't get here until the skeletons were picked by scavengers. Maybe they were in a hurry."

"Maybe they just suck at their jobs."

"That's a possibility. There is something about this that smacks of incompetence. A rush job, at the very least." Milton bent down and picked up a piece of the dirty gray armor that lay broken around a goblin corpse. He turned it over in his hand, inspecting it closely. "Someone wanted us to believe they fought these goblins. Whoever that is failed at what should have been a fairly simple tactic."

"Are you saying we have been overestimating them?" asked Harrison. "Because they did a pretty competent job of abducting those girls from our own headquarters."

"Respectfully, sir, they did not," said Milton. "If you and the director had not been under that curse, that would all have gone down a lot differently. You missed some obvious clues, like Sergeant Crenshaw going AWOL and your son running away. And the decision to put all the women on the seventh floor instead of scattering them to safe houses virtually guaranteed their abduction. You did that at Agent Kestrel's suggestion, which never would have happened if you were at one hundred percent."

Harrison scowled at the reminder of the enormous role he played in the fiasco at NCSA. "What's your point?"

"Only that they succeeded because of their plan to hamstring our best and brightest. This was not a master plan. It was a brute force attack that worked because they had one good idea, and they got lucky. I think we should consider the possibility that we are dealing with a very powerful but very amateur group."

"Does that make them less dangerous?" asked Harrison.

"More," said Milton simply.

Sparky chose that moment to appear from behind a house. She flew to Milton, where she paused in a hover and saluted.

"Don't do that, Agent Sparky."

"Righto," she said. "Just letting you know I'm finished with the perimeter thingy you wanted me to do. There's no one within at least two miles of this place."

"Thank you," said Milton.

"What's our next step?" asked Harrison.

"We set up a base here," said Milton. "I want these houses scoured for any clue that will lead us to where they went. Sparky, please tell the wizard he's up. If there was magic used here, I want to know how much and what kind. Assistant Director, I would be grateful if you would inform Mrs. Mendoza-Cody that we will likely be needing her talents very shortly."

"Can you be more specific?"

"Trust me, as soon as I know what we need, you two will be the first to know."

Harrison nodded. "You headed back to the flier?" he said to the pixie.

"Yup," she said.

They excused themselves. Hadley followed, at a tasteful distance, observing their environs instead of trying to interact with them. Walking through the deserted compound littered with staged carnage, Harrison felt less like talking than he thought he would. Sparky chose to break the awkward silence. "Dorothy is awesome, you know."

"Of course I know," he said. "Why do you say that?"

"Because if I had to pick one person to watch after my little kid, if I ever had a little kid, which I don't, but if I did, it would totally be her."

"Really?" said Harrison. Dorothy had always amazed him with her intellect, even at fourteen years old. And he absolutely trusted her with Melody. Dorothy adored her and would do anything to keep her safe. But he never would have chosen to thrust her into a situation as random and perilous as this one, and he had no way to predict how she would rise to that occasion.

"Really," said Sparky. "That one has some strength, I have to say. Did I tell you she killed a goblin?"

That brought him up short. "What? Dorothy? By herself?"

Sparky nodded vigorously. "No lie! Stabbed him right through the gut with a sword. I wasn't there, but I saw him on the lawn. Looked awful."

"Oh, shit!" said Harrison. "I did see that! That was her?"

"She says so. Like I said, wasn't there, didn't see it. Anyway, my point is, she's awesome."

Harrison mulled this over, entirely unsure what to do with it. It did indeed reassure him to know Melody had been put into the hands of someone so devoted to her safety. Unfortunately, with them now both captured, that no longer felt like the defining feature of their situation. He chose to take Sparky's comments as the pep talk they seemed meant to be.

Harrison approached the flier. Several collapsible chairs had been set up on the ground near where they landed. Apryl, Sarah and Claudia occupied three of the chairs. The latter two sat silently with vacant expressions, each fearing for the fate of a missing loved one. He wished he had words of comfort beyond the news they were staying in this place to hunt for clues.

Apryl sat with eyes closed, awake, but evidently more at peace. He crouched by her side, and took her hand. Her head rolled in his direction, and her eyes fluttered open. "Hey."

"Hi there. Are you still picking up signals from Melody?"

"Yes," she said. "Same as before. She's fine. Not even scared."

Aplomado emerged from the inside of the flier at that moment. "Actually, there has been a change. Melody and Dorothy are now exhibiting signs of the same physical perfection as the others."

This got Claudia's attention. "But that's a good thing, right?"

"It is a thing," said Aplomado. "Whether it is good or bad remains entirely to be seen."

Sarah stood at this and walked away. She stayed in sight, but planted herself at the far side of the flier, on the ground near one of the landing struts.

"Are you required to be insensitive?" asked Harrison. "Because I have to say, that was brilliantly done, if so."

The wizard ignored Harrison. "You are here to collect me?" he said to Sparky.

"Uh… yeah," she said. "Milton—"

"Needs me to scan the compound for traces of magic. Already in progress. I can discuss it with him if he would like."

"I would like," said Harrison. "If you're there, you can't be here."

Aplomado offered Harrison a nod far more dismissive than courteous and departed. Sparky zipped away ahead of him.

Apryl looked in Sarah's direction. "You need to talk to her."

"I know," said Harrison. "What do I say?"

"That her little boy is going to be fine," she said. "And you say that whether you believe it or not, because it's what she needs to hear. Yes, she will see right through that. She needs to hear it anyway."

"Can you say that to me too?" asked Claudia. "Tell me Dorothy is going to be okay?"

Harrison smiled at that. "You know damn well she will be. By now she's probably engineering a coup, and seizing power from whoever is in charge over there."

"That's so like her," said Claudia.

"Isn't it?" said Harrison.

Claudia found the will to smile. "You know what? That does help, even though I know you're bullshitting me."

"See?" Apryl shooed him away. "Get over there."

Harrison stood. "I'm supposed to tell you Milton says we're going to need your powers soon. And no, he didn't say why, and no, he didn't say which powers."

"Message received. Go talk to Sarah."

"I'm going."

Harrison made his way to the other side of the flier, down the dirt road there, where Sarah sat on the bare ground, looking away. He sat as well, resting his hands on the earth, packed hard and dry. Gravel poked him through his pants. He gazed off in the same direction as Sarah, at lushly wooded mountains, the Mahoosucs, a northern extension of the Appalachians, and familiar territory. They reminded him of the Berkshires near where he grew up. He took a moment to drink in their beauty before speaking. "He's going to be okay."

She did not look at him. "Apryl sent you over here."

"She sure did."

"That was probably the right thing to do," she said. "Thank you."

"I really do believe it, you know. We are going to find these people, and we are going to get our children back."

"I know that," said Sarah. "I have faith in this group. I have faith in you. But even if... even when I get Adler back, Warren might still die. I left my husband in a hospital in a coma to go on this mission. He would do the same if our places were reversed. But I might never see him again. It's been four weeks, Harrison. The longer it goes, the worse his chances are. I even looked into getting a court to override his 'do not magically heal' order, and it turns out at this point it wouldn't matter. Crow was right about magic and brain damage. Either he comes out of it naturally, or he doesn't come out at all. I might never get to hold him again."

Harrison struggled for the right words. "I want to promise that you will."

"But you can't."

"No," he said. "I can't. I don't know what to say."

"I don't think I need you to say anything," she said. "I just needed someone to hear it."

He nodded. "Fair enough. Do you need to be alone?"

"Not necessarily. Is the wizard still over there?"

"Nope," said Harrison. "He's off offending someone else entirely."

Sarah made a sound somewhere between a laugh and a sigh. "Good."

Harrison stood, and held his hand out. She took it, and he pulled her up. He looked back to Apryl and Claudia. Dallas had emerged from the flier, and stood awkwardly nearby.

"Great," said Harrison. "Dallas got bored. I wonder what fight he's going to pick with me now."

"Stop letting that buffoon get to you," said Sarah.

"Yeah, I know. When this is over, he'll go back to his pathetic life. His first opportunity to be a real field agent, and he's already blown it. I kind of feel sorry for him, when I'm not thinking of punching him in the face."

Hadley had taken one of the chairs. While it surely looked empty to everyone else, Dallas walked by it twice, and hesitated before continuing to pace. Hadley wore a sort of bemused deadpan, and Harrison suspected he took some degree of joy in finding an entertaining aspect of his ghostliness.

Sarah returned to her own seat next to Apryl, who took her hand. "I'm okay."

Apryl nodded.

"What's happening now?" asked Claudia. "How soon are we leaving?"

"Not sure," said Harrison. "Milton says we're setting up a base here to look for clues. I imagine it will be at least a day, maybe more. Hopefully, the next move will be in the direction of our people."

"That's crap," said Dallas. "This was a bust. We should go home. Regroup from there."

"No," said Harrison, concentrating on patience. "We should stay here, because it's the only place we know they've been, and because those are our orders."

"If we go home, we might miss something here," said Apryl. "Wouldn't you rather we find a clue than start over from scratch?"

"Yeah," said Dallas, "I guess so."

"Thank you," said Harrison.

"For what?" asked Dallas, his tone shifting fluidly from concessional to confrontational.

Harrison had directed his gratitude to Apryl for nudging Dallas in the direction of reason, but he chose to use this misunderstanding as an opportunity for dialog. "Thank you for agreeing with the plan to stay here."

"Stay here?" said Dallas. "That's stupid. We need to move on. What are we waiting for?"

Apryl gave Harrison a look of confused resignation.

Claudia rolled her eyes.

Harrison frowned. "Hang on," he whispered. Dallas had grown no closer to being less difficult, but something in his words finally tipped a scale in Harrison's perception of his behavior. Still looking at Dallas, he said to Apryl, "We should move on. We're not going to find anything else here."

"What are you talking about?" said Dallas. "The boss says we stay here, we stay here."

Harrison looked Dallas in the eyes. "We should stay here."

Stay here?" said Dallas. "Are you nuts? What if those goblins come back?"

The others watched this exchange with various signs of concern and confusion. Harrison forged ahead. He looked at Sarah. "My, you are looking lovely today, Dr. Logan."

He shifted his gaze to Dallas, now checking out Sarah in an obvious and creepy manner. After a moment of this, he declared, "Those pants make your ass look fat."

Sarah's jaw dropped.

Claudia rose, and moved to Harrison's side. "What the fuck is happening right now?"

Harrison responded by holding up a finger, signaling her to be quiet. He walked right up to Dallas, and stood inches from his face. Looking into the eyes of this man, he found no madness, only steely resolve.

"Duck season," said Harrison.

Dallas narrowed his eyes. Through clenched teeth, he said, "Rabbit season."

Harrison closed his eyes, and rubbed his temples. "God damn it. How did we miss this?"

"He's cursed," said Apryl.

"Wow," said Claudia. "Good one. I thought he was just an asshole."

"To be fair…" Harrison glared at Dallas. "He is kind of an asshole. Absolutely the first choice for hiding a spell like this, because no one would think twice about his behavior." He shook his head. "No, that's a cop-out. We still should have caught this. Do you remember a wizard?" he asked Dallas. "Bald? Lots of tattoos?"

"Leave me alone," said Dallas.

"Answer the question," said Apryl firmly.

"Yes," said Dallas, panic evident in his eyes. "I met him a day or two before those bats came. Kind of a creep. I forget what he told me. You're saying he cursed me?"

Harrison turned around. "Someone who isn't me, please tell this man to wait in the flier. I need to go find a wizard I don't like, and ask him to fix this."

"Don't look at me," said Sarah. "He called me fat."

Apryl stood. "I have this. Dallas, come inside, please."

"Yeah," he said, clearly bewildered. "All right."

As they climbed into the hatch, Harrison wondered about the type of foe who would try to sabotage a mission by planting someone cursed to irritate exactly one member of it. It might have been more effective if Harrison had taken the leadership role instead of Milton, but even then, its effect would chiefly have been one of inconvenience. Milton's observations about their foe being amateur rang more true, and his comment stood out, that their clumsiness might make them more dangerous.

PROFESSOR

"Sacrifice us?"

Dorothy looked into Siobhan's eyes, hunting for any sign she understood the meaning of her own words, and found none.

"That's right," said Siobhan, with a casual sort of cheer.

"Do you even hear what you're saying?" asked Dorothy.

Siobhan took her hand, gently. "You'll understand soon."

Dorothy understood nothing at that moment but her need to get Melody, Ian and Adler away from this place. She had no idea how she would accomplish that, let alone her secondary goal of freeing all the adults, and the children she didn't know, but her obligation to those three superseded everything. "What will I understand?" she asked cautiously.

"That things need to be put right," said Siobhan. "The professor will explain it all when you meet him."

Professor Heatherington. This was the third time Dorothy had heard him named or referenced. Absent alternative evidence, she assumed he led this operation. Exactly what that meant remained to be seen. "When will I meet him?"

"That's where we're headed right now," said Siobhan.

Dorothy steeled herself for the probability they intended to brainwash her. Siobhan and Jessica both showed complete loyalty to a man who had been open with them about his plan to murder them. The fact this loyalty took hold in so short a time implied something at work here far beyond simple cult mentality.

Professor Heatherington, or someone else, had ensorcelled them.

The name conjured images for Dorothy of a mad scientist, and with it flashed before her eyes multiple instruments of laboratory torture. As casually as she could, she inspected Siobhan for signs of scarring or burns, with no idea what to look for. What she could see of Siobhan's skin seemed healthy and uninjured, and nothing in her gait suggested anything other than comfort and happiness. Whatever they had done to her hadn't left a mark, or had been healed.

They ascended a set of concrete stairs, and emerged on a promenade of empty concession stands. Assorted canopies—those few not tattered beyond legibility—advertised foods no longer available, in the form of hot dogs, cold beer, ice cream and French fries. They strolled past this ghost town of fast food, which served to remind Dorothy she had not eaten breakfast, while also bringing to her attention an anxiety-induced lack of appetite.

They entered a corridor, found another flight of stairs, and made their way upward arriving at office space, presumably the former headquarters of whoever once managed the stadium. Its new proprietor chose to use this same space as his command center. Or perhaps he lived here. Or maybe only interviews, torture and forced behavior modification took place here. The chill of early morning air cooled the perspiration accumulating on her brow.

"I can't go in with you." Siobhan offered this with no trace of foreboding, which somehow made it more frightening.

"I understand." Impulsively, Dorothy pulled Siobhan into a hug. Though no longer the person she had known for years, she still wore the face of her dear friend. After this meeting, that might not matter to her the same way. One last grasp at human contact before the plunge. "Will I see you soon?"

Siobhan giggled. "You sure will. I'm going to find you a bunk. When you're done here, come find me and I'll show you your room and give you a tour of the building."

Dorothy nodded, and rubbed Siobhan's shoulders. She turned, took a deep breath, and opened the door.

Floor to ceiling windows looked out over the stadium from the enormous office. Outside, workers continued to clear brush, though they hadn't progressed to the point of clarifying the type of field they worked, or their purpose in doing so. Dorothy did not imagine they planned to mow it and paint it for some regulation sport. Against her will, she conjured the image of fifty-odd altars laid out on the grass, with her sisters, the children, and herself stretched out on them, knives in their hearts.

By the windows, facing away from Dorothy, stood the woman who had brought them here. Until the previous day, Dorothy had known this person as NCSA Agent Felicia Kestrel, Harrison's administrative assistant, his right hand for several years. Now it appeared she had been a mole that entire time. She wondered if Harrison knew yet, or if his trusted aide continued to feed him disinformation. Felicia turned away from the window long enough to give Dorothy a cruel smile, before turning her attention back to the field.

Across the room from the door behind a large, wooden desk sat a figure dressed in a tan frock coat, red waistcoat, and gold ascot around a white, wing-collar shirt. A moss-colored, reptilian head contrasted this attire. Occupied with writing something in quill pen, the creature did not yet appear to have noticed Dorothy enter the room. She felt no rush to call attention to herself. He lifted his quill to refresh it in an inkwell with his right hand, covered in—or perhaps made of—polished brass. It glinted in the sunlight coming in the windows.

"Do come in, Miss O'Neill." He spoke in a Scottish accent, with a lilt, and did not look up from his papers.

She crossed the room at a slow pace, attempting to give herself time to plan something, though she had no idea what. As she drew closer, a faint, irregular ticking noise grew louder, the only sound in the room apart from the scratching of the creature's pen. Both sounds issued from the actions of the metal hand. She stopped about three feet from the desk, and stood in silent apprehension.

After making a few final, flourishing strokes, he put the pen down. As he looked up, she watched the scaly skin of his face move, and tried to place it. Not a lizard, not a snake, not a crocodile. Something else. He returned her gaze through a pair of mismatched eyes, on the right a yellow-green orb with a vertical black slit that narrowed in response to the sunlight, the other black glass, mounted in a brass frame, itself covered in tiny gears and pins whose function she wouldn't dare to guess. The prosthesis appeared to be implanted in his head.

"Good day." He stood, wiped his metal hand on the side of his coat, and extended it across the desk. "Basil Heatherington, at your service."

She considered her options. Touching that hand was not her first choice. "I don't feel very served," she said simply. The boldness of her words did not hit her until they had already left her mouth.

He stood in silence for a moment, his reptilian features impossible to read. Eventually, he withdrew his hand. "Yes, well, as pleasantries go, it does lack something in the literal sense. Do sit, please." He gestured to a wooden armchair on her side of the desk, upholstered in red velvet.

240

They each took their seats. "I trust you have not been mistreated?" He glanced at Felicia on that question, who did not move to acknowledge it.

"Apart from the abduction itself, no," said Dorothy.

"Couldn't be helped," he said. "But I am glad you are otherwise unharmed."

"What is going to happen to us?"

The Professor drummed his fingers on the surface of the desk, the tapping sound mixed in with a staccato, trilled ticking. "You do cut right to the heart, Miss O'Neill. I suppose you've had more time than most to prepare for this meeting." The gears on his facial prosthesis spun, and a pink filter rotated down to cover the glass eye. A dim light pulsed softly from it. "You will be staying with us for some time. Perhaps days, perhaps weeks. During that time, you will be treated with kindness, and given every reasonable comfort and liberty."

Dorothy felt a dull throbbing in the back of her head. The brainwashing had begun, a product of this device. Perhaps magic, perhaps technology. Either way, she had no defense against it. She looked away, even closed her eyes, but the sensation did not change, nor did he attempt to redirect her. Whatever that eye did to her did not require direct visual stimulus.

"I will of course ask that you not leave this facility," he continued. "Everything you could possibly need is right here, and we wouldn't want you to be separated from your sisters and cousins."

"And son," added Felicia, nonchalantly.

"Quite so," said Heatherington. "And son. For the duration of your stay, you will be asked to contribute to the community from whatever skills you possess."

The throbbing in Dorothy's head increased. She resisted, but had no illusion that simply willing herself not to be affected would work. So far, she still possessed all her faculties. That would change any second. As she thought this, she whispered, so softly no one else could possibly hear. Her lips did not move, as she formed words from complex and minuscule motions of her tongue. The words came without thought, and when she tried to identify them, she found they were not words at all, simply highly specific nonsense syllables. But she recognized them and understood them, and though not from any language she herself spoke, she knew their meaning to be simple:

You will not have my mind. You will not have my mind.

"At the end of your stay, you and all of Mayhem's Children are to be offered up, so the world may be restored to its proper state. Know that you give yourselves for a truly noble purpose. The stain of science is to be wiped away, and the glory of the fantastic will be renewed and purified."

She heard these words, and took in their meaning, confirming Siobhan's revelation they would all be sacrificed. This creature wanted to eliminate all traces of the world of Dorothy's birth. Their lives would be given to separate the blended worlds, and from the sound of it, only one world would survive the split. She heard all of this. And she heard herself whispering, more clearly than the damning news. *You will not have my mind.*

"Do you have any questions?"

Dorothy opened her eyes. The pink filter had retracted again, the pulsing light gone. She had now been indoctrinated to the sickening cult of Professor Basil Heatherington, and assigned her role as sacrificial lamb to the cause of killing everyone from her own version of Earth. As she looked into his monstrous and artificial eyes, she saw only reptilian abomination. He was not her leader. Nothing but a beast, to be defeated, broken, and destroyed.

He did not have her mind.

And he did not know that.

She smiled sweetly at him. "No questions, Professor. Thank you."

"Splendid," he said. "Then you should run along and find Siobhan. She will show you around, and help you find a new job here."

She stood. "That sounds lovely."

He sighed. "I am so glad you've come aboard, Miss O'Neill. I do hope you find a role in our community to your liking."

"Oh, I am quite sure I will. I know that when I find my contribution, my calling here, it will be my utmost pleasure to carry it out." Beaming, she curtsied and drifted out of the room. Once in the hallway, and about ten paces away from the door, she lifted her hand to look upon the small red book now in it. She would find Siobhan as instructed, but not dally with her. Afterward, Dorothy needed to find somewhere safe and private.

She had reading to do.

[47]

LILAC AND CINNAMON

"This is beyond me."

Dallas sat patiently in a passenger seat inside the flier as Aplomado examined him. At these words, his patience apparently reached its limit. "Beyond you? What does that mean?" He looked at Milton plaintively. "What does that mean?"

"It means this curse was placed on you by a spellcaster of significantly more power than I," said Aplomado. "There are safeguards I cannot lift. I could attempt to break through them, but it would likely kill you."

"Don't!" shouted Dallas.

Milton put his hand on Dallas's shoulder. "He's not going to."

"I would not attempt it even if you ordered it," said the wizard. "Once we return to New Chicago, Mallory should be able to lift this. She is far more adept than I at this sort of removal. Until then, you will have to carry it."

Harrison watched all of this in silence. Dallas would immediately and angrily contradict any contribution he had to offer, and he didn't want to add more senseless stress to the proceedings.

"Carry it?" said Dallas. "What does that mean? Is this gonna hurt me? I want it out!"

"Relax, Special Agent," said Milton. "It's not going to damage anything but Cody's peace of mind." He looked to Aplomado.

The wizard nodded.

Milton looked at Harrison with steely eyes. "It's a pity Mallory wasn't available for this assignment. Apparently, she's busy for the next ten months."

"Mallory is working on something as important as we are," said Harrison. In truth, she was working on something most people would consider significantly more important, trying to find a way to prevent the Mayhespheres from killing everything on the planet. Harrison ranked it as about equal with saving his children. "It was the right call."

"All your calls suck," said Dallas.

"You're doing it again," said Milton.

Dallas slapped his hand over his mouth, then seemed to recognize it was a pointless gesture. "Aw, dang it!"

"It's all right, Rutherford," said Milton. "We're not going to make any more headway on this right now. You should get yourself some fresh air."

Dallas stood and inched his way past Harrison. Neither said anything until he was out the hatch.

"You still think these guys are amateurs?" asked Harrison.

"Absolutely," said Milton. "If anything, I'm even more convinced now."

"Whoever laid that curse was no amateur," said Aplomado. "It is a network of complex threads spun at a level I have not seen outside of a simulation. Mallory might be able to lift it, but I doubt even she has the wit to create something like this herself."

"I don't mean the spell," said Milton. "I mean the plan. It's needlessly complicated, and served no tangible purpose. Why go to all this trouble just to annoy Cody?"

"If I had been the one making tactical decisions, it would have caused a serious problem."

"If you had been making tactical decisions, how long would you have put up with that kind of back-talk?" asked Milton.

"About five seconds," said Harrison. "By now Dallas would be locked in the cargo hold."

"Which is exactly where I would have put him if he directed that behavior to me," said Milton. "I didn't intervene because your disagreements with agents are not mine to question. But if a subordinate did that to me, there would be a reckoning, and I wouldn't waste any time bringing it down on his head."

"You're saying this is another botch job?"

"There was no conceivable way this curse was going to interfere with the mission," said Milton. "And even if it were possible, that plan hinged on the fact of you being in command of it and choosing to bring Dallas in the first place."

"Which I wouldn't have," said Harrison.

"All this cost us was fifteen minutes, and we picked up significant intel," said Milton. "So yes, on the whole, I would say this was a botch job."

"What intel?" said Harrison.

"They have a master wizard," said Aplomado.

"And a leader who is a terrible tactician," said Milton. "I'm sure they didn't want us to know either of those things, and now we do."

"Can you check everyone else for curses?" Harrison asked Aplomado.

"I can check," said the wizard, "but I cannot make any guarantees of being able to do anything about whatever I find."

"Knowing would be helpful," said Milton. "Get on that, please."

Aplomado nodded, and stepped out.

Harrison watched him go through the hatch, and as he got beyond earshot, asked softly, "What if he's cursed, too?"

Milton pursed his lips. "I guess we will just have to hope he isn't. Unless you have a better idea?"

Before Harrison could respond to this, Sparky zipped in the hatch. "You should come outside."

"Who?" asked Harrison.

"Both of you," she said.

Harrison filed out the hatch, with Milton close behind.

Her back to them, and standing away from the flier, close to the main gate, Apryl stretched out her arms. Strands of her hair levitated outward, some faintly glowing.

"What's happening here?" asked Milton. He looked at Aplomado, whose look of bafflement brought Harrison no small degree of joy.

"I truly do not know," said the wizard.

"Hey sweetie," said Harrison loudly. "Whatcha doin'?"

"I can smell her!" she called.

Sarah held back, looking entirely confused and uncomfortable, as did the several agents who had returned from scouting the compound. As the only two people there who had ever seen Apryl like this, Harrison and Claudia were naturally unperturbed.

"She can smell her?" said Milton. "What the hell does that mean?"

"Melody," said Harrison. "I'll take this one. I think Apryl is shifting to auto-pilot."

"Auto-pilot?"

"I've seen this before. If I'm right, she's letting her instincts take over."

"And then what?" asked Milton.

Harrison shrugged. "And then we'll get some more answers, I guess." He walked to her. "What does she smell like?"

"Like lilac." She closed her eyes. "Or cinnamon. It keeps changing." More of her hair strayed outward and up.

Claudia fidgeted, looking back and forth between Harrison and Apryl. "Is she going to teleport?"

"I don't know. Are you going to teleport?" he asked Apryl directly.

"Maybe," she said.

Claudia twitched.

"Do you know where she is?" he asked.

"No. Maybe. It's not cinnamon anymore."

She was beginning to come detached from her surroundings. He had seen this happen only a few times in the eight years they had been together. The first time she teleported an entire lifeboat and its passengers into a cave halfway around the world, to flee a sea serpent. If she was gearing up for a similar jump now, in search of Melody, it could take her anywhere.

"What does she smell like now?" he asked.

"She smells like..." Apryl halted there. Seconds later she tried again. "She..." Again she got stuck. Finally, her eyes snapping open, Apryl shouted, "She smells like Faerie!"

The glow enhancing the tips of her dancing hair exploded into a full-blown halo, and Harrison took a step back to shield his eyes. In the instant before throwing his hand up in front of his face, he caught a glimpse of Claudia lunging at his wife. With a crackle, and a *whoosh*, they both disappeared.

He sprinted back to the flier.

"What just happened?" said Milton.

"They've gone to wherever Melody is. Or to wherever Apryl thinks she is, or feels she is. Can we track her?" Harrison directed this last question at Aplomado, who had been able to find a randomly appearing and disappearing cabin in a matter of minutes with the right resources.

The wizard did not respond. He stared at the polished patch of dirt road where two women had vanished.

"Gerry!" snapped Harrison. "Can you track her?"

Aplomado locked eyes with Harrison, with a bewilderment that no longer amused him. Quietly, the wizard said, "No."

48

CLAUDIA

Hiding places for Dorothy turned out to be plentiful. The stadium had been built to accommodate tens of thousands of fans. By Dorothy's quick estimate, no more than two hundred people and creatures occupied it now. The original building itself housed scores of vendors with empty kitchens, storage areas, locker rooms, offices, box seats and suites, the clubhouse, the press box, and assorted rooms whose purpose she did not grasp.

Whatever this facility had been before Mayhem, its structure had undergone radical changes, both inside and out. Concrete walkways alternated with cobblestone alleys. Some doors had been replaced with wrought iron gates. Gargoyles sat perched atop seats. Whether these changes had been caused by the Mayhem Wave or had been put into place deliberately after the fact was impossible to discern and beside the point. A plethora of rooms, chambers and catacombs existed where they most likely had not originally, and while some had been converted into living quarters and workspaces, still more had been left open and empty. Opportunities to slip away for an hour or two of quiet reading abounded.

The more time Dorothy spent with her book, the more sense it made to her. She still had no way of knowing what language it represented, but that didn't stop her from reading entire passages and sections—mostly in the form of teachings of skills well outside her background knowledge— and committing them to memory. The trick for how to hide the book itself was one of the first and easiest she learned, a simple matter of absorbing it directly into her hand, and releasing it when she wanted to read it. The fact she considered this impossibility to be "simple" did not escape her notice.

She found the spell for resisting hypnosis, both common and magical, recognizing the nonsense syllables she had chanted in whispers to protect herself earlier. That one had come naturally to her, and she recalled for the first time in years having been told at fourteen years of age she possessed a natural resistance to magical mind control. It had protected her from a patch of carnivorous crystals once, and helped break the power of a sentient house attempting to brainwash her into despair. Seeing a spell here in black and white that offered the same protection, she wondered how many more of this book's secrets already resided in her.

Apart from Siobhan and Jessica, Dorothy had encountered about a half dozen of the other captives so far, but none she knew as well as those two. They were all equally pleasant, most hugged her, and none showed signs of understanding Dorothy did not share their state of mind.

Close to noon, her hunger finally caught up with her, as did her concern for the children. She felt her time with the book gave her strength to protect them but none of that would matter if she lost track of them. Reasoning the school would have a lunch break, she went there to cover both bases. She found Jessica reading a story to a group of children sitting on the floor. Melody got up to run to Dorothy without asking permission. Jessica smiled, and kept reading.

"Dorrie," whispered Melody. "Are we staying here?"

Dorothy weighed possible answers to this question. She wanted to reassure Melody, but she also didn't want to tip her hand. The fact she retained full possession of her own mind would only give her an advantage as long as no one else knew. Sadly, that would have to include her little sister. "I think so," she whispered back. "Do you like it here?"

"I want to go home," said Melody.

Dorothy did not get a chance to respond to that.

"Hey there!" said Jessica as the children got up after she finished the book. "How are you settling in?"

The notion of captivity as the sort of thing one settled into gave Dorothy the willies. "Pretty well so far. I've been strolling around the building. Interesting choice to house a community."

"They needed the field," said Jessica. She did not elaborate, which suited Dorothy fine as she did not want to know the details yet. "Did they find you a job yet? Please say no."

"No," said Dorothy. "Siobhan was going to ask around to see where I was needed."

Jessica clapped gleefully. "You're needed right here! We could use another teacher. Please say you'll stay."

"I'm not sure it's up to me," said Dorothy.

"I'll talk to the professor! I'm sure he'll say yes." Jessica spontaneously grabbed Dorothy in a warm embrace. "I'm so glad you're here."

"Me too," said Dorothy, patting Jessica on the back. It was true, but for reasons entirely different than Jessica thought.

A few dozen humans worked for the Professor in addition to the assortment of goblins, and most of them took lunch with the captives in the clubhouse. None of the women seemed to think twice about that, but Dorothy saw it differently. Any adult there she did not know by name had come to this place by choice, and should be considered an enemy. This included Jessica's co-teacher. Though cordial and pleasant to her, Dorothy saw him only as a participant in their upcoming murders.

In the lunch line, Dorothy finally had her reunions with all twenty-eight of her adopted sisters, all delighted to see her, though some more than others. Whatever conditioning they had been through, it had not altered the fact of her personal relationships with them. The ones she barely knew said nothing to her beyond sincerely wishing her a happy stay there. Her close friends fawned over her. Jessica and Siobhan had already had their turns with her. Britney Hinson squealed loudly in delight the second she saw Dorothy, and charged her to give her a hug. Christine Rivera and Meghan Rosso were similarly enthusiastic, though less flamboyant and physical about it.

In the midst of this reunion, someone shouted Dorothy's name from across the clubhouse, Delight overwhelmed her on seeing Mitchell Bell, her adopted brother. That delight lasted as long as it took him to race across the room and pick her up in a bear hug.

"You made it! I'm so glad you're here!" he said.

His fantastic grin at the sight of her dashed Dorothy's vain hope he would somehow be immune to the brainwashing. She nearly cracked at that moment, but found the willpower to keep from breaking down in tears.

That group of her friends and brother insisted on sitting with her at lunch, putting to the test Dorothy's ability to maintain the façade of mind control. Would they know her well enough to see her fatuous happiness as a sham? Half an hour into this ruse, she ruled that none of them had any idea. That would make things easier, though she still had a lot of work ahead of her.

These six would be the first of her allies, once she learned how to reverse the conditioning. Surely if she could learn to shield herself from it, freeing the others should be possible. She would start with her closest friends, and one other. Rebecca Wheeler had always been the strongest of them. They would need a leader, because phase two of Dorothy's evolving plan consisted of escape, if necessary by killing their captors, which would require organization. Her plan also hinged on Harrison and Claudia arriving at the most dramatically opportune moment and rescuing them. One thing at a time.

After the meal, most of the people filed out to go back to whatever jobs they had, and the teachers led the children outside for recess. Sensing an opportunity to speak away from prying ears with the ones she knew, Dorothy went with them. Once outside, in the light of day, she finally recognized the stadium. The patch of cleared meadow on the ground, exposed the shape of the surrounding stands, arranged in a ring, heavily weighted to one side. On the other side, a high green wall patched over a break in the seats. Directly below the enormous press box, a broad net separated the fans from the field of play. Weeds and small trees had completely overtaken the ground, burying beneath them a baseball diamond.

The children spread out on the field, some running and chasing each other, others strolling and chatting. All stayed well clear of the workers, human and goblin, still engaged in the process of brush-clearing. Several children had already claimed the one exposed dugout as a fort, the other still completely covered in overgrowth. Melody isolated herself from the pack. She found an open spot of clean field, and sat. Dorothy meandered over to her, taking care to make it not seem urgent to anyone watching her, and sat with her.

"Hey, Little," she said.

"Hi, Dorrie," said Melody.

"You don't want to play with your new friends?" Dorothy gauged Melody's reaction to this probe. She needed to know what indoctrination the children had been given. Adler did not seem brainwashed, but his earlier question about his parents being there gave her pause.

Melody shrugged. "They're not my friends."

"Why not?" asked Dorothy. "You don't like them?"

Melody shrugged again. "I like them. Are we supposed to be here?"

As Dorothy adjusted to the sudden change of topic, a breeze caught Melody's hair, and as it flicked, a tiny amethyst sparkle flashed from underneath it. A trick of the light perhaps, but when it happened a second time, she gently brushed Melody's hair away from her face, surreptitiously feeling for an object in there that might reflect sunlight. She found nothing.

"All the other kids are out here," said Dorothy. "I think we're fine."

"I don't mean the field," said Melody. "I mean this place."

Tricky question. Dorothy wanted to answer honestly, but part of her feared a trap. If she opened up to this five-year-old girl, she might expose her freedom from the conditioning. She also vehemently disliked the idea of lying to Melody to support whatever positive spin the people around her had been putting on her captivity. She chose a compromise. "I'm not sure. Everyone here seems happy. Are you sad?"

Melody shrugged once more. "How did we get here?"

That one Dorothy felt comfortable answering with fact. "We flew here in a bag, carried by a giant bat."

"That's what I thought."

"Why did you ask that?"

"The other kids came here with their mommies. They told me my mommy brought me here, too, but I thought we came here in a bag."

"We did," said Dorothy. Melody's tale included two important revelations. The children were being given false memories to placate them, and Melody had been able to resist it. "Did you argue with your teachers? Is that why you're sad?"

"No," said Melody. "I'm sad because they confused me."

Dorothy put her arm around her. "Hey. I've got you. You and I know the truth, right?"

Melody nodded.

"Well then, that's all that matters. If anyone tells you differently, you just…" She got stuck there, trying to decide what Melody should do. "Just be okay with it. It doesn't matter if they're wrong, and it's not worth fighting about. Okay?"

"Okay."

"Adler says his mommy brought him here," said Melody. "Did she?"

Not good. "I don't know, honey," she lied. "Maybe he's confused. If that's what he wants to think, you should probably let him think it." As she said that, she caught sight of Ian. He too had chosen solitude for his recess, but exercised that by wandering to the edge of the overgrowth, where he whacked weeds with a stick. "Is it okay if I go talk to Ian, sweetie? Or do you need me to stay with you? I won't go anywhere if you're scared."

Melody rolled her eyes at that. "I'm not scared. I'm sad. That's different."

Dorothy laughed. "I can stay with you if you need me to."

"You can talk to Ian. He's sad too."

"For the same reason?" asked Dorothy.

Melody shrugged, and said no more.

"I'll be back. If you feel lonely come get me, okay?"

"Okay."

Dorothy stood, and on her way up, caught another flash of pale purple coming from her sister. It gave her pause, but she let it go. She walked straight to Ian, again trying to make it seem as casual as possible. "Hey there. How are you doing?"

"They don't know what to do with me." He did not look up, and punctuated this comment with a loud *whack* against an enormous thistle.

"What do you mean?"

"I'm the oldest kid," he said. "It's freaking them out."

"Really?" asked Dorothy. "Why?"

"I don't know. They also told me something weird"

Red flag. "What did they tell you?"

"They told Melody and me that our mothers brought us here. I told them they were wrong, that you're her sister, not her mother. Then they said her mother brought her here, and my mother brought me here. And I said I know my mother brought me here, but we all came together, but you're not her mother. And then they said I didn't come here with you, I came here with my mother. And I said I know I came here with my mother. And they said I didn't come here with you. They kept saying it over and over. That I didn't come here with you, I came here with my mother. It made no sense." Ian's activity with the whacking stick grew more pronounced the further he got into his circular tale.

"Were they trying to say I'm not your mother?"

"I guess. I don't think they knew what they were trying to say. It made me crazy. Then they got mad and told me to stop talking about it."

"Jessica got mad?"

"No," said Ian. "She was nice. The other one got mad. The guy."

More revelations. Evidently the false memory trick backfired on Ian in an unexpected way. He understood Dorothy's legal claim to parenthood over him, and the conditioning reinforced that. "Do you remember the bat?"

"That's the other thing!" he shouted. "They tried to tell me there was no bat! They said I made it up!"

"You didn't make it up," said Dorothy. This was better than she hoped. The false memory they attempted to implant was meant to be a pleasant lie to make him complacent. Instead, they had given him a paradox; he had both come here with his mother and not with Dorothy. In the face of that contradiction, he rejected it, at least the parts that made no sense to him. The part about Dorothy being his mother was now apparently set in stone for him, though. As this young man she had only known a month expressed his commitment to her as his family, she found herself taken by the reality of it. This was no legal fiction, the way Harrison had employed it to save all her sisters in Texas. This was her son.

"Listen, Ian," she said. "I understand you are feeling frustrated right now, but I need to ask you to do something, and it won't be easy. I need you to let this go. They might try to tell you about how you got here a different way than they already did, and I want you not to argue with them about it. Can you do that for me?"

"But they're wrong!" he cried.

Dorothy took pride in his preadolescent drive for justice. "Even if they are wrong, I still need you to go along with it. I promise we will set them straight before we leave here. But for now, I need us all to avoid getting into fights over things like this. Can you promise me you'll wait it out?"

He frowned. "Yeah, I promise."

"Good. There's one other thing I have to ask you, and I want you to know it's okay with me if you say no, and I'm so sorry I am even bringing this up. I am asking because I need to know where we stand here." She paused. "If the time comes when I ask you to break something, will you be able to do it?"

He flinched at this. "I don't like that."

"I know." She put her hand on his shoulder. "And believe me, I am sorry. If you can't, you can't, and I won't ask again. But I am asking now. Do you think you would be able to break something if I need you to?"

"I'll try." It came out in a bit of a squeak.

"That's all I will ask," she said. "But the other thing I need right now. No fighting about anything, right?"

"Right."

She held out her hand. "Shake on it?"

He spat in his palm and wetly slapped and grabbed her hand, then pumped once vigorously before letting go.

"All right." She wiped her palm on Strontium's borrowed skirt, silently groaning at the prospect of having to undo so much of the witch's upbringing of the boy, starting with sealing promises with spit. Ew.

"Dotty."

Dorothy jumped. Claudia's voice sounded as clearly in her skull as if spoken at her point blank.

"Oops. Try not to act surprised. Should have started with that. Sorry."

"Can you hear that?" she whispered to Ian.

"Hear what?" he asked.

"I'm in the dugout," came the voice. "Nod if you think you can get here without drawing attention."

She hesitated, then nodded.

Ian frowned. "What?"

Dorothy pulled him into a hug. "Nothing at all, dear." She kissed him on the forehead, then pulled back to look in his eyes. "Are you going to be all right?"

"I think so."

"Good. I need to go for a walk. Clear my head a bit. Can we talk some more about this later?"

"Sure." Ian resumed his weed-whacking activity, with the same intensity as before.

Dorothy walked toward the open dugout, currently occupied by three children, and under siege by three more.

"Not that one," said the voice.

Dorothy halted. She looked at the dugout completely covered in weeds and brambles. Even if she could hack through that, every rational part of her mind told her this was a test. If she went there, Felicia would be waiting with her assortment of knives to explain to her what they did to people they couldn't brainwash.

But the voice belonged to Claudia. No threat of violence would keep Dorothy away from knowing if it was really her.

As casually as she could muster, she strolled across the partially cleared ballpark. It took her an agonizing full minute, possibly two, possibly a thousand, but she made it to the border between cleared ground and wild tangle. She paused there, pretending to notice a fascinating weed. Plucking a frond from it, she held it up to the sun in mock inspection, which afforded her the opportunity to spin in a slow circle, and check for watchers.

Jessica and her partner had begun to herd kids back to the building. Apart from them, only the workers occupied the field, all busily engaged. She swept the press box and every other window on that side of the park, which she discovered she now had the ability to do in extreme magnification after whispering a simple spell. That caught her by surprise, but she recovered, and inwardly thanked the book, once again.

Certain no one had eyes on her, she smoothly pushed through the

254

brush, and emerged in the dugout. It happened so quickly she had a flash of panic she might have torn up her clothes or scratched her skin to shreds, but on inspection found no damage to either.

"Hey," said Claudia.

Dorothy spun. Claudia stood there, a look of combined joy and worry on her face. Dorothy jumped into her arms, and held on for dear life. Claudia returned the hug, and then some. For the first time in her life, Dorothy's heart outraced her head. Overcome with elation, she took Claudia's face in her hands and kissed her.

With that contact, Dorothy's sense of well-being soared. Claudia being here fixed everything. She had never been so happy to see someone, and as she basked in the warmth of that thought, she found herself admitting the only two things that had kept her moving through these challenging and terrifying weeks were her need to protect her little sister, and the thought of seeing Claudia again. The mental image of this meeting had sustained her, and brought forth a courage she did not know she possessed, that sense of security now tightly bound in Claudia's embrace. And as Dorothy's entire body begin to tingle, she realized she was still kissing Claudia. And Claudia was kissing back.

Then her head finally caught up to her heart.

Dorothy snapped away, the wide-eyed look of astonishment on Claudia's face surely mirrored in her own, probably to greater effect. "Oh, my!" She gasped for air. "Oh, my God."

For a second, neither of them spoke. Finally, Claudia offered, "We don't have to talk about this."

A generous out, but Dorothy wanted no part of it. "Yes, we do!"

"Okay," said Claudia. Again they stood in shocked silence, until Claudia attempted to break it. "Um…"

"Oh, my God," said Dorothy. "I think I love you."

"I love you, too." No hesitation.

Dorothy's heart leapt as those words triggered an adrenaline surge, and she regretted blurting her feelings in the heat of her confusion. "Claudia…" She fumbled for the words. "I'm not a lesbian."

Claudia smiled. "I can work with that."

Warmth spread across Dorothy's face, surely into an absurdly obvious blush. She held up her hands. "I can't… I can't do this right now. This is too big. We need to table this until we're not in real and immediate danger anymore. Can we do that? Can we talk about this later?"

"Later is good," said Claudia. "I like later."

"Okay," said Dorothy, still panting. "Good."

"Okay then," said Claudia.

"How did you find us?" asked Dorothy, desperate to fill the ensuing silence with any other subject.

"I didn't." Claudia pointed to the bench behind her, where lay a prone and unconscious Apryl. "She did."

Dorothy took a moment to absorb the implications. "It's just the two of you? Does Harrison even know where you are?"

"I have no idea. It was just going to be Apryl, but when I realized she was homing in on you, I grabbed her."

Dorothy sat beside Apryl on the bench, and felt her forehead. "Does this happen to her when she teleports?"

"Not always," said Claudia, "but yeah."

"The women are all brainwashed," said Dorothy. "Right now, the three of us are the only people here who have their own minds. I can't risk either of you getting caught, so you're going to have to stay here for now. I will try to get food and water to you."

"What are we going to do?"

Dorothy thought on that. Her resources had now tripled, perhaps more than tripled depending on Apryl. Even without Harrison, she might still have enough opportunity to begin a plan of action. "There is a small army of very angry women being held here. They just don't know they are angry yet. What are we going to do?" She peered through the brambles that held them secret for now.

"We are going to wake them up."

[PART 3]
PROTÉGÉE

49

NEEDLE MEETS HAYSTACK

Harrison stared at the spot where his wife stood only a few moments before, a circular patch in the packed dirt road, about four feet across and smooth. Individual chunks of embedded gravel sparkled at him, scoured to a shine. "When you say you can't track her, you mean you need more resources, right?" He asked Aplomado. "Do we call Larson? Do you need to get back to Esoteric yourself?"

The wizard shook his head. "This is not about resources. Your wife operates within a system of parameters we have never successfully isolated. Her abilities may be the single most random phenomenon currently under study at Esoteric, and I probably should not have to add how extreme a statement that is."

Milton pulled a communicator from a pouch on his belt. "Mrs. Mendoza-Cody? Special Agent de Queiroz? Status, please."

"That's a waste of your time," said Aplomado. "Her abilities are all based around an internal power source of extraordinary magnitude. The primary manifestation is disruption of other power sources. Their communicators are most likely lumps of slag right now."

Harrison had witnessed that talent before, when Apryl inadvertently exploded a ship's engine. He had used it himself when temporarily imbued with her powers, to destroy Ru'opihm's weapons factory. The batteries in the pen-sized communicators never stood a chance.

"Is that something we can use?" asked Harrison. "If she's disrupting power sources, is that the sort of thing that might be detectable?"

"I do not believe so," said Aplomado. "Disruption of power sources has been a globally common phenomenon for some years now. It would be difficult to attribute a cause to your wife."

"I don't understand what that means," said Milton.

"The energy demands of the post-Mayhem world are significant," said the wizard. "And the means for producing that energy, in most cases, is based on found technologies. Some have been reverse-engineered, some are in use without a full understanding of their workings, some are based in magic. There are probably thousands of such generators and power stations scattered across the globe."

"That's part of how we've located other rising nations," said Harrison. As the first and largest of the new countries, New Chicago had long since established itself as a self-sustaining entity in terms of energy production and consumption. For the first two years after the Wave, severed power lines continued to carry energy from their original sources, stolen directly through time, across universes, and sustained with the energy of the Static Mayhem Pulse itself. The same effect sustained all manner of running water pipes. Eventually, those sources of energy and water petered out, but by then New Chicago had become a nation of nearly a million inhabitants, under a government that had been working on the problem of what to do when that happened.

They met some of their power needs with fossil fuels, but most energy came from solar gathering stations and turbines capturing the currents of the Great Lakes and their various rivers, based on advanced technologies left in the wake of the Wave. Other energy needs were addressed with magical solutions; the Department of Esoteric Studies facility was independently powered by a reactor that drew its power entirely from found magic wands and other enchanted objects, serving the dual purpose of keeping the lights on, and keeping those artifacts out of circulation.

"Indeed," said Aplomado. "However, probabilistically, we can expect a dozen detectable disruptions today alone, all of which will be in small sovereign nations who will not invite us to investigate their difficulties."

"It's a place to start," said Milton.

"It is a dead end. It is, of course, your prerogative to pursue it. I predict it will take two weeks to discover that none of those disruptions will be traceable to the assistant director's wife."

"He's right," said Hadley. "There's a good chance she won't have caused enough of a disruption to detect at all. If you put your energy in that direction, you are going to get bogged down in a wild goose chase."

"Hadley says you're right," said Harrison.

"Tell him I know I am right," said Aplomado.

"I'm standing right here," said Hadley.

"What do we do now?" asked Sarah, eyes wide, tone edgy.

"This doesn't change anything," said Milton. "Our purpose here is to look for clues as to their destination, which we will continue to do. If that doesn't work out for us, we regroup, but those two being out there does not affect any of that. If anything, they will give us an advantage by being on the inside." He looked at Harrison with steely and commanding eyes. "De Queiroz is a trained field agent. Mrs. Mendoza-Cody is one of the most powerful humans on the planet. They'll take care of themselves. For now, we stay on mission."

In Milton's shoes, Harrison would say those exact same things. That didn't make it easier to embrace the reality that his adopted children, his one true daughter by blood, and now his wife, had all fallen into the hands of the enemy.

"Understood," he said.

[50]

FAERIE REDUX

As Dorothy and Melody made their way down the seats, Dorothy struggled not to look around them for prying eyes. Melody was supposed to be in bed, but Dorothy convinced Brooke Witherspoon, in charge of bedtime for the children, she and Melody wanted to go for a stroll before sundown. The general assumption that Dorothy was under the mind control rendered her immune to suspicion so far, especially from the other women. Brooke happily released them, on the promise Dorothy would bring Melody back before dark. She didn't imagine she would be able to sustain this ruse for more than a day or two at most. Hopefully, she wouldn't need to.

They came down as close as they could to the dugout to minimize the amount of distance they would need to cross over open ground. Dorothy had cast an eye repellant spell over them to avoid being seen. Anyone who attempted to look at them would find their attention strongly drawn in the other direction, assuming she understood it correctly, and made no mistakes casting it.

"Okay, Little," said Dorothy. "I have a surprise for you, but you have to make me a promise. Can you promise me that no matter what you see, you can stay quiet?"

"I promise," said Melody.

"I mean it, little girl," said Dorothy. "Even if you feel like shouting for joy, you have to keep it to a whisper. Do you understand?"

She perked up. "Is it a happy surprise?"

"It is a very happy surprise, but I need you to be extra special quiet about it. It has to be our secret, and if anyone hears you, it will give it away."

"I promise," said Melody, with a new seriousness in her voice. Dorothy hoped it would be enough.

They got to the front row, and Dorothy lifted Melody up and planted her on the wall. "Wait here." She handed her a paper bag, containing supplies for the fugitives. She climbed over the five-foot barrier, then picked Melody up and set her down on the weeds. "All right. We're going to go into that bush." She pointed at the overgrown dugout. "I'm going to carry you. When we get inside, you'll see the surprise, and you will be very, very, very quiet. Right?"

"Right!" said Melody, loudly enough to make Dorothy flinch.

"How about we start the quiet right now." She picked up her little sister, who wrapped her arms around Dorothy's neck, and held tight. As before, Dorothy pushed effortlessly through the overgrowth. This time she paid better attention to her own behavior, and caught herself muttering the gibberish composing the spell to protect herself and Melody from thorns and branches. The fact she now did these things, only sometimes aware of it, did not bother her at all, and she made a mental note of that, as it didn't seem like her.

They emerged in the dugout, now getting dark in the early evening twilight. Dorothy's admonishment that Melody stay quiet turned out to be pointless.

"Melody?" said Apryl, with no regard for volume.

Melody's head popped up and around to find the voice.

"Baby!" cried Apryl.

"Mommy!" Melody dropped to the floor and ran into her mother's arms. Dorothy cringed at the sounds. Apryl did not rise, even at the sight of her daughter. Melody and Apryl held each other and rocked.

"Dorothy O'Neill, you are my favorite person in the entire world right now," said Apryl. It sounded sluggish. That didn't stop Dorothy from choking up.

"I do what I can," she said.

"Hey, tell me that's food." Claudia pointed to the bag. Her tone was short, and distant. Apparently, they had now come full circle back to awkward. Dorothy did not intend to stand for that, but first things first.

She reached in, pulled out a wrapped sandwich, and handed it to Claudia, who opened it and began devouring. Dorothy reached in again and pulled out a juice box.

"Fank you!" said Claudia around her food, snatching the drink.

Dorothy gave her a moment to navigate the straw, swallow her bite of sandwich, and take a sip of the juice, before producing the next item. Claudia's eyes went wide as Dorothy pulled out a roll of toilet paper.

"Oh, my God! I love you!" Claudia took the roll of paper, admiring it for a moment, before her face sank. "Fuck. Sorry about that."

"No," said Dorothy.

Claudia frowned. "No?"

"No, we are not doing this." She put the bag down, and held out her hands to Claudia, palms up. After allowing her to stare at them for a few seconds, she said, "Take them."

Claudia put down her sandwich and took them, apprehensively.

"I am very, very happy to see you. That has to be more important than whatever happens next. I refuse to let you retreat into your awkward defensive nonsense. You mean the world to me, and now I have to reevaluate what that even means. I have a lot of new things to think about, and a lot of feelings that caught us both by surprise. And I'm still sorting out how I want to express those feelings."

"Do you want to try kissing me again?" asked Claudia, with a deviously innocent smile.

Dorothy laughed. "A little. Don't push it though."

"Come again?" said Apryl.

Dorothy could not decide if she found the look of astonishment on Apryl's face embarrassing or amusing. She sighed, ruled Apryl family, and forged ahead. "Welcome to my identity crisis, Apryl."

"This is the best day ever," said Apryl. "Carry on, you two. Pretend I'm not here."

"Perhaps I could get you some popcorn?" said Dorothy.

"Actually, Apryl," said Claudia. "I think for the moment we're done." She gave Dorothy's hands a squeeze and let go. Claudia offered Dorothy a warm smile, then took another huge bite of her sandwich.

"Rats," said Apryl.

"I'm going to try to get you out of here tonight." Dorothy sat down next to Apryl on the bench and handed her a sandwich and a juice box. "There's a storage closet near one of the locker rooms that looks like no one is using it."

"I guess that's a step up," said Claudia.

"I don't suppose you can teleport?" Dorothy asked Apryl.

She shook her head. "Maybe once I rest a bit. Getting here took a lot out of me. Totally worth it, though." She hugged Melody tighter.

"Well, I may be able to sneak you in on foot. I'm working on a spell that makes people look away from me. If we sneak out of here after midnight when everyone is asleep, the spell might be able to deflect the few people still up."

Claudia and Apryl stared at Dorothy, with flat expressions impossible for her to read. Their lack of enthusiasm about getting out from under this bush struck her as odd. Before she could ask if they had questions, Claudia said, "Spell?"

"Oh," said Dorothy. "Um… Yes. Spell. I have this book… It's difficult to explain, but Melody and I met this witch when we first left New Chicago."

"Good witch?" asked Apryl. "Bad witch?"

"She said those aren't really meaningful designations. But good. Definitely good. She took care of us until the goblins came. Then she disappeared." She hesitated there, trying to decide whether the word "died" applied. "She left me this book." Dorothy opened her right palm, and the book appeared in it.

Apryl gasped.

"It's okay. Really. It's been helping me keep Melody and Ian safe. It protected me from the mind control thing the Professor did to everyone else."

"Slow down," said Claudia. "Professor? Ian? Mind control? Goblins?"

"I know. It's a lot to take in all at once. Let me focus on getting you out of this shrub first. I promise I will explain everything."

"Is it… changing you?" asked Apryl.

Dorothy almost said no, on pure reflex, but caught herself. It was most certainly changing her, but not in the way Apryl meant. "Do I seem different to you?"

"Well," said Claudia, "if you're asking, I gotta say that's a new look for you."

Dorothy glanced down at her own clothes. She still wore the frilly skirt, shawl, and knee boots she borrowed from Strontium, the same garments she wore when she executed her first goblin. And yet they were entirely free of blood. Made of silk, or something like it, they had somehow carried her into and out of the briars surrounding this dugout twice now without so much as a run or a pill. Surely a new look for her, to say the least, but it didn't make her a different person. "Okay, fine. Picture me out of these clothes."

Claudia grinned.

Dorothy blushed again. "Picture me wearing something else, please. Do I seem any different to you? Apryl, do you still trust me?"

"You brought me back my baby," she said. "You get all the trust you want."

"Dorrie took care of us," said Melody.

"Hold on to that, please," said Dorothy. "I don't know if these are just tricks I'm learning, or if there's something bigger at work here. But I promise you I have done nothing with this book but help you, and help the children, and I am going to use it to free all of them, with your help."

Apryl kissed Melody on the forehead, and lurched back in surprise. "Hey, you're tingly."

"Mm hmm," said Melody, snuggling further into her mother's arms.

"Why is she tingly?" Apryl asked Dorothy. "How long has she been like this?"

"I don't know." Dorothy leaned in and kissed Melody on the forehead herself. Her sister's skin buzzed against her lips like a live battery. "Wow. I have no idea."

"Did the witch do this?"

"No," said Dorothy. "Strontium said we were both cursed when we found her. Something about a bad judgment spell. She was able to clear me of it, but Melody wasn't showing any of the correct symptoms. She did say Melody was affected by it somehow, but she didn't seem to think it was anything dangerous."

"Strontium?" asked Claudia.

"The witch. Don't ask," said Dorothy in response to Claudia's amused expression.

"As soon as we get home, we get you to a wizard," said Apryl to Melody.

"Okay," said Melody.

In that moment, in the half-light of the dugout, Melody's hair glinted purple again, This time the light clearly issued from strands of her hair itself, not some jewel embedded in it.

"You're sparkling," said Apryl.

"You saw that too?" asked Dorothy.

"So did I," said Claudia.

Apryl gently took a handful of Melody's hair and held it up to her nose. "That's the smell!"

"What smell?" asked Melody.

"It's how I found you," said Apryl. "I could sense you. And then I smelled something I couldn't place, but I knew it was you, and it took me straight here."

"What do I smell like?" she asked.

Apryl stroked her daughter's hair. "Baby, you've got Faerie in you."

[51]

SCORCHED EARTH

Harrison trudged through the forest. The brush here did not resemble what he remembered from his youth, hiking through the mountains of New England. Familiar trees, ferns, mosses and other low-lying plants abounded, but interspersed among bushes with broad, purple leaves, randomly distributed bamboo, bonsai palm trees, and other assorted floral wildlife that ran from absurd to intimidating. Some of this was native to the magical world, brought here by the Mayhem Wave, while others were hybrids, mutant offspring of the mundane and the fantastic. Passing through it, particularly when forced to come into physical contact with the bizarre plants, he wished he had a machete. He ever so briefly toyed with the idea of using Bess to cut a path, but didn't risk offending her.

"How much farther?" he asked.

"This would really go much more quickly if you would just fly," said Sparky.

Jacobs, one of the two NCSA agents who accompanied Harrison and Sarah on this guided trek, laughed at that.

"No, really though," said Harrison.

"I dunno," said the pixie. "Half a mile maybe? Maybe less? I seriously have no intuitive grasp of how you people measure distance."

"Great," he said.

The four of them soldiered on, toward some clue Sparky discovered in the forest but declined to describe, in typical pixie obfuscation. Hadley walked with them, passing intangibly through trees as he went.

267

Harrison looked to Sarah. "How are you holding up?"

"Are we talking about the hike, the quest for my son, or my comatose husband?" she asked. Harrison did not detect bitterness, only a request for clarity.

"I meant the hike, but you can answer any one of those."

"My feet are getting sore, I am in constant state of anxiety that we will never find him, and I wish I were back at the hospital right now," she said.

Harrison addressed the only thing on that list he had any control over. "Do you need to rest?"

She shook her head. "I need this. Let's keep moving."

"What's that up ahead?" asked Jacobs. "Those black trees."

Harrison squinted forward. At least a football field away stood a line of trees, branchless and stark black. "Is that it?" he asked Sparky.

"Hang on." She zipped upward. A couple seconds later she returned. "Yep."

"Good."

They drew nearer to the trees, not only branchless, but also considerably shorter than all their neighbors. The reason for that became clear when they crossed the line. Beyond the blackened trees lay a patch of bare, charred ground, in a circle roughly one hundred feet across.

"Holy shit," Harrison whispered. "This is the thing you said was too complicated to explain?"

"I was afraid I'd say it wrong," she said. "Is it important? It looks important."

"I have no idea." Harrison pulled out his communicator. "Milton, we're here. I am looking at section of forest that has been burned to the ground."

"Forest fire?" came Milton's voice over the tiny speaker.

"I don't think so. It's circular, and extremely well contained. Whatever burned here was hot enough to destroy everything on the ground, but the trees outside the boundary are untouched."

"How big is it? Could it be a blast from a rocket or some other aircraft?"

"Don't know. My guess would be not, because it looks too big, but I'm really not an expert at this sort of forensics. Hang on a second, let me check something." Harrison drew Bess from her sheath. As he held her out at arm's length, looking at the reflection of the ground in her blade that showed a light green tint indicating the presence of magic, she spoke to him.

This is dragon fire, she said.

Harrison nearly dropped the sword. He hadn't expected so concrete and immediate an answer, let alone that revelation. "Are you sure?"

Most definitely. I have slain many dragons. The signs of their activity are unmistakable.

"Jacobs and Clark," he said to the two agents with them, "I need you to get samples of the burnt soil, and the charred wood." He pulled out his communicator again. "Milton, Bess says this is the work of a dragon."

"A dragon!" cried Clark, looking skyward.

"Get it together, Agent," said Harrison. "You have a job to do."

"She's sure of that?" asked Milton.

"Says she is," said Harrison. "She tends to be reliable on this sort of thing. I have Clark and Jacobs collecting samples, in case we need them."

"I'm sending Aplomado to you," said Milton. "Stay put."

"Great," said Harrison.

"A.D. Cody? Have a look at this." Jacobs pointed to one of the trees at the edge of the circle. As Harrison crossed the gap, tiny coals crunched under his feet.

"What do you see?" he asked.

"This," said Jacobs. "What do you make of it?"

Harrison scanned the burned tree looking for whatever singled it out. Near the top, a mark in the shape of an X had been gouged there. "Check the other trees. See if there's anything else like this. And get pictures, please."

"What do you think it means?" asked Jacobs.

Harrison traced the mark with his eyes, looking for anything to give it meaning. "I don't even have a guess. Maybe nothing. Let me know what else you find."

Jacobs nodded, and began systematically inspecting the tops of the trees. Harrison worked in the opposite direction. About ten minutes into that task, he discovered another possible mark, three scratches, in a pattern than did not form a recognizable letter or symbol. He took a picture of it with his phone. Behind him came a loud crunching noise, and he spun to find Aplomado crouched with his head down, one hand on the ground, the other extended for balance.

"Holy shit!" said Harrison. "Did you seriously jump the whole way here?"

In response, still looking down, the wizard held up the index finger of his free hand, to buy silence, time, or perhaps both. Shortly, he stood, and brushed black dirt off the hand that was on the ground.

"I did," he said, sounding out of breath. Harrison found something about Aplomado having physical limitations quite satisfying. "What do you have for me?" asked the wizard.

"You're looking at it." Harrison extended his arms and spun in a circle.

Aplomado made a similar but slower sweep. "Dragon."

"Way ahead of you."

"Really," said the wizard. "European or Chinese?"

"European," guessed Harrison without pause. The gamble paid off, as Aplomado frowned, unable to patronize him.

"What variety?" asked Aplomado.

Damn. "I'm hoping you can tell me. I don't know what nuances to look for."

"It was a meaningless question," said Aplomado. "Each European dragon is unique. They do not come in varieties. Good guess on European though. A Chinese dragon would never be able to burn this hot or this precisely." The wizard picked up a fragment of debris, which he crumbled in his fingers and scrutinized.

"Why would a dragon do this kind of damage to a forest?"

"This is a goblin bone," said Aplomado, holding up a scorched object. To Harrison's eyes, it looked no different from a stick. "Speculating on a dragon's motives is generally futile. This could have been a focused attack, a temper tantrum, or simple boredom." He sniffed the burnt bone before dropping it into his sleeve.

Harrison frowned. "What are you doing with that bone?"

Aplomado ignored the question. "Dragons do not generally consider goblins to be food, sport or threat. The most reasonable explanation would be that this goblin either said the wrong thing, or was in the wrong place at the wrong time when a dragon had an episode of moodiness. It all depends on which dragon this was." He knelt and brushed the ashes on the ground with his fingertips.

"How many dragons are there?" asked Harrison.

"At present, twenty-three European and sixty-one Chinese," said Aplomado without looking up. "At least on record. There could be ten times that many Europeans as yet undiscovered. They do tend to stay hidden unless provoked."

"Do you think this dragon has anything to do with whoever took our people?" asked Harrison.

"Difficult to say. This site is close enough to the village to make it plausible, but far enough away to be a coincidence. I would be more convinced if there had been dragon tracks or droppings anywhere near the settlement, but we would have noticed those right away."

"But it's possible."

Aplomado sighed loudly. "Yes, Mr. Cody. It is 'possible.' On balance, I do recommend that we pursue this lead."

Harrison took that for the sliver of hope it provided him. "Are you able to track a dragon?"

Aplomado looked up, and offered Harrison the rare and sinister sight of him smiling. "I am. I most certainly am."

REBECCA

Well past midnight, Dorothy returned to the dugout. She slipped past the thorns and branches again, and found Claudia sitting up waiting for her. Apryl had gone back to sleep. "How is she doing?"

"Kind of spotty," said Claudia. "This is the third time she's dozed off since you left. I get she's tired, but I've never seen her this wiped out after a jump before. Part of my plan kind of hinged on her kicking lots of ass when we got here, so I'm getting a teensy bit nervous."

Dorothy sat beside Claudia on the bench. They both stared straight ahead at the bushes covering them. On the other side of that barrier, the stadium lights shone down on the field, lighting the way for workers clearing brush on the graveyard shift. Enough of that light filtered into their hideout for them to see.

"We should talk," said Dorothy, still looking away.

"I thought you wanted to wait until we weren't, you know, likely to die any minute."

"Yes, well, I changed my mind," said Dorothy. "If something does happen to either of us, and we never talked about this… I don't want that."

"Oh."

Neither of them looked at each other. Finally, Claudia ventured, "You're not gay."

"Not as a rule, no."

After a beat, Claudia said, "I get it. No big deal."

Dorothy finally turned to look at Claudia, who continued to stare ahead, an unreadable expression on her face. She took Claudia's hand, warm, and soft, and tense. "Claudia, look at me."

Claudia turned to face her, with numb eyes.

Dorothy tried to form the words, but they wouldn't come to her. Finally, out of a simple inability to express it any other way, she leaned in and kissed her. Unlike before, this was deliberate, meaningful, tender, and brief. Dorothy's heart rate picked up a bit, and she suspected a new blush in her cheeks, hopefully invisible in the dim light. When she pulled away, Claudia had gone from stoic to surprised.

"Really?" said Claudia.

"Yes. Really." At that, Dorothy ran out of words again. She waited for Claudia to break the silence, which she did.

"You have no idea how much I want to get naked with you right now."

The flood of heat to her cheeks confirmed a blush no doubt visible in any light. "Actually, I kind of do, but that's out of the question at the moment."

"Are you sure about this?" asked Claudia.

"No," said Dorothy. "It's new, and it's scary, and it's confusing. But I haven't been able to stop thinking about you since we went on the run. And now that you're here, I cannot imagine a life without you in every moment of it."

"Wow." Claudia sat for a moment, her customary sharp wit apparently overcome. "Me too. I mean the not being able to stop thinking about you. And the life thing."

"I know. Melody… kind of outed you."

Claudia frowned. "What does that mean?"

"She told me you loved me. It was right after you let it slip. She heard me say I love you, too, and she told me you loved me, only she had no idea it was you on the phone."

"How did she…?" Claudia stopped mid question. "Harrison. That dick."

"Don't. I'm glad she told me. It was a shock at first, but it helped me understand you, and why we've been at each other's throats for so long. And it's been on my mind this entire time we've been apart. All I could think of was how much I wanted to see you again, and I let myself believe that I wanted that in spite of what I knew. But now I think I wanted it because I knew." She looked down. "I'm rambling again, aren't I?"

Claudia squeezed her hand. The contact gave her chills. "No, you're good."

Dorothy looked into her eyes. "I don't want to do anything about this until we're safe at home. But I needed you to know how I feel." To punctuate this, she kissed Claudia again, softly. "I think it's safe to say I am going to be very awkward at this. I was bad enough at straight sex. This is going to open up a whole new world of embarrassment for me. I trust you, I really do, but I can't afford to be this self-conscious right now. So, no funny business until we make it out of here. Then I'm all over you. Deal?"

"Deal." Claudia grinned. "You better believe I'm gonna get us out of this one. I've never been this motivated in my life."

"See that you do." After a beat, Dorothy said, "I don't know what I'm going to tell my mother about you. This is going to be a lot for her to adjust to."

"Is it because I'm Brazilian?"

Dorothy stared at her in the best deadpan she could manage. "Yes, Claudia. It's because you're Brazilian."

"Mom always hoped you'd settle down with a nice Irish girl?"

Dorothy laughed at that, then lifted the hand she held and kissed it. "We need to get back to business."

"Yes, ma'am," said Claudia.

Dorothy leaned down and pulled a pair of wire cutters out of her boot. "This was the best I could do. Do you want to wake Apryl, or cut a hole in that bush?"

Claudia held out her hand. "I'll do the bush. Why do we need to cut it anyway? You've gone in and out a bunch of times."

"I think I've been using magic to slip past the branches. I can't carry all three of us through there, though."

Claudia met this with a stare.

"Please don't let this bother you. I promise I'm not turning into a monster."

"Sorry," said Claudia. "It's just pretty new."

"Well, I guess we both have new things to get used to then, don't we?"

Claudia smiled. "Touché."

"Darn right."

Claudia went to work on the branches. Dorothy slid down the bench to the sleeping Apryl, and shook her shoulder. "Hey, sleepyhead. I need you to get up. We're moving."

"Five more minutes," mumbled Apryl.

Dorothy shook her again. "Nope. Sorry. Rise and shine."

"Mm," Apryl complained. After a couple more shakes, she sat up. "What time is it?"

"No idea. Late."

"Melody?"

274

"Safe in bed, along with all the other children." For an instant, Dorothy reconsidered her use of the word "safe," but did not correct herself. Convincing Apryl to let Melody return to the group to avoid suspicion had been a battle.

"Okay," said Apryl. "Are we going now?"

"Yes. Can you stand?"

"Dunno. Haven't tried yet." Apryl pushed off from the bench to her feet. She swooned. Dorothy caught her. "Whoa. Head rush."

"I have you," said Dorothy.

The light from the field poured into the dugout more dramatically as Claudia made headway through the overgrowth. Dorothy walked Apryl to the passage. "I need both of you to stay extremely close to me, and hold my hands. "There are workers out there. They didn't see me come in here, and I want to keep it that way. Ready?" They both nodded. "Good." Dorothy escorted them through the gap, onto the lawn of shorn weeds. They still had about twenty yards to cross before they made it to cover.

"Green Monster," said Apryl.

Dorothy's heart leapt. She frantically looked around, trying to spot the Professor. If he caught them now, their hopes would all come to an end. "Where?" she whispered.

Apryl pointed. "There."

Dorothy looked up at the left field wall, painted a loud green, and towering over much of the stadium.

Apryl hocked and spat on the ground.

"What are you doing?" whispered Dorothy.

Apryl scowled and pouted. "This is Fenway Park," said the New Yorker.

With Apryl and Claudia safely tucked away in the promised storage closet, Dorothy proceeded to the second part of her mission for the night. Many of the kidnapped women shared sleeping quarters, but not all of them. Fortunately, Rebecca Wheeler occupied a single by herself. Dorothy slipped in without difficulty, and pulled up a chair next to Rebecca's bed. Steeling herself for a high stakes gamble, she shook her shoulder.

"Becca?" she said.

"What?" said Rebecca, eyes still shut.

"Are you awake?"

Rebecca groaned. "I am now."

"I'm sorry," said Dorothy. "I couldn't sleep, and I needed someone to talk to."

Rebecca grumbled, and muttered a few incoherent words, before sitting up. "What's the matter?" Even in her half-awake state, she managed to make the question sound both professional and compassionate. The others looked up to her and followed her because of this quality, the reason Dorothy chose to free her first. Unexpectedly, Dorothy now found herself aware of another quality in Rebecca that had eluded her for years: how pretty she was. Dorothy made a mental note her heart now gave her brain permission to notice new things, and forged ahead.

"I just feel nervous about being here," said Dorothy.

"You have nothing to worry about," said Rebecca patiently.

"Neither do you," said Dorothy. "Not anymore."

As Rebecca took in those words with a ponderous look on her face, Dorothy began to chant. The language was the same string of nonsense sounds she had been hearing in her head for the past two days, both from her reading of the words of that language in her book, and from her involuntary vocalizations of them. Now she chanted them deliberately, and while she wouldn't be able to explain how, she knew the literal translation of her words. *They will not have your mind.*

Rebecca's face cycled through irritation to confusion, until landing on shock. "They will not have my mind," she whispered.

Hearing it in English felt bizarre to Dorothy, but she did not flinch from her chant.

After nearly a minute of this, a tear ran down Rebecca's face. "Is my husband dead?" she asked in a tone both weak and desperate.

Dorothy had not anticipated this question. "I'm so sorry, Becca. I don't know. How are you feeling?"

"Okay, I think."

"How much do you remember of the last four weeks?"

"All of it. We're in a baseball stadium. There's a lizard who wants to kill us for some important spell. And until right now, I was somehow okay with that."

"It's some form of mind control," said Dorothy.

"I think they killed my husband," said Rebecca.

"I hope that isn't true. But right now, we need to get everyone away from here and back home."

"How many of us are there now? How many are free?"

"You were the first I woke up," said Dorothy. "So, two."

Rebecca climbed out of bed. "Then you need to tell me everything you know. And then we need to start waking them all up."

Rebecca's resolve gratified Dorothy. If Blake were indeed dead, there would be time for mourning later. For now, they would have to prioritize breaking the other women free of the conditioning. "Can you get dressed?" asked Dorothy.

"Where are we going?" she asked.

"To a storage closet downstairs. We have a lot of planning to do."

[53]

UNFINISHED BUSINESS

Smoke rose from the pile of goblin corpses. With Aplomado now devoted to locating the dragon, the remainder of the team cleaned up the camp. While the goblins had been relatively odorless lying dead in the open, burning them resulted in an unholy stench that rendered the entire area unsuitable for occupation. Aplomado did what he could to provide a sweeping breeze to take it away, but it barely made a dent. The team returned indoors. Some sealed themselves in the abandoned houses, others retreated to the calm of the passenger cabin in the flyer. Harrison gazed out the window at the puffs of green cloud rising irregularly from the mound of carcasses. The worst of it apparently over, perhaps in another hour or two he could venture outside.

"It's your move," said Hadley.

This nudge brought Harrison's attention back inside, and he looked down at the chessboard represented on the tablet screen at his lap. His queen was gone, and Hadley had pinned his lone remaining bishop. All hope had been lost for at least three moves.

"What do you think of Aplomado?" asked Harrison.

"I think he's patronizing," said Hadley. "Why?"

Harrison thought back to Aplomado pocketing the goblin bone at the patch of burned forest. That bone was evidence of something, and he didn't like not having access to it. He shook his head. "Nothing." He returned his attention to the chess board. "I'm just getting twitchy, I guess. Pawn to queen's knight six." The move played out in animation on the screen.

"You'll never get that piece across the board, you know," said Hadley. "And by the way, rook to king's rook one."

Harrison repeated it for the tablet to hear, and Hadley's rook shuffled to the end of the board, to wait for the futility of Harrison promoting his pawn to queen, only to watch Hadley take it on the next move.

"Resign," said Harrison. The screen shifted to a victory celebration for black, with a prompt to restart the game. He declined. "You know, you don't have to stay in here. Unless you can smell that. Can you?"

"No," said Hadley. "I could choose to smell it, I suppose, but I'm not inclined to do that."

"Why are you here, then?" Across the aisle, Agents Clark and Meredith glanced his way, inadequately concealing their obvious suspicion he was talking to himself, rather than an invisible ghost.

"I can't stray from your side," said Hadley. "We've been over this."

Harrison turned in his seat to better face him. Hadley's ghost still wore the Hawaiian shirt he had on when he first appeared. An interesting choice. That shirt had been Hadley's attempt to dress inconspicuously when they set out on their mission to find the cause of the Mayhem Wave. He died in a different shirt on that mission.

"Okay," said Harrison, "broader question. Why are you here?"

Hadley frowned. "I'm not sure. We've been over that as well."

"But it has something to do with this mission."

"I believe so, yes."

Harrison watched Hadley's face carefully. Perhaps they should have looked for clues there instead of on this protracted snark hunt. "Are you really Hadley?"

"That's a very good question," he said. "I believe so, but there are many factors that could account for that belief that do not require it to be true. I do have Hadley Tucker's memories, although to be specific, I have the memories he shared with you. I do recall other events beyond what you would require for evidence of my identity, but there is no reliable way to determine if those are real, or filler." As he spoke, his pace picked up, and his tone became more animated. "I suppose I could be a construct, given enough memory information to simulate Hadley Tucker's life without actually living it. It's possible that I was designed to believe myself to be Hadley Tucker, and that belief would override contradictions that might present themselves. It's also possible that I am only simulating self-awareness, and that I've been designed to mimic it by an elaborate set of predetermined responses. We could verify that by performing a Turing test on me, I suppose. We would want to do that at Esoteric. Might be worth looking into when we get back."

"Oh, my God," said Harrison. "You are so obviously Hadley. You're the only person I know who could get this enthusiastic over testing his own existence."

"That's a fair observation. We can put that in the column of evidence for my being real. We should keep a tally of points for and against until we can run a proper test."

"Why don't we go ahead and assume that you really are you," said Harrison. "I'm much more interested in the answer to the question of why you came back."

"I really couldn't say," said Hadley.

"Hm," said Harrison. "When I suggest that you might not be real, you throw out a ton of speculations and talk about tests, but when I ask you why you're here at all, you don't want to talk about it."

"I suppose that's right."

"Come on, Hadley. That doesn't seem weird to you? Where's your curiosity?"

Hadley did not respond, other than to look at Harrison in obvious confusion.

"All right, you say you have some connection to this mission, right?"

"Yes," said Hadley.

"Fine," said Harrison. "Then I'm giving you an assignment. I need you to find out why you're haunting me. Put that brain of yours to work. Treat this question like any other problem you have to solve. If you were sent here, I want to know by whom. If you weren't sent here by anyone, I want to know what it is about this mission that brought you back from nothingness."

Hadley hesitated.

Before Harrison had a chance to pursue it further, an unexpected voice came from his communicator.

"Harrison?"

"Larson?"

"Yes, it's me. You were right."

He shook his head, trying to think back on all the things he could have been right about. "Remind me what we're talking about."

"The Mayhespheres. There's a pattern to the pulsing that goes beyond the mathematical models we first attributed to it. We ran thousands of simulations to find a match, and the best fit indicates that someone is deliberately pumping energy into them, and then withdrawing it."

"There's no chance it could be random?" he asked.

"The surges coincide with abductions of your children, to within six hours of when the NCSA thinks they happened," said Larson. "The largest one by far happened at the time of the seventh floor break-in. And the strength of the surges is roughly quantifiable as proportionate to the number of abductees in each case. You might also want to know that we have reconstructed possible evidence of several abductions that predate the ones we know about, assuming the pattern holds."

"Oh, my God," said Harrison.

"Yes," said Larson. "I knew you would want to know, because I know how much you enjoy being right."

"Is that a joke?"

She paused. "Attempted. That's not really in my skill set either."

"Larson, you're telling me we are working on the same case from two different ends. Is that correct?"

"I believe so, yes," she said. "At least, that's the model that seems to best explain the data. I have people combing the prophecy database to look for a match."

"We have a prophecy database?"

"It's incomplete, but yes, we do. Mostly prophecies from non-real sources, but you'd be surprised how much real world prophetic text has turned out to be relevant in the last nine years. Even sources that have been long debunked or even admitted to be frauds include a lot of valid references to non-real events."

Having personally met characters from Shakespeare's *A Midsummer Night's Dream*, this notion surprised Harrison less than Larson could know. "You're hoping to find a prophecy that will help us find the kidnappers?"

"Nothing that specific, I'm afraid. We're looking for any language that could be interpreted as a reference to the Mayhespheres, cross-referenced with any description of a kidnapping. Hopefully we will see something that shows a pattern similar to what we can already observe. To confirm, the most recent pulse was two days ago. Was there another abduction?"

"That would correspond to Melody and Dorothy," he said.

"I'm sorry, how many people did you say?"

"Two," said Harrison. "How many does your math tell you?"

"Closer to five," she said.

Before Harrison had a chance to form the right question about that, Milton came in through the side hatch. In the seconds it stood open, the hatch brought into the flier the horrible stink of the bonfire outside. A quiet whirring indicated the flier's internal ventilation system attempting to purge the air. The hatch opened again, emphasizing the futility of this gesture, as Dallas and Jacobs came in, found seats, and buckled up.

"What's going on?" asked Harrison.

"We're breaking camp," said Milton. "I want to be in the air in fifteen minutes. Just waiting on a few details."

"Harrison?" came Larson's voice.

"Sorry," he said into his communicator. "We're moving on. Please let me know the second you find a prophecy that makes any sense out of this."

"Understood," she said.

"We have a solid lead?" Harrison asked Milton.

"I sure hope so," said Milton. "Aplomado found your dragon."

RISE AND SHINE

J essica successfully lobbied to have Dorothy join the teaching staff at the tiny school. Apart from the two of them, the only other teacher was the man Dorothy had seen earlier. He introduced himself as Paul, and offered no last name. While pleasant enough, he carried himself in a manner noticeably different than what Dorothy had seen in her twenty-eight sisters, exposing him as here by his own free will. His social appeal could not counter his certain role as an accomplice to Dorothy's upcoming murder. Pretending to get along with him pushed her acting abilities to their limit.

Given the small class of students who ran from infant to nearly eleven, instruction in this classroom was varied. It struck Dorothy as odd they would go to this much trouble to maintain the charade of educating these children, when every one of them would be killed before their next birthday. Perhaps the spell required them to be knowledgeable. Perhaps their lessons included preparation for the sacrifice, though Dorothy observed no evidence of this.

Halfway through the morning, Jessica took the children out to the field for recess. The human and goblin workforce continued to expand the boundary between overgrowth and mowed lawn at a remarkable rate. Jessica took the baby in a stroller for a walk while the others stayed with Paul close to the seats, and Dorothy took this opportunity to speak with her alone.

"What do you think of him?" asked Jessica once they were out of earshot.

Dorothy looked back over her shoulder. "Paul? He seems nice enough." She looked back to Jessica, who wore a dreamy expression on her face.

"I think he likes me," she said.

Dorothy contained her horror. "Really?"

Jessica nodded with a smile. "I think he's going to ask me out." Her giddiness masked her obvious failure to consider what "out" could possibly mean in this context.

Dorothy responded with a string of nonsense.

Jessica stopped walking. "What?"

Dorothy repeated the chant.

Jessica gasped.

"They will not have your mind," said Dorothy in plain English.

"Oh, shit," whispered Jessica.

"Keep smiling and keep walking," said Dorothy.

They continued their stroll in silence. After a bit, Jessica said feebly, "I was going to have sex with him."

"Well," said Dorothy, "now you're not."

At lunch, Dorothy sat with the same group of people who had surrounded her the day before. They all had the same cheery, vacuous manner as then, other than Jessica, her happiness obviously strained, though only Dorothy would detect that. They spoke of their jobs in the laundry room, and the kitchen, and running errands for the professor, with the shallow banter of adolescents who find the fact of their occupations more interesting than the tasks themselves.

At the end of their meal, Britney Hinson excused herself with a cheery smile. "I need to go see what Felicia needs me to do next." Britney took the role in this community of gofer to the assassin, a position Dorothy did not envy, but which left her sisters in awe of the prestige it implied.

"Is it all right if I go with her?" Dorothy asked Jessica. "I'm still trying to get a feel for the layout of the building. Besides, I want to say hello to Agent Kestrel."

Britney giggled. "You really do not want to call her that." In her youthful fire, Britney's comment seemed like a dare. To punctuate this remark, she shook her head with a grin, bouncing her blonde curls. The hairstyle was an affectation, and her freely admitted attempt to make herself look like Shirley Temple. It worked.

Dorothy feigned innocent surprise. "Oh, I wouldn't want to offend! Maybe you could tell me a few things about her before we get there? I'm trying so hard to make a good impression." As much as this felt to Dorothy like laying it on too thick, Britney seemed delighted.

"Oh, she is the best!" she said. "You should see what she can do with a knife!"

Dorothy was quite certain she did not want to see that. "Can I go?"

"Sure," said Jessica. She clutched Dorothy's hand, and forced a grin. "Hurry back though, okay?"

"Will do," said Dorothy, getting up from the table.

Two minutes later, well out of view of the others, Dorothy whispered a few words in Britney's ear. After a moment of shock, she embraced Dorothy and cried.

<hr/>

Shortly after noon, Dorothy found Meg Rosso cleaning bathrooms on the upper level.

"Hey," said Meg. "I thought you were going to see Felicia."

"Oh, I decided to wander a bit instead," she said. "This is what they have you doing?"

"Yeah," said Meg. "It's not so bad. At least they have me doing the human toilets. Keri has to do the ones on the lower levels the goblins use. No, thank you."

"Ew."

"I know. How's the school?"

Dorothy shrugged. "It's a good job. I get to work with Jessica, and I love the kids."

"That's nice for you." Meg set down her brush, and flushed a toilet she had finished scrubbing. "I have a few loads of laundry to move along. Do you want to give me a hand before you go back?"

Dorothy smiled. "I'd love that." She took Meg's hand, and began the chant.

Meg's eyes flew open in confusion, and she tried to pull away.

Dorothy held tight, and tugged her in closer, as she chanted more loudly. As she encountered her first sign of resistance in this task, the sense of ease that had been building inside her shattered.

"No..." said Meg. "Don't..."

"They will not have your mind!"

Meg yanked her hand away, and Dorothy braced herself to block her from fleeing. Instead, Meg spun around and vomited violently into the newly shiny toilet. Dorothy sat on the floor and held Meg's hair as she coughed, choked, and cried. Finally, Meg pulled herself away from the bowl and slumped against a wall. Dorothy handed her some paper towels, which she used to wipe her mouth and left crumpled on the floor.

"Can I kill them?' she asked.

"Maybe," said Dorothy.

"Good."

≡≡≡

Dorothy found Mitchell later that afternoon, walking the seats. As the only adult male abductee, he was a bit of an anomaly in the community. Being several years younger than all the women also resulted in mixed success for him socially. After a few false starts in finding a role to play there, his eventual assignment basically amounted to looking busy and keeping to himself. They gave him the title of Roving Security Monitor, his job to walk the grounds throughout the day, and mark boxes on a checklist of places he had to visit at specific times. A pointless task, but it provided valuable exercise, and like everyone else there, he had no complaints.

As Mitchell found the row and seat number on his checklist and marked it secure at the specified time, Dorothy caught up to him, and planted herself in the seat. "Hey there, runt."

"You're in my seat, punk," he said.

She scooted over one and patted the newly empty seat.

Mitchell looked conflicted for a moment, then put his clipboard checklist on the ground and sat next to her. They both gazed out on the partially defoliated ballpark.

"I tried to call you the day the bats came for you," she said. "Did you get my message?"

He turned to face her. "You did? No, I lost my phone. You called me?"

"Yeah. I needed a buddy. Stupid Brad broke up with me, and I needed someone to lean on."

"Oh, Dorothy, I'm sorry," he said. "You do know I just would have made fun of you, right?"

She smiled. "I was counting on it. Jerk."

He looked back out onto the field. "That would have been great. God, I hated that guy."

She sat up at this. "Really? Why?"

"He never treated you like you mattered."

Dorothy rolled those words around in her head. After a bit, she began her chant. Mitchell gave her no reaction. As the volume and intensity increased, he turned his head her way, a look of curiosity on his face. Finally, calmly, she declared, "They will not have your mind."

His look of curiosity changed to one of surprise, then disappointment. He looked back out onto the field.

"God damn it," he said. "I should have known this was too good to be true."

<hr>

Christine Rivera hummed to herself as she chopped carrots. The joy these women took in their jobs gave Dorothy a sick feeling of remorse. Surely they were happier now than they would be before this was all over. Before Meg fought off the cure she offered, Dorothy assumed this would all be about liberation, but now she accepted that for some, this would be nothing but pain. Jessica lost her prospective boyfriend. Britney now feared the woman whose praises she had sung only that morning. Whatever loss Meg had suffered, she wouldn't discuss it. Mitchell found disappointment at the loss of a refreshingly simple lifestyle. Now Chris would be hurt in some unpredictable way, and this was all just the beginning. Dorothy had two dozen worlds yet to shatter.

"Hi, Chris," said Dorothy. She and Meg stood in the door to the kitchen. Chris was alone here, but would only be so for minutes. The rest of the kitchen staff had gone on break, but Chris didn't take breaks. She loved her work that much, as she told them all over lunch.

"Hi." Christine offered a nervous smile.

Mitchell came to the door and nodded. Meg closed it, leaving him on the other side as a lookout. "Do it," she said to Dorothy. "We don't have much time."

Dorothy flinched at the bitterness in Meg's voice, and hoped Chris was too far gone to detect it. This would be hard enough.

"Do what?" said Chris. She stopped chopping, but still clutched the knife.

Dorothy carefully pulled up a stool, sat next to her, and began the chant.

Chris frowned in confusion. "What are you doing?" The knuckles on her knife hand went white.

Dorothy continued to chant.

"What does that mean?" Chris stood and backed away, fear in her eyes, the knife still in her hand, inching up to a defensive position.

"They will not have your mind," Dorothy hissed. This was the most difficult wakeup call so far, for reasons she could not discern. Christine did not resist the way Meg had, but Dorothy could feel the spell had no effect.

Chris's eyes went a bit wider, and she lowered the knife. "They don't."

Dorothy stopped chanting. Tears formed in Christine's eyes.

"They don't?" asked Meg.

Chris shook her head. "No. You too?"

"Just now," said Meg. "Dorothy woke me up."

The knife hit the concrete floor with a resounding clatter. "How many?"

"Becca, Jess, Britney and Mitchell," said Dorothy. "And me."

The tears broke and streamed down her face. "It's so hard. I'm so scared. They all think I'm like them. It's so hard."

"Are they any others who weren't affected?" asked Dorothy.

"I don't know," said Christine.

Dorothy hopped down from the stool and held out her arms. Chris ran into them and curled into a ball. Shorter than Dorothy, Chris sobbed directly into her chest. She had never been under control. Dorothy welcomed this news. They might already have aces up their sleeve. All they had to do was find them.

<hr style="width:20%;text-align:center"/>

Late that afternoon, Siobhan dropped by the school to check on Dorothy. "How are you settling in?"

Again, that phrase gave Dorothy an unpleasant rush. "Good. I like the school. And Jess let me go wandering for a bit, so I could get used to the building. Everyone seems so happy here."

Siobhan raised an eyebrow. "Did she?" She looked at Jessica, who did not notice the scrutiny. "Well, I'm glad you're fitting in. You should probably stick to your job from now on, though. The Professor does like things to run smoothly."

"Oh, I will," said Dorothy. "Tell him I am sorry."

"No need," said Siobhan. "Just don't do it again."

"Hi, Siobhan," said Jessica, walking up to her.

"Hello, Jess," said Siobhan.

"Hey, Paul says he'll watch the kids for half an hour or so. I thought it might be fun if the three of us went for a walk and caught up."

Siobhan pursed her lips. "Hmm. Maybe that would be fun." She took Dorothy's hands in her cold palms. "I have missed you, Dorothy. The Professor says you had a bit of an adventure before you got here. I'd love to hear about it."

"Sure," said Dorothy, sensing a double opportunity. Heatherington evidently wanted Siobhan to pump Dorothy for information about Ian, or Strontium, or anything else Felicia reported about their encounter that piqued his interest. She couldn't have asked for a better chance to get Siobhan alone.

"Let's walk," said Siobhan.

Jessica waved at Paul. Dorothy blew Melody a kiss as she watched them leave. Melody put her finger to her lips, and Dorothy nodded. The incredible grace with which this little girl handled the demands being put on her baffled Dorothy, and filled her with pride. No amount of ice cream could possibly serve as a proportionate reward.

Out on the cobblestone walkway, Siobhan said, "So, tell me about your travels."

"I met a witch." Dorothy and Jessica had Siobhan flanked. She showed no sign of concern about that.

"A witch!" she exclaimed. "Why, that's wonderful! Tell me about her!"

Dorothy began the chant.

Siobhan laughed. "Is that witchcraft?"

Dorothy increased the intensity of her words.

Siobhan clapped. "Oh, that's delightful! Is that a witch thing? Did she teach you that?"

"They will not have your mind," said Dorothy.

Siobhan's face fell. "What are you doing?"

Jessica took Siobhan's arm and held it firmly. She did not seem to notice. Dorothy continued to chant, looking directly into Siobhan's eyes.

"What are you doing? Stop!" Siobhan tried to wrench her arm away, but Jessica outmuscled her.

"They will not have your mind!" In that moment, Dorothy recoiled as the thread that bound Siobhan to these monsters snapped, the first time in this process she experienced that sensation, and it stung.

"No!" Siobhan finally ripped her arm away from Jessica's grasp. She fell to her knees, palms on the ground, and panted. "What have you done?"

"It's all right," said Dorothy. "You're free now. It's going to be okay."

Siobhan looked up from her crouch. Panic boiled in her eyes. "What have you done to me?"

Jessica looked at Dorothy in alarm. "What do we do now?"

Dorothy knelt down next to Siobhan, and said to her softly, "I know this is hard on you, but you're free now. Your mind is your own."

"No!" shouted Siobhan. "Fix it! Put it back!"

"Siobhan," said Dorothy with as much patience as she could strain through the fear now overwhelming her. "The professor was controlling you. He was going to kill you."

Siobhan glared at her with a darkness she had never seen before in those child-like, green eyes. "Oh, Dorothy. What made you think I don't want to die?"

[55]

LAIR

"There. See it?"

Harrison strained to find the cave opening from his hiding place behind a large rock. "No."

Sparky groaned. "Ugh. It's right there." She pointed again, to the collection of rocks and brush that completely concealed an entrance.

"Harrison," whispered Sarah. She had her back flattened against the rock, and had made no attempts to peer over it. "I don't want to be here."

"You don't have to whisper," said Sparky. "He's not going to hear us from this distance."

"I'm sorry, Sarah," said Harrison. "I promise we'll get you out of here as soon as possible."

"Don't promise things you cannot deliver, Mr. Cody." Aplomado crouched with them, concealed behind the rock, showing no indication of anything other than boredom. "The four of us are the only ones in the party with any hope of confronting a dragon. You're needed here, whether you want that or not."

Harrison patted Bess for reassurance. Of all of them, this task might well end up being his. Bess was the only one here with dragon-killing experience. "Do you have a plan for how to tackle this thing once we know it's here?"

"Of course," said Aplomado. "A simple spell of illusion will make the dragon appear to be a grandfather clock. One glance from Agent Logan should be sufficient at that point."

"Should I lure it out?" asked Sparky. "I bet I could get his attention."

291

She squinted in the direction of the cave Harrison could not see, and held her fists in front of her face.

"Please don't," said Sarah.

"Perhaps not," said Aplomado, "but it would be helpful if you would confirm the dragon is present. Are you able to get into and out of that cave without attracting his notice?"

"You want me to scout for you?"

"That is the idea, yes."

She scratched her head. "I guess so. How exactly does one go about not attracting someone's notice? That seems weird to me."

"Typically, you would achieve that by a combination of silence and stealth," said Aplomado. "Are you able to be quiet?"

"No idea. Never tried that before."

"Won't he smell her?" asked Harrison.

"Pixies are not on the dragon food chain," said the wizard. "Even if she does have a scent he can detect, he likely wouldn't make anything of it."

"Okay." Sparky counted off items on her fingers. "Quiet. Hide. Don't fart. Got it. See you in a bit." She zipped away, leaving a faint, orange trail that led into the opening, finally allowing Harrison to see it.

She was gone for more than ten minutes. During that time, no one spoke. Sarah got increasingly agitated the longer they waited. Aplomado seemed increasingly bored. Finally, with no warning, an orange flash of light shot from the mouth of the cave, and Sparky returned in a manner anything but stealthy.

"What did you see?" asked Aplomado.

"Dragon," said Sparky. "Big one, too. He was asleep when I got there, but he's awake now. I suck at not being noticed, by the way."

Sarah clutched Harrison's arm at this news.

"Is he coming out?" asked Harrison, his hand already on Bess's hilt.

"No, actually," said Sparky. "He wants you to come in."

"That will not happen," said Aplomado.

"Wasn't talking to you," said Sparky. "He said he wants to talk to Harrison. Requested him by name."

Aplomado and Sarah stared at Harrison, in differing degrees of shock. He in turn stared at the slender opening to the dragon's lair.

"You've got to be freaking kidding me."

The entrance to the cave was alarmingly vertical and slippery. Harrison did not fondly recall his one experience spelunking in college, and this reinforced that mild trauma. He slid into the crack and landed with a thud on a pile of leaves and other detritus that had fallen into this first chamber. A glance up at his only means of egress confirmed sufficient holds to pull himself out, which he hoped he would be doing soon. No one accompanied him to the cave apart from Bess.

His headlamp cut through the cold, moist darkness. It shone mostly on smooth rock, in the form of an irregular tunnel leading farther into the ground. Sweeping the light across the floor revealed a smattering of broken artifacts, no doubt pillaged by the beast deliberately or accidentally in his travels. It also exposed a considerable quantity of bones, a small but non-zero fraction of those clearly human.

Harrison passed through two more chambers before he found the beast. Long before he saw him, the rustling sound of enormous wings shifting in an enclosed space, and the bellows-like sound of his breathing, carried through the cave. He stepped from the chill into a warm, dry chamber. Curled up against the far wall, facing away from him, sat a scaly, reptilian form the size of a bus.

"Gustav?" asked Harrison.

"Vhat do you vant?" asked the dragon in an exhausted tone, not at all the reaction of a dragon happy to see an old friend. Even so, Harrison allowed himself a moment of relief at the familiar voice.

"Hey, I'm sorry to bother you. I think there's been a misunderstanding." In truth, he only hoped that, but it occurred to him at that moment to confirm his theory by gripping Bess and silently asking her if this dragon scorched the circle in Maine.

I do not believe so, she told him.

Inwardly, Harrison swore. Though relieved to hear Gustav was not the enemy they sought, this entire diversion now officially wasted time they did not have. Given Gustav's home territory in the land that used to be upstate New York, it now appeared Aplomado might have picked the closest dragon from simple convenience. Laziness brought them here, not evidence. As he mulled that over, other events compelled him to consider an alternative explanation; perhaps Aplomado deliberately led them here to waste that time, or to frame this bystander. The longer this mission went, the less sense Aplomado's actions made.

"Are you here to kill me?" asked Gustav.

"No." Harrison shook off his nagging suspicion for the moment. "You know I wouldn't."

"Then vhy are you drawing your tiny sword?"

Harrison released his hold on Bess. Gustav still faced away from him, unclear whether he had sensed Harrison's actions, or guessed correctly.

He preferred not to take the chance either way. "I'm not. I was asking her a question."

"Vhat did you ask her?"

"If you're the dragon who left a circle of charred ground in a forest about fifty miles from here," he said.

"Ah." With that, Gustav shifted his weight and smoothly rotated his body to look at Harrison. More snake-like than anything else, the motion made Harrison nervous in ways he did not want to be. "Am I?"

"She says no."

"And vhat if I vas? Vhat then?"

Harrison gulped. "I would ask you if you knew where my daughter is."

"Dat doesn't sound so good."

"It's not," said Harrison. "Thirty-two people have been kidnapped. Most of them are my children by adoption. We traced them to a village in Maine, but they were already gone. Then we found the burn, and our wizard said he could track the dragon that did it."

"A dragon vould never take so many prisoners," said Gustav. "Dere vould be no point. Vhatever dragon sign you saw must have been unrelated to your missing family."

"You sure about that?"

"No," said the dragon. "But it's none of my business anyvay. If you're not going to kill me, you should probably go now."

"Are you okay here?" asked Harrison. Part of this question came from genuine concern over a creature whom he considered an ally, if not a true friend. Part of it came from the concern that this dragon might still pose a threat to his people.

In response, Gustav shrugged both his forelimbs and his wings. "I suppose. Have to find a new hiding place now, though."

"Sorry about that," said Harrison.

"It's all right." The dragon followed this with a sigh so heavy sparks drifted from his nostrils, and the temperature in the cave went up another notch. "I miss the vorld the vay it used to be."

"As do I," said Harrison.

56

SIOBHAN

"Now what do we do?"

Claudia voiced what Dorothy thought but did not dare speak. The small group of women (and one man) she had freed from Heatherington's mind control—and the one she hadn't needed to—sat on assorted boxes and other objects in a room not designed for meetings. Siobhan sat away from the group, curled into a ball in a far corner. Despite her horror at losing the comfort of her mind-controlled delirium, she offered no resistance to accompanying the others.

"We stick to the plan as best as we are able," said Dorothy. "At least that's what I think. Becca?"

Rebecca stood near the door, facing away from the group, chewing a fingernail. "Hmm?" She looked up. "Sorry, what?"

"Should we stick to the plan?" repeated Dorothy. "Can we still make it work?"

"I don't know. What does everyone else think?"

"I don't see how," said Jessica. "It's not going to take long for the Professor to figure out she's missing. Do you think he won't tear this place apart looking for her?"

"We could kill her," said Meg. "Make it look like an accident. Maybe he won't suspect."

"Whoa," said Mitchell, with wide eyes.

"Are you fucking crazy?" said Claudia. "We're not killing Siobhan!"

Dorothy took her hand to settle her down.

Siobhan watched this exchange, looking from speaker to speaker with interest. That the topic had turned to murdering her did not appear to change the intensity of this behavior.

"Why not?" asked Meg. "She wants us all dead, including herself."

"She's not herself," said Britney, close to tears.

"Sure she is," said Meg.

"We are not killing her," said Dorothy. "This is not up for discussion. We need to be focusing our energy on our real enemies."

"Our real enemy is sitting right here!" said Meg. "She wants this! We can't let her out of this room now. She'll go right back to that reptile and tell him everything to get her bliss back."

"Can't you see she's been brainwashed?" said Britney.

"This isn't the same as—"

"It's Siobhan! Doesn't that mean any—"

"Don't defend her!"

"Stop! Just stop!" shouted Dorothy. The clamoring died down. Dorothy looked to Becca, who had drifted away again. "Dinner is in less than two hours. If we don't have a fix for this problem by then we are all in big trouble, so let's keep our eyes on the target, please." She leaned over and whispered in Claudia's ear, "Take over for a minute, would you?"

Claudia nodded.

Dorothy kissed her on the cheek and stood up.

Claudia met this gesture with raised eyebrows.

Dorothy smiled at her and rubbed her shoulder before stepping away. She made her way to the other side of the storage room where Becca stood in a world of her own. "Come with me, please," she said quietly.

Becca followed her out the door without question.

"Are you up to this?" asked Dorothy when they were both out in the hall.

"Up to what?" asked Becca.

"These women look up to you, Rebecca. I woke you up first for a reason. We need you sharp right now."

"Blake is dead."

Dorothy hesitated. "You don't know that."

"I asked Claudia."

"Oh." Dorothy had no adequate follow up remark.

"I'm pregnant, Dorothy."

Dorothy gasped. "Oh, Becca, I'm so sorry. I didn't know."

"No one does. The only person we've told so far is Dad."

"Becca, I don't know what to say."

"You don't have to say anything," said Rebecca. "My husband is dead, and I am carrying his baby. There's nothing else to say. Whatever you expect from me right now, I'm not going to be able to do it."

Dreading the heartlessness of her own words, Dorothy pressed on. "They're going to expect you to be their rock. What are you going to tell them?"

"I'm not going to tell them anything. And neither are you."

"But—"

"No," said Becca. "I'm sorry, but no. You want me to be their den mother again, and I can't."

"You got them through hell once before."

"That was eight years ago! They were children. I was the closest thing they had to an adult. And that was hard, Dorothy. I had to take care of them all, and there was no one to take care of me. I was seventeen, for God's sake. I did it because I had to, and if it had gone on much longer, I don't know that I would have been able to keep it up."

"They need a leader."

"They have a leader."

Dorothy took a step back. "Me? I'm younger than almost all of them!"

"You're also smarter, and braver, and…" She twirled her hands around, trying to finish the sentence. "Witchier. They all defer to you now. Don't you see that?"

Dorothy thought about it. "No."

"Well, start looking for it, because they are. They barely even know I'm here. Dorothy, this isn't what I did for them. I never led a rebellion. I had two dozen children whose lives had turned into a nightmare of abandonment and sexual abuse, and it was all I could do to help them feel like there was still someone who cared about them." She paused there. "Maybe I was their best hope for a mother figure then, but they need a different kind of mother now. I don't have any idea how to lead them into a fight. Like it or not, that's you. That's always been you."

Dorothy took a deep breath, bracing herself for the reality of Becca's words. Since leaving her home she had already taken on the mantle of motherhood. Apparently, it now extended to two-dozen grown women.

Claudia poked her head out the door. "Hey, Dotty, we need you back here. They're asking questions I can't answer."

Becca looked at Dorothy and spread her hands.

"I'll be right there," she said.

"Told you," said Becca.

"So you did."

When they returned to the storage room, all eyes went to Dorothy, including Siobhan's. It was a striking nuance for Dorothy to have missed before. Confronted with it now, she had no way to deny it.

"We need a decision," said Jessica.

"Very well," said Dorothy, in her best command voice. "First of all, there will be no violence. No matter what she has done, Siobhan is our sister. I won't stand for any further suggestion of harm against her. Is that understood?" She meant this last question for all, but directed it at Meg.

"Got it," she said. Whatever confrontation Dorothy expected did not come through in Meg's tone.

"Good. Second, I have to believe this isn't what she really wants. I think it's safe to say she is suicidal, and I think it's safe to say that has been true for some time, long before this drama started. But the Siobhan I know would never wish harm on any of us." Dorothy hesitated. She looked directly at Siobhan, uncertain if what needed to be said could be said in front of her. "Siobhan has been fragile for as long as I have known her, and now I think she is broken. I think the mind control found her in the right state of vulnerability to welcome it, to allow her death to be someone else's decision. The curse or hypnotism or whatever it was is clear now. I am certain of that. But it left her in a state of damage I cannot correct with magic, at least not with what little magic I know so far."

"Then what do we do with her?" asked Christine.

"For now, we keep her here. We'll take turns watching her, bringing her food and escorting her to the bathroom." If Siobhan had opinions about this plan, she showed no sign.

"In two hours, everyone will know she's missing," said Britney.

"No, they won't," said Dorothy. "I'm going to take care of that loose end right now."

"By doing what?" asked Claudia.

"I'm going to go have a chat with Professor Heatherington."

———

After making several inquiries of multiple people (and goblins), Dorothy found the Professor on the field, inspecting the work being done there. Since the day before, the amount of cleared ground had greatly increased. Two men had begun painting white lines on the razed weeds, in patterns that did not yet make sense to her, and she chose not to be curious about their significance.

"Professor!" she called to him with as vapid a smile as she could manage.

He waved to her. The dark wizard who zapped Sparky when Felicia came to the cabin to abduct her and the children stood with him. Though grateful for the news from Claudia that Sparky survived the attack with no lasting harm, she found this dark mage frightening. She had seen him several times since her arrival here, and every time he looked at her she felt covered in bugs.

"How are you settling in?" asked the reptile when she got close enough for conversation. She wondered how many times she would need to hear that question before it stopped making her sick.

"Very well, thank you," she said. "I'm so glad I finally found you. Siobhan wanted me to give you a message."

"Indeed?" he said. "What message?"

"She wanted to apologize for not checking in with you at all this afternoon."

"Oh!" he said. "I suppose she hasn't, has she? I've been so engaged with the work here I didn't even realize. Is everything all right?"

"Well, yes and no," she said. "I'm afraid she says she won't be able to run your errands for the next four days or so."

"Oh, really?" The ticking from the Professor's brass hand became rapid and loud as he crossed his arms. "And why is that?"

"She's having some girl issues," said Dorothy.

"Well, I hardly see that as something that would take days to sort out. Surely there are people she can talk to? What am I supposed to do without my gofer while she has her bout of moodiness?"

"Um," said Dorothy. "I'm not quite sure you're hearing this properly. She's having some... *mammal* girl issues."

His one real eye went wide in sudden and uncomfortable understanding. "Oh! Oh, my! Ah, yes, well..."

"She wanted me to tell you it was nothing personal, but she wasn't sure how someone of your species would react to the smell of blood—"

"Yes! Thank you!" He waved her away frantically. The sound of his metal hand accelerated to a cacophonous whirring, with intermittent pings and hisses. In his animated reaction, the sleeve of his coat slipped down, revealing the brass extended to at least his forearm. "That will do! Please tell her... I hope she feels better soon. Rest up, drink plenty of fluids, that sort of thing. Stay in her room. No need to come back to work until she feels ready."

Dorothy smiled. "I will tell her. Thank you!" She turned on her heel and walked away.

"Naturally, she will need someone to cover her duties during this time," he said to Dorothy's back. "You'll do nicely."

Heart pounding, she turned back to face him, a fully artificial grin pasted to her face. "Why, it would be my pleasure and honor, sir."

"Pish posh, girl," he said. "Do call me Basil."

"Thank you... Basil," she forced out.

"You are dismissed for the nonce," he said. "I will summon you as needed."

She bowed to take her leave. As she straightened up, the sorcerer stared at her. He narrowed his eyes, and his thin lips stretched into an indecipherable smile.

57

BLOWOUT

Scaling his way out of Gustav's cave drew Harrison's attention to his missing finger more than usual. What spare purchase he could gain on the smooth, cold rock automatically suffered from a ten percent disadvantage. When he finally did emerge from the cool pit to the warm blast of spring air, he rolled over onto his back and lay there with his nine numb fingers resting on his belly. Hadley stood over him.

"Did you really stay up here the whole time?" asked Harrison.

"I have a thing about dragons," said the ghost.

Harrison was too tired to press. After a few minutes of panting, and regaining his bearings, he pushed himself up and hiked back to the rock that served as a duck blind for his team.

"What's the story?" asked Sarah in a small voice.

"Red herring." Harrison walked up to Aplomado and said, "Congratulations on finding literally the only dragon on the planet I am absolutely certain would never target my family."

The wizard raised an eyebrow. "What did you find down there?"

"An exhausted dragon, who has no idea where my children are, and would very much like to be left alone. He also said a dragon would never abduct people like that. That it would make no sense for a dragon to keep so many prisoners."

"And you believe him?"

"We're acquainted," said Harrison.

"Yes, I heard all about that while you were in the cave," said Aplomado.

"You do realize your friend down there is an undocumented dragon, do you not?"

"Classified, not undocumented," said Harrison. "Need to know. Which, apparently, you don't."

"Harrison," said Hadley, "maybe you should take a break for a bit."

Harrison ignored the ghost. "And I don't appreciate you hanging whatever accusation that is on me, when the real issue at hand is that you led us to the wrong place."

"Were there any human remains down there?"

This brought Harrison up short. "What?"

"It's a simple question," said Aplomado. "Did you see human remains in that cave? Skulls? Partial skeletons?"

"I don't know," Harrison lied. He knew Gustav well enough to understand the dragon as an excellent judge of character. The human bones in that cave disturbed him on a basic level, but those skeletons could not have belonged to innocents. "What does that have to do with anything?"

"You've been harboring an undocumented dragon for nine years, Mr. Cody. "

"I told you he's not undocumented," said Harrison with rapidly increasing wariness. "Baker has met him. So has de Queiroz. I'd show you the file, but you're not cleared for it."

"A dragon," continued Aplomado, without acknowledgment of Harrison's claim, "whose fire, as near as I can detect it, closely resembles that of dragon activity near the last known location of our quarry."

"Or so you claim. Bess disagrees. That sounds like wizard-speak for you not being able to tell the difference between two dragons. Which is your job, I might add."

"This entire event began with the abduction of your children, and now it has led us to a dragon you have kept secret for a very long time."

Harrison took one step closer to the wizard, in an aggressive stance. "Where are you going with this, Gerry?"

"I can't say for sure," said the wizard calmly. "I think it might be best if I interviewed this dragon myself."

"No," said Harrison, struck by the mental image of Aplomado's interview going wrong, and ending with a deceased dragon. If he had something to hide about this misdirection, that would surely be the way to hide it.

"Don't we have bigger priorities right now?" said Sarah.

"Hey, gray guy," said Sparky. "I talked to Gustav, too. I really don't think—"

"Please silence your pixie," said Aplomado.

"Hey, now!" said Sparky, hands on hips.

"You are way out of line, wizard," said Harrison. "We are done here. Get back to the flier, right now."

"I don't think so."

"I'm not asking. You don't ever seem to have understood this, but I'm your superior. You can start toeing the line right now, or I'll have you brought up on charges."

"If there is any question of malfeasance, I am well within my rights to disregard your directives." Aplomado's demeanor remained frustratingly cool, while he pushed Harrison to the brink of reason. "Step aside, Mr. Cody."

"Not happening."

Aplomado took a step back, and reached into one of his loose sleeves. Harrison took a step back, and drew Bess.

"Harrison!" shouted Sarah.

"You may want to get in there," said Hadley to Sparky.

"No dice, dead man," she said. "The last time I had dealings with a wizard it left me out of sorts."

Be sure you want this, said Bess. If this goes to melee, one of you could die.

Harrison ignored them all. "Stand down, Gerry."

Aplomado produced a small wand from his cloak, and raised both arms.

Harrison's hand tingled as Bess asserted control over his motor functions.

"Stop!" shouted Sarah.

Bess released Harrison. He had a moment of panic she had taken Sarah's interjection as an order, leaving him at the complete mercy of the wizard. But as he stood his ground, Aplomado had stopped moving. Harrison waited a few seconds in caution. The wizard did not blink. He stepped closer, gingerly. The folds of Aplomado's robe had stopped responding to the slight breeze, or to gravity.

"You did this to him," he said to Sarah.

Glaring at him, she held out her hand. "Give me the sword."

Harrison glanced down at Bess. "She doesn't like to be passed around."

"Give... me... the sword." The words came out through clenched teeth.

Harrison complied. As he handed Bess to her, pommel first, she took the hilt and tensed even further. She gasped. Harrison recalled the first time Bess spoke to his mind, and did not envy her the experience.

"Oh!" she said, looking at the blade. "I know. I'm sorry. Just for a moment." As gently as possible, she laid the sword on the ground.

The pain of the slap shocked Harrison nearly as much as the sound of it. Sarah gave him about two seconds to acclimate to the intense sting on the side of his face. Then she slapped him again. Harder.

"You stupid, self-centered son of a bitch. How exactly do you plan on finding your wife now?" She pointed to the frozen wizard. "Do you know what that was? That was the best hope we had for finding my son, and rescuing him from monsters. You know what it is now?"

Harrison did not offer a guess.

"Now it's a doorstop. I don't know how to undo this. He is now stuck like that until the people back home finally figure out what it is I do, so they can reverse it. And by the time they do that, my son will be dead. I want you to look at that statue. Look long and hard, Harrison, because you did that. And you did it to protect some dragon over my only child."

"I don't trust him," said Harrison. "I don't believe for a second he gives a rat's ass about any of our children, and as of this incident, I think we should consider the possibility he's another mole."

"Well, I guess we'll never know now, will we?" She turned her back on him, and began the long trek back to the flier.

"Thank you for saving me," he tried.

"Don't thank me!" she shouted. "I was trying to freeze you both!"

58

GETTING ORGANIZED

Apryl stared dumbfounded at Dorothy. "Mammal issues?"

"Unbelievable," said Claudia. The three of them sat in their windowless supply room. Christine took the first shift watching Siobhan, who had been moved to a separate location in the basement. The others had gone back to their routines, blending back in with their mind controlled sisters.

"You do know that almost thirty women have been here for four weeks," said Apryl. "Almost all of them have probably had their periods by now. Some of them might already be synchronizing."

Dorothy held up her hands. "Yes, I know that. Fortunately, he didn't."

"That was a pretty ballsy risk to take," said Claudia with a grin, and a pride in her voice Dorothy found gratifying.

"Well, it only bought us four days," said Dorothy. "Whatever we do next has to happen quickly."

"How soon do you want to wake up the rest of them?" asked Claudia.

"Tonight. We don't dare wait longer than that." Dorothy put her hand on Apryl's shoulder. "How are you doing?"

Apryl frowned. "I don't know. Tired still. Something about this trip hit me hard. It feels different than usual."

"I need to know if you can teleport yet."

"I don't know. I don't think so."

"Then we'll have to assume that's an asset we don't have," said Dorothy. "What about your other abilities?"

"I honestly don't know," said Apryl. "I haven't tried anything since we got here."

"Anything you can tell me as soon as possible would be helpful," said Dorothy.

"I'll do some experimenting today," said Apryl, in a tone Dorothy thought sounded defeated. Her physical limitations could prove her more a liability than an advantage in their escape attempt, but Dorothy couldn't waste energy worrying about that. She had at best two or three days to form and execute a plan that would get approximately forty women and children away from this nest of monsters without the threat of being recaptured.

"Please do. But don't knock yourself out. We need you healthy more than we need your power." Dorothy hoped that last part did not sound like the lie it obviously was. "Claudia, you're the closest thing we have to an actual tactician. Do you have any thoughts?"

"Not really. My NCSA experience mostly involves waiting around for someone to tell me where and when to use my power."

"That's okay. I have some ideas. And now that I am working directly for the professor, I have some access I might be able to exploit. I need some time to think. If you come up with anything, please bring it to me."

"Okey dokey."

Dorothy sighed. "And now I have to have a conversation with our suicidal train wreck, on the topic of what happens to her next."

"Good luck with that," said Claudia.

"I'll need it," said Dorothy.

Apryl got up and went to the corner, where she stretched out on her makeshift bed.

"You all right?" asked Dorothy.

"Just need to rest," she said. Within seconds, she was snoring.

"This has me very worried," said Dorothy.

"No shit," said Claudia. "She's as bad as she was when we first got here. Sometimes I swear she sounds like she's drunk."

"I can't fixate on this problem right now." Dorothy took Claudia's hand. "Thank you for being my rock. Don't tell the others, but this feels like I have bitten off more than I can chew."

"It doesn't show."

"Really?"

Claudia laughed. "Mostly. I see it, but they don't know you like I do."

Dorothy stood, and pulled Claudia into a hug, drawing strength from her.

"Wanna make out?" Claudia whispered in her ear.

Dorothy laughed. "No time." She let go.

"You kissed me in front of the others," said Claudia.

"Did I?"

"Yeah." Claudia smiled. "It was pretty cool."

"You mean that peck on the cheek?"

"Yeah. Thanks."

"For kissing you?" asked Dorothy.

"For not hiding it. I know that's going to be tricky for you. It just meant a lot to me."

Dorothy took Claudia's hands. "I said this was scary. I never said I wanted to hide it. This is all new territory for me, and I have no idea what adjusting to it is going to be like. But the one thing I want you and anyone else who is even remotely curious to know is that I am not ashamed of what's happening here. And I really and truly am not invested in what other people think about it. We live in a world filled with things far more unusual than two women in a loving relationship, and most people know that by now. Whatever hang-ups other people have are their problem, not ours." With that, she tapped her lips.

Claudia smiled and kissed her.

It surprised Dorothy to find this becoming comfortable and natural. After a couple seconds, they both broke away. "Besides, it's not like I have a social circle who are going to be shocked by this."

Claudia laughed. "We really should get you one of those."

"Maybe." She let go, reluctantly. "Off to talk to Siobhan now. Really not looking forward to this."

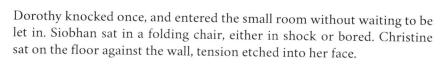

Dorothy knocked once, and entered the small room without waiting to be let in. Siobhan sat in a folding chair, either in shock or bored. Christine sat on the floor against the wall, tension etched into her face.

"May we have a moment, Chris?" asked Dorothy.

Christine nodded and stood. "I'll be right outside." She stepped out and closed the door behind her.

"What are you going to do with me?" asked Siobhan, with no fear in her voice.

"I truly do not know," said Dorothy. "What would you like me to do with you?"

"I truly do not care," said Siobhan.

"That's not helpful. Neither is it true, or you wouldn't have asked. Here's my problem, Siobhan: Very shortly, I intend to leave this place, and when I go I will be taking all the people who were brought here against their will. I would very much like you to be in that party. Is that what you want?"

Siobhan shrugged, and offered no further response.

"Well, that poses a problem," said Dorothy. "If you're still committed to being sacrificed, that leaves me with the choice of abandoning you here to die, or dragging you away in the hope that you won't get us all killed. You can see my difficulty."

Siobhan glared at Dorothy for a few seconds, then turned her head away.

"Do you really want to die so badly you're willing to take us all with you?" asked Dorothy. "That doesn't seem very fair. And it doesn't sound like the Siobhan I know."

"You don't understand," said Siobhan.

"No, I don't," said Dorothy. "You're right about that. I don't understand. Maybe this doesn't mean anything to you anymore, but we all care about you."

"Meg doesn't."

"Yes, she does. She's frightened and angry, and she feels betrayed, which to be blunt is quite understandable. What she really wants—what we all want—is to have you back, safe and healthy."

Siobhan said nothing.

Dorothy considered several possible approaches toward reasoning with her, before finally conceding there would be no resolution in this conversation. "I'm not ready to give up on you," she said, and left the room.

Shortly after midnight, Dorothy, Jessica, and Meg went room to room and systematically brought every one of Harrison's daughters out of their imposed complacency. They brought a bucket, a box of tissues, and a roll of duct tape. In each room, Meg and Jess sat on either side of a bed, firmly gripping the arms of the afflicted, while Dorothy whispered the spell into their ears as they slept. After freeing each victim from the mind control, they treated them with profuse kindness, gave them a brief update on their situation, and asked them to go into the next day as though nothing had changed. Four of them turned out to be unaffected, and had been

308

pretending the entire time, now overwhelmed in their relief at no longer being alone. The bucket proved necessary for only two people, but the box of tissues was completely consumed. Thankfully, not a single episode required the use of duct tape.

Very few of them got any more sleep that night.

[59]

BREADCRUMBS

"Are you in trouble?" asked Sparky.

Harrison would have preferred to hike back to the flier in solitude. The presence of a ghost who couldn't leave his side and a pixie with no sense of personal boundaries made it trickier to take a moment to collect himself. Whatever happened next would be awful, up to and including the possibility of his arrest. "Probably."

"It totally wasn't your fault," said Sparky. "I'll back you up on that. So will the ghost, right ghost?"

"They can't hear me," said Hadley.

"Well, I'll tell them you back him up," said Sparky. "That should do it, right?"

"Leave it alone," said Harrison. "The priority now is finding Apryl and the others. Any discipline is going to have to wait. I hope."

When they arrived at the flier, they found Agents Clark and Hitchcock waiting on the ground. For a moment, Harrison imagined they would take him into custody, but they nodded as he walked past them and entered the hatch. Inside, Sarah sat in the rear. She did not make eye contact. Dallas played a game on a tablet. Milton sat at the pilot's station, looking intently at a monitor, with Jacobs and Meredith standing behind him. None of them looked up as Harrison approached. Jacobs pointed at the monitor. "There."

Milton touched a control and the image on the screen zoomed in on a photo from the circle of charred ground they discovered earlier. It showed a close-up of one of the burnt trees. "How many of these did you find?"

"I found four," said Jacobs. "Cody found at least one."

"What are we looking at?" asked Harrison.

Milton looked up from the monitor. "Those markings you and Jacobs saw on the trees."

"Aplomado didn't think they were significant," said Harrison.

"Well, his opinions aren't really part of the equation anymore," said Milton.

Harrison tensed. He did not want to have this conversation in front of the two agents, but he didn't want to presume to dismiss them. "I assume Sarah brought you up to speed on that?"

"Yes, she did," said Milton.

"Is Harrison in trouble?" asked Sparky from over Harrison's shoulder.

Milton frowned. "Should he be?"

"No!" said Sparky. "He totally didn't do anything wrong! The gray guy attacked him!"

"I know," said Milton. "And Logan has already taken full responsibility for Aplomado's condition. She said you only drew your sword after he assumed an attack posture. Unless you have something to add that contradicts that, I wasn't planning to do anything but debrief you."

"No, that's right." Harrison looked back to where Sarah sat. She continued to ignore him. "What exactly does 'full responsibility' mean?"

"Beats me," said Milton. "I've never been involved in an internal investigation before, so I guess I'll find out. As for now, my primary concern is that we had a rogue wizard attempting to bypass chain of command. Given we already know Rutherford was compromised, I'd say you probably made the right call, even if it does turn out he was just overstepping his assignment. I think the most likely explanation for his behavior is arrogance, and a disregard for proper communication, but that still makes him a liability. Either way, with him now neutralized, everything else is paperwork as far as I'm concerned. Logan did tell me she tried to freeze both of you, though. I'd say she's lucky that didn't work on you. Any thoughts on why?"

"No," said Harrison. "Maybe because we're both telekinetics? I really couldn't say. I'm not even sure why it worked on Gerry at all."

"Well, that will be some more fun for your people at Esoteric." Milton returned his attention to the screen. "Tell me what Aplomado said about these markings."

Meredith stepped aside to let Harrison get closer to the monitor. "He said they were meaningless. Not dragon-related, not magical, possibly tribal markings."

"What tribe does he think lives in the forests of Maine?"

"I don't know."

"Hey." Sparky pointed to the monitor. "That's a breadcrumb glyph."

Harrison waited for the explanation.

Sparky flew closer to the screen and examined it, rocking her head back and forth.

"A what?" said Milton finally.

"Breadcrumb," said the pixie. "That's super-weird."

"No one knows what you're talking about, Sparky," said Harrison.

"Oh!" said the pixie. "Yeah, no. You wouldn't. It's a Faerie thing."

"Are we talking about a tribe of faeries?" asked Jacobs.

"What?" said Sparky with a baffled look on her face. "No. They're just markers."

"Agent Sparky," said Harrison. "You're doing that pixie thing. We need clarity here. Please tell us what a breadcrumb glyph is, and why this one is weird."

"Let me see if I can dumb it down." She tapped her head. "Breadcrumb glyphs are markers. They lead the way back to Faerie, which can be very helpful if the entrance has moved, which it used to do a lot. Not so much lately. But anyway, you can stick them to trees, or rocks, or anything that doesn't move. Well, I mean, you can't do that, but I could if I needed to."

"Why is it weird?" said Milton.

"Seriously? Look at it." She pointed to the screen again.

Harrison scanned the image, trying to see what she could possibly mean.

"Can you see it?" she asked.

"I can see the marking, if that's what you mean," said Harrison.

"See?" she said. "That's weird!"

"We shouldn't be able to see it?" asked Milton.

"No, and it certainly shouldn't be showing up on your techno-whatever. They're totally invisible to anybody not from Faerie."

"We both saw them before we took these pictures," said Jacobs.

"Well, that's weird," repeated Sparky.

"Maybe the dragon fire made them visible," said Harrison.

"I don't see how," said Sparky. "Once you get past the magic, they're nothing but marks. Dragon fire should have burned them clean off."

"What if they were made after the dragon burnt the trees?" asked Harrison.

"That's a good question," said Sparky. "Maybe that would work.

Dragon fire is a different kind of magic, and those trees would still be sticky with it. If I tried to put a glyph on one, the magics might cancel out and make it visible. I'm totally guessing, though."

"So am I," said Harrison. "But the last word Apryl said before she vanished was Faerie. Could she have done this?"

Sparky shrugged. "I don't understand most of what she does. It's not a complicated spell, if that's what you're asking."

"I don't see how this helps us," said Milton. "There are only five markings in that forest. Are they supposed to spell out a word or something?"

"No, they don't spell. They point," said Sparky. "You don't read them, you follow them."

"They lead in a circle," said Milton.

Harrison shook his head. "The ones we can see lead in a circle. What if there are others we can't see?"

"There should be hundreds," said Sparky. "But there weren't. I was there, remember? I would have seen them."

"You would have seen them if a faerie had put them there," said Harrison. "If these are Apryl's, they might be different."

"I guess," she said. "If they're hers, and they're out there, there's probably some way to find them, but I have no idea what it is. Too bad we don't have a wizard."

Harrison felt that comment like a punch to the gut.

"Is there really no way to unfreeze him?" asked Hitchcock.

"I don't know," said Milton. "I don't think anyone really understands the telekinetics or what they can do. I tried to talk to Logan about it, but she is very shaken right now. She said as far as she knows, until the people at Esoteric make some new discovery, Aplomado will be locked in that pose."

"Oh, no way," said Harrison. "It can't be that easy."

Milton circled the motionless form of the wizard. "You really think this will work?"

"I definitely think it will work, and I feel like an idiot for not thinking of this on my own. Our powers are based on unconscious understandings of the nature of the objects we can move. For Sarah it's clocks. The trick to making them work on other stuff is to let ourselves believe the other stuff is somehow the same. Maybe Sarah can freeze things that aren't clocks by letting herself believe they have a clockiness to them, or whatever you want to call it."

"He's a sundial," said Sarah.

"What does that mean?" asked Milton.

She pointed. "Look at him. He's standing on a patch of flat ground with his hands pointed straight up. See the shadow?" She waved her arm in the direction of Aplomado's shadow. It had not moved in the several hours since she froze him, now pointing in a direction contradicted by the position of the sun, and the shadows of everyone else standing there.. "That's how I decided to see him, which made him a clock. I didn't give it a lot of thought, honestly. I was too angry at the time, but that's how I did it."

"Huh," said Harrison. "You ever try that before?"

"No," said Sarah, "and I don't ever want to try that again."

"Well, that illustrates my point," said Harrison. "I have used my unlocking ability on things that were not literal locks. It's a matter of perceiving whatever I am trying to affect as a lock. It's usually extremely difficult, but you don't get much more locked than this. That might even be why it didn't work on me. I can't be locked by anything."

"I hope you're right," said Sarah.

"Everybody stand back," said Harrison. "He's still going to be in attack mode. I don't want anyone getting hurt."

"What about you getting hurt?" asked Sarah.

Though silently appreciating her concern in the face of her anger at him, he did not respond. He cracked his knuckles, and rested one hand on Aplomado's shoulder.

The wizard collapsed, unconscious.

"Oh, shit," said Harrison.

"Is he breathing?" asked Milton.

Harrison checked. "Yes."

"Well, let's call this a win and get him back to the flier then."

Clark and Meredith lifted him onto a stretcher. They had barely taken the first step back to the flier when Aplomado rolled off, hit the ground, and leapt fifty feet into the air. He disappeared into the trees.

"Damn it!" said Harrison.

"Go!" shouted Milton to Sparky.

She zipped into the trees in Aplomado's last known direction.

Sarah walked up to Harrison. "I'm glad he's not dead, at least."

"Me too." He put his arm around her. "I'm sorry about earlier."

"I love that you just apologized for getting slapped in the face."

"I had it coming."

"You most certainly did."

Sparky reappeared. "Found him."

"How is he?" asked Milton.

"Unhappy," she said. "But he's being pretty professional about it. I told him about the glyphs—"

As she said this, a sound like millions of tiny wind chimes marked a sudden and dramatic change in the forest. Gradually, Aplomado's spell to render the glyphs visible took hold. Hundreds of trees now showed markings carved into them, glowing in an assortment of colors.

"Are those the glyphs?" asked Milton.

"Yeah," said Sparky, with a wide-eyed look of amazement. "Wow. That's a lot more than I expected."

"Wait," said Milton. "They're here? I thought they were back at the fire site. That's fifty miles from here."

"That's really, really a lot more than I expected," said Sparky.

"Is that important?" asked Harrison.

"I guess it depends if these are Apryl's, and how strong she is. If she dumped this much energy into making glyphs, she's not going to be good for much else for a while."

"I don't like the sound of that," said Harrison.

"Maybe it's not so bad," she said. "I mean, fifty miles worth of glyphs could be doable, I guess. Kind of weird they're not in a line, though."

Harrison looked around, seeing signs of them in every direction from where he stood. "I thought they were just supposed to be directional markers."

"They are," said Aplomado, having returned through the glowing forest. "Now that I know what I am looking for, I can detect them with ease. You are right to think these are your wife's work."

"No hard feelings?" said Harrison experimentally.

Aplomado ignored the overture. "These markings lead from the village where she disappeared, in a spiral band that is over two miles wide."

"You can tell all that from the ground?" said Milton.

"As I said, now that I know what to look for, yes," said Aplomado.

"Where do they go?" asked Harrison.

"Boston," said the wizard.

[60]

THE PLAN

The daily routine did not change. Apart from kitchen staff who had to start their day earlier, everyone rose at seven o'clock. Breakfast was served at eight. The women and children filed in to the dining area, sat with their usual mealtime companions, and engaged in banter about their work, or whatever other interests they usually shared. A casual observer would have been hard pressed to distinguish differences in behavior for these women from the previous day at the same time. The only evidence lay in the quantity of served food that went uneaten and discarded at the end of the meal. Had anyone taken note of that, they might have posed questions about the collective lack of appetite among the adults.

Dorothy and Jessica took the children from the dining area to the school. They made a show of their shallow conversation and vacuous happiness at their situation. If Paul detected a change in Jessica's demeanor, he gave no sign. Shortly before lunch, Dorothy asked Jessica if she could take a break and go for a walk, citing a vague need for fresh air and alone time. As part of the show for Paul, Jessica responded with a perfunctory expression of concern about Dorothy's well-being, to which she gave a stock answer that she would be fine.

Having slipped away, Dorothy made her way down to the storage room, grateful for the astonishing lack of supervision that went along with the assumption that everyone in this facility was either here by choice or under mind control. She tapped gently on the door before opening it. Claudia and Apryl were both sitting on the floor, looking at a notebook. Dorothy handed them each a sandwich.

"How are they all doing?" asked Claudia.

"Remarkably well," said Dorothy. "So far everyone is doing a great job of pretending nothing has changed. I doubt they will be able to sustain it long, though."

"Hopefully they won't have to," said Apryl. "I think we have a workable escape plan."

Dorothy sat down next to Claudia and turned the notebook to face her. She read a list of bullet points, and studied a set of sketches. "Did you add anything since last night?"

"Nothing new," said Claudia. "We've been putting together a timeline. You're going to need to talk to Ian today. Without him, this may not work at all."

Dorothy closed the notebook and pushed it aside. "Run me through it. Every step, without looking."

"We have four obstacles to clear," said Claudia. "First, the goblins. There are about thirty of those, and most of them are still working on clearing the field, but they're fighters, and we need to assume they will fight us."

"Solution?"

"Poison. Christine is going to start sneaking sugar into their food tonight. By two days from now, most of them will be too sick to stand. She's going to mask it with horseradish, habanero, and any other strong spices she can use."

"All right," said Dorothy. "That's one. What are the other three?"

"Tim the wizard," said Apryl. "He's mine. We think his power source is the staff he carries. Without it, he shouldn't have the energy needed to work his magic."

"How sure are you that you can take it out?"

"I've been practicing on batteries. They are getting easier to explode. By two days from now, I should have the strength to take out something as big as the staff." As the first ability Apryl manifested, she could provide a power source for machinery or magic. She could also destroy existing power sources by overloading them. For sheer offensive capability, she offered their best chance of disabling the wizard.

"Let's hope that's right," said Dorothy. "Two down. Next?"

"Felicia," said Claudia. "She's mine. First Ian softens her up by shattering every one of the fifty million blades she carries. With luck that will cut her up pretty bad right there. Then I come in with my concussive voice trick and rupture her eardrums. After that it's a matter of overwhelming her with numbers and beating the snot out of her."

"We can't risk Ian being hurt," said Dorothy. "That concern overrides everything else. He's not only our ace in the hole, he's also my son. You get him out of there the second those blades are broken."

"Jess is on that. Grabbing him and running is the only thing she's going to do in this whole plan." She put her hand on Dorothy's knee. "I won't let anything happen to your boy."

Dorothy took Claudia's hand and gave it a squeeze. "Good. Three down."

"The professor," said Claudia. "He's yours. I would say how you're going to take care of that, but you haven't told us yet."

"Anti-reptile spell." Dorothy held out her hand, palm up, and the red book materialized in it. "I've been researching ways to neutralize reptiles. There are a few options. By this time tomorrow I will have picked one."

"You make it sound simple," said Apryl.

"It is simple." She shook her head. "No, wait, that's not right. It's not simple, but I can do it."

"You sure you're okay with the whole witchy thing?" asked Claudia. "If you aren't up to this—"

"I don't have a choice, Claudia. I have to be up for it, or every one of these women and children will die, and that reptile will destroy everything and everyone not from his world." She meant it as a simple statement of reality. But with those words out her mouth, she felt confronted for the first time by the scale of their goal, and the possibility they would fail.

"You'll be fine," said Apryl.

Dorothy nodded, but as she looked into Apryl's eyes for the support she offered, all she could see were the bags under them.

Outside, after lunch, Dorothy took Ian for a stroll around the field. With the plant growth nearly cleared, some of the goblin workforce had begun to dig holes near the outfield walls.

"Can you keep a secret?" she asked him.

"Are we going to escape?"

"What makes you say that?"

He shrugged. "I dunno. I just want to go home."

For Ian, home meant a Random Cabin now lost to them. The life he knew had already ended, no matter what happened next. She considered lying to him to win his allegiance, but she needed his trust. "We can't go back to the cabin."

"How come?"

"Because I don't know where it is. But I do want to take you away from here. We have a very nice home waiting for us in the city of New Chicago. I think you're going to be happy there."

"I don't think you were always my mom." He looked confused by his own statement. "You and Melody didn't always live with us, did you?"

"No. I've only been your mother for the last few days. And we've only been together for a few weeks." She took his hand. "But I am your mother now, Ian. And I love you. And I promise this will all make sense soon. Okay?"

"Okay," he said softly. "I love you too."

Dorothy felt a cascade of warmth. Her commitment to taking care of this sweet child meant more to her than a simple inherited responsibility. The next request stung her inside. "Ian, do you remember when I asked if you would be able to break something if I needed you to?" She braced herself for his anxiety.

"I'll do it," he said.

"Are you sure?"

"If you need me to, I'll do it."

"I'm very glad to hear that," said Dorothy.

"I should warn you I can't break people, or anything natural. It only works on man-made stuff. I can't hurt anyone with it, even by accident."

The seriousness of his tone tugged at her heart, and she wondered if she heard relief in his voice, or apology. She thought back to the goblin armor, and how the shrapnel of it exploding off him didn't hit anyone, or even leave a mark on him. "Ian, I would never ask you to hurt anyone." She left unspoken the hurting would be her job.

"What do you need me to break?"

Dorothy took a deep breath, and put her hand on his shoulder. "I'm afraid it's going to be quite a bit."

"I'm not scared."

She found the truth of this in his eyes, and hoped he could sustain that bravery. "Do you remember Felicia?"

"The lady with the knives." For an instant, it looked like his courage wavered, but it passed. "You want me to break the knives."

"Yes, I do."

"Good. What else?"

"There are two trucks parked outside behind the stands." The Professor and his lackeys had transported this entire operation here in those tractor-trailers. Though she had never been near them, anyone willing to climb to the roof could see them.

"You want me to break the trucks?"

"Just one," she said. "We're going to use the other one to drive away from here. Can you break one without breaking the other?"

"I think so," he said. "Is that all?"

"No." Dorothy hesitated, giving herself one last chance to think of an alternative to the next part of the plan, and came up empty. "I want you to break this building."

"The whole thing?" he asked, with no surprise in his voice.

"Once we are out, yes. Do you think you can break something this large?"

"Yeah." No hesitation.

"Ian," said Dorothy, "have you ever broken anything this size before?"

"I think so. It's hard to remember. You and Strontium never told me what really happened, just that we had to run."

Dorothy suspected the story behind their Random Cabin journey went something like this, but hearing it confirmed, and hearing the pain in his voice over not knowing the details of his own acts of destruction broke her heart. "That was just her, Ian. I wasn't there yet."

"Oh, yeah," he said. "I forgot."

"Dorrie!" Melody called her and jogged across the field toward them.

"Hey, Little!" Dorothy crouched down and held out her arms. Melody hopped into them and grabbed her in a bear hug. The little girl's cheek tingled electrically against hers.

"Are you talking about escaping?" Melody whispered in Dorothy's ear.

Both the question and the stealth with which she asked it caught Dorothy off guard. She chose to respond with a silent nod.

Still clinging tightly, Melody whispered, "I want in."

Dorothy entered the room they had converted to a holding cell for Siobhan. Apart from bathroom breaks under escort every few hours, she had not moved from her chair.

Britney, taking her turn at guard duty, sat in another chair doing a crossword puzzle. "Do you need me to step outside?"

"No, I won't be long." Dorothy walked over to Siobhan's chair and crouched down next to it. Siobhan looked sleep-deprived, adding another layer to Dorothy's guilt. "Hello, Siobhan."

"Mmm?" she said, appearing half alert at best.

"I'm only here to share some things, and I don't need you to respond."

Siobhan's glassy eyes refocused themselves into a glare.

"Very shortly, we will all be leaving this place. I have given a lot of thought to the question of what we will do with you, and I want you to know I intend to take you with us, even though I think that's not what you want. Am I right about that, at least? Do you want to stay here?"

Siobhan hesitated, then shrugged.

"Fair enough. I think you are in a lot of pain right now, and I think it may be that you have been in a lot of pain the entire time I have known you. I want you to know I don't blame you for feeling the way you do. But I also want you to know that you have options. When we get back to New Chicago, I am going to make it my mission to get you the help you need. I think you have been hiding for a very long time. But I can see you now, Siobhan, and what I see makes me very sad. You are my friend, you are my sister, and I... we all love you."

Dorothy stood. "And I want you to know that if you still feel this way after you've had a chance at some solid, constructive treatment, if you still want to die so badly you would wipe out half the world to make it happen, if you still feel that way..." She leaned down and placed a light kiss on Siobhan's forehead.

"If you still feel that way," she said softly, "I will kill you."

Without waiting for a reaction from either Siobhan or Britney, Dorothy turned her back on them and walked out the door.

CAPTAIN

"That's Fenway Park!" shouted Harrison. A high altitude recon image on the flier's monitor showed the glowing breadcrumb glyphs terminating at a large structure surrounding a field.

"How can you tell?" asked Milton dryly.

"Green Monster!" Harrison pointed to the screen. "And see that dot? That's the red seat!"

"Harrison, that's Boston below us," said Milton. "Obviously, it's Fenway."

"Oh," said Harrison, deflated. "Right."

"Did you just use sarcasm?" asked Spark with a delighted grin. "I wouldn't have thought you were any good at that."

"I have my moments. The more important information for those of us who aren't Red Sox fans is the strength of the enemy." Milton pointed to the field. "Are those goblins?"

Harrison squinted. "Hard to say. Either goblins or something roughly person-sized. I count at least two dozen."

"It's more." Milton touched a control in front of him. "Director? Any word on our backup?"

After a few seconds, Alec's voice came over a speaker. "The army is sending you a platoon. Expect to rendezvous in two hours."

"Ah," said Milton. "I was expecting it to be our people. This would be a lot easier with a clear chain of command."

"Which is why you've been reinstated to active duty, and promoted to captain," said Alec. "You're welcome, by the way. Their C.O. is a Lieutenant Davies. He will transfer command as soon as they get there."

"Respectfully, sir, the NCSA—"

"Does not have trebuchets, and we're a little short on crossbows. Is there a problem here, Agent?"

Milton hesitated. "I don't know if you are aware of the circumstances surrounding my discharge."

"I am well aware, and I just spent thirty minutes convincing the Commander in Chief that your discharge was absolute bollocks. If you have something to add in contradiction, you will really have to take it up with him once you get back."

After a silence surely not as long as it felt to Harrison, Milton said, "Understood. Heading for the rendezvous coordinates now." He tapped a switch to cut the line. In response to Harrison's quizzical expression, he said flatly, "Don't ask."

"Don't tell?" said Harrison.

"Exactly," said Milton, without breaking his deadpan.

After a moment to absorb that, Harrison said, "We're good here."

"I wouldn't work for you if I thought otherwise, Assistant Director."

"All right then," said Harrison. "So... what's the plan when they get here?"

"Still working on that," said Milton. "I was hoping for a frontal assault, but that was when I thought we could catch them off guard. At this point, I'm pretty sure any element of surprise we might have enjoyed is pretty well spent."

Harrison looked out the window once again at the mile-wide trail of glowing treetops that led to the enemy's doorstep.

[62]

ESCAPE

With only a few hours until Dorothy would lead all the prisoners to freedom, and as she, Claudia, and Apryl went over the details for what must have been the twentieth time that day, a knock came on the storage room door. Jessica poked her head inside. "We have a problem."

"What is it?" asked Dorothy.

"I have no idea. There's something in the forest and it's getting a lot of attention. We were all ordered inside. They still aren't supervising us, though. I thought maybe you and I could sneak up to the roof?"

"Maybe," said Dorothy. "I can move around more or less unseen, but if everyone is on alert, that might not be as easy."

"Everyone is outside," said Jessica.

"Then let's go." Dorothy stood.

Claudia grabbed her hand and pulled herself up.

"You can't come—"

Claudia cut her sentence short with a kiss. "I know. That's to remind you to come back safe, please."

"We will," said Dorothy. She and Jessica slipped into the hall, and made their way up the stairs.

"So," said Jessica one flight up. "You and Claudia?"

"Yes," said Dorothy.

"How long has that been going on?"

"Only since she got here," said Dorothy. "Or nine years, depending how you want to count."

"Wow. I really did not see that coming."

"I think it's fair to say no one saw this coming," said Dorothy.

"I'm happy for you," said Jessica.

"So am I. Here's hoping we all make it out of here. If I die two days after finally figuring out what I want, I am going to feel extremely swindled."

They made it to the roof without incident. They also found several others had beaten them there, including the Professor and the wizard.

"Do not make a sound," whispered Dorothy. "And do not let go of my hand."

Jessica nodded, fear obvious in her eyes. As long as they maintained contact, the spell deflecting everyone's gazes away from Dorothy would protect Jessica as well.

Dorothy led her to the edge of the roof, into a stretch as far away from the cluster of gawking goblins as she could. They peered over the edge. Jessica gasped, and Dorothy gave her hand a squeeze.

The entire forest glowed.

Dorothy looked as far out in every direction as she could see. Though limited to one side of the building, the glow emanated from thousands of trees, stretching to the horizon. Without thinking, she zoomed in on some of them, and found the light did not come from the trees themselves, per se. Each radiant treetop bore a symbol burned or etched into the wood. Simple, crude collections of short, straight lines, some looked like letters, most did not. Except they did. Not English, but a language she understood nevertheless. They spelled out, over and over, "This way."

"That can't be good," whispered Dorothy.

"Are you telling me you don't know what this is?" asked Professor Heatherington.

Dorothy turned to look at him and nearly fell off the roof before remembering she had focused her eyes for long distance.

"Reptiles in mirror may be closer than they appear," she whispered. Refocusing, she could see he was about thirty feet away from her. "Or farther."

"What?" whispered Jessica.

"Shh!" said Dorothy.

"Absolutely no idea," said Tim, the wizard, with no sign of alarm, and perhaps a touch of amusement.

The reptile's artificial eye glowed, first taking on a magenta hue, then switching to aqua. He made a clicking noise with his mouth. "Bah! It looks the same no matter how I filter it."

"How many functions does that eye have?" asked Tim, with feigned nonchalance.

"I'm sure you'd like to know," answered the professor with equal dryness. He pointed back to the forest. "Is that harmful?"

"Not as far as I can tell from here," said the wizard. "Send some goblins out and see how they fare."

The Professor looked around him and singled out two goblins leaning over the edge. "You two! Go outside! Find out what this is all about."

"Wot?" said one of them. "Hell no, I won't do that! You don't pay me enough to mess with magic stuff! Besides..." He clutched his stomach, "I ain't feelin' so good."

"Tim?" said the professor.

The wizard waved his staff in the direction of the goblin and made a smooth, sweeping motion, launching him well into the forest. A delayed scream came from his direction, and then a crash. Tim and the Professor leaned over the edge to look for him.

"Well?" said the reptile.

"Quite dead. I suppose that could have been the fall, though." Without looking, Tim causally flicked another goblin into the trees. Another cry. Another crash. The wizard craned his neck. "Ooh. That one is still alive."

"I say!" shouted the Professor, his hands cupped around his mouth. "You down there! Are you feeling any ill effects from the lights?"

No reply.

"Blast!" The Professor looked around him. Half of the goblins had rushed to the edge to see the show. The others had already fled down the stairs. "There's nothing for it. We're just going to have to send them out the door. Come along." He pushed his way past the wretched creatures around him. Several of them held their stomachs, wincing. Christine's sugar had started to do its stuff.

As Tim turned to follow his master, his eyes swept across where Dorothy and Jessica stood.

And stopped there.

Dorothy's heart pounded. The spell she had cast was meant to direct gazes away from her. Not invisibility, just eye repellant. That Tim looked directly at them meant he certainly saw them. Neither woman moved.

He smiled faintly, and looked away.

Once they had all left Dorothy and Jessica behind on the roof, Jessica said, "Did he see us? I think he saw us."

"No," lied Dorothy. "It's fine. Let's go downstairs."

"What does this mean?" asked Jessica, looking at the glowing symbols in the trees.

"It means we aren't waiting until tomorrow," said Dorothy. "Our escape starts now."

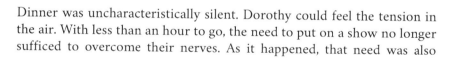

For the next two hours, Dorothy wandered the building, checking in on everyone, pretending to be nervous about whatever was happening outside, and pretending not to know what it was. The others followed her lead. Varying degrees of anxiety and outright fear showed in their eyes, but none of them gave her cause to believe they would crack. These women were survivors, which made Dorothy simultaneously proud of them, and sad for what it had taken to forge that strength. Every time she encountered abductees, she gave them three simple instructions:

"We are leaving tonight. Check in with Claudia for the plan. Pass it on."

Right before dinner, she returned to the storage room. Claudia and Apryl were running through their checklist. "How many of them have been down here?" asked Dorothy.

"All twenty-seven, plus Mitchell," said Claudia. "Here's the list of assignments." She tore a sheet out of the notebook and handed it to Dorothy.

She glanced over the tasks each woman had been given. "How are they doing?"

"Some of them are pissed, some of them are scared shitless. About what you'd expect. They're all ready, though. I have the tougher ones herding the timid ones. If everyone sticks with her buddy and sticks to the plan, we'll all make it out."

"This is good. This is very good." She put the list down. "Ninety minutes to go. I have to go make an appearance at dinner. I will see you at the back door."

Claudia stood to give her a hug. "I love you," she whispered in Dorothy's ear.

"I love you, too," said Dorothy. She tried to shake the foreboding sensation they exchanged that sentiment because they knew it would be their last chance.

Dinner was uncharacteristically silent. Dorothy could feel the tension in the air. With less than an hour to go, the need to put on a show no longer sufficed to overcome their nerves. As it happened, that need was also moot, as all the people who worked for the Professor were out on the field, working through the meal. Whatever they had seen in the forest had spooked their master into keeping all his prisoners inside and all his men out.

The women scraped their barely touched plates into the trash and filed out of the dining area in small groups. Ostensibly, they would all head back to their rooms for the evening. Apart from the ones assigned to round up the children, they did go back to their rooms, but only to wait out the remaining minutes before making their dash for the exit and the truck. Dorothy had that much time to find and take out Heatherington.

From the windows of the clubhouse, she could not find him on the field supervising the labor. That meant he would be in his office. Dorothy lifted her hand and the book appeared. She reread a spell she had now spent two days memorizing. It would transform that abomination into a common lizard. And she would have no trouble killing a common lizard.

Cloaked in her eye repellant spell, Dorothy ascended to the Professor's office. By now, Claudia would be on the move with Ian, Jessica, Kari and Emily, hunting Felicia. The assassin kept a surprisingly reliable schedule of rounds. While still under mind control, and Felicia's gofer, Britney came to know her routine, from which she never wavered. That information proved to be a key ingredient in the escape plan. Felicia's primary purpose was simple security, a task she no doubt found horribly boring in that it consisted of guarding entirely compliant captives. She would soon find it less boring. Disarmed and deafened, she would have to contend with Kari, the marine sergeant; Emily, the police officer; and Claudia, the secret agent. All three planned to subdue her regardless of how far they had to go to do that.

Apryl would perform her task from the safety of their hideout. She did not need physical contact, nor even proximity to take out Tim's power source. As long as he stayed somewhere in the building, her ability would work on his staff.

Dorothy reached the Professor's office. She knocked on the closed door.

"Enter," he said from within.

She found him standing at the window, looking out on the field, still a great deal of activity underway down there. He looked over his shoulder to her. "Miss O'Neill. Do come in. How may I help you?"

She crossed the room, shutting out his saccharine pleasantries. The spell she memorized and rehearsed now came sluggishly to her lips, but she found it, and began the chant. As she rolled through the intricate hand motions that went with it, it became a dance.

"Good gracious," he said. "What are you doing?"

On her second iteration through the phrase, she raised her voice. She continued to walk toward him, arms now making broader versions of the hand motions. She felt herself falling into the magic, as the line between volition and instinct blurred. Her hands glowed a pale red.

"Miss O'Neill!" he demanded. "I asked you what you are doing!"

She charged him, shouting the words of the chant. In English, she screamed, "Lizard!" directly into his face from inches away.

Everything stopped. Her hands no longer glowed, and she fell silent. She looked for any trace of change in this reptile's appearance or bearing, and found none. The small lizard she expected to see remained a man-sized, green-scaled monster.

Then he hit her.

In the slow-motion sensation of the moment, the staccato ticking of his prosthetic hand and the wind-up for the powerful backswing telegraphed its cold sting against her body. When it did connect, it flashed her back to a moment in her childhood when she was accidentally thrown from a bicycle. Her collision with the pavement brought with it five stitches and a broken clavicle. This pain resembled that only in type. In magnitude, no comparison. The blow struck her in the ribcage, and effortlessly lifted her off her feet. She perceived her moments of freefall with alarming precision, but had no sense she traveled at a speed sufficient to shatter plate glass.

As she passed through the window, dozens of tiny glass knives appeared around her and nipped at her flesh. Her prevailing thoughts centered on the danger to her eyes, but she could find no way to effectively shield them. Satisfied they had come through the ordeal uninjured, she took note of her distance above the ground. Never particularly athletic, she could not fathom the prospect of somehow moving her body in a way that would save her life, but when she hit the grass, she did so at exactly the correct angle to disperse her momentum into the yard-long divots she backwardly gouged into the earth with the soles of her boots. She threw her arms out in front of her when she toppled forward, and finished on her hands and knees. She looked up, having fallen at least four stories, and at least a hundred feet horizontally.

The Professor stood in the window, with his coat and shirt off, extending enormous, green, leathery wings.

"Oh," she whimpered. "Not fair."

As he swooped down, he revealed his prosthetic hand was in fact a prosthetic arm, the brass extending to cover his entire shoulder. She pulled herself up, with both a stabbing in her feet, most likely from breaking them as she fell, and a sharp burning in her side, surely a broken rib. In the seconds she had to prepare, she produced the book and shouted, "Tell me about dragons!" It opened and spread itself to a page with illustrations of winged, fire-breathing beasts, and she frantically read the spells for how to contend with them. She had just enough time to learn exactly one of those before he landed and strode across the field. She braced herself, and began the incantation.

A white-hot lance sliced through her left shoulder. Her concentration shattered, she cried and fell to the ground. Panting, she looked to the source of her pain, a throwing dagger embedded in her. She touched the handle, sending new shoots of agony through her body. As she desperately fought against blacking out, a boot came down on her left arm and held it in place. The boot was covered in blades, some cracked and shattered, and spattered with blood.

"You don't want to pull that out," said Felicia. "Not unless you want to bleed to death."

With a loud *thump* to her right, the dark wizard crouched down next to her with a sinister smile. "Most impressive, little girl." Pressing her arm down, he waved his staff over it. With a hum that vibrated the ground under her, the book appeared in her hand. He took it from her, and absorbed it into himself exactly the way she had. He laughed. "Most impressive indeed."

BACKUP

The military flier arrived early in the evening, the same approximate design as the one from the NCSA, but three times as big. When the evacuation finally came, this craft would be more than up to the task of ferrying thirty people to freedom. As it came in and slowed to a hover before setting down near them, Harrison took his eyes away from the window.

Milton stood at the hatch. "Walk with me, please."

"Right," said Harrison.

"Sparky," said Milton. "I'm going out there to assume command of the troops that just got here. I need you to do a quick recon of that stadium. Can you report back here in ten minutes?"

"Um..." said the pixie.

"Yes?"

"She's not very good at getting in and out unnoticed," said Harrison.

"I'm really not," she said.

"Then don't go in," said Milton. "Do a quick pass around the building. Tell me anything you see."

"They're going to spot me," she said.

"Sparky, that ballpark is sitting at the end of spiral of glowing trees, miles long. They know we're coming. They probably already know we're here. We do not have the element of surprise, but they still do unless we can get a solid handle on just what we are up against. Do you understand?"

She bit her lip. "The thing is... You see, there's this wizard."

"Yes?" said Milton.

"Well, he took me out like it was nothing. Back at the cabin, I mean. If he sees me, I won't make it back here in ten minutes. Like, I won't make it back at all."

"I have faith in you."

She stared at him. "You're really going to make me go over there."

"I am. On the double, please."

"If I get killed, you are going to be in so much trouble." She zipped out the hatch, leaving an orange trail of sparks behind her.

"Come on," said Milton. He and Harrison left the flier, and crossed the ground to the army transport. Halfway there, they met up with an officer and two soldiers.

"Captain Milton?" said the officer.

"Yes. Lieutenant Davies, I presume?"

"Yes, sir." He held out a small box. "I am authorized to give you these."

Milton took the box, opened it, and pulled out a set of captain's bars. He pinned them to his collar.

Davies waited for Milton to finish putting the bars in place, then saluted.

Milton returned the formal gesture. "How many men in that thing?"

"Twenty-six men, four centaurs, sir. Also, four trebuchets and two catapults. I understand we may be storming the stadium?"

"Possibly. I'm waiting on a report from one of my agents."

As he said this, Sparky's bright orange streak appeared. She stopped short in front of his face.

Both soldiers with Davies drew their swords and assumed defensive positions.

"Stand down. This pixie works for me." Milton looked at Sparky. "That was a very short ten minutes."

"I panicked, okay?"

"Probably not, but it is what it is. What did you see?"

"Somebody exploded a truck!" she said. "It was all crunched and burny. There's a second one that looks like nobody has touched yet."

"Is that it?"

"No," said Sparky. "I also saw a lot of sick goblins. Something is really going around there. Can't say I've ever seen that much goblin puke all at once before."

"Charming," said Harrison.

"Sick goblins, exploded truck. Is that it?" asked Milton.

"Oh, I doubt it," said the pixie. "But I didn't go inside. There's probably a lot more falling apart in there than what I saw. Something is definitely going down."

"That could be Apryl and Claudia," said Harrison.

"Whatever it is, we're going to take advantage of it. Davies, I need you to take that transport and do a low flyover above the field. Then land it right on their doorstep."

"Yes, sir," said the lieutenant. "Are we going to launch an assault?"

"Negative," said Milton. "There are thirty-two hostages in there, two of whom are children. If they are having a crisis, an assault might panic the enemy into doing something awful. Our top goal is still the safety of those hostages. I want to announce our presence, then negotiate for their release."

"So we won't be attacking?" asked Davies.

"No," said Milton. "We are going to set up a siege."

[64]

CAVALRY

"Hold still. This may hurt a bit." Felicia grabbed the hilt of the dagger lodged in Dorothy's shoulder, and turned it.

Dorothy screamed. Tears flooded from her eyes, as the pain she endured began to dim them. She fought to stay conscious, and succeeded, barely.

After a few seconds of toying with her, and with a slight giggle, Felicia yanked the knife from her flesh. As promised, it gushed blood. The healer laid her hand over the open wound and pressed.

In the pain from sealing the gash and repairing the blood vessels within, Dorothy longed for the simplicity of Felicia twisting the blade into her. She gasped for air, dimly aware these inhalations were but desperate pauses between shrieks. Her vision went truly dark, and as she thought she would slip away and never wake, a voice beckoned her back.

"Don't leave us, little girl," said Tim. "You're made of more solid stuff than this. Surely a touch of searing agony is not sufficient to do you in."

The taunt pulled her back from the brink of oblivion. "You should be so lucky," she managed to say with a weak, raspy voice.

The wizard laughed heartily. "Delightful! Oh, I do like this one, Basil. May I keep her?"

"She dies with the rest," said the Professor.

"Bah. Such a waste."

"Nothing of the sort," said Heatherington. "After how many we lost in that foolish escape attempt, we need every sacrifice we still have."

Through her pain, Dorothy struggled to contain her terror at that

334

statement. The notion her poor planning had now cost lives overwhelmed her. That those deaths might include Melody, or Ian, or Claudia...

"Just how many did we lose, Professor?" asked Felicia, her tone catty, rather than concerned.

"I'm sure I don't know," he said. "We're still counting bodies."

Felicia laughed at this. "Oh, Basil, give it a rest. Counting bodies? Please. Who is this show for? Her?" She clarified this statement by grinding the toe of her boot into Dorothy's shoulder wound.

The pain which had started moving in the direction of tolerable fired back up, and Dorothy shrieked again. But that cry also disguised a spark of hope. Heatherington's claim of deaths was a bluff. More importantly, he and Felicia were, on some level, at odds with each other. While she loudly and tearfully proclaimed herself broken and in despair, she analyzed this information for ways she could turn it to her advantage.

"This is the best they have to offer." Felicia dug her toe in deeper. "And look at her. She is pathetic."

"She is magnificent," said Tim. "Did you see how gracefully she tumbled from that window? That was a second order slow descent spell. This one has talent. With a little reconditioning, she could be very useful."

"I said no," said the Professor.

Dorothy's head began to clear. When she nearly blacked out from the pain, she lost all sense of her surroundings, apart from the voices of her enemies. She still lay on her back in the field. The presence of both Felicia and Tim meant that Claudia and Apryl had failed in their own assignments, perhaps as spectacularly as she had. "That spell should have worked," she said feebly, too late realizing she spoke it aloud.

"What were you trying to do?" whispered Tim in her ear.

She gave him silence in return.

"What spell does she mean?" he asked Heatherington.

"I haven't a clue," he said. "She spouted some arcane nonsense and waved her hands about. Then she shouted 'Lizard!' at me. Naturally, I struck her."

Felicia laughed. "The nerve!"

"Quite so!" said the Professor.

"You tried to simplify him," Tim said softly to Dorothy. "You thought he was a reptile. Oh, you really are something."

"He's a dragon," said Dorothy, in a flimsy attempt to take control of the conversation.

"Half-dragon," said the Professor.

She found this piece of information genuinely confusing, and she rolled her head to get a better look at him. He stood a few feet away from her, still shirtless, his enormous wings tucked close to his sides.

"And half human," said Tim with a bemused smile.

"How is that possible?" she asked, her voice barely a groan.

Heatherington looked away from her. "It's complicated."

"What's that sound?"

Felicia asked the question moments before the rumble penetrated Dorothy's addled head. She looked up, tracking Felicia's gaze to a point in the sky with nothing in it. The rumble grew louder. Both Felicia and Tim backed away from Dorothy's supine form to scan the sky. She propped herself up on her elbows, silently cursing the pain in her shoulder. Finally, the source of the sound revealed itself. A massive, olive-green shape emerged from the edge of the stadium, and swept over the field. As it passed between her and the evening sun, the size of the shadow it cast indicated how low it flew.

"NCSA?" said Tim.

"They don't have anything that big. That's military." As Felicia said that, another, smaller flier appeared at a higher altitude, also moving its way across the sky. "That one is NCSA."

"This is a problem," said Heatherington.

"They have a wizard," said Tim, watching the smaller flier.

"A good one?" asked Felicia.

"Hard to know from here. All I can tell is there is a spellcaster in the smaller vehicle. You know their people better than I. Do they have a wizard powerful enough to be a threat?"

"I can think of three. Worst possible scenario would be Mallory. Apart from her, Aplomado or Eleonora would pose a challenge. They have no one else of your caliber, as far as I know."

The two fliers smoothly crossed the length of the field, then dipped below the outfield wall. Dorothy imagined them setting down in the forest just beyond the stadium, and Harrison knocking on the front door any second now. "You're finished," she said hoarsely.

The Professor whirled on her. "Hardly!" he snorted. "Lock her up!" he snapped at Felicia.

The assassin punched Dorothy in the shoulder, hard enough to finally throw her pain past a reasonable threshold for consciousness. As she blacked out, a pair of giant reptilian wings beat furiously before her eyes, and the professor launched himself skyward.

[65]

ERROR

A pair of centaurs hauled heavy equipment down the ramp of the larger flier. Several human soldiers assembled a trebuchet from components of ceramic and steel. Harrison had never seen one of these in action before, and as much as the mixed aesthetic of archaic weaponry fashioned with advanced technology fascinated him, all he could think about were the cases of cannonballs these war machines would fling, and that one could land on his daughter or his wife without anyone knowing until they were dug from the rubble.

Milton's voice issued from Harrison's communicator, shattering his ruminations. "Cody, I need you inside."

He drew the device from his pocket, grateful for the distraction. "On my way."

"Is Sparky with you?"

Harrison looked around. A familiar orange glow hovered near Sarah. "No, but I can see her."

"Bring her, please. And Dr. Tucker, as well."

"Will do." Harrison went to round up Sparky first.

Sarah sat in one of the collapsible chairs, eating a sandwich. "How soon before we can go in and get our children?"

"I don't know," said Harrison. "Kind of hoping that's what I'm about to find out. Milton wants to see you and me, Sparky."

"Is he going to ask me to do another one of those recon whatevers? Because I'm not doing it."

"He didn't say. All I know is he wants to see you and me and Hadley."

337

"Hadley?" said Sparky. "What the hell for?"

"Again," said Harrison patiently, "I do not know."

"Please tell him I would like to rescue my son now," said Sarah before taking another bite of her sandwich.

"I think he knows, but I'll bring it up anyway."

From there, they went to collect Hadley, a spectator to the trebuchet construction. Harrison took a moment to admire the work himself. In the wake of the Mayhem Wave, with gun powder and other explosives rendered useless, the modern trebuchet proved to be the most effective long-range, heavy ordinance weapon. Simple in design, it was essentially a lever, with a counterweight hoisted on the long arm, then released, to propel a projectile mounted on the short arm in a net. The sling action of the fabric as the arm flipped around added to the momentum of the shot, increasing the range. As much as these war machines were simply arms for throwing stones, their gleaming metal frames and crisp nylon slings lent them an air of formidability, as did the sight of centaurs manually operating the winches that pulled the counterweight high over their heads, and dropping enormous stone spheres into the nets, ready for action.

As Harrison and Sparky got closer to the half-built trebuchet, one of the centaurs intercepted them and blocked Harrison's path. "I'll need you to stand back, sir."

"I'm not trying to interfere with your work, Sergeant," said Harrison. "There's a ghost watching you build that thing, and I need to talk to him."

The centaur took in this new information, looking back and forth from Harrison to the partially built trebuchet. "The ghost should not be there."

"May I tell him that, please? This comes from Captain Milton. He wants to talk to the ghost."

"Understood." The centaur stepped aside.

"Hadley!" called Harrison. "Come here!"

With no sense of transition, Hadley went from fifty feet away to less than a foot from Harrison, looking straight at him. "What do you need?"

"Shit!" shouted Harrison.

The centaur looked his way in concern, or perhaps annoyance, before returning to his work.

"Sorry, I didn't know you could do that," said Harrison. "Milton wants to see you."

"He won't be able to," said Hadley.

Harrison shook his head. "Not see. Wrong word. He wants me to bring you to him."

Hadley frowned. "Why?"

"He won't tell you," said Sparky. "Don't let it bother you. He won't tell me either."

"Because I don't know. Can we please just go?" Without waiting for either of them, Harrison turned on his heel and made for the NCSA flier. While he had faith in Apryl's ability to take care of herself, and while he had Aplomado's reassurances that all the abductees remained healthy, the separation from his family still wore him down. He needed this to end, and soon.

Inside the flier, he found Milton studying a floor plan of the stadium. "What's the plan?"

"We're going to negotiate for the release of your children," said Milton.

"By lobbing missiles at them?"

Milton looked up from his screen and met Harrison's eyes. "Yes. As soon as the artillery is set up, I want to send in a few warning shots. Whatever disarray they are experiencing in there is about to become more pronounced."

"What if you hit our own people?" Harrison strained to keep the anxiety out of his voice.

"We're going to take out the press box," said Milton. "It makes a great target, and it's likely to be uninhabited."

"Likely?" said Harrison. "What if that's where they're keeping the hostages?"

"That's where you two come in," said Milton. "Dr. Tucker? Are you here?"

"He's here," said Harrison. "To my left."

Milton faced what surely appeared to him to be an empty space, and continued. "You are the only one of us who can slip in and out of there completely undetected. I need you to find our people, and report their location back to me. Can you do that?"

"Please tell him he is doing a remarkable job of simulating eye contact," said Hadley. "And yes, I can do that."

"He says yes," said Harrison.

"Excellent," said Milton. "How soon can you get started?"

"Apparently now," said Harrison. "He just disappeared."

"Good. Sparky?"

"Sir! Yes sir!" The pixie affected a salute.

"Do not mock the salute, Agent. While Dr. Tucker is searching for our people, I need you to confirm they are not in the press box. We are about to send some fairly large munitions into that structure, and I want to be sure we are not putting our own in jeopardy."

"Do I have to do this?" She pouted.

"Yes," he said. "Just confirm the press box is empty, or give me a count of how many are in there. How quickly can you do that?"

"Seconds," she said, and was gone.

"So," said Harrison, "did you need me for anything, or were you only interested in my sidekicks?"

"Actually, I do need to have a conversation with you. Have a seat." Milton gestured to the co-pilot's chair, which Harrison apprehensively took. "I got a message from Larson this morning. She thinks she has an idea what these abductions are all about."

"Why didn't she contact me directly? Liaising between departments is my job."

"Because she thought it might compromise you, and she wanted it to be my call whether to bring it to you."

Harrison's heart accelerated. Images of Melody and Apryl flashed before him, and he pushed past them. "Tell me."

"Mallory found something in the prophecy database she believes is a reference to Melody." He paused here. "Am I okay to go on?"

"Fuck," said Harrison, blood pounding in his ears. "Is she sure?"

"No, but she thinks it's very likely. Do you want to hear this? Do you want to recuse yourself from the mission?"

"This has always been about Melody, David. I have to hear it."

Milton picked up a tablet and read from the screen. "The actual text is a bit garbled, and in a language we've only partially decoded. The parts Mallory has translated with certainty refer to a 'Child of Mayhem,' who has the power to split worlds. The prophecy itself predates the Mayhem event, which she says makes it more credible."

"How do we know this is Melody, and what does Mallory mean about splitting worlds?"

"They're still working out that second part, but if I understand correctly it's either a metaphor for political power, or it describes a literal force of destruction. She says there's also a possibility the intended meaning is the exact opposite, describing a unifying force."

Harrison put his hands up. "I'm sorry. Can we cut to the chase? How does this help us?"

Milton set the tablet down. "The bottom line is that Mallory and Larson theorize the reason all those women were abducted is that our enemy is going to try to harness that power, to literally split the two worlds apart, and destroy our world. And she thinks they are going to tap into the Mayhespheres to do it. She said you would know what that meant."

Harrison nodded, numbly. "Will that work?"

"Thankfully, no," said Milton. "According to what they can glean, what you did with the counter-bomb was permanent in every sense. The worlds cannot be separated. Unfortunately, they are also telling me that another project they are working on, something with the sun, will become impossible to fix if the splitting is even attempted. The enemy has already been tapping energy out of the Mayhespheres as part of the abductions. The giant bats, the weird storm over New Chicago, all that stuff is part of the same process. Every time they do that, it widens the gap between the Mayhespheres, and if they push it too far, it might not be possible to pull them back together before the outer one swallows the sun. Honestly, a lot of that went over my head, but I think that's the gist."

"I understand most of it. But if this is just over some prophecy about Melody..." Harrison paused there, queasy with anxiety at hearing the words from his own mouth. Through the sour taste of bile, he forged on. "Why were all the others taken too?"

"Mallory isn't sure, but she thinks it may have been a misreading of the prophecy as the plural, 'Mayhem's Children.' If they thought they needed more than one they might have thought they needed to take anyone who could plausibly fit that description."

Harrison stared, dumbfounded. "You're saying they took all those people by mistake."

"A clerical error, essentially, yes. And if they knew enough to identify Melody, they might have linked her to any child of any surviving telekinetic."

"Which is why they took Adler," said Harrison.

"And which also might explain why all the captives are still in perfect health. Larson thinks there are still telekinetics we haven't yet accounted for. In nine years, it's likely some of them may have had children. The enemy may be waiting until they have every one of those before they make their move, and keeping the ones they have in peak condition using a healer while they wait. Unfortunately, as we don't know how many children we're talking about, or where they are, that's just a shot in the dark."

"I'll take it," said Harrison. "What exactly will it entail for them to make that move?"

"It's not clear." Milton paused there. "Mallory is not ruling out the possibility of human sacrifice."

Blood pounded sharply in Harrison's head at the unsurprising but dreaded words. "Then we have to get them out of there!"

Milton put his hand on Harrison's shoulder. "That was always the plan. This information has now given us a little more to work with if we're going to negotiate their release."

"How soon before these negotiations begin?"

Sparky chose that moment to return from her assignment. "It's empty."

"Good," said Milton. "Then the negotiations begin right now."

[66]

WHISPERS

Dorothy clawed her way back to consciousness as Felicia pulled her to her feet, using her wounded arm. She found the strength not to howl in pain, but barely. Felicia, apparently unsatisfied with this response, punched her in the shoulder. Between the wound and the effects of the healing, every touch felt as sharp as the original stab. She screamed.

"That's better." Holding Dorothy's arm behind her back to keep her in a perpetual state of pain, Felicia pushed her across the field toward the seats. Tim the wizard did not follow them, no doubt considering her helpless with the loss of her spell book. And rightly so.

When they got out of earshot, Dorothy said, "He's not very bright, is he? Your dragon boss?"

Felicia stopped walking, and spun Dorothy around to face her. She glanced surreptitiously upward at the professor, perched on the outfield wall. The conflict between the two of them obvious, Dorothy prepared herself to probe the chink in that armor. When Felicia looked back to her again, she did so with eyes torn by doubt. She grinned and patted Dorothy on the cheek.

"Are you actually trying to manipulate me? That is so precious."

Dorothy's heart sank. "All right. You don't have to be a bitch about it."

"Now, that's the first thing you've said that does impress me. And, yes, I do." She punctuated this last remark with another punch to the shoulder. This time, Dorothy managed to stifle her reaction to a whimper.

Felicia took her to the basement, and pinned her against a wall as she unlocked a closet door. "You know, you do have some promise, I'll give you that. Tim says you're good with the magic. That's new for you, isn't it?"

Dorothy, still pressed against the wall, did not respond.

Felicia leaned in close and whispered in her ear. "No. He's not very bright. He makes mistakes. And those mistakes represent opportunities." She gently turned Dorothy around to look her in the eye. Softly, she said, "Given the right opportunity, and given the right…" She looked Dorothy over, top to bottom. "…allies, things could change here very suddenly."

Dorothy took a moment to let those words sink in. "Are you trying to manipulate me?" she asked, putting on her best mischievous smile. "Why, that's adorable."

Her bravado earned her another punch to the knife wound. The new spike of pain ignited a sudden and focused rage, and she lashed out with her uninjured arm, attempting to punch Felicia in the stomach. She regretted the desperate and pointless gesture before her hand even connected, in anticipation of the inevitable retaliation. The action produced a loud *thud*, like a single stroke on a bass drum.

Felicia flew backward, slamming gracelessly into the far wall and collapsing to the floor. She gasped repeatedly as she struggled to get to her feet, the wind knocked out of her.

Dorothy looked down at her own hand in shock. It still faced outward, palm open. Whatever she had thrown at Felicia, it wasn't a punch.

The assassin pushed herself onto her knees, and stumbled again, still wheezing desperately. She looked up at Dorothy, a mixture of surprise, anger, and fear in her eyes.

Dorothy kicked her in the face.

As Felicia lay panting on the floor, still conscious but incapacitated, Dorothy opened the closet hurriedly, to look for something to restrain her, or kill her, with no clear preference. The dim light from the bare bulb overhead revealed shelves filled with cleaning supplies, and two cowering people.

"Dorothy?" cried one of them.

"You're alive!" said the other.

Britney Hinson and Anna Bruce gawked at her with a combination of despair and hope. She needed to push them toward the latter.

"Help me!" She pointed to Felicia. "Quickly! I need rope or tape!"

They both jumped up and pulled supplies off the shelves onto the floor. "Duct tape!" said Anna, tossing it to her.

Dorothy ripped the shrink wrap off the roll of tape, kicking Felicia in the head again for good measure. She dropped her knees onto Felicia's back and bound her wrists behind her, wrapping tape around them several times. She repeated this on her ankles.

"Kill you..." said Felicia groggily.

"There, there," said Dorothy.

Sheathed blades covered Felicia's outfit, including the katana strapped to her back under her bound arms. Dorothy reached for the hilt of the sword. As her hand drew nearer to it, it put out a cluster of tiny green sparks. She leapt back. "Don't touch the sword," she said to the other two. "Is there a bucket in there?"

"Yes." Britney pulled it out and dropped it on the floor next to Felicia's head with a metallic *bang*. "What did you do to her?"

"Something magic. I don't know." Dorothy reached for one of Felicia's smaller knives. No sparks this time. She drew it from its sheath and dropped it in the bucket. Twelve more knives went in with it, most of them already chipped or cracked. "Help me get her in the closet."

Anna and Britney hesitantly reached for Felicia's shoulders and ankles as Dorothy fished the key from her pocket. Felicia thrashed as soon as they touched her and they both leapt back. Dorothy pulled a tiny knife from the bucket and sliced a shallow incision across Felicia's cheek. She cried out in rage.

"The next one goes in your eye," said Dorothy.

"Jesus!" said Anna.

Dorothy held out a hand for silence. She ripped another length of tape off the roll and applied it to Felicia's mouth, also partially covering the bleeding wound on her cheek, then crouched to Felicia's face, pointing the dagger at her eye, which threw out daggers of its own. "Both of you grab her legs and pull."

They dragged her into the closet, where they dropped her legs, sprang over her and dashed into the hall. Dorothy took one last look at Felicia, and the dark promise in her eyes, before turning the light off and closing the door. She locked the deadbolt with the key, which she dropped into the bucket with the knives.

Anna and Britney looked at her with wide, frightened eyes.

"We have to assume that won't hold her long," said Dorothy. "We have however much time it takes for her to wiggle out of that tape. What happened with the escape?"

"We don't know," said Britney. "We made it as far as the truck, but there were men there, and some goblins. We tried to run, but they got us. I don't know how many. Some of them might have made it to the woods, but I just don't know."

"The children?" asked Dorothy.

Britney gave her a confused shrug, and looked at Anna.

"I don't think any of the children made it that far," said Anna. "I didn't see any."

Dorothy's chest tightened. This meant either excellent or terrible news. She dreaded her next question. "Claudia?"

"I didn't see her there either," said Anna.

"Maybe she got away," said Britney.

Dorothy nodded, trying to think of ways to force bravery through her fear. The escape plan had gone south in every possible way. Apryl's attempt to overload Tim's staff did not work. Claudia's role of bringing Ian to shatter Felicia's weapons and then overwhelm her did not work, although some of Felicia's blades were clearly fractured.

She rubbed her recently injured and repaired shoulder. The throwing knife was whole enough. And she still wore an unbroken sword on her back. Dorothy did not look closely enough to confirm it suffered no damage, but sensed it had not from her brief encounter with it. So, some tiny fraction of their plan had worked.

Then it hit her. That part of the plan included Felicia being knocked off her guard by cuts from the shrapnel of her exploding knives. But a fluke aspect of Ian's power guaranteed that none of those metal fragments would hurt her. Ian could not hurt anyone, even by accident. He said it right to her, and she completely missed the connection until this moment. One tiny detail escaped her, leaving one third of the plan in ruins. And she misidentified what manner of creature the professor was, leading to her use the wrong spell against him. Two details, two thirds of the plan shot. As she tried to imagine how to take blame for the failure of the third component—disarming Tim—she caught herself up short. Self-recrimination served no purpose. Learn. Move on.

"You said you made it to the truck," said Dorothy. "How many trucks were there?"

Britney and Anna looked at each other. "There was just one truck," said Britney.

"And some wreckage," said Anna. "Is that what you mean?"

So, Ian had managed to take out one of the trucks. That was something. He must have done that before they went looking for Felicia.

"What are we going to do?" asked Britney, anxiety in her eyes.

Dorothy had no words of reassurance for her. By now, their captors knew the mind control was no longer in effect. Claudia was either dead or captured. A small chance remained Apryl was still in hiding, but she had no way to communicate with her.

"I don't know," said Dorothy. "I need time to think, and we are too exposed here. Come on."

She picked up the bucket of knives and led them farther down the hall. A minute or so later they found themselves in a partially demolished candlepin bowling alley. Hardwood planks, ripped up from the floors, sat in neat piles covered in dust. The stadium owners probably intended to be repurpose them nine years earlier, before the Mayhem Wave rendered whatever plans for them irrelevant. Disarray dominated the area, with no signs of activity from Basil's people.

"This will do," said Dorothy, taking it all in. "Is there anything to write with in here? I need you to make a list of people you saw captured, especially if they were injured. Can you do that?"

"Here's a pencil," said Anna, holding it up.

"Can we write on the wall?" asked Britney.

"Yes. Good," said Dorothy. "While you're doing that, I need to concentrate. Can you give me five minutes?"

"Sure," said Britney. She and Anna crouched close together and whispered names. In truth, Dorothy had no need for such a list, but she did need some uninterrupted focus, and those two needed to feel useful.

She curled up in a ball, and tried to remember incantations. Tim had taken her book from her, but the book wasn't the weapon, was it? The book gave her information. She used what she learned to do those things. And he couldn't take that from her, could he? Obviously, she learned something that allowed her to throw Felicia like a rag doll with a single gesture. It was impossible for her to recall that spell. The content she picked out of that book happened at a level not quite conscious. She muttered a few disconnected phrases she recalled, but without access to the book, the memorized words sounded like nonsense to her. And as much as she tried to stay on task, her thoughts kept running back to Claudia. After a solid minute of whispering gibberish, she switched to English.

"Please be alive, Claudia. Please be alive. Please be alive." She took her already nearly silent words down a notch in volume to prevent the others from knowing how desperate she truly was. "Please be alive, Claudia. Please be alive."

Dotty? Is that you?

Dorothy's eyes snapped open. The voice had sounded in her head crisply, and she looked up to see if the others had heard it. Engrossed in their list, they paid no attention to her.

Dotty? Are you trying to talk to me? Tell me I'm not crazy.

Warm tears drew trails down both her cheeks. "I love you so much," she whispered.

Holy fuck! It is you! Where are you?

"In the basement. Where are you?"

They put us in a bathroom and jammed the door. There's nine of us down here, including Apryl. Are you alone?

"I have Britney and Anna," said Dorothy.

"Are you talking to us?" asked Anna.

Dorothy held up a hand, now aware she had gone from a whisper to a normal speaking voice. "What happened?" she asked Claudia.

Bitch's sword wouldn't break. He was able to do the smaller knives, but she had plenty of time to figure it out and defend herself. Cut us up pretty bad. We're okay now. No, I'm talking to Dotty. I don't know how, I just am. Apryl says hello.

Dorothy laughed. "Tell her I said hello. Do you have Ian?"

No. They took him away and put him with the kids. They said he'd be safer there, like I believe that.

"They still don't know what he can do?"

No clue. Bitch came after me first then Keri. She never touched the boy.

"That's good. We might still have a secret weapon. And Harrison is here."

What? Here? Why isn't he breaking us out?

"I don't know what's happening outside. I just saw the fliers."

"Who are you talking to?" asked Anna. Dorothy took a moment to pay attention to her cellmates, both obviously shaken by what must have appeared to be Dorothy's ramblings.

"I'm talking to Claudia," she said.

"How?" asked Anna. "Are you doing magic?"

"I think so," said Dorothy.

A distant but extremely loud *bang* sounded outside the bowling alley. Everyone jumped.

What the fuck was that?

"You heard it too?"

Yes, I heard it! The whole room shook!

"Stay here," said Dorothy to Anna and Britney. She bolted back into the hall. Another *bang*, closer, louder, and more familiar.

Fuck! What do we do?

"Sit tight!" said Dorothy. "I have this."

She made straight for the closet where they had stored Felicia. In front of it stood Ian, his hands spread out in front of him, and rage in his eyes.

Further down the hall lay piles of rubble. A small band of children and three women stood clustered behind him, covering their eyes in anticipation.

"Not that one!" shouted Dorothy.

Ian looked up, surprise in his eyes, and dropped his hands. "Mom?" He ran to her, and she scooped him into her arms.

"Dorrie?" cried Melody, pushing her way past the other children.

"Little!" cried Dorothy, drawing her into a group hug with the boy. She felt the tingle of contact, stronger now, and ignored it. "Oh, thank God."

Melody pulled away and looked Dorothy in the eyes.

Dorothy gasped. Melody's eyes were purple, and ever so slightly sparkly, but the sheer joy in her smile offset that shock.

"Where's my mommy?" she asked calmly.

"Bathroom," said Dorothy.

Melody stood and took Dorothy's hand. "Let's go get her."

[67]

TRUCE

H arrison watched in boyish fascination as an eighty-pound stone sphere, lobbed from a nylon net at the end of a steel arm, sailed over the outfield wall in a graceful arc before plowing through the center of the press box. Underwhelming destruction resulted, as the ball hit nothing but window. Apart from the vaguely satisfying and distant tinkle of breaking glass, they had nothing to show for the shot but a hole.

"Bring it down a bit," said Milton to the soldiers loading the next trebuchet. "See if you can take out the floor."

"And this is absolutely necessary?" asked Harrison.

"I know we're pounding your childhood stomping ground, Harrison," said Milton. "I will try to keep the destruction to a minimum, but I won't spare it out of sentimentality. These people need to fear us as quickly as possible."

A second projectile went over the wall. This one clipped the lower edge of the box with a loud crash. Wood, glass, and desk fragments spilled out of the hole onto the seats below.

"Better," said Milton. "Six more shots, then hold fire."

"Yes, sir." The centaur sergeant trotted around the siege engines supervising their operation.

"I have a message to broadcast," said Milton to Harrison. "You're welcome to stay here and spectate if you want."

"No, I want to hear their reply," said Harrison.

The two walked to the NCSA flier, Harrison occasionally turning at the sound of a counterweight being released. Once inside, they took the pilots' seats, and Milton opened a recording.

"Attention occupants of Fenway Park: This is Captain David Milton of the New Chicago Armed Forces. You are hereby ordered to surrender your hostages immediately. Please be advised we are aware of the prophecy you seek to fulfill, and that our research indicates your plan is based on faulty information, and will not work. If you harm the hostages in any way, the worlds will remain merged, we will still be here, and we will destroy you. End recording. Playback."

The flier's internal speaker repeated Milton's words back to him. Satisfied, he instructed the onboard computer, "Broadcast that over the external public address every five minutes until further notice." A few seconds later, the recording rolled out in its first loud iteration.

Forty minutes and twenty-four stone missiles later, they got a reply.

<hr />

Both parties agreed to hold negotiations on the field. The late afternoon gave way to evening, and the arc lights compensated for the diminished sunlight. In the interest of avoiding an ambush, Milton's party came over the wall in the NSCA flier. He brought all the telekinetics, the wizard, the pixie, twelve human soldiers with repeating crossbows, and two centaurs carrying shields and assorted weapons. Should their hosts attempt to gain an advantage by killing the lights after the sun went down, the flier's floodlights, already illuminated and more powerful than the ones overhead, would take up the task of keeping the environment in day-like brightness.

Harrison emerged from the flier. Two figures sat at a table set up on the grass. One stood to greet them, looking for all the world like a crocodile dressed in Victorian finery.

"What is that?" whispered Harrison to Aplomado.

"Half-dragon," said the wizard. "Watch that one. Under the fancy dress you'll find he has a pair of wings that will give him a distinct advantage if this comes to blows."

"Terrific. What about the other one?" Harrison looked at the other person sitting at the table. Unlike the half-dragon, this one did not stand. He appeared human, with a pale bald head covered in tattoos. None bore an identifiable image, just vague forms and swirls.

Aplomado frowned at that. "Wizard, I believe. Difficult to say what order. Something pre-Mayhem, though. A non-real indigenous."

"You look nervous," said Harrison, in the first time he could recall expressing concern for Aplomado. The wizard did not respond.

"Good evening!" said the half-dragon as they approached the table. "Professor Basil Heatherington, at your service." The professor had a mechanical hand, and a large prosthetic eye made of brass and glass. Absurdly, atop his head perched a brown leather top hat, with a pair of antique motoring goggles mounted to the band. Given the shape of the monster's head, and the size of his artificial eye, they could only have been ornamental.

"Captain David Milton," said Milton.

"And friends," added the Professor.

"Naturally," said Milton. There were only three chairs set up on their side of the table. Milton took the center seat, and gestured for Harrison and Aplomado to join him. Sarah, Dallas, and the soldiers remained standing. Sparky landed on the table and sat down cross-legged.

"Before I entertain whatever you have come to offer, I must insist on a guarantee of immunity from retaliation after anything that is decided here," opened Heatherington.

"And I'm sure you can appreciate that I may not be authorized to make such a guarantee without contacting my government," said Milton. "In any case, that's the sort of detail I feel should come at the end of these talks, not the beginning."

"Very well. In that case, the first thing I would like from you is the research that shows our plan—whatever you think that is—won't work. If I am satisfied we are talking about the same thing, and that you are correct, we will be able to proceed."

"All right. In exchange for that research, I would like to see our people, to be certain they are still alive and well. In fact…" Milton leaned forward. "I'm going to have to insist they be brought out and seated in those bleachers, so they will be in my sight the entire time we talk."

Harrison could not read the facial expressions of this creature, but the hesitant pause at this request was unmistakable.

"That can be arranged," said the half-dragon. He turned to the wizard. "Tim, have our guests brought to the field, please, and ask them to sit together in the seats."

The tattooed wizard nodded silently, stood, and drifted away. At no point did he look in Harrison's direction, making him feel annoyingly invisible. With that thought now risen to the top of his head, another realization struck him. He looked around the field.

"Excuse us for a moment, while we wait for them to arrive." Milton stood. "I need to speak with my consultants."

"Of course," said Heatherington.

Milton tugged on Harrison's shirt sleeve, breaking him out of his ruminations. He stood, and they took a few steps away from the table.

"What did you see?" whispered Milton, facing away from their hosts.

"What do you mean?" asked Harrison.

"I saw you looking around. I assumed you noticed something. No?"

"No. I mean, yes, I noticed something, and I can't believe I didn't notice it before." Harrison took one last look around the field. "Hadley never came back."

BREAKOUT

"Get back from the door!" shouted Meghan. "Cover your eyes!" Dorothy hung back as Ian walked up to the door, held up his hands, spread his fingers and pushed. Still at least two feet from the door, he never made direct contact with it. It shattered with a loud *bang* that echoed down the hall. The fragments fell neatly downward and to the sides. Several startled women peered through the open doorway. Melody walked right past them, calling for her mother. Mitchell approached the new opening, and held his hand out to assist. The prisoners came out of their bathroom cell one at a time, shaken but unharmed. Claudia was the fourth one out the door. She looked around her at the large number of people who had gathered.

"Is this everyone?" she asked.

"We're still missing four." Dorothy pulled Claudia into an embrace and kissed her. "That's for not dying," she whispered in her ear.

"That can be for anything you want it to," said Claudia.

Apryl emerged from the bathroom holding Melody. "Her eyes are purple. What do we know about that?"

"No idea," said Dorothy. "I saw it too. She seems okay, otherwise. Does she seem okay to you?"

"So far."

"Do we have a plan?" asked Claudia.

"Find the others," said Dorothy, raising her voice so everyone could hear. "Then find a way to get to Harrison. He's here to rescue us. We need to do whatever it takes to make that easy. We stay together. Everyone got that?"

Lots of nods, and a few yeses. Dorothy took in the sight of her responsibility. Twenty-six women, one young man, and sixteen children all looking at her with expectation in their eyes.

"We're going to do this buddy system. Every adult find another adult, and every pair of adults take at least one child."

Claudia took Dorothy's hand and held it over her head. Her other hand she held out to Ian, who took it. Several more pairs of clasped hands went up. Dorothy waited until everyone was accounted for.

"Good. Do not get separated. How many of you have weapons?"

A few swords went up, and one spear, all gathered from one of the store rooms Ian broke into. "All right. One weapon per group, as far as they will go. Make sure whoever has it is going to be okay using it."

A few women passed swords to others. Mitchell experimented with swishing a sword back and forth, and Dorothy silently hoped he would not have to use it. Her little brother had risen to this crisis admirably, but he had no violence in him.

"We have four more people to break out, and then we head for the surface." She bent down to speak to Ian. "Are you okay?"

He nodded.

"I'm going to keep you close to me. If we find any goblins or people other than ourselves, you'll need to break their weapons and their armor. Can you do that?"

"I couldn't break that lady's sword," he said with a mixture of fear and anger.

"I know. Just do your best." Dorothy stood. "All right, people, let's do this." She meant it as a simple instruction, but the determination in their eyes told her they heard it as a rallying cry. Their failed escape attempt had done nothing to demoralize them. If anything, it strengthened their resolve to be free. With Harrison and the NCSA here, they had a solid chance at achieving that now.

Dorothy hoped that would be enough. To pull this off, they would all need to be at their best, and they could not afford more surprises. She held on to that idea as they went forth to find the remaining four captives, and she did everything she could not to obsess on the fact one of those four was Siobhan.

Three destroyed doors later, they found all four of them. Ashley Adams and Taylor Richardson came out the door first, and Dorothy assigned them as escape buddies. She cautiously entered the room to get the other two.

Siobhan lay on her side in the corner of the empty room, curled up in a ball. Becca sat on the floor next to her, stroking her head. "You might not want to come in here," she said softly to Dorothy.

"Becca, we're leaving," said Dorothy. "We need you to come."

"I thought we tried that already."

"The NCSA is here. And we have swords. And Ian isn't holding back anymore. At this point I wouldn't be surprised if he brought this whole arena down." She paused there, seeing Siobhan's shivering form. "Is she going to be okay?"

"Anyone's guess," said Becca. "She had a breakdown when we tried to take her with us, and when we were caught, she begged the goblins to take her to Basil."

Dorothy shook her head helplessly. "I don't know how to fix this."

"Then don't worry about it. I'll take care of her."

"Well, you can best take care of her by getting her on her feet and out this door," said Dorothy. "You're her escape buddy now. Don't get separated."

"Right," said Becca. "Come on, honey. We have to go."

Siobhan shook her head and curled into a tighter ball, sobbing.

Dorothy turned her back on them, then paused in the door. She came back into the room and crouched near Siobhan. "Dad is here. He loves you, and he misses you, and he wants to take you home. Can we table everything else for now and focus on that?"

Siobhan looked up with saturated, red eyes. "Dad?"

"Please, honey," said Becca. "Let's go find him, okay?"

Siobhan's lip trembled, and she broke into another round of tears, but through them, she nodded. That would have to do for the time being.

Dorothy stood and walked to the door.

In the hall, two unarmed men stood with their hands in the air, surrounded by a dozen women pointing swords at them. "Wonderful." Dorothy walked up to one of them. "You are not locking us up again. If you're lucky, locking you up is all we will do to you."

"We're not here to lock you up," he said. "We were told to let you out and bring you up to the seats."

Dorothy's eyes narrowed. "Why?"

"Your people are here. They wanted to see that you were all still alive."

Dorothy took the closest sword, and pointed it at his neck. He gulped. "If our people are here, why aren't they down here to let us out instead of you?"

"I think they're still negotiating. You can probably ask them yourself when you get up there."

Dorothy lowered the sword. "Negotiating?" she said, nonplussed. "Negotiating. That son of a bitch."

[69]

NEGOTIATIONS

For about fifteen minutes after the wizard left to round up the hostages, Milton and the Professor went back and forth laying down ground rules. Harrison knew nothing about diplomacy, and had no way of knowing if Milton's ease with the process came from training, experience, or simple intuition, but things did seem to be moving in the right direction. The half-dragon appeared to find their evidence against his plan working to be persuasive. Both sides offered veiled threats of violence, in consistently polite tones, and after several such exchanges it became obvious the two sides were evenly enough matched in strength that physical conflict could end in mutual devastation.

Halfway through a hypothetical scenario regarding transfer of the prisoners to Milton's custody, they begin to emerge from below. Dorothy and Claudia arrived first, walking hand in hand up the stairs from beneath the stands. Dorothy towed a young boy. From this distance, Harrison could not identify him as Adler, and he looked to Sarah, who saw the same thing, with a look of unmasked and severe anxiety.

"Excuse me," said Harrison to Milton and the Professor. "I'm sorry to interrupt. I can see our people now, and I would like to interview them right away. May I?"

The half-dragon looked over his shoulder at the people filling the seats. When he looked back to Harrison, he appeared to make his best—but still horrific—attempt at a smile. "Naturally. They are all in perfect health. We have nothing to hide on that count. Please do see for yourself."

Harrison turned to Sarah. "Special Agent Logan, will you join—"

That was as far as he got before she bolted across the lawn.

Harrison leapt up to catch her before she alarmed anyone, but no one else on either side seemed to take issue with her behavior. He jogged after her to catch up, and now saw both the boy he spotted earlier and Adler. In addition to the women, and Mitchell, at least a dozen other children had taken seats.

Melody came out, hand in hand with Apryl, and he sprinted.

"Adler!" shouted Sarah, running at top speed. Her son stood and ran down the seats to the wall. From the other direction, she slammed into it, then grabbed him under the shoulders and pulled him over it into a tight embrace. They both fell to their knees.

Harrison did a headcount as he ran. Twice, he lost count, but there seemed to be the correct number of adults there. Given the additional children, he would have to confirm them all as the people he had come to rescue, but he took a great deal of hope and comfort in seeing so many of them, and they appeared to be sound. When he reached the wall, he rested his hand on Sarah's head. She and Adler still knelt in each other's arms.

Apryl walked down the steps to where he stood, lifted Melody up, and sat her on the wall. He took her, and she threw her arms around his neck, resting her head on his shoulder.

"Is she okay?" he asked Apryl.

"Her eyes are purple. Otherwise, yes." She leaned over the wall, grabbed his face, and kissed him with gusto. "Thanks for coming," she said when she finally came up for air.

"I love you," he said.

"Damn straight."

"Is everyone here?" he asked.

"Yes, plus fourteen children we didn't know about. Are we leaving?"

"Yes. Working on that."

"Good." She held her arms out. Harrison passed her his daughter after kissing her on the forehead, which resulted in a small static electric shock. As he handed her over, he saw the amethyst sparkle in her eyes, and found it inexplicably familiar.

"Wow. Have her eyes ever done that before?"

"No," said Apryl. "I have decided not to panic about it."

"Good plan." He touched Melody on the nose, and his finger tingled. The shock he felt earlier was likely magical then, not electric. "As soon as we get home, we're taking you for a checkup, young lady."

"Okay," said Melody.

Behind Apryl, Dorothy said something to Mitchell. Harrison had a flash of profound relief at the sight of both his adopted children alive and seemingly well, and impatiently hoped for a chance to speak with them soon. Mitchell nodded to Dorothy, and she made her way down the stairs, dressed in a frilly top, a skirt, and tall leather boots. He had never given her appearance much thought, mostly because she tended to dress in ways designed not to attract attention. She had a hard look in her eyes, and the closer she got, the less he recognized her.

"May I have a moment with your husband?" she asked Apryl when she got to the wall.

"Sure." Apryl looked back to Harrison. "This one has been the glue holding us all together. I'm putting that out there in case you forget to tell her how proud you are of her."

He smiled at that. "I'll try to remember."

Apryl walked back up the aisle.

"Are you all right?" he asked Dorothy.

"As well as can be expected," she said. "I've been through a lot."

"Thank you for keeping Melody safe. How is Mitchell doing?"

"Why are we still here?"

"We're getting there," he said. "It shouldn't be long."

She crossed her arms. "Negotiations going well?"

"They seem to be."

"Uh-huh. About that. Why are you negotiating with these animals?"

This took him by surprise. "As opposed to leaving you here?"

She leaned over the wall and stared him down. "As opposed to killing them." This close, the weariness and bitterness in her eyes shone through. These past few weeks had aged her considerably.

"If this turns into a fight, I can't guarantee the safety of any of the people sitting behind you," he said. "I can't even promise we would win. Dorothy, please, sit tight. We're trying to get you out of here."

"Harrison," she said through clenched teeth, "stop trying to get us out of here, and get us out of here."

As he tried to figure out a possible response to that, the ground under his feet vibrated slightly. It grew to a soft rumble. Well behind Dorothy and all the people sitting in the stands, a loose chunk of the press box broke free, and came crashing down onto the seats, triggering several frightened cries. With a loud *thump*, the earth beneath Harrison shifted enough to make him wobble.

Dorothy grabbed the wall as she too lost her balance. Once stable, she whirled around and shouted, "Ian?"

The boy Harrison had mistaken for Adler earlier shouted, "It's not me!"

Though not sure what that exchange meant, Harrison had some guesses. He looked back at the negotiating table. Milton stood with his arms out and his palms upward in a gesture of peace, with Aplomado nowhere in sight. The half-dragon stood, and leaned over the table.

"Not good," said Harrison. Another *thump* sounded, and the jolt was enough this time to topple him to his knees. Several people screamed.

One more *thump* followed, this time a familiar one, as Aplomado landed to his right at the end of one of his leaps.

"What's happening?" he asked the wizard.

"Unclear. Captain Milton is trying to explain this is not our doing. Their wizard is missing. We need to find him and bring him back to the table." He looked at Dorothy. "Witch, I need you. Come with me."

"Excuse me?" she asked, with wide eyes.

"Slow down!" said Harrison.

"There really isn't time for further explanation, Cody."

"I'm sorry," said Dorothy, "did you just call me Witch?"

"I did," said Aplomado.

She scowled at him. "I have a name."

Aplomado closed his eyes and held up his hand for silence. "He is under the seats. Come." He vaulted over the wall, and ran to the steps that led down.

"Apparently, I have witch things to do. Take care of the others." Dorothy ran after Aplomado.

"Witch things?" said Harrison. He looked back to the negotiating table, where the half-dragon waved his arms. Milton also gestured, though with less animation. As Harrison decided he needed to get back there, and as he opened his mouth to say as much to Sarah, the reptile lunged, and swiped the air with a broad and powerful backhand. A stream of colorful sparks flew away from that strike in a tall arc. As Harrison made the connection that his pixie had just been batted across the ballpark, a wide stream of orange flame jetted out from the Professor's mouth and engulfed his captain.

[70]

TIM

Dorothy followed Aplomado downward. At first, she simply took on faith he knew where he was going, but then she felt the pull. It taunted her. Somewhere in this building, Tim was toying with forces whose destructive effects had already become evident outside, and whose scope she intuitively knew to be orders of magnitude beyond anything she had experienced in her brief stint as a vessel for magic. As much as she truly desired to stay detached, and focus on containing whatever new threat this posed, two thoughts dominated her consciousness now: the unbridled thrill of realization her connection to magic was clearly still intact, and the rage the bastard still had her book.

As she ran, the floor beneath her feet vibrated, and by the time she heard the rumble, she lost her balance. She dropped to her knees as the wall to her left split with a deafening *crack*. The jolt left a fissure at least six inches wide that ran from floor to ceiling, and beyond, with nothing visible through it but dust and smoke.

Aplomado crouched and ran his fingers along the floor. She stood and bolted to him. As she got to his side, he lifted his right hand, made a circular gesture in the air with it, and brought it down with a hard slap on the floor. Cracks radiated forward from the point of impact, and as those cracks united, the concrete crumbled to gravel, and dropped out to form a triangular hole.

"Down," he said, then stepped into the hole and disappeared.

Without pause, she followed. She landed with ease and grace one floor down, inches away from the wizard. Looking away from her, he held a hand up. She stayed still and quiet.

Dorothy took in her surroundings, including a bank of cubbies, each holding a Red Sox uniform. Aplomado had his ear to the floor. "Are we in a locker room?" she whispered.

Without responding, he waved and slapped the floor again. Cracks riddled the surface, and a larger hole dropped out. The wizard jumped into it. Dorothy sighed, and followed again.

This drop went considerably longer than one floor. Dorothy found herself in a vast chamber, fifty feet top to bottom. She slowed her descent instinctively. On her way down, she passed friezes carved ornately into curved marble walls. They depicted scenes of horror. Fierce monsters terrorized, attacked, and devoured a variety of hapless humans. A brutish demon tore the wings off multiple faeries, and threw their flightless forms onto a heap. Dozens of torches mounted in sconces illuminated these frights, and rendered them even more disturbing by the flickering shadows.

On the far wall, under an enormous and jagged arch, sat an altar. Above this altar, his arms spread wide and his head lolled in apparent unconsciousness, hovered a man she did not recognize, dressed in a bright Hawaiian shirt.

She touched down softly next to Aplomado and pointed. "Who is that?"

Aplomado followed her finger and gaze. "Who is what?"

"Who is the invisible man?" came a familiar voice from the chamber.

Dorothy tried to track the source of the sound, but could not.

"The invisible man is Tim, the vermin wizard," she said. Her taunt did not flush him out. "I meant the floating man." She pointed again.

"The mundane cannot see him, little witch," came Tim's echoing voice.

"Hadley Tucker," said Aplomado, turning in a slow circle, palms out in front of him. "He is a ghost. Do not be distracted by him."

"Can you really not see him?" asked Dorothy.

"I really cannot."

"The gray falcon is not like you and me, little witch," said Tim.

"What is he talking about?" asked Dorothy.

"I have no idea," said Aplomado. He threw one of his hands out, and a blue flash of light shot from it, striking a wall. The sound of Tim's laughter resounded in the chamber.

"I'm nothing like you!" shouted Dorothy. Aplomado's sudden but completely ineffectual attack snapped her back to the realization she did not know her purpose here. She had assumed it would come intuitively, but so far the only thing her intuition told her was to be afraid.

"Really, little witch," said Tim. "Why the charade? Who is the show for? This mundane? Soon Aplomado the Pretender will be dead. And I already know who you are. The game has run its course."

With another rumble, a chunk of the ceiling broke free and came crashing to the floor, a few feet from where Dorothy stood. As that happened, the floating man Aplomado had called Hadley Tucker glowed white. His eyes snapped open, and he uttered a feeble and short scream. It did not sound at all human.

"Is the ghost supposed to scream?" asked Dorothy, trying to keep the rising fear out of her voice.

"No," said Aplomado. "Did he?"

"I think so," said Dorothy.

Aplomado threw his palm out again. A green flash of light struck a wall and sheared the head off a frieze monster.

"You're getting cold, pretender," said Tim. "This isn't very good spo—"

Aplomado smoothly reached behind himself without looking, curled his arm and drew it inward. There was a loud *crackle* and *buzz*, as tiny bolts of yellow lightning swirled around his arm, and then around the exposed form of Tim.

The dark wizard shrieked. Aplomado wrapped his arm around Tim's neck, and he tightened his grip. Tim choked, dropping his staff to the floor. Aplomado kicked it away, then clamped the fingers of his free hand onto Tim's scalp. The tattoos there pulsed in a deep red. Tim cried out in agony, and dropped to his knees. Aplomado released his grip on the dark wizard's throat, and intensified the pain channeled through his fingers to Tim's pate. The tattoos glowed more brightly.

"What are you doing down here?" asked Aplomado.

"You will get nothing from me, mundane. You—" Tim screamed once more as Aplomado lashed out with more pain.

"What are you doing to him?" asked Dorothy.

He ignored the question. "What are you doing with Tucker's ghost?" As he asked this, the color of Tim's tattoos phased from red to white, and a dull look came over his face.

"I need his power," said Tim.

"What power?"

"The power of the slain. The power of the lone kill. He is unique."

"How is this connected to the prophecy?" asked Aplomado. "What are you doing down here?"

"There is no prophecy," said Tim.

Aplomado came up short at that. "Explain."

"I used the dragon. Fed him a false prophecy. Made him believe in the Child of Mayhem."

"Why?" asked Aplomado.

"Bait."

One of the tattoos on Tim's scalp faded to black, slithered off his head and coiled itself around Aplomado's wrist. The shock of that sensation caused him to lose his grip, and as he clawed at his wrist, the thin black line snaked up his arm into his robe. It emerged at the collar, wrapping itself smoothly around his throat. Aplomado's skin compressed under it as it constricted.

Tim stood, brushed himself off and strolled to where his staff lay on the floor of the chamber. Aplomado dropped to his knees, eyes closed and hands out.

"Stupid mundane," said Tim. "Did you really believe you were a wizard? Did they really tell you that you could learn what I do? It would almost be endearing if it weren't so pathetic."

Aplomado gasped for air, his face turning blue. Still, he remained calm.

Dorothy tried to think of something, anything she might have learned from Strontium's book to break a curse like this, but she came up blank. "Stop it! You don't have to do this!"

"Oh, I know," said Tim with a smile. He pointed his staff at Aplomado, and a shimmering beam emanated from it, touching the black band around his neck. Aplomado's eyes snapped open, which they remained, long after he fell to the floor, and long after his last breath hissed through his lips.

"Well, where were we?" He stepped over Aplomado's body and took Dorothy's hand. "Ah, yes, the game."

The feel of his icy, slimy touch sickened her. As she held her nausea in check, and she looked over the body of the wizard who only minutes ago had called her to action, she numbly detached herself from her immediate predicament. In a voice more courageous than justified, with a calm that was entirely inappropriate, she asked, "What prophecy?"

"Oh!" He released her hand. "That! The prophecy. Well, you see, I couldn't just take the child myself. That would have been too obvious."

At the word "child," Dorothy felt a chill. "You said Child of Mayhem. Who is that?"

Tim laughed. "Your precious purple sister. Or would be, if there were such a thing."

Dorothy took a step back. Melody's changes, her eyes, her hair, which had long been cause for concern, now seemed foreboding. "What did you do to her?"

Tim held his hands out in mock innocence. "Not a thing, I assure you. Well, I suppose I set the ball in motion with that bad judgment spell, but you can hardly blame me for that. Any direct exposure to magic would have done this to her, sooner or later. I must say it has been amusing to watch her transformation from afar. If she survives, I may keep her."

"I don't understand." Dorothy fought past panic, and a desperate desire to find Melody and somehow save her from forces she couldn't fathom. "What does Child of Mayhem mean? What is the prophecy?"

"There is no prophecy!" Tim snapped. "Do listen, little witch. There is no Child of Mayhem. Your little girl's condition is an amusing but completely irrelevant coincidence. Had I foreseen it, I would have used it, but as it happened I didn't need to. Basil took to my bait greedily enough without the additional evidence."

Dorothy struggled to comprehend this. "What's happening to her?"

Tim shrugged. "That's really not for me to say. Wouldn't want to spoil the surprise, after all. I'm sure you'll find it delightful." He offered a smile drenched in mock friendliness.

She pushed aside her immediate concern for Melody's well-being, knowing that down that road she would only find emotional vulnerability. At that moment, she needed her strength. "You created a prophecy as a hoax?"

"Yes! As I said, a simple kidnapping would never have been sufficient bait for your knight, Cody. It had to appear to be a grand master plan with all sorts of detail, and a conspiracy. And for that to work, I needed a figurehead. A cult leader of sorts. Enter Basil. Half-dragons are very fierce, but grossly susceptible to guile, alas for him. Planting that prophecy was child's play. Leading him to it was a bit of work, but once he 'found' it, and had a chance to imagine a world wiped clean of all the mundanes, his ego took over from there. It was quite a stroke of luck he misread the prophecy to mean children instead of child. Once we had forty instead of one, the scale of this operation guaranteed a rescue mission. I almost wish I had thought of that myself, but no matter, it worked."

"You never wanted us," said Dorothy, with an odd mixture of confusion and relief Melody was never truly a target. "You were just trying to lure the NCSA?"

"Cody, specifically, yes. And it worked beautifully."

"I don't understand," said Dorothy. "Why bother with all of this, if none of it was real? Why lure Harrison at all? Why not just capture him instead of all of us?"

"Because the only way for me to get what I needed from him was for him to bring it to me. It was never possible for me to take it. Believe me, I tried."

All of this, all the terror, the killing, the enslavement, had only ever been a ruse. Dorothy felt a bitterness at being made a pawn that drove her onward. "But what does Harrison have that you could possibly need?"

Tim pointed back to the altar. "That ghost. The most important ghost in all of history. Do you know who that is?"

Dorothy had heard the name Hadley Tucker before, but she never knew the man. She knew him only as a friend of Harrison's, and the man who died on the Static Mayhem Bomb mission. "No."

"That, little witch, is the only mundane human ever to die by the direct hand of Ru'opihm." Tim made a gun gesture with his thumb and forefinger, and pointed it at Hadley. "Shot him right in the neck. Pow."

Dorothy had definitely heard the name Ru'opihm. Hearing it now gave her a chill. "That makes him important?"

"That makes him a source of fantastic power. Harnessing it was the only difficulty. It took me years to pull him together into a coherent specter. And even then, he would never come to me. He was always drawn to Cody, the man who cost him his life. So, I planted the prophecy, magically back-dated it for authenticity, and waited for Basil and Cody to do the rest of the work for me." He looked back at the immobilized ghost. "Dr. Tucker here has the power to split worlds. Amazing, really. All that power for destruction bound up in such an unassuming spirit. So much chaos, and so little desire to use his gift. The only possible obstacle to my plans was that oaf Rutherford. Equally powerful, in his own way, and equally oblivious to its use. His ability to force order from chaos could quite handily have ruined all my plans. Happily, he was easy enough to neutralize. It is extraordinary to me how quickly mundanes degrade to simpering fools in the distraction of a simple spell of Oppositional Defiance."

"And now that you have Hadley and his power, what are you doing with him?" She looked at the damage already done to just this room, and thought back on the cracks in the walls, and the quake in the stadium.

"Very much the same as Basil intended, actually," said Tim. "I am going to use him to destroy the mundane world and all its natives. Of course, most magical natives will not survive the process either. I never did share that with Basil. It probably would not have been well received."

Dorothy's jaw dropped. She had been given only a few days to acclimate to the idea these monsters intended to kill half a world. Now Tim confronted her with the reality he didn't plan to stop at half. "Why are you doing this?"

"Why, to free my master, of course."

Dorothy gasped. All of this sprang from a desperate attempt to serve a force for evil that had been painstakingly imprisoned, and the walls of that prison shorn up by the sacrifice of any hope the two worlds would go back to their earlier states. He sought to invalidate everything Harrison had done eight years earlier, when he saved what remained of both worlds. What promises did Ru'opihm make to this man, to make him believe life in the world that remained would be worth living? And now he casually shared that intent with someone who had every reason to kill him for it. "Why are you telling me all of this?"

"Because, as I said, I know who you really are. This has all been such a burden to carry, and I don't mind saying it is a relief to share it with someone. I know you may not agree with my goals or my methods, and I may yet have to kill you, but at least I know that you of all people will understand."

"Understand? You madman! You are about to destroy my world and everyone left on it! You want me to understand that?"

"Little witch, the only world I am destroying is the mundane. Yours will still carry on, albeit a bit worse for wear."

"The mundane world is my world!"

At this, Tim finally halted his rambling confession. He looked her closely in the eyes. "You don't know, do you?"

This question somehow made her more nervous than anything else she had heard from him. "Don't know what?"

"You don't know who you are. You still think you are that mundane girl who left her city a month ago. You think that everything you can do now is all skills you learned from reading a book, as though somehow the level of expertise you demonstrate over and over could be achieved with no instruction, no training, no practice. That makes sense to you."

"And you have an explanation that makes more sense?"

He shook his head in awe. "You truly do not know you are Strontium."

[71]

BREAKING THINGS

In the second it took Harrison to fully grasp the situation, and as he tried to reconcile the sight of Milton inside a ball of fire, several of the soldiers unleashed their crossbows at the Professor. Two of the bolts found their marks, but succeeded only in tearing his jacket as they glanced off the scales underneath.

The half-dragon tore his garments off, exposing the wings Aplomado warned had been hidden beneath, much bigger than Harrison expected. With a huge, sweeping flap, the Professor took to the sky, shooting fire at his opponents. Milton had anticipated the possibility of dragon fire, and a magical shield Aplomado had put in place around the flier protected the soldiers who stayed close to it. When Basil's fire breath struck it, the flames flattened and splashed outward. They had all been given additional protections individually, but it remained to be seen if Milton's would protect him at point blank range.

The centaur sergeant launched a spear at the airborne half-dragon, but he saw it, or sensed it, and managed to turn in time to catch it. Unfortunately, that gave Harrison an opportunity to observe how well the individual protections against fire worked up close. As Heatherington roasted the centaur alive, he lobbed the spear at the flier, where it had no difficulty penetrating the fire shield, and buried itself in the chest of one of the soldiers.

Behind Harrison came screams. Several of the women stood and looked around them in obvious fright. "Apryl! We need to get these people out of here! Can you get them to the army flier? It's parked just outside the outfield wall."

Still holding Melody, she looked over her shoulder. "Everyone stay together! Stay with your buddy! Keep your children close!" Claudia took the hand of the boy he had seen with Dorothy earlier, and she ran with him down the steps toward the wall. Apryl turned back to Harrison. "I can take them out through the building."

"No!" said Melody. "We'll be trapped!"

Perhaps it was her tone. Perhaps it was the fact of her suddenly taking charge. Perhaps it was that in the evening light, even under the glare of the arc lamps, Melody put off a faint purple aura. Whatever the reason, Apryl gently set Melody down, with a look of awe, or perhaps fear.

As Claudia and the boy got to the front row of seats, Melody said calmly, "Ian, make us a door." She pointed to the outfield wall.

The boy nodded, closed his eyes, and balled his hands into fists which he curled up to his chest. He took a deep breath, and after a protracted moment of inactivity, he threw his arms forward, splaying his fingers.

The Green Monster exploded.

Tons of fragments of metal and wood flew upward and outward, the resulting *boom* sufficient to prompt another round of screams, but they stopped once everyone looked in the same direction. The rubble settled, revealing the army flier outside the arena.

"Holy shit," said Harrison.

"Is she glowing?" asked Claudia, pointing at Melody.

"I think so," said Apryl.

"We'll sort that out later," said Harrison, having no idea what he meant by sorting it out, and less of an idea what he meant by later. "Right now we need to get everyone through that wall. Can you take them?" he asked Apryl.

"No," said Melody. "She's the Power. We need her here."

"Okay," said Claudia. "She's freaking me out now."

Harrison held up his hand for silence. Whatever was happening to his five-year-old daughter went beyond his ability to identify or cope with at that moment. A fire-breathing monster bore down on the men and centaurs who had come to defend them, and they were not faring well against it. They had no time to argue. "Claudia, can you take point on this? Ian?" he said to the boy. "Is that right?" Ian nodded. "Can you stay with her? Use that trick again if you have to?"

"I'm waiting for my escape buddy," said Claudia.

"Oh for... Claudia! We need to get moving! She's got a new buddy now, that asshole wizard. She'll be okay."

"Fine," said Claudia, crossing her arms. "Then I'm waiting for my girlfriend."

"I... Wait, what?" said Harrison.

"And I'm waiting for my mother," said Ian.

Too many things came at Harrison too quickly for him to absorb them. He abandoned debate. "Okay, Claudia, yes, Ian, no. Mitchell!" Mitchell deftly climbed over a row of seats and stood at attention in front of Harrison. Suddenly recognizing these words as the first he had spoken to his adopted son since arriving, he put his hands on Mitchell's shoulders. "How are you holding up?"

"What do you need me to do?" he asked with a resolve Harrison had never seen in his eyes before.

"You are now Ian's escape buddy."

Britney came up behind Mitchell and took his hand.

"You both are. I need you to get him out of here." To Ian, he said, "I need you to make more doors. You have my word I will get Dorothy out of here safe and sound. Can you do that for me?"

Ian nodded.

That settled, Harrison looked up to find them a leader. "Becca!" He found her, already standing, a few rows back. Next to her, Siobhan, looking haggard and frightened, clutched Becca's hand. At Harrison's call they both came down the stairs.

"I need to you take everyone out that opening," he said, pointing to the remains of the enormous wall. "Walk them through the stands as far as you can. That will be less conspicuous. You'll get as far as the bullpen, and then Ian will have to break you through it. That will make some noise, so you're going to have to make a run for it from there. Are you up for this?"

She looked behind her at all the people who had just been put in her care. Again. "I'm going to have to be." She looked at Siobhan. "I'm pregnant." Siobhan's look of shell-shock took on a new nuance of surprise. "I know you don't care if you live or die, but I also know you care about me, and I need you to help me protect my baby. You got that?"

Siobhan nodded dumbly.

"Good, because I need you to pull it together right now."

Whatever was happening between Becca and Siobhan would be one more thing Harrison would ask about if they all made it home alive. For now, he contented himself to have something resembling a plan. "Can you do this in the dark?"

"It's not dark," she said.

Harrison looked at Apryl.

She nodded. "It will be."

371

"Oh, boy," said Becca. Turning around, she called, "Everyone, grab your buddy and your kids! We're heading through the stands to that hole in the wall! Make sure you all grab hands right now, because it's about to get very dark!" General murmur ensued, followed by pairs of linked hands rising from the crowd.

"Do it," said Harrison.

Apryl leaned on the wall, and closed her eyes. After a few moments' concentration, she hunched down and grimaced.

The arc lights exploded. They burst like impossibly large popcorn as they blew randomly and in rapid sequence. The entire process took no more than five seconds, though it seemed considerably longer. Somewhere, whatever power source provided this arena with energy had just been overloaded and destroyed. With the main source of light gone, it was now obvious that evening had progressed past dusk. The moon cast enough light to see, but no more. The flood lights on the NCSA flier continued to shine. Someone inside increased their brightness after the arc lights went, adding a new advantage to the soldiers, the flier now so bright by comparison to its surroundings as to make it difficult to look directly at it.

"Go," said Harrison to Becca.

"Stay close, people," she said, and led them out.

Over by the flier, a small battle raged on between the soldiers and the few goblins still healthy enough to fight. They had all fallen back to within the shield now, and while goblins could walk through it, close quarters put them at a disadvantage. Heatherington circled overhead, repeatedly testing the strength of the shield with shots of fire, but either through cowardice or lack of interest, declined to cross the shield himself. As Harrison was about to tell Sarah to take Adler and run with the others, the half-dragon apparently remembered about him, because he stopped in midair and made straight for the stands. They would never outrun him, and the wall would not provide adequate cover for those still behind it.

His back to the soldiers, Basil presented them with a new assault opportunity they did not waste. A dozen arrows and spears flew to him. Most found their marks, and were either deflected by his dragon scales or shattered by them. Even his wings were impenetrable.

"Can you cut that skin?" Harrison asked his sword, clutching her hilt.

Unknown, said Bess. Unlikely.

"What do we have, people?" He looked around them trying to calculate some way one of them could use their abilities to attack this monster. Melody's aura, barely visible in the bright light, had grown overwhelmingly brilliant, to the point where she now acted as a beacon

372

leading the beast straight to them. She had her arms out, and looked like she intended to find a way to take the Professor on by herself.

Harrison looked back. A winged silhouette, backlit by the flier flood lights, reared back to strike. He drew Bess, somehow hoping she would find some way to deflect the oncoming blast of fire, but before he could ask her directly, an orange streak of light darted straight into the half-dragon's mouth. Momentarily thrown, the Professor grabbed his throat. With a loud *pop*, orange sparks shot from his mouth in every direction. It looked nothing like the fire he had spouted earlier. In fact, it looked alarmingly familiar.

"Sparky?" cried Harrison. "Sparky!"

Heatherington lost his air balance, and came crashing to the ground, where he rolled to a stop about ten feet in front of them.

Harrison held Bess out in front of himself, pointed at their foe. "Too much to hope he's dead?"

Indeed, said Bess.

Heatherington pulled himself to his feet, coughing loudly. In a wheezing growl, he said, "That was good. You slew my fire. Alas for you, I still have claws and teeth."

"I have teeth of my own," said Harrison, waving Bess.

Heatherington brought his hands together and cracked his knuckles. From this distance, and without the jacket, the half-dragon clearly had an entirely prosthetic arm, gleaming brass, and ticking loudly as it moved.

"Clockwork!" shouted Sarah.

Heatherington shrieked. His artificial arm had gone completely stiff, and he dropped to his knees, clutching that shoulder.

Sarah's mind had identified his prosthesis as something enough like a clock for her to stop it. Harrison could only imagine the pain he would be feeling, as that part of his body slowed down in time to the point of immobility, while still being attached to him. As he mentally celebrated their victory over this beast, the ticking started up again. Heatherington's artificial eye glowed a bright piercing blue. His arm moved freely once more, and he stood with what must have been a smug grin through all those teeth. The artificial eye mounted in his head faded.

"Well," said the half-dragon. "That was interesting."

"Stop!" shouted Sarah. Her voice cracked in obvious desperation.

Again, the Professor's arm seized up, and again, he shook it off. His eye glowed even brighter this time, and right before his arm returned to normal movement, the half-dragon's body experienced a highly accelerated spasm. He growled, evidently less amused than the first time.

"Harrison?" asked Sarah nervously.

"I don't know!" he said, holding Bess straight out.

"It's the eyepiece," said Melody.

"I can see that, sweetheart," said Harrison without turning around. "What does it do?"

"It does a lot of things," said the little girl.

The professor advanced.

"Hit him again!" shouted Harrison to Sarah

"Stop!" she shrieked.

Once again, accompanying the bright blue glow of his artificial eye, Heatherington experienced momentary acceleration. Whatever the device did, the effect reversed the power being thrown at him. Time around him sped up instead of slowing down, and it affected his whole body, not just the clockwork arm.

"Hey Professor!" shouted Harrison. "That's a great trick, but it won't work on me!"

"What are you doing?" asked Sarah, panic edging itself into her voice.

"Stay with me, Sarah." He lifted his hand out to the Professor. "Bring it on! I'm going to unlock you, stem to stern!"

"What is that even supposed to mean?" asked the half-dragon. It sounded like bravado, but for the slight hesitance in his voice.

"I don't know, Puff! Why don't we find out together?" With that, Harrison relaxed his body and handed motor control to Bess. She took over Harrison and charged the beast, ducking and sliding underneath the telegraphed roundhouse of his huge, clawed hand. Heatherington's artificial eye glowed bright blue, as Harrison hoped. Rolling underneath the professor, Harrison reached out and grabbed his ankle.

The half-dragon froze again, this time over his whole body, as Harrison used his unlocking ability to lock him in place. The eyepiece became a tiny, brilliant, blue nova in its attempt to counter Harrison's attack, but only made it more effective.

"Sarah!" shouted Harrison, rolling away. "Throw everything you've got at him! Now!"

Sarah, still holding her son, threw her gaze upon this monster.

Still locked in place, and his eyepiece working at what must have been the upper limit of its function, Heatherington now felt the weight of Sarah's power in reverse. Rather than slow time to a halt, it accelerated, at an astonishing rate. It took only a few seconds for the creature to shrivel to a dead husk, in the agonizing process of dehydration.

Heatherington's body mummified, and crumbled to dust. The artificial arm and eye hit the lawn with a soft *thud*. For a few moments, they continued to demonstrate a kind of life, but the twitching arm ground to halt with a flurry of ever-slowing ticks. Seconds later, the tiny blue sun faded to a simple, black glass marble.

Panting, Harrison stood. His thoughts turned to Sparky, who had apparently flown directly into the Professor's mouth to extinguish his flame. Before he could form the question to Bess on the topic of Sparky's possible survival, the short sword reestablished control of his actions, spinning him around, ducking, and parrying. His arm tensed with the ring of metal hitting metal, and as he pressed his sword against another, Felicia's hateful eyes glared back at him from the other side of it.

"We're not through," she said.

We are in trouble, said Bess.

"She only has one sword this time," said Harrison.

I have history with this blade, said Bess. And he despises me.

[72]

WITCH

Dorothy heard the words over and over. Each time she mentally repeated them, she attempted to assign new meaning to them, and failed.

You are Strontium.

"That's impossible," she said, finally and weakly.

"Have you met the world lately?" scoffed Tim.

"I know who I am," said Dorothy.

"Really, you don't. I've been watching you. How long have you been using magic? How long since you first opened this?" He held out his hand, and the red book phased into being in his palm. "A week? Less?"

Dorothy stared at the book. Her relationship with it suddenly seemed preposterous. It represented years of learning, and she had absorbed it all in a matter of days, reading a language she did not know, in an alphabet that resembled nothing more than random squiggles. "I would like that back, please." Her attempt at confidence was transparent, even to herself.

"I do not doubt it." The book vanished back into his hand. "But that will not happen today. Still, 'Dorothy,' tell me this: do you even need it?"

Her heart skipped at the question. "I don't know what you mean."

"Yes, you do. This book is the source of all your magic, or so you believe. And yet..." He pointed to Aplomado's still form on the floor. "This mundane thought you were a witch, did he not? Why would that be?"

"I have no idea," said Dorothy.

"Yet you followed him into my sanctum. Were you planning to hide behind him?"

Dorothy said nothing.

Tim looked down and shook his head. He mumbled something, but she could not make out words. Without warning, he looked up, thrust his staff in her direction and shouted a word she did not recognize. A bolt of red lightning sprang from its tip, headed straight for her eyes.

She cried out, closed her eyes, and threw her hands up. A few seconds passed with no obvious effects, and when she opened her eyes, her hands were spread out and parallel to each other in front of her face. Between them hovered a ball of red energy, attached to her fingertips by slender, crackling threads.

"Well, that is impressive," said Tim. "The light was harmless, but I feel it made my point."

She brought her hands together and closed them around the ball of red lightning. It was warm and tingly, and she absorbed its energy.

"Is that a thing you knew how to do growing up in your mundane city?"

"New Chicago is not mundane," she said. "It is a mixed community."

He laughed. "I stand corrected."

She stared at his smug grin, wanting to punch it. "Tell me what I am."

"Oh!" He stepped back. "Is that what you want? I can do that for you, of course, but this seems a bit too easy. Surely we should have done a lot more dancing before we arrived at this point in our discussion. If I tell you now, I would hardly expect you to believe me. Typically, there would be a period of breaking first. Denial, rage, and the like. Eventually you would beg me for the truth, but not now. Not yet."

"Just tell me," she said. "We can do the breaking after."

He laughed again. "Oh, I do like your moxie, little girl. All right, here's what you are: Your name is Strontium."

"My name is Dorothy O'Neill."

"Dorothy O'Neill is dead!" he shouted, anger in his voice for the first time. "You wear her body, but her soul went up in flames, sacrificed to kill a single, insignificant goblin. Typical ruthlessness for you, I might add. I wonder if she knew how easy it was for you to cast away her life like that to achieve such a meager goal. But I digress. Your name, want it or not, is Strontium. You are a witch, of an order whose name is known only to those in it, although I am sure it is not a very interesting one. You are ninety-three years old, or at least you were before you took this form. Like me, you found yourself stranded in this mixed world nearly a decade ago. Unlike me, you chose to hide. Until we picked you up in that cabin, I was not even aware you had survived."

Dorothy searched her heart, looking for truth in this. That he would know Strontium personally provided no evidence he spoke the truth, but it nagged her. "That's not consistent with what I already know about myself. Why should I believe you?"

"Oh, little girl," he said. "Let me be perfectly clear. I am in no way invested in whether you believe me. As long as you remain in denial, you will never have access to your full power, and so you remain no threat to me. If you do choose to believe, and embrace who you are, the Strontium I know is enough of a survivor to join me, and add her power to mine. Either way I have the advantage. So, understand what I share with you is only what you ask for, and I share it only because I find it entertaining to do so."

"That doesn't answer my question," said Dorothy.

"All right," said Tim. "You should believe me because you want to believe me. It is no more complicated than that."

Dorothy considered this, and found truth in it. "What happened that day?"

"The day you switched places?"

Dorothy hesitated. "Yes."

"A simple spell, really," said Tim. "You traded minds with the O'Neill girl. Any novice can do it, and it requires no consent. Normally, that effect is temporary. A day, at best."

"Unless one of the two dies," said Dorothy.

"Is that your memory returning?" he asked.

"It's an inference."

He bowed. "Forgive my underestimation of your insight. And yes, you are quite correct. Dorothy's death in your body sealed the spell."

"Then why don't I remember any of this?" she asked. "It doesn't seem like a very good spell if the participants don't even realize it happened. Doesn't that defeat the point?"

"It would indeed. I should, perhaps, share with you another detail about yourself." Tim took two steps toward her and leaned forward. She held up her arms to defend against an attack, but he merely put the back of his hand to the side of his mouth in a comedic gesture of discretion. "You are not a very competent witch," he whispered loudly.

At those words, something stirred in the catacombs of her consciousness, and she heard a voice in her head, Strontium's voice, speak a single word. "Duh."

Dorothy gasped.

"Aha," said Tim. "That got through. Am I correct?"

"I'm not her." A bead of sweat formed on her brow, and she wiped it away.

"You don't sound quite as certain as before," he said.

"I... I'm not. Her. I'm not her."

He tapped his chin. "Hmm. Perhaps this was a mistake. You should have let me break you first, I think. This would have been easier on you. We should stop here." He turned his back on her.

"No!" she shouted. "I'm not her! She wouldn't do that to Dorothy! To me!"

"You should probably sort out what you want to call yourself." He approached Hadley. The ghost still hung suspended over the altar, looking barely coherent, and in pain. "For now, I have work to do. If you survive it, we will continue our talk." He pushed his hand into Hadley's ethereal torso, and turned it.

Hadley screamed. Overhead, distant explosions sounded.

Whatever Dorothy's thoughts on her own identity, she would have to set them aside. She needed to do the right thing now, in no small part because she had no faith that once she understood the whole truth she would do the right thing later. She closed her eyes and took a deep breath. A warmth formed in her hand, and when she opened her eyes to look at it, she saw it in the form of the lightning ball she had observed earlier. It tingled, but made no appreciable noise. Cautiously, she pulled her hand back, and launched the object at the back of Tim's head. It passed through the wizard with no effect, and dissipated upon hitting the far wall on the other side of him.

"I did tell you that was harmless," he said without turning around. "At some point, you are going to have to accept that I am telling you the truth."

At that moment, Strontium emerged.

Dorothy could feel her, something she could not define, just a presence that harkened back to the feeling she had every time she had been in the same room as her witch sister. Strontium was here, and had always been, and occupied the same space Dorothy did. "You piece of dung," said Dorothy, but not in her own voice.

"How dare you call me incompetent!" shouted Strontium.

She threw herself on him. Her twenty-three-year-old body surprised her with its agility and strength. Strontium had never been a feeble woman, even in her old age, but this new body was fit and vital in ways she had to reach back sixty years to recall. She struck Tim in the back with far more force than she intended, and they both flew forward, tumbling into Hadley's intangible form, and out the other side. They hit the floor hard, and Strontium intuitively expected severe pain that never came, Dorothy's body too hearty to be hurt so by a simple fall.

Tim rolled away from her, still holding his staff, and swung it around toward her face.

Strontium shouted a single syllable, and the wood rebounded hard off a point in space less than a foot from her head. "You tried to club me?" she shouted. "Don't you know who I am?" She threw her arm forward, made a grabbing motion, and pulled. A sphere of stone melted away from the wall and hurtled itself toward her opponent. He dodged, parried with the staff, and sent it directly into Strontium's face.

This time the pain did come. The stone struck her beneath her left eye, knocking her off her feet. Her head hit the floor, and she felt dizzy and nauseous. She tried to rise, but could not orient herself.

Tim planted his foot on her chest, and pointed the tip of his staff directly at her head. He leaned forward, putting his entire weight on her right breast.

The pain went beyond what she could endure, and she nearly blacked out, but willed herself to stay conscious.

"Perhaps telling you was a terrible mistake after all. I thought you would be more reasonable than this. No matter. The mistake is easily enough corrected."

The tip of his staff vibrated. Strontium recognized it as the buildup to a spell meant to decapitate her. He would need to be that brutal to defeat a witch of her level, but it would work beautifully. With only moments to act, she grabbed his foot with her left hand, and dug her nails in. He responded by grinding it into her breast, which earned a scream. Forcing herself past the agony, she raised her free hand, and reached for Tim's staff. He laughed.

"It won't work for you," he said. "Even if you could take it from me, which you cannot. This staff is your doom, not your savior."

"It's not..." She gasped. Tried again. "It's not your staff I want."

Tim's hand glowed red. His smile faded to a look of confusion, then one of worry. The staff ceased in its vibrations, and Tim's fingers flew open, releasing it. The wooden rod struck Strontium in the face as it fell to the floor. She ignored the new and relatively minuscule sensation of pain it caused. Red sparks formed in Tim's open hand. One by one, randomly and sporadically, they leaped to Strontium's hand.

In Tim's panic at this new development, he relaxed the pressure on her chest, and she seized the moment, toppling him to the floor. He lay there, eyes rolled up into his head, quivering in spasms, as a stream of sparkly energy shot from his hand to Strontium's. Picking up speed, the sparks cohered, resolving themselves into a small, red, leather-bound book. Its energy spent, Tim's arm collapsed.

Strontium stood, clutching the book to her bruised and sore chest. Her head cleared. Her old life came back to her in bits and pieces. Her years in the secret coven. The Mayhem event that ripped that life away from her. Finding Ian. Traveling with him for years in the cabin to keep him safe. Meeting Dorothy, and finding in her a kindred spirit, dearer than she could ever admit.

"Strontium?" Dorothy's voice called her from the depths of her mind, no fear in her tone, only relief. "I thought I'd lost you."

"I'm here, child."

Tim screamed, a guttural, rage-filled cry. The staff flew to his hand, and he pointed it at her head. With barely a thought, she held up the book, which opened itself to a page facing the wizard.

There was a flash, as Tim's spell launched from his staff, and a *boom* as it rebounded off the book. When the smoke cleared, his headless body lay next to his shattered staff.

Strontium felt nothing for the victory. "Dorothy? Can you hear me, child?"

"Strontium?" came the voice. "What's happening? He said you stole my body?"

"Do you believe him?" asked Strontium.

After a brief pause, the voice came back. "No."

Strontium laughed. "Well, good on that, at least. You and I need a little sit down, I think."

"Dorothy," said Hadley weakly.

"Half right. Dorothy's not here at the moment. I'm Strontium."

"Strontium then," he said. "I need you."

She sighed. "That sit down'll have to wait. You trust me for now?" Strontium felt Dorothy nod, and nodded in return. She pulled herself together, and gave Hadley a smile. "All right, ghost. I'll have you down from there in a jiff."

He shook his head. "You don't understand. Tim's spell..."

Strontium shook her head as this ghost, tortured and used, tried to pull together a coherent sentence about Tim's plan to destroy a world, kill nearly every living thing on it, and unleash the very essence of evil onto the universe. "He's dead," she assured him.

"It doesn't matter," he said. "It's already started."

[73]

MAURICE ET PIERRE

"**R**un!" shouted Harrison.

Felicia leaped back, then attacked again. Harrison dodged her stroke and lunged, a move he and Bess had used successfully against many opponents over the years. Felicia spun in a complete circle, and effortlessly deflected his attack.

"I hope you weren't talking to me," she said.

"I wasn't, but you're welcome to run if the mood strikes you."

She laughed. "No, I think I'd prefer to kill you."

Harrison rolled out of reach an instant before she brought her blade around, narrowly missing his scalp. "Run!" he repeated.

Felicia stood just out of range, her sword arm extended, and stared him down. Her weapon was a katana, identical to the wakizashi in storage back at the NCSA, but nearly twice as long. When they first met in combat, Felicia carried both swords, but Harrison relieved her of the shorter one. In theory, this should give him a new advantage. And yet, Bess still said they were in trouble.

Harrison looked to the stands. His family and friends still waited there, terrible at following instructions. Harrison experimented with fleeing, to draw Felicia away from them. He bolted for the dugout, then gracefully vaulted to its roof and turned around. Felicia pursued him. Mission accomplished.

"Tell me about the sword," he said in the few seconds he had bought.

His name is Maurice, said Bess.

"Why does a Japanese sword have a French name?" he asked.

382

I do not know what those words mean.

"Never mind." As Felicia reached the dugout, Harrison sprang upward and back, making his way up the seats.

"I hear my old job is available again," she said. "Be honest. Should I apply?"

The jab hit its mark. Harrison still had not had time to process the attack on Milton, and still did not know whether he survived it. Now his inevitable feelings of responsibility and guilt kicked in. He refused to grant her that advantage. "Why are you doing this? Your boss is dead. Even if you kill me, you're through here. Why did you sign on with this madness in the first place? He was trying to kill every survivor from our world."

"Your world," she said. "Not mine."

"What?" said Harrison.

You truly should have seen that coming, said Bess.

"Is that what this is about?" said Harrison. "You can't go back, Felicia. This is the world we have now."

"Thanks to you."

He tried switching gears. "How are you planning to carry on with your dead boss's masterplan, Felicia? From where I stand, this project just lost all its assets."

"So many questions," she said. "I believe I will decline to answer them, but I will share this: the only dead boss I see here is the one in front of me. I never worked for that snake."

"Who do you work for?"

"I work for no one!" she shouted. "I used that monster. He gave me an opportunity, and I took it. Do you have any idea what the last nine years have been like for me? Can you even guess? This is who I am, Cody. It's who I have been since I was twelve years old. I am exceptionally skilled at what I do, and I love my work. But ever since Mayhem, I have been in limbo. Do you know how long it takes to establish a proper assassin's guild from nothing? In this world, the answer is forever. There is no demand for people like me. The entire globe is covered in sparkling new democracies and tribal enclaves. There is no social structure that supports people like me. There isn't even any decent organized crime. You want to know why I signed on with Professor Dimwit the Dragon? Because he gave me the first real contract I've had, and it made me feel alive again. For the past three years, I have had purpose. And today, once again, Harrison Cody has taken that away from me."

"Yes, you should apply," said Harrison.

Felicia paused. "What did you say?"

"Your old job," he said. "We're hiring. I've seen your work, so we can skip the résumé."

"I don't know what kind of joke—"

"No joke!" he insisted. "You want a purpose, and I can give you one. Do you really not understand the NCSA needs people with your experience? Even the good guys need assassins, Felicia. We used to call them sharpshooters, or snipers, or whatever euphemism you want to use for professional killer. You know the kinds of strings I can pull, Felicia. This is no joke. With two phone calls I can get you a pardon and a job, no questions asked."

Captain..., said Bess.

Harrison slapped the blade against his leg to silence her.

"What do you say, Felicia?" The assassin stared him down, but some small part of that glare softened. Trying not to move his lips, Harrison whispered, "Is she less dangerous with only one sword?"

More, said Bess.

"How?" asked Harrison.

Pierre was a friend. He allowed me to disarm her when we last faced her. If he had not done so, you would be dead now. Maurice will not hesitate to flay you alive and split me to the hilt.

"Who's better?" he whispered. "You or Maurice?"

Bess did not respond.

"Fuck," whispered Harrison. "What's it going to be, Felicia?" he called. For a moment, he truly thought she would take the bait.

Then she charged.

Harrison, with Bess in command, did a double back-flip up five rows of seats then spun around and skipped up four more. It took effort to suppress the thrill ride component of working with Bess. "Are we running or fighting?" he asked the sword.

The former, said Bess. Combat will not end well. We should draw her to the troops and let the crossbows even our odds.

"We're headed in the wrong direction for that," said Harrison.

"Are you talking to your sword?" asked Felicia. "That's so dear. What is she telling you?"

"That Maurice is a girly name for a katana!" shouted Harrison.

She froze, and scowled at her sword. "Really?" she said to it. "That would have been nice to know earlier."

"Trouble in paradise?" Harrison glanced in the direction of the flier. The glare from the flood lights obscured how the battle there had progressed.

"Evidently Bess is quite the heartbreaker," said Felicia.

Harrison groaned. "Seriously?" he said to Bess.

She did not respond in words, but he felt her give the enchanted short sword equivalent of a shrug.

"Maybe we should let these two work out their issues without us," said Felicia, in either a joke or an obvious ploy. If they both dropped their swords, Felicia would use one of a hundred other ways to kill him, and he didn't have a viable defensive move without Bess in his hand. He looked down to the ball field. If he could make it to open ground, he could probably outrun her to the flier, almost certainly his only hope of survival.

"Can we make that leap?" With nine rows of seats and a dugout from where he stood to the ground, he would have to push his body beyond its known limits just to make the jump, and he would have to land and roll just right to keep moving.

I hope so, said Bess. She took over.

He charged down the stands, planting his feet on seatbacks. Five steps in, he launched himself forward and upward, tucking and tumbling forward to minimize his size as a target, and to use angular momentum to propel himself farther.

Felicia collided with him in midair. He kicked her away, and had the tiniest fraction of a second to congratulate himself for doing so successfully.

Then her sword arm came around.

Harrison watched in terrifying slow motion as Bess, his only means of attack, defense, or survival, flew away from him in a steep parabola.

The leap was not a total failure in that he did make it the whole way to the grass. Without Bess to guide his descent, the roll was considerably clumsier than planned, and did not finish in a sprint to the flier. He ended up face down in the scratchy weeds. Only when he tried to push himself up to his knees did he come to understand the stroke that knocked Bess from his grip had also severed his right hand.

With no clear sense of how to survive such a wound, he did his best to stop the bleeding by clamping the stump under his left arm. The pain had not yet registered. Instead, he found himself in the grip of a growing euphoria. It barely registered when Felicia landed on her feet next to him, and put the point of her katana on his sternum.

"Well, that was fun," she said. "I can't decide whether to finish you off, or simply wait for the bleed-out. Probably wait, I suppose. This will be my last professional kill for some time. Best to savor it, don't you think?"

Unsure how to answer the question, Harrison struggled to find the words. It seemed somehow urgent for him to have an opinion on the manner of his own murder. Images of his family danced in front of him, and he had just enough awareness to hope they weren't watching this. Melody deserved a better childhood than one scarred by the image of her father's final, pathetic moments. His mind replaced that picture with one of Apryl, Melody and himself, on a picnic, or at the beach, or riding a carousel. They blurred together, and felt like the same event. Dorothy was there, happy, holding Claudia, the love of her life. Harrison felt great joy the two of them had found each other in the face of this impossibly difficult circumstance, and as he congratulated them, Claudia spoke to him.

"Harrison?" she said. "Harrison! Oh, fuck! Apryl! Get over here!"

These were not the words of warmth he expected, and as he tried to focus on Claudia's face, she dropped the impaled body of Felicia to the ground, Bess buried in the assassin's back, to the hilt.

"She cut off his fucking hand! Sarah! Find it! Oh, fuck." Claudia dropped to her knees and stroked Harrison's hair. "Hang in there, boss. Sarah! Fucking hurry!"

As his wife arrived, looking more beautiful than he could ever recall, and holding his baby Melody, Harrison slipped into icy blackness. The last thing his eyes registered was Melody's halo, brilliant amethyst, and radiating purest Faerie magic.

74

ANCHOR

Strontium took a moment to get her bearings. Still reassembling her memories, she tried to clarify to herself exactly where she was. Dorothy had spent the past few days living in a sports arena called Fenway Park. This chamber was somewhere beneath that stadium. Strontium had lived in the mixed world long enough to know baseball, and that such a room as this would never have been part of the original design. Indeed, she now recalled many nuances of this ballpark—random gargoyles, cobblestones where there should have been concrete—likely elements of the magical world.

She looked around, studying the wall friezes. They depicted familiar stories from her childhood. Dark stories. This troubling cavern was Tim's sanctum. The other modifications to Fenway must also have been his doing.

"What spell did he cast?" she asked Hadley.

"Not my area of expertise, I'm sorry to say," said the ghost.

"But he needed to create this place to cast it," she said.

"I really wouldn't know," said Hadley.

"Just thinking aloud, boy. I'm going to need to step inside for a bit. You okay with that?"

"Step inside what?"

"You." She walked up to his intangible form, and took a step forward.

Strontium's perceptions shifted. Merged with Hadley's ghost, she saw the walls of the chamber in their full horror. The friezes, which she earlier perceived as static representations, sprang to life. Scenes of torture now included animated violence and tiny screams.

"Oho," said Strontium. "This is about the beasties." She narrowed her eyes and concentrated. The chamber shrank away from her, replaced by an aerial view of Fenway. She saw a flash of light, a few hundred yards outside the park. A second later followed the distant *boom*, and the chamber rattled. She panned back further until she could see all of New England. Pinpoints of red light appeared and disappeared at random. She adjusted her perception to look for patterns, and found these ground explosions to be laid out in a spider-like web. Pulling back further, she saw that web cover the globe.

Tim had set into motion a spell to crack the Earth open. And if Strontium read these walls correctly, those cracks were about to birth a demon horde that would likely torture, kill, and eat the majority of the world's population, both mundane and magical.

"Well, piss." Strontium stepped out of Hadley's body, and shook her head to readjust to her normal perception of her surroundings. "Ghost, we have a problem."

"That part is obvious," said Hadley. "Do we have a solution?"

"He used you to power a spell to make demons," she said. "Lots of them. He's right about you, by the way. Never seen a ghost like you before. Not that you want to know this, but Ru'opihm charged you up, but good. Lotta bad mojo stored in you."

"I'm the power source?"

"Yepper," she said.

"Then kill me," said Hadley. "Will that fix it?"

"You're dead already, boy. How much more killed do you think I can make you?"

"Poor choice of words," said Hadley. "Can you destroy a ghost? Sever the connection?"

"Destroying you would take more punch than I pack. I have another idea." She stepped back inside him. Once again, her view of the world took on a broader scope. She panned back to see the whole Earth, and spun it in her mind, searching for the best alternative. "Not sure if you can hear this, but I'm going to try to reroute you. The spell is too big for me to shut down, but I might be able to divert what you're feeding it and starve it to death."

Hadley did not respond, at least not in a way that Strontium could hear.

She continued to scan the globe. She needed to find an opportunity to cast a spell that would require a great deal of energy while still not having an appreciable effect on its environment. She had no idea what that would look like, but she trusted she would know it when she saw it. If she could do that, she would try to redirect the energy coming from Hadley's ghost to fuel that spell, instead of Tim's demon spell. She wouldn't have to try to stop the unstoppable; it would simply burn itself out.

Finding no ready opportunity for giant spell-casting on the surface, she scoured the Earth's oceans. She considered the possibility of casting a spell to heat the entire body of water by one degree, which would surely take enough energy to serve her purpose, but closer inspection showed her several hundred species of marine critter that would die from that minuscule change. Making it colder posed the same problem. Panic crept into the proceedings as she felt herself already running out of ideas.

She pushed, hard. The Earth shrank to a dot. As she reoriented herself to the view of this corner of the universe, she picked up her search again. Perhaps she could cast a spell to another planet. And perhaps it wouldn't matter if that spell did catastrophic damage to a lifeless space rock. She rotated her view to find other dots like the Earth dot, and ways she could funnel energy to them.

And, as she ran out of ideas, she remembered she had more than one mind to work with. "Dorothy?"

"I'm here," came the voice.

"I'm in a bit of a pickle, child. Do you know what's happening?"

"I heard everything," said Dorothy. "But I can't see."

"That's all right," said Strontium. "In just a sec, I'm going to let go. Give you your eyes back. We need a place to throw this energy, and I don't know what I'm looking at. I need you to take the reins."

"Wait," said Dorothy. "I don't understand. Isn't this something a witch should do?"

"Oh, sister. We really do need to talk."

With those words, Strontium's consciousness faded to background noise. Dorothy felt a rush of upward motion and emergence, like a diver resurfacing. She gasped.

"Oh, God," she said. "Where am I? What am I supposed to do?"

Surrounded by stars, she somehow intuitively identified one of the specks in front of her as Earth. From there, she found the sun and several more planets. She tried to look at her hand, to see if she really was somehow floating free millions of miles above the ecliptic plane. Waving her hand in front of her face produced no interruption in the view, so she ruled this a vision, not literal reality.

"I'm supposed to cast a spell. I remember that much. Something big." As she said these words, instructions formed in her mind. She needed to find a place to dump this energy where it would do the least amount of damage. Strontium was banking on Dorothy's knowledge of astronomy to find an appropriate target. With a moment's reluctance, but the grim understanding that a sacrifice would be inevitable, she chose to destroy Pluto.

She zoomed out, searching for the icy rock, and only then saw something she could not explain. A roughly circular region of space appeared a subtlety different shade of black from its surroundings. A ring of yet another shade of black enclosed that. She had no clear way to describe the difference, but to her it was obvious and bright.

"Well, that can't be right. Am I supposed to fix that?"

No one answered, but she felt a sudden nudge in the back of her mind. Without words, Strontium impelled her toward those rings. The gesture held a quality of approval as though this new task presented a far better idea than her plans for poor Pluto.

"Wait," said Dorothy. "I know what this is. It's the blast waves of the two mayhem bombs!" An unfamiliar word formed in the back of her head. "Mayhespheres? Is that right? They're still out there?" She scrutinized the circles in space, confused by her ease at identifying them, but certain of their identity nevertheless. She pulled at them with her thoughts, and felt them, both soft as putty, with a smell about them like overripe fruit. "Something's not right. Someone has been picking at these."

Again, she felt a nudge, and a sense of approval. Bit by bit, she understood both her task, and her relationship with Strontium. The body-switching story was a lie, but a lie is often the easiest place to hide a truth. She felt another nudge, and got back to work.

The Mayhem Waves needed repair. And a spell of certain doom and great magnitude needed to be diverted. She would solve both problems with one action.

She cracked knuckles she could not see, waved invisible arms, and recited memorized incantations with meanings unknown to her, even though she now understood how she had been able to memorize them.

Before her eyes, the tiny blue dot of Earth extended a slender blue thread in the direction of the ring. It took several minutes for it to reach the edge of the anomaly, which at this scale meant it traveled at the speed of light. As it ponderously made its way across the sky, she found the vision tranquil.

That tranquility shattered when it touched the ring. A scream formed inside her head, louder and clearer than Strontium's voice had been. Covering her ears had no effect. As it grew in intensity, her grip slipped.

Strontium kicked her, just hard enough to keep her on track. She hunkered down and endured.

Dorothy had never repaired a Mayhesphere before, so she had no way to know how much it would hurt. The quality to this pain had no analog in her experience. It best reminded her of hanging from a cliff by her thumbs, while being hacked away in random places by tiny razors. If she let go, she would, at best, have to start over from scratch.

By the time she had been working on the problem for an hour, she came to understand that if she let go, she would die.

She took what gratification she could find in watching the gradual success of her efforts. The blue thread that stretched from the Earth to the Mayhespheres had begun to knit them together. She looped it around the inner sphere, then made a pass around the outer and pulled. She had to do these motions without letting go of her cliff face. Occasionally she would pull the thread past the wrong section, and would have to take out a dozen stitches to do over, being careful not to tear the fabric.

After a few hours, the bugs came. In their assault, she longed for the early stages when she merely felt cut by razors. They rotated tactics, sometimes attacking in a swarm, sometimes buzzing in her ears. They found the most tender places on her skin, and drove their stingers and proboscises in where they would do the worst damage. Every sting and bite came away both painful and itchy. Still she held on.

And at every stage of the process, every obstacle and every resultant torture, exactly one thought drove her to the next step: if she did not do this right, if she did not save the world, she would never see Claudia again. She held that thought close to her, and it supported her against the cliff like a climbing rope. She would not, could not die. Not after finally finding this love that had evaded her all these years. The injustice would be intolerable.

Finally, an eternity later, she pulled the last stitch through. The rings dissipated, and the circle of differently black space faded to match its surroundings.

She found herself on the floor of Tim's sanctum, looking at the ceiling, suddenly aware of a sharp pain on the side of her face, and a deep ache radiating from her right breast.

"Strontium?" she croaked. Clearing her throat, she tried again. "Strontium? It's time for that talk."

"You did good, child," came a voice from within herself. She smiled at both the relief to hear her friend, and the praise.

"Something tells me I couldn't have done it without you," said Dorothy.

"Then something is telling you nonsense," came the voice.

"You're not dead, are you?" asked Dorothy.

"Not hardly," said Strontium. "Just laying low. Burning that goblin took a piece out of me more than I expected. Time was I could have reconstituted that body in half an hour."

"Is that why you took over my body?" asked Dorothy. "To recuperate?" Her voice carried no judgment, just curiosity.

"Took over? Pish posh, I was barely awake in there. Damn near slept through this whole hootenanny."

Dorothy laughed, then frowned. "Wait, if you weren't in charge, how was I doing magic?"

"By doing magic, I reckon," said Strontium. "I have some recall of passing you whispers along the road by way of suggestion, but you were driving that whole time."

"But the book—"

"Is yours. Never seen anyone take so quickly to it, either. You're a sharp tack. Spotted those sphere things all on your own, I might add. Can't believe I missed that. You've got the knack, child."

Dorothy took a moment for all of this to sink in. "Are you going to be in here forever now?"

"Nah," said Strontium. "I'll find my way out. May take a bit, though. At least I know where I am now. Soon as I get my body up and running, I'll skedaddle. Meantime, you'll barely know I'm here."

Dorothy smiled. "I don't mind knowing you're there." She waited for a reply, and got none.

Sitting up sent new waves of pain through her body from the physical injuries she sustained at Tim's hands. She looked around her. Two bodies lay on the floor, one of which had no head. The intact one belonged to Aplomado, and she remembered seeing him fall, strangled by a magical tattoo. Cautiously, she felt his wrist, unable to find a pulse, though surprised to find it warm. She poked at the tattoo still wrapped around his neck, and it wriggled.

"Off!" she shouted at it.

It unwrapped and fell to the floor, a harmless looking, quivering black curve. She picked it up from both ends and bit a chunk out of the middle, which she spat onto the floor. It left a tarry aftertaste in her mouth.

Aplomado gasped, and sat up. "How did you know I was alive?"

"You're welcome," she said. "And I didn't. What was that?"

"An induced trance. Evidently the dark wizard had further plans for me, never to be realized, I see." He nodded in the direction of the decapitated mage. "How were you able to break the curse?"

"I have the echo of a vanished witch inside me," she said. "She tells me things I can't hear, and then I do things I can't do. But you already knew that, didn't you?"

"I did," he said. "Not the details, but the general fact, yes."

"Well, like it or not, I'm a witch now," said Dorothy. "And I want to know what I'm doing. The way I see it, you owe me at least one favor. Do you do private tutoring?"

"I do." He held out his hand. Dorothy took it, and he pulled her close, looping his arm around her waist. He looked up at the triangular hole he had created in the ceiling earlier. "This is your first lesson. Do pay attention."

Dorothy took one last look around the room. "Wasn't there a ghost here when we came in?"

Holding her tightly, Aplomado jumped.

75

PIXIE REDUX

Harrison woke screaming. Four soldiers held him down, aggravating the shooting agony in his wrist.

Apryl stroked his face. "Shhh. Hey, baby, I've got you." She kissed him, momentarily distracting him from his pain. Then it came back, and he twisted his face away from her to scream again.

"You can let him up now," said someone, a woman's voice he did not recognize. The four soldiers each released a limb, and Harrison instinctively grabbed his stump with his remaining hand. To his surprise, he found another hand there. He surveyed the hideous scar of melted skin that went the whole way around his wrist. The pain came not from the injury, but from the healing.

"Ow!"

Apryl kissed him again. "I know."

"Ow," he said with less rage.

"Yes."

He sat up. Mid-morning sunlight covered the middle of the field, where he recuperated on a collapsible cot. Apryl, Sarah, Mitchell, and Claudia stood or sat around him, along with soldiers whose names he did not know, and one odd looking woman, presumably the local healer. "How long was I out?"

"I don't know," said Apryl. "At least twelve hours, I think. We only just found your hand about ten minutes ago. You were very lucky, you know. It was under a seat."

"Twelve hours?" He looked over his wrist again. "How did I survive the night? Why didn't I bleed to death?"

Apryl looked at him uncomfortably, and opened her mouth to say something, but didn't, or couldn't, finish the thought.

Sarah spoke up. "Melody cauterized your stump."

Harrison took a moment to absorb that. "*Melody* cauterized it?"

Sarah bit her lip. "Maybe cauterized is the wrong word."

"She used magic," said Apryl.

"What kind of magic?" asked Harrison nervously.

"I don't know," said Apryl. "Purple magic? She touched your stump and the bleeding stopped. There were purple lights. I don't know how to explain it better than that."

He looked around him, acutely aware for the first time of Melody's absence. "Where is she?"

"Looking for Sparky," said Apryl. "She insisted. She's with Adler and a couple of the soldiers, combing the weeds."

"Sparky," said Harrison. "Right. What happened to Sparky?"

"We don't know," said Claudia. "I saw her do that thing to Basil, to put out his fire, and figured she was dead, but Melody says she's out there somewhere."

"So, Adler's okay?" Harrison asked Sarah.

"Yes," she said. "Thank you so much."

"Me? You're the dragon slayer! We should all be thanking you!"

She smiled. "I suppose. How did you even know that was going to work?"

"I had no idea that was going to work. I just do some of my best guessing under pressure. It looked like his eye-piece was reversing our powers, not negating them. It seemed like the thing to try. Good thing it did, because I had no plan B." Harrison waited for congratulations or mockery of his stupid luck, but Sarah's gaze had drifted over to the weeds where her boy helped to search for a pixie.

"Well," she said after taking a deep breath, "all we need to do now is get his father back on his feet, and we'll be a family again."

"Are you going to let Adler see him?"

"Hell yes, I'm going to let Adler see him! I hope he has better luck talking Warren out of his coma than I have."

"I hope so, too." Harrison flopped back down on his back. "Did we get all twenty-eight out?" he asked Claudia. "Did they all make it?"

"Yeah," said Claudia, shifting uncomfortably. "I don't know how much you picked up on this last night, but Siobhan is kind of a mess. All twenty-eight of them were under mind control, but it looks like she actually wanted to go through with being sacrificed, even after Dorothy freed her."

"Oh, fuck."

"Yeah. Becca wants to take care of her. I have no idea how someone recovers from something like that."

"Let's stay on top of that. I want her hospitalized when we get back. Gotta add that to my to-do list." He took a deep breath before pushing forward with his next question. "Milton?"

"He's going to need some skin grafts when we get home," said Claudia. "A few more seconds and he would have been a goner."

Harrison released a profound sigh, his guilt over Milton's possible death replaced by the much preferable guilt over his injury. "Who did we lose?"

"The army guys lost five men and one centaur. Maybe Sparky, if we can't find her. Maybe Aplomado. Maybe Dorothy."

Harrison sat up. "Dorothy? What happened?" As he tried to juggle the depth of his feelings at this news, he saw Claudia's emotionless face in a new light. "Oh, God, Claudia. I'm sorry. Are you…?"

"Don't worry about it," she said coldly. "It's okay. We both knew this could happen. That's why…" She stopped there, her face tightening. She took Harrison's good hand and squeezed it hard. "You know," she said, sniffing, "for a little while there, I finally got what I always wanted. She loved. She told me she loved me. It was real, Harrison. Took us forever to find that out, but at least we knew." She sniffed again, and wiped her eyes with the heel of her palm. "Would have been nice to hear it one more time, though," she said through a forced laugh.

"Hey," said Harrison. "Let's not give up yet, okay?"

Claudia's tears broke through. "I know. The army guys are looking for her inside the building. She never came back from looking for that bad wizard. Neither did he. I'm trying to stay optimistic."

"Do." He gave her hand a squeeze. To Apryl, he said, "I want to see Melody."

She kissed him on the forehead. "I'll get her. You okay here?"

"For now, I think," he said. "We did win last night, right?"

"Oh, yes. We won." She walked off to get her daughter.

"Hey kid," said Harrison to Mitchell, who had been hanging back. "How are you doing?"

"I'm good," he said, stepping closer, hesitantly. "How's your hand?"

"Ask me again in a week."

"Ha. Right." Mitchell shuffled awkwardly. "They told me I could wait here until you woke up. I just wanted to thank you for rescuing me. Again."

"I owe you a ball game."

"I'm pretty sure this counts," said Mitchell.

Harrison laughed. "Did you call your dad yet?"

Mitchell nodded. "We talked for about an hour this morning. He thought I ran away. I don't think I'm ever going to leave my house again after this."

"I'm sure he'll be happy to know that."

"Oh, he was. He actually offered to help me get an apartment. When I told him I wanted to stay at home he totally started crying. I'm pretty sure I can milk this for a while." He laughed, but turned his head to wipe away a tear of his own, less subtly than he probably imagined.

"Hey," said Dallas.

Harrison rolled over to see him. He looked sheepish, and worn out, and Harrison tried to remember what role Dallas had played in the battle.

"You here to argue with me?" asked Harrison. "Because I have to say, that's not how I want to spend today."

"Naw," said Dallas. "Just wanna say I'm sorry. The curse thing wore off. Centaur says that might mean the wizard who put it on me is dead or something. But it's off. Just thought you should know."

"Thanks," said Harrison. He and Dallas looked at each other awkwardly, with Harrison unsure how to dismiss him kindly.

"You need anything?" said Dallas.

Harrison sighed. "Yeah. I need my daughters to be okay. I need my wrist to stop hurting." He looked around him, at the ruins of Fenway Park. "And I need this place fixed up. Damn it, would you look at what we did here? This is one of my favorite childhood memories, and we found it just in time to wreck it. Can you get on that?"

Dallas laughed, which Harrison considered polite in light of the weakness of his joke. "Yeah. Feel better." He held out his hand to shake Harrison's, then pulled it back, eyeing the painful scar on Harrison's wrist, and just waved instead.

As Dallas walked away, Harrison's wife returned, with Melody in tow. His daughter looked normal for a little girl who had only twelve hours before that saved his life with unexplained magic. She held something in both hands, and when they got close enough he recognized it.

"Sparky?" he said.

The pixie lay on her back, across both of Melody's outstretched hands.

"Is she alive?" asked Harrison.

Without sitting up, Sparky raised one hand, and gave a thumbs-up.

"Do you need a healer?"

She pointed her thumb down.

"Do you just want to find a comfortable place to lie down, and have people bring you grapes?"

Both thumbs went up.

He laughed. "Get her set up with a pillow in the flier," he said to a soldier.

"Yes sir." He held out his hands, and Melody gently transferred the pixie to him.

"And how are you?" Harrison asked Melody.

"Good," she said, smiling.

"I hear you made me better last night."

"Uh huh."

"Do you know how you did that?" he asked.

She shrugged. "Not really."

"Is she acting like herself?" he asked Apryl.

"Absolutely. You'd never know anything was different to talk to her. Right, honey?" Apryl mussed Melody's hair, and Harrison noticed it had taken on a purple tint, like her eyes, and the halo he had seen last night.

"We'll take her to Esoteric first thing when we get back," he said. "There are good people there. We'll figure this out."

"I know," said Apryl. "I have decided not to worry. It wasn't an easy decision, but I'm sticking to it."

"Good. Hey, what do we know about all those other children?"

"You mean what are we going to do with a hundred and one Dalmatians?" she asked.

He smiled. "Something like that."

"Jessica and a few of the women have taken over there. She was their teacher here, so they trust her. Some of the kids are old enough to tell us where they came from, some aren't. I'm not sure what they're going to do about those. Find them new parents, maybe?" She kissed Harrison on the forehead. "Whatever happens, there are people who will take care of them. You've done plenty by rescuing them. It can be someone else's job from here."

"What's he doing?" asked Melody. She pointed to the rubble at the base of the gaping hole that used to be the Green Monster. Dallas picked up chunks and dropped them, over and over again.

"I have no idea," said Harrison. "Did he lose something last night?"

"If he did, he didn't lose it there," said Sarah. "He spent the entire battle hiding under the negotiating table. He's lucky he wasn't killed."

Harrison shook his head. "Poor guy. This is all so far beyond him. We should have left him home."

"No, wait, really," said Claudia. "What is he doing?"

Dallas had gotten down on his knees, and he thrust both hands into the shattered wood and metal fragments. After a few seconds, they shifted and moved. The Green Monster rose up, particle by particle. Considering the complexity, the process moved swiftly, although it took a full two minutes for the wall to grow to its original height. The paint shone brighter on that section of wall than anywhere else in the park, and as Dallas continued to press his hands into the ground at the base of the wall, that brightness radiated outward in a wave.

The weeds below him dissolved, leaving a smooth warning track. Farther out, the lawn purified itself, with non-grass plants disappearing, and the remaining grass cut to a uniform length. As the effect spread farther, it resolved itself to the checkerboard pattern so beloved of groundskeepers. A baseball diamond appeared from under dissolving weeds, and a pitcher's mound rose in the middle of the infield.

The shattered arc lights overhead reassembled themselves from glass shards that flew straight up from where they fell. The pulverized press box reconstituted itself from crumbled debris levitating up from the stands.

For twenty minutes, this wave of restoration swept around Fenway Park. When Dallas finally stood, he did so in a ballpark that looked exactly like Harrison's memories of it, though with perhaps a great deal more luster.

"Order from chaos," said Harrison. "Son of a bitch."

"That," said Claudia, "is literally the coolest thing I have ever seen."

"No," corrected Apryl, pointing to the stands. "That is the coolest thing you have ever seen."

Claudia turned around, and tore across the field. Two soldiers led Dorothy and Aplomado up from under the stands. They both looked hurt and exhausted, and they leaned on each other as they walked. The sight of his adopted daughter alive flooded Harrison with warmth, as did the sight of Claudia running into her arms.

"Mommy?" said Melody. "Daddy?"

Overwhelmed with happiness at that moment, Harrison looked at his little girl. She had a curious smile on her face, a mixture of wonder and mischief. "What is it, honey?"

"I don't know." She giggled, and spun in a circle. In the instant she had her back to him, Harrison's heart nearly stopped.

"Harrison?" said Apryl, clutching his hand. Pain shot through his wrist. He ignored it.

"I see them," he said.

Everyone did.

A pair of oversized, purple butterfly wings unfurled around Melody's torso.

Still squeezing Harrison's hand, Apryl whispered, "There are no pixies on my side of the family."

"Look!" Melody shouted with utter delight, and lifted into the air.

76

EVER AFTER

As Dorothy emerged up from under the stands, she shielded her eyes against the morning sunlight. She had spent the entire night underground, saving the world. She assumed the passage of time had been an illusion, a consequence of her hard labor, but it had in fact been hours. Her exhaustion certainly made more sense in that light.

As her first order of business, she needed to find Claudia, a task greatly simplified by the sight of Claudia charging across the field toward her. She gently pushed Aplomado away from her, and did her best at running down the aisle to the wall, which she carefully climbed over. As she hit the ground, Claudia crashed into her and held her in a bear hug.

"Ow!" Dorothy cried, as sharp pains shot through her injured breast. Claudia jumped back, a look of fear on her face.

"What?" she said.

Dorothy pouted. "My boob hurts." After an awkward moment of uncertainty, she laughed. "Oh, I don't care." She threw her arms around Claudia and kissed her with all the pent-up emotion of a world-threatening crisis, now resolved.

"I love you," they said simultaneously, when they finally both came up for air.

"I thought you were dead," said Claudia.

"I thought I was dead too," said Dorothy. "Long story."

"I killed someone," said Claudia.

"So did I."

Claudia's eyes went wide, and she gently stroked Dorothy's cheek. Reminded of the pain by her touch, Dorothy flinched.

"Are you okay?" asked Claudia.

"I'll live. Which is good news because I very much have something to live for."

Claudia smiled and kissed her again.

"You saved me down there," said Dorothy. "You should know that."

"Me?" said Claudia. "How?"

Dorothy considered the explanation. "It's complicated, but I just... I had an impossible job, and the thought of you is what kept me going."

"Really?"

"Really. I love you, Claudia. It turns out I've always loved you." She smiled. "Surprise!" Dorothy took Claudia in her arms again, finding a way to favor her bruised breast and still hold her. "So," she whispered in Claudia's ear. "About what happens next..."

"We should wait until you're feeling better," said Claudia softly.

Dorothy laughed. "Actually, no, we shouldn't, but that's not what I'm talking about."

"Oh," said Claudia. "Bigger stuff?"

"Something like that," said Dorothy. "It turns out I have this son to raise. Is it too early to talk about starting a family?"

Claudia laughed. "I'm so in. You sure about this?"

"Never surer," said Dorothy, and held her close again.

EPILOGUE

M elody's life suddenly made sense to her. She had never understood why she could see things no one else seemed to see, or why she understood things everyone else found confusing.

That day she saw the funny lights in Daddy's office, something happened to her. Something happened to everyone, really, but only Melody noticed. Mommy and Daddy and Dorrie and that funny English guy all started acting weird, and Melody wanted to say something, but no one ever understood her when she tried to talk about things like that. It was so much easier to pretend to be a regular little girl.

But that day, the lights did something to her too. Not the thing they were supposed to do. That's what the pretty old witch said. Something else. It made her purple. And sparkly. And magical.

It made her a pixie.

But not a real pixie. A kind of half-pixie. Except it didn't make her that. Deep down, she was always that. She knew it, though she didn't know how exactly. But now it all made sense. The lights didn't change her, they just found something hidden. Found it by accident. Now she knew. She was a pixie-girl. And that meant something else, too.

Mommy wasn't a pixie.

Daddy wasn't a pixie.

Everyone always said she had Mommy's nose, and Daddy's chin.

Some day she would have to find out whose wings she had.

ACKNOWLEDGMENTS

Many thanks to Guinevere Crescenzi whose invitation into her writers group kicked me into gear as a novelist for the first time in my life. Thanks also to Steve Carabello and Kate McGourty, whose continued contributions in that group helped sculpt this book.

I continue to be grateful for the feedback of my many, many beta readers. Their input has ranged from general comments about how well the story came together, to comprehensive nitpicking over every imaginable detail. They should all recognize some of their contributions in the final draft. Special thanks go out to Dorian Hart, Jeanne Kramer-Smyth, Josh Bluestein, and Matthew Cox, whose questions and suggestions were particularly influential in my revisions.

Extra special thanks to beta reader extraordinaire Lori Bentley-Law, who provided immediate feedback chapter by chapter as I worked through the first draft. Her collaboration lit a fire under me like nothing else during those four months, and made the process a true joy for me.

I do not make a habit of basing my characters on real people. For this book, there are three exceptions, loosely based on my wife, Annelisa Aubry-Walton, and my daughters, Delphi and Aenea. Thanks go to all of them for providing such entertaining templates, as well as for reading my various drafts and opining on how I navigated those characters, hopefully to their satisfaction. Matching them to their counterparts is left as an exercise for the reader.

Though the first draft of Mayhem's Children rolled out in only a few months, it took me ten years to get past my first scene. At issue was the third act of my outline, which remained blank, the only example of writer's block I have ever truly experienced. Credit for pushing me over that hurdle goes exclusively to my brother-in-law, Timothy Blodgett. In a single conversation over roasted marshmallows one evening, Tim offered an idea for how to resolve the complicated mess of my plot in a way that was both elegant and unique. His suggestion opened me up to revisit that story from a new angle, and it flowed out easily after that point. He likely won't recognize his twist in the final draft, as very little of his original suggestion survived in the details. However, the spirit of what he offered remains in there, and was absolutely the driving force that got me to dust this thing off and actually write it. Any villains in the book who happen to share his first name should be viewed as purely coincidental.

Finally, I am eternally grateful to Karen Escovitz, who stepped in to be my sensitivity reader as I made my first foray into telling a same-sex love story. Anything in that relationship that feels authentic to the reader is surely the result of her advice. Conversely, if any aspect of it doesn't track for you, it means I didn't ask the right questions.

ABOUT THE AUTHOR

Edward Aubry is a graduate of Wesleyan University, with a degree in music composition. Improbably, this preceded a career as a teacher of high school mathematics and creative writing.

He now lives in rural Pennsylvania with his wife and three spectacular daughters, where he fills his non-teaching hours spinning tales of time-travel, wise-cracking pixies, and an assortment of other impossible things.

ALSO BY EDWARD AUBRY

Unhappenings

When Nigel is visited by two people from his future, he hopes they can explain why his past keeps rewriting itself. His search for answers takes him fifty-two years forward in time, where he meets Helen, brilliant, hilarious and beautiful. Unfortunately, that meeting has triggered events that will cause millions to die. Desperate to find a solution, he discovers the role his future self has played all along.

The Mayhem Wave Series

On May 30, 2004, the world suddenly transformed into a bizarre landscape populated with advanced technology, dragons, magic and destruction. Now what few humans remain must start over, braving wilderness, dangerous beasts, and new and powerful enemies.

Prelude to Mayhem

Static Mayhem

Mayhem's Children

Balance of Mayhem

Made in the
USA
Middletown, DE

76371850R00246